Table of Contents

DISCLAIMER

The characters herein do not relate to, nor are they based upon, any living person other than myself. (And Molly and Ziggy.)
Even then, any association is very loose and tenuous, more 'inspired by' than based upon... anyway, you probably want to get on and read the book now...

PROLOGUE

'Is that better ... or worse, Mrs Harkins?'
'Yes.'
"Yes?"
Oh my dearie goodness me ...
Mrs Harkins is a sweet old lady - she's also a nightmare to try and test subjectively. Luckily, I have magic powers, (and a retinoscope), so we can dispense with her questionable input. Let's see what she can read on the chart with a minus 3.25 lens.

'H...A...Y...O...U...Y'

Yes! Five letters out of six - near enough. Pretty good actually considering she's developed some early cataract since I saw her last.
'Will I be able to see the television any clearer with my new glasses, Mr Rogers?'
Mrs Harkins is housebound due to rheumatoid arthritis, which is why she needs a home visit for her eye test; daytime television in all its sorry entirety, and Jeremy Kyle in particular, are a big part of her life.
'A lot better, Mrs Harkins. We will have to keep an eye on those cataracts, but I think new specs will do the trick for now.'
What's she laughing about?
'Oh, you are funny Mr Rogers. Keep an eye on - my eyes. That's priceless.'
Glad I'm entertaining you.
One of these days I'm going to write a book.

After she's chosen her new glasses and I've given her a quick bit of advice on the dry eyes – i.e. try actually remembering to put the drops in – I'm off – early finish today, personal business awaits.
I can't really remember the last time I worked on a Sunday, but Mrs Harkins lives just five minutes from the Garden Centre, so it seemed a waste not to include her when I was coming here anyway.
Back in the car I pull off my tie - (I know, I know ... but the old ones like it, it helps get their confidence) – and switch my 'Mr Bean' tweed jacket for a light, sporty number from the Debenhams select range that also happened to be in the sale.
I'm a bit early, as planned, which is good – I wouldn't want to keep my date waiting.

ONE

'Hi' says I.

'Uh... Hi' says she.

Good start...

'So - you're Diane, then?'

'Yes - you must be Mark?'

The introductory handshake feels strange. We already know each other - or do we? Familiarity is vying with anonymity.

'What made you choose a Garden Centre to meet in?' she asks.

'It's handy for us both, it's a public place, and the coffee's supposed to be good - shall we go try some?

'Funny,' she remarks as we head for the café. 'I haven't seen any plants yet.'

She's right; china ornaments, books, toys - this place seems to specialise in everything except horticulture. As for the café - Jamie Oliver would be proud to work in this set-up. Looking around, scratching my scalp, I ask:

'Where's the coffee?'

Diane shakes her head; her eyes join mine on a journey past the 'Design Your Own Pizza' counter, the 'Fresh Home-Made Soup' cauldron, a gigantic pan of 'Just-Created Crepe'... ah, there - just beyond the 'Roasted-Venison Carvery' - a mass of taps and spouts that might be a drinks station. Grabbing a wooden tray, Diane scurrying behind me, I manage to outflank an approaching herd of OAPs and order two coffees. The plump lady in green-striped white needs more detail.

'Is that Americano, Latte, Espresso, Macchiato...?'

My mouth is open but wordless, so Diane takes over.

'Two Macchiatos,' she clarifies before adding to me: 'Is that alright?'

'Fine, I'm sure it will be - em, let's grab a table.'

Shoulder to shoulder we fight our way through the crowd to a free space. Sunday afternoon in a garden centre; café's a madhouse, plants are going paranoid because nobody's talking to them.

Safely seated, a veil of calm materialises to separate us from the melee all around. We're both starting to relax a little I think. The trauma of meeting is behind us, neither of us has turned out to have two heads, and we're settled in a shared private space where we can focus our full attention on one another.

Diane's a bonny lass I find myself thinking as my eyes follow ochre and silver streaks to their soft resting place on slim shoulders. I like the way she dresses; her clothes are colourful and well tailored, and she looks comfortable in them. She's got a nice smile too…oops.

'Sorry - was I staring?'

'That's okay, guess you've got every right to inspect the goods…oh, now I'm sorry. It's just so weird this, don't you think? Doesn't help that I'm totally inexperienced - how many Internet dates have you been on, Mark?'

Quite a lot…

'Not many.'

She brings her elbows up on the table, leans her chin on her hands.

'Come on then - what caught your interest when you read my profile?'

Your photo.

'Oh I don't know, you just seemed like an intelligent, honest sort of person…what about you? What was the first thing about me that made you want to know more?'

'That's easy, it was your name...'

Ah, my name. Yes, Mark Rogers – has a certain ring about it, rolls off the tongue so easily…what's she saying now?

'…you see, I have a cat called Markus, so I thought, what a coincidence, must mean something…'

Her cat?

'And you're a Nurse?'

'Yes, I work at the Royal. I'm a bit puzzled about what you do, Mark. What's an Optometrist?'

'A lot of people have trouble with that. I used to be an Optician.'

'Really? What made you change your job?'

Is she joking? No, she isn't.

'I didn't, an Optician IS an Optometrist. They changed our title a few years back, so that the public wouldn't get confused…now everybody spends hours walking the streets, passing loads of Optometrists' shops, looking for an Optician…'

She's laughing. That's good.

'Don't you get a bit fed up spending all day in a dark little room looking at people's eyes?'

'Not me. I'm a Domiciliary Optometrist - means I go out to housebound people with suitcases full of portable equipment. It's been nearly ten years since I've worked in a high street practice – I'd be a bit lost now, fetching things out of drawers and cupboards instead of suitcases.'

Laughing again…

'Is it mainly old people you see?'

'Mostly, but I've got a fair number of younger ones too – well, younger as in between 40 and 60 – people with MS, or learning difficulties, or injuries that have made them housebound.'

'I had to work in the eye department for a few months when I was training – I hated it. The thought of touching an eye…'

Yes – that's why we have Ophthalmoscopes, love...

'How old did you say your girls were, Mark?'

'Zoe's fifteen, and Kara's nineteen. They were both from my first marriage, to Claire. Zoe's still at school of course, and Kara's studying in Glasgow to be a Vet.'

'Glasgow's quite handy – take you what, about an hour to get through there? You did say you live just outside Haddington, didn't you?'

Let's change the subject.

'That's right – what's Gorebridge like? I don't think I've ever been there.'

'Oh, it's just a little place – suits me alright though. I've only been married once. Matthew and I were together for eighteen years, and it's been barely six months since we split up, so this is all very strange for me.'

'Funnily enough it's not much over six months since my second marriage broke up.'

'Another coincidence.' She sees that I'm puzzled. 'You know, like the name thing – Marcus and Mark…'

Oh yes – the cat…

We've reached that mandatory point where it becomes obligatory to re-hash our previous failed attempts at romance. Forming a new bond seems to necessitate examining the reasons for past failure, all of which lie fairly and squarely at the feet of preceding partners. It's like saying, well, I never did anything wrong, and you never did anything wrong, so it can work with us.

Mind you, those preceding partners are probably sitting in some other coffee venue right now doing exactly the same thing.

Diane's telling me more about her ex-husband.

'For most of the eighteen years we were married he worked abroad, so I only saw him one week out of every month.'

'So it won't have made much difference when he left, then?'

'Anyway … it was quite a good arrangement really, kept things fresh between us, you know? Then out of the blue comes Veronica. Twenty years younger than him, with an IQ smaller than her bra-size – which doesn't, incidentally, make her THAT thick. What comes over men when they hit their forties?'

'I suppose they…no, no idea really what men like that are thinking of.'

'It kind of took my confidence in myself away – still haven't really got it back, if I'm honest.'

Her voice went quiet when she said that, sitting here amongst all this noise and bustle, and I felt my sword arm twitch involuntarily.

'Anyway Mark, what about you, what went wrong with your second marriage?'

I find this bit hard; there were a lot of problems between Sally and me, but the one that instigated our separation is the same story as Diane just told. In reverse. This is not something I can talk about very easily. Wounded male pride, feelings of inadequacy – I've done the whole shrink routine on myself over and over, but the words still get lost on the way from my brain to my mouth. Maybe I can lead up to it…

'Looking back now, I think we weren't compatible in the first place. We were just both used to being married, and we rushed into things too fast. It was coming apart long before…'

'Before what?'

'Before…well, same as happened to you.'

'You had an affair?'

She looks shocked, so I answer in a rush.

'No, not me. Her.'

I can feel my face heating up like a griddle, and I'm relieved when her expression softens.

'You sound so defensive. Look, I know what it's like, how it makes you feel...you don't need to be embarrassed or ashamed. It wasn't your fault.'

So distracted am I by the tear formation in her inner canthi that I barely notice when she reaches for my hand, not until the jolt of contact surges up my arm like a defibrillator discharging.

'We seem to have a lot in common,' she says, an ironic harmony playing in her words.

My eyes are fixed on our ten co-habiting fingers. I'm trying to work out whose hand it is that's shaking. Listening to my voice, I think it must be mine.

'We ... do.'

Her eyes are smouldering black, (full pupil dilation if you want to be technical about it), and her grip on my fingers is reminiscent of a hungry python. Then she lets go, leans back, and the sense of loss startles me.

'So, what do you like to do for fun?' she inquires, but there's no suggestion of mischief; we're back to the interview. She giggles when I call it that.

'Well it's true. I've met a lot - a couple - of people who made it feel like an interview. I swear those women had a clipboard hidden under the table, so they could tick off the questions. What kind of music do you like...?'

'If you could travel anywhere in the world, where would it be?' she puts in, and giggles again. An army of ants rush down my spine.

My turn.

'What was your most embarrassing moment?'

'Not telling.'

'Okay, what do you do to keep fit?'

'Pilates, Zumba, Kick-Boxing and Women's Rugby.'

She throws that back without a twitch of facial muscle. You'd need to have read a few dating-site profiles to appreciate the joke. She can't maintain the straight face though, and after a moment we're both laughing. Reaching out, I re-capture her hand.

'For fun…' I start, watching her eyes widen, '…I like dancing, going to gigs, listening to music, meeting up with friends…'

'Stop.' Now she's wiping tears from her cheeks. 'What the hell are intelligent people like us doing on a Dating Site?'

My other hand joins the first, making a sandwich with Diane's, and I suck in a lungful of coffee-flavoured air. Can I really say this, without sounding stupid?

'Looking for each other?'

There's a wee moment of eye contact and something passes wordlessly between us, while a bloody big butterfly beats its wings in time with my heartbeat. I lean forward, unaware that the table has started to tilt. Then her hands rip free of mine and she squeals in shock. Well, you do when a half-full cup of cold coffee lands in your lap.

'Sorry, sorry…here, let me…'

I'm on my feet, grabbing a handful of napkins from the metal dispenser on our unbalanced table. Crouching at Diane's side, I start rubbing vigorously at the damp stain on the crotch of her jeans. After a moment I stop, suddenly, and slowly raise my eyes. Two blue lasers return my gaze, and her cheeks are burning too.

'Sorry, I…'

Now she's on her feet, and the atmosphere has lost every shred of blooming romance.

'I think I'd better go … it's just one of those things, don't worry, but I need to go home and change.'

Her tone has all the accusation her words lack.

'Of course – I'll walk you to your car.'

The walk is more like a sprint, and I don't know whether I'm imagining the soggy swishing sounds as her legs propel her over the asphalt to a blue Mazda that looks like its last clean was in the showroom. She fumbles her keys from her bag, opens the door. I can't let it end like this.

'Look, I'm really sorry about tipping that coffee over you - and I just didn't think, I was trying to dry you off...'

She's looking at me like I'm a particularly vague crossword clue.

'It's alright, really - but I have to go now. I feel very uncomfortable...'

Is that because of the wet crotch, or because I started rubbing it?

'I was hoping we could meet up again,' I blurt quickly, as the car door closes. The engine starts, then the window slides open. Well, half open.

'E Mail me,' she says, then leaves the car park like the Starship Enterprise breaking orbit.

"E Mail me." In other words...

All those meetings with women who'd lied about everything from their age to their shoe size, and finally I meet somebody I really like.

Then I blow it. Totally.

Story of my life.

Back at the Caravan Park, at least my dogs are pleased to see me.

Yes, I live on a Caravan Park.

Dogs are wonderful; unlike wives they're never moody, they don't hold grudges, and especially unlike wives, they always give you an excited, delighted 'welcome home.'

My two are both Tibetan breeds, so that's what I call them. 'The Tibetans.'

Ziggy, the smaller, six years old and pure white, is a Lhasa Apso. Historical rumour has it they were bred for guard duty in Tibetan Monasteries, though some sources claim their major role was to keep the cloisters clear of vermin. I treat this last with some scepticism, since Ziggy regularly used to lose stare-downs with rabbits. That was until she became stone-blind a few months ago, due to an untreatable congenital condition. Having a blind dog does not exactly inspire confidence in my professional abilities.

Molly, jet-black, five years old and twice Ziggy's size, is a Tibetan Terrier. Her breed's claim to fame is described in the archives as 'mountain herding dogs.' When I got her, I was looking for a dog with intelligence and character.

'Oh, she's got those alright' her breeder informed me in a hushed tone, going on to confide that TTs are better known as 'Tibetan Terrorists.'

'They have a reputation for being untrainable,' she said.

Unfortunately Molly overheard this, and decided to live up to it. At the moment she's making four-foot vertical leaps through the air directly in front of me, barking happily, and grabbing mouthfuls of the new jacket I bought to impress my latest online date.

It doesn't look like I'll be wearing that jumper in public again.

Ziggy has wandered out to the wooden verandah that runs along the side of our Caravan to relieve herself. She finds Molly's excesses embarrassing.

Living in a Caravan on a Holiday Park has a number of disadvantages, but it's much more comfortable than most people imagine. I've had reactions like 'Isn't it cold in winter?' and 'What if you need the loo in the middle of the night?'

This baby cost forty grand; it's got (bottled) gas central heating, and the plumbing includes an extra en-suite shower-room off the main bedroom. I actually like living here, though it's not exactly through choice.

Basically, my ex got the flat, and I got the holiday home.

Still, the dogs were happy, since to compensate for their narrow wooden garden there's miles of grassy walking-land all around. Despite being just five minutes from Haddington, Greenacres (what genius thought that one up?) Caravan Park feels like it's in the middle of nowhere. In summer the air smells of trees and barbecue charcoal, and there's a big sense of community here, a contributory factor to this being the common eccentricity of people who regularly write large cheques for 'Site Fees' and other thinly disguised extortion demands. The attraction of a place like this is ethereal, but I think a lot of it's to do with letting go of the stresses of outside life. As soon as I swipe my keycard to lift the barriers at the entrance I feel a sense of sanctuary; even the noise here is quiet.

I'm not the only person who has made their 'home' (as opposed to 'holiday home') on the Site, but perhaps not surprisingly we're in a very small minority.

Before taking Molly and Ziggy on their nightly patrol, I need to check for telephone messages. Today might be Sunday, but the older ones have no respect for the sacredness of my weekend. Sure enough the dial tone on the phone is blipping, so I press '1' to hear the message.

'Mr Rogers, it's Mrs Forsyth. My eye's awful red and sore, will you call me back? My number's...'

Oh Mrs Forsyth, I practically know your number by heart.

Mrs Forsyth is totally hypochondriac about her eyes. Probably about the rest of her as well. Under the General Ophthalmic Services, the arm of the NHS that pays me, she's allowed one 'proper' visit a year, but there is provision to attend emergencies in-between.

Mrs Forsyth has an emergency most weeks.

She lives a little over an hour away from here, so my input at short notice like this is limited to telephone diagnosis and advice – bit of an Optometric NHS 24. She would love for me to arrange her a hospital bed, but the Hospital wouldn't be too chuffed when she arrived. Mrs Forsyth suffers from Blepharitis, which is most easily described as 'Dandruff' of the eyelashes. It can become uncomfortable, but when Mrs Forsyth applies her usual amplification-ratio to the symptoms they sound more like Uveitis, or Keratitis, or even Acute Glaucoma.

But it's just Blepharitis.

Allowing myself a groan, I dial her number.

'Oh Mr Rogers, it was so painful, I was so worried….'

'Yes…how is it now though, Mrs Forsyth?'

'Oh, it's much better since it was washed out.'

'You washed it out? What with?'

'I don't know, it was the nice paramedic man who did it.'

My grip on the phone tightens.

'Paramedic? How did a paramedic come to be washing out your eye?'

I know the answer before she tells me.

'Oh Mr Rogers, it was so sore, and you weren't in, so I dialled 999…'

'You dialled 999,' I repeat. 'For Blepharitis?'

'Yes.'

She's getting quite excited in the telling of this adventure.

'They were awful good, just like you. They said they thought it would be alright after they'd washed it out, and do you know, it has been much better.'

I start calculating how much it has cost the NHS to send an emergency vehicle staffed by skilled paramedics to pour some saline over Mrs Forsyth's eye. Then I decide not to, it's just too depressing.

'Well I'm glad you're feeling better now, Mrs Forsyth. Um - don't hesitate to call if you've any further problems.'

'I wont,' she croons.

Yes love, I know you wont.

Still shaking my head, I take Molly and Ziggy for their walk.

Dogs walked and fed, a microwave ready-meal consumed, (it looked distinctly inferior to what was in the dogs' bowls), nice glass of malt-whisky poured...

...I may be broke, but there's a limit to the depths I'm prepared to sink.

Actually, this is my third glass of Glenfiddich. I'm hardly noticing it go down, busy as I am obsessing over my ridiculous behaviour with Diane at the end.

These 'dates' are usually comfortable enough one-time interludes, sometimes more interesting, just occasionally waking-nightmares - but I haven't ever come back with a woman lodged in my head like this. Diane got to me a bit.

I really liked her.

It's difficult enough normally to know what sort of protocol to follow if you're interested. Contact them too soon, and you're 'desperate.' Leave it too long, and you're 'obviously not that interested.' It's a no-win situation. It doesn't need the complication of having acted like a moron. Chances are she's not interested in hearing from me again, but … faint heart and all that…

Right. Sod it. Laptop open – Internet connection active. One thing, I'm better at composing emails than I am at saying the right things in person. (Worrying)

From: Mark.Rogers@yahoo.com

To: Diane.Wells@btinternet.com

Subject: This afternoon

Hi Diane

Hope you made it home ok. Without any traffic hassle or anything.

DELETE

Hi Diane

DELETE

Diane

Just want to say how much I enjoyed meeting you this after. It didn't end very well – I'm a clumsy idiot, in more ways than one.

I'm sorry.
I'm still hoping you might want to meet up again; perhaps if I were to sit at a separate table? I'd really like to take you for a proper meal, and prove to you that I can be a normal human being. It was all your fault anyway for being so attractive and overloading my senses. :)

It is a bit weird this meeting off the Internet thing, and I know I made it even weirder, but honestly and joking aside it was all down to nerves - if we meet again, it'll be as real people who've met before, and that'll make it so different.

If you don't reply I'll quite understand…

…but I hope you will.

Mark (x)

TWO

The next day, Monday, is passing slowly. Monday is my 'scheduling' day - when I phone my housebound patients to arrange the week's appointments. You'd think it would be easy to make appointments with people who are housebound i.e. at home all the time.
Well it's not.
Just a few examples of the obstacles I regularly run into:

Oh, I've got my hairdresser coming in then.
No,that's my lunchtime. (Meals on wheels/communal dining room in sheltered housing)
That's my day-centre day
My daughter comes to take me shopping on a Tuesday
The Nurse /GP /Chiropodist /Dentist /Fortune-Teller is coming then...

Housebound people have the busiest calendars of anybody I know.

My territory is quite big; I go to Falkirk and Stirling, all of the Lothians, Fife, and the Scottish Borders. Preferably not all on the same day. Somehow I have to put together my patients' limited windows of availability in an order that doesn't have me zig-zagging across several counties like a demented roadrunner.

This is stressful enough in itself, but considering Diane hasn't answered my email...I'm not in the best of moods.

The dogs sense my melancholy, and sensibly limit their demands for food/treats to once an hour.

At least, since my business is going down the tubes, it means I'm finished by lunchtime.

I'm living under the axe of my soon-to-be ex-wife's demands for the equivalent of a lottery win. Almost as bad, my solicitor demands payment of his £300 an hour on a monthly basis. I'm not sure how well Mr Diggins is handling my case, but he's knowledgeable enough to appreciate the necessity of getting his cash in quick while I've still got some left to give him.

My tawdry share of the money I earn has led me to question the point of putting a lot of effort into padding everyone else's coffers. The one-time workaholic now can't get too excited about chasing up examination recalls, reminding other professionals who refer patients to me that they should keep doing so, and all the other activities necessary to keep work flowing in. My new mantra is 'I'll get round to that tomorrow.'

Simple logic tells me that the more 'they' take off me, the more I need to earn to stay afloat…

…but…

…I can't be bothered.

So my business is slowly going down the tubes.

Thinking this through depresses me, and my inbox is still Diane-less. The only practical course of action is to go to the pub.

'For lunch' is how I sanitise it to the dogs, who anyway seem unperturbed by my imminent departure. Probably because I will be taking my miserable mood out with me.

One advantage of living on a Caravan Site is having a pub/restaurant within walking distance of your home. They call it 'The Club.' This is because of its exclusivity - members only. If you're not a member, all is not lost - you can be signed in up to four times. The staff will sign you in.

After being signed in four times, you will be offered a free membership.

'Pint please, Eric.'

Eric is the manager of the Club. The barman too. Sometimes he brings the food. I understand he has to help out with the cooking occasionally. Come to think of it, I can't remember seeing any other staff in here...?

Caravan Sites take the management of overheads seriously. Once they've raked in the cash like a croupier at a roulette table, they don't like parting with any of it.

Tom appears at my side - he must have come in practically right behind me -and he catches Eric's eye.

'I'll get that, Eric.'

Tom is a wiry little man with a face that resembles a brillo pad. Whatever the temperature, he always wears short-sleeved shirts over his jeans; I think this is to show off matching bird tattoos on each of his forearms. Yes, birds, and no, I've no idea what breed they are. Knowing Tom, probably pterodactyls.

Tom and his wife Kathy have become my best mates since my marriage broke up. This was a time when, like most separated people, I suddenly became an embarrassment to the majority of 'our' former friends. Tom and Kathy however never liked Sally, and I think they're quite proud of me for coming round to their way of thinking. Both are just a little older than me, and they don't actually live on the Caravan Site, though they're here so much you'd think they did. I really like them, but I worry about drinking with them. Unlike me, they can drink all night and still find their way home.

I try to protest Tom's hijacking of my order, because if he pays for this drink, I'll then have to buy a round for him and Kathy, after which they'll insist I'm owed one...and at the end, I won't be able to find my way home...

No good, he's having none of it. Grinning stupidly, he ruffles my scalp.

'It's all grown back then.'

'Tom, I finished my chemotherapy four months ago and my hair's been back for three. Well, when I say back…'

'You sure it's all back?' he asks, peering suspiciously at the top of my head.

I decide to ignore that.

We carry the drinks to a table, where Kathy jumps off her seat to give me a big hug. Kathy's attractive in an earthy sort of way, probably not nearly so stout as the baggy clothes she wears make her look, but she's strong.

'Come and sit down doll. Tell us how your check-up went.'

Have to get my lungs re-inflated first.

'It was fine. I got another scan and it was all clear, just like the last one. Not a trace of cellular mutiny, to quote Doctor Gordon.'

Tom makes a face; it would be unkind to say it's hard to tell.

'So does that mean you're cured?'

'Well, I feel cured. But it seems it's eight years before you can really say you're cured.'

'So it could still come back, then?'

He didn't really deserve that nasty jab from Kathy's stiletto.

'How's work going luv?' she asks over Tom's squeals.

'Still struggling a bit – I'm just not getting the numbers I used to have.'

'No wonder after being off for two months. You were lucky you had any customers left to go back to.'

'It's not just that, Kathy. This thing with Sally – between knowing she's going to annex most of my liquid assets, and paying my lawyer, it just doesn't seem worth the trouble to try and get my earnings up. I never see any of what I do make, so what's the point in making more?'

Kathy's face darkens. 'She's just a bloody scrounger, that one. Lived off her mother until you were daft enough to take her on, then decides she can vamoose with her fancy man and take your money with her. Makes me sick.'
Can't argue.
Tom sets off for the bar to get another round, ignoring my protestations that it's my turn. He seems to be limping slightly.
'What about the anaemia, how's that?'
'I'm still a bit anaemic, but I don't think Doctor Gordon is too worried about it.'
Kathy tuts. 'You don't eat properly – in fact, you don't look after yourself at all. Them dogs eat better than you do.'
She drains the last of her lager, then glares at Tom's back while he and Eric discuss last night's 'big match'. He'll be a while yet – Eric is bored and eager to chat. Caravan parks are pretty empty places outside of weekends and school holidays.
'How'd your date go yesterday?'
'Don't ask.'
Why's she laughing like that?
'Messed up again, did you? Oh Mark, you're such a wally around a pretty face, why couldn't you have done something daft when you met Sally?'
'I did. I met her.'
Suddenly the bottom of my glass has grabbed my whole attention. Wisely Kathy decides not to pursue that topic, or maybe it's the shock of Tom re-appearing with her drink. We were talking about my illness when he went to the bar, and of course he expects time to have stood still while he was away, especially since he's still got tuppence-worth to put in. Funny how fascinating cancer is to people who don't have it – something to do with the eternal struggle with mortality, I think. Sort of rehearsal stuff.

'I thought chemo was pretty horrible, like throwing up all the time – you never seemed to have much of that. Well, except that night we took you to Haddington, but after five pints with whisky chasers…'
Don't remind me.
'Chemo's pretty sophisticated stuff these days, they give you all sorts of drugs to control the side effects. It wasn't really uncomfortable at all, and I was getting it in a big room with about twenty other folk; they all seemed fine too.'
We all agree modern medicine is wonderful before I set off to find Eric. I've got to buy at least one round, and going to the bar when everybody's glass is full seems to be my only hope.
After that drink I say goodbye. Every time I meet up with Tom and Kathy in here I start making plans to escape while I'm still sober – but usually the drink makes me forget those plans. Luckily today I've remembered while I'm still ambulant – if only just.
I've also just remembered that I forgot to have the lunch I went for.

The dogs are pleased as ever to see me; no recriminations for my lapse in sobriety, and they show incredible agility (or in Ziggy's case, intuition) as they avoid the random motion of my feet.
On my way to collapse on the couch, I take a quick peek at the computer screen.
One new message.
Diane.

From: Diane.Wells@btinternet.com

To: Mark.Rogers@yahoo.com

Subject: Re: This afternoon

Hi Mark

I'm sorry too, I think I over-reacted a bit to a simple accident, and I know you were just trying to help… I did actually enjoy meeting you, you're different, but even despite that…JOKE! Look, if you really fancy meeting up again, I'm up for it. Meal sounds great – you say when and where, and I'll see you there.

Diane x

It takes a minute to sink in before I let rip with a whoop of delight, the seismic shock of which sends both dogs a foot into the air.

Pity Ziggy was on the sofa; it meant the floor was further away…

oops…

THREE

Next day arrives too quickly. Mornings and I are not the best of friends, unlike sleep, with which I have an intimate relationship.

On waking, I love to float in that unique state of tranquillity at the outer-edge of sleep. I use two alarm clocks - one leaves me time to float, the second wakes me half an hour later from the inevitable return to oblivion. Then I drag myself through to the kitchen for my first cup of coffee.

Producing enough coffee to supply a packed Starbucks, walking the dogs and giving them their cornflakes, tidying myself up enough to avoid scaring the old folks; that all takes nearly two hours. It's a paradox, but morning-phobic people have to get up at the crack of dawn. Sally was the opposite. She never got up until the last moment, then she blasted into the day like a bungee jumper. My early morning alarm calls made her furious.

Most housebound people refuse to accept visitors before 10.00am; I don't think they can be morning people either.

It's now 9.55 and I'm outside the door of my first patient in Falkirk, pressing the doorbell button.

I hate doorbells.

It's a less than fifty-fifty chance whether they're working, people never change the batteries in the damn things. Trouble is the bell box is usually so far from the front door that I can never tell whether it's rung or not. I'd rather just bang the door with the flat of my hand, but then I'd get:

'Why didn't you use the doorbell...?'

So I press the button, and I wait...

...and wait...

Most of my patients are riddled with arthritis, and piloting a Zimmer to the door can take a while. Knocking prematurely sounds like 'hurry up'; if they panic and try to rush, they could end up on the floor in a knot of flesh and aluminium, at which point I would be obliged to kick the door down and untangle them...

So I make myself wait for about three minutes, knowing that if the doorbell wasn't working, nobody even knows that I'm here.

Three minutes is a long time...

Mrs Rutherford makes it to the door in two. It takes her as long again to unlock it. Twice I hear the keys drop to the floor; picking them back up sounds like a rescue operation in a collapsed coal mine.

Straight away I see that Mrs Rutherford is MRS Rutherford; there'll be no casual use of first names here. She's wearing a slightly hairy Marks & Spencer suit that looks more abrasive than sandpaper, and her hair is lacquered to a metallic finish. I find myself surprised that it isn't MISS Rutherford.

'Mr Rogers! DO come in. Oh my, are you moving in? What a load you're carrying.'

I shuffle the strap of my shoulder bag out of the furrow it's ploughed in my flesh; not easy when you've also got a suitcase in each hand.

'Yes Mrs Rutherford, I'll be staying for a couple of weeks if that's alright.'

I'm trying to make it sound like I'm saying that for the first time.

'Oh my, you must be very fit.'

Yes, and getting fitter all the time you keep me standing here holding this lot.

My first mission-objective is to get some drops into Mrs Rutherford's eyes – I need her pupils dilated, and unlike Sunday at the Garden Centre, I don't see that happening as a result of romantic interplay.

The drops take time to have an effect so they have to go in as soon as possible, allowing them to work while I'm setting up my equipment. From a purely ergonomic point of view, I'd really like to pop the drops in at the front door, but I suspect the patients would find this sort of attack unacceptable. So I waste four minutes imitating a snail while Mrs Rutherford lifts and lowers her Zimmer and leads me to her sitting room. Yes, I know it only took her two minutes to answer the doorbell, but on the way back she chats to me, and each time she speaks the Zimmer goes down and stays down until our verbal exchange is complete.

Mrs Rutherford's hallway is huge and the flock wallpaper is long past reflecting light. In the sitting room it's just a little brighter thanks to a plant-lined bay window, though the sunlight is strictly rationed by curtains that would feel at home in the Edinburgh Playhouse. There are several wooden tribal masks decorating the walls, and herds of china elephants and other exotic animals roam a marble meadow on her mantelpiece. The little table beside Mrs Rutherford's leather-upholstered chair holds the only picture in the room, a yellowed photo of a middle-aged man in military uniform.

Finally Mrs Rutherford has got herself seated, I've removed an ancient pair of fake-tortoiseshell specs, and after a quick check of her pupils my little plastic applicator of 0.5% tropicamide drops is making its final approach past heavily painted-on eyebrows.

First drop goes into the right eye, then very quickly a second in the left – needs to be fast before she realises how badly they sting. That's when their eyes close up tighter than the shutters over an off-licence window.

Doesn't matter how often I hear it, I still jump at the noise my patients emit at this point. Reminds me of being on the platform at Prestonpans Railway Station while the London express is shooting through.

'Oh – that NIPS, Mr Rogers.'

Such a proper lady; it's not uncommon to hear the 'F' word at this point…

'Some people feel it more than others, Mrs Rutherford. It's all to do with the relative ph values of your tears and the drops; this varies widely amongst individual patients...'

That might be true, I'm not really sure, but a bit of gobbledegook distracts them. Now I start speaking slowly, using a firm tone:

'…good thing is, it only nips for a moment, in fact…'

- my words grow softer, coming still further apart ' –

…there, see, it's better already…'

Technically, that's hypnotic suggestion.

Not sure if it's ethical, but it works.

While Mrs Rutherford's assaulted ocular tissue cools off, I set about turning her sitting room into an Optometric consulting room. Finding a power outlet for my little electronic test chart is always a trial. I know before I ask that she's going to insist I consider the spare socket right beside her. They always do that; just doesn't seem to occur to them that it wouldn't be much of a test if I placed the chart three inches from their eyes instead of three metres.

I have to negotiate though; if I just pull a plug out of whichever socket I fancy using, I run the risk of de-programming a satellite-box, or disabling an oxygen-pump. I'm never sure which of those gaffes would upset them most.

Finally I'm ready, and I start to shine my various lights at Mrs Rutherford's eyes, noting the results on my clipboard.

'Oh, you are writing a lot. There's nothing wrong, is there?'

'Absolutely not, Mrs Rutherford. Nowadays I have to write it down when I find that an eye is healthy. For example, if I don't say that you haven't got cataracts, it can legally be assumed that I haven't looked for them.'

'Isn't that a bit silly?'

'Just a bit.'

'I mean, isn't that the same as putting down what you DON'T need on your shopping list? Like 'bread not needed, because there's still half a loaf left.' Isn't that an awful waste of your time?'

Out of the mouths of - OAPs.

Mrs Rutherford is 92, which means her ocular condition is quite remarkable. The lenses of her eyes are totally transparent, and I can't see anything to worry me on her retinae. She confirms these observations by reading right down the chart to the second-bottom line. With a patient of this age, I'm happy if they get as far as the middle line. Problem is, I'm not finding any refractive change from her old spectacles.

'So, Mrs Rutherford, just tell me again about your vision problems. Is it distance things that are blurred, like television, or is your difficulty more with reading?'

'Oh both, Mr Rogers, but more the reading. And I do so love to read.'

She said that last quite wistfully.

'Mmm ... did the deterioration happen gradually, or was it sudden?'

'It wasn't sudden, it's been like this for a while now. I didn't know you could come out to the house until the nurse told me, or I would have called you months ago.'

'Any double vision at all?'

This is a common problem with near vision in the elderly patient, but her cover test looked normal.

'Oh no, nothing like that.'

Based on my examination and this little exchange, the cause of her near difficulties must be inadequate lighting when she's reading. As eyes age they need more light for detailed tasks, something most people are totally ignorant of.

Two problems with this theory. First off, it doesn't explain the problem with watching television. Second is the state-of-the-art halogen reading-lamp standing next to her chair.

Mind you...

'Mrs Rutherford, when you're reading, do you actually turn your reading lamp on?'

'OF COURSE I turn it on. What possible use could it have if it weren't turned on?'

OK, just asking.

Well, that's that. I'm stumped.

'I'm sorry Mrs Rutherford, but I can't find any underlying reason for your difficulties. Your eyes and sight are really very good, and I don't understand why you're finding it hard to read.'

An exasperated sniff. She lifts her own spectacles from the little table with the photo where I'd laid them for safekeeping and very carefully, using both hands, puts them back on. Then she produces a book from somewhere inside her chair, something by Jane Austen.

'I'll show you, Mr Rogers. There - see - I can barely make out the words.'

A quick peek tells me the words in her book are normal size, possibly even a shade larger than average, and the print isn't faded. This doesn't make sense; she was reading much smaller print quite easily through trial lenses of the same power as her specs.

Enlightenment tends to be a sudden experience. It can be embarrassing in its simplicity.

When I measured the power of Mrs Rutherford's old spectacles I noticed the Focimeter image was a little faint and distorted, but I didn't give it much thought. My equipment lives in the car, and sometimes there's a cold snap during the night; when that happens, the instruments suffer from condensation at the beginning of the day. But – this is June.

Murmuring 'May I?' and lifting Mrs Rutherford's spectacles from their perch on her nose, I have to resist an urge to tap my fingers on her steel-spun hair. Holding the spectacles up to the light from the window, and peering over the top of my own rimless specs to use the magnification gifted to me by myopia, I can see a telltale dull mosaic.

There's several layers of clear hair-lacquer on her lenses.

'Mrs Rutherford, I presume you have a hairdresser who comes to the house. What do you do with your spectacles while she's spraying your hair with lacquer?'

Her head comes up sharply.

'Why, I take them off, of course. I put them down on this little table beside me, right here.'

Where the clouds of lacquer settle gently on the lenses, building up a layer at a time with each visit from the hairdresser. Coating the precise optical surfaces with an irregular, light-scattering film. Causing a gradual impairment to detail.

She's sceptical about this.

'But I clean them every day with a soft cloth.'

After hunting in one of my bags, I bring out an aerosol spray loaded with solvent and give Mrs Rutherford's spectacle lenses a good dousing, followed by an equally extreme scrub with my Selvyt cloth.

'Ordinary cleaning doesn't have any effect on hair lacquer Mrs Rutherford, it takes something much more powerful to shift it. Here...'

I hand back her spectacles.

'...try your book now.'

Watching her reaction as she welcomes Jane Austen back into her lonely life sends a surge of pride through me. I've just done myself out of a good sale, but I don't care. It's times like these when I love my job. Time to pack up.

'What are you doing, Mr Rogers?'

'Well Mrs Rutherford, that's me done. Problem solved, your glasses won't need to be changed after all.'

'Ah, but while I intend to take steps to prevent this happening again, supposing it somehow does? Then I would have to wait until you had time to come back and clean my glasses again, and also I would like to have a means of confirming that it was the same problem. No, I think I shall ask you to make me an additional pair of spectacles, Mr Rogers. A spare pair. Would that be alright?'

The rest of the day's patients prove more routine and by three o'clock I've worked my way back to Edinburgh, where I have an appointment with my solicitor. His office is on Leith Walk, just far enough out of the city centre to make parking possible without diminishing his fees.

Sitting opposite Mr Diggins in his office I feel quite proud of the polished-oak flooring, and the limited edition prints looking down on a miniature forest of palm trees. I even take some pride in Mr Diggins' pinstripe suit, tailored to perfection about four inches of waistline ago.

After all, I've paid for most of it.

It came as a shock to discover I needed a solicitor at all. Since Sally came to the marriage with no assets, I had assumed that mine would be safe. The nightmare began when it was explained to me that everything I acquired before our marriage would remain my sole property, with the exception of anything that had been careless enough to 'change its persona.'

The flat where the couple take up residence for example (my flat) automatically becomes a 'matrimonial home.' If you take the accountant's advice and make your wife a partner for tax reasons, then it doesn't matter whether all she's ever done is answer the phone now and again. She still owns half your business. I could go on...

I'm here to be told the details of Sally's latest proposal to settle our dispute over my money. Mr Diggins is snatching worried glances over the top of his varifocal spectacles, being obviously as skilled in their use as he is at managing my case.

The best way to choose a professional is by recommendation. Unfortunately, any friends whose marriages founder while your's is still afloat are promptly excommunicated. So when your own marital bliss turns sour, you don't have anybody to ask for advice about divorce lawyers.

This left me choosing Mr Diggins on the basis of his firm's sleek image, and even because of his exorbitant fees. I'm beginning to suspect that he's better at marketing than he is at law. Lately, I've even begun to wonder whose side he's on.

'Would you like a coffee, Mr Rogers?'

That means bad news. I decline; a cup of coffee in here would cost me around £10.

'Now, as you know, I have received a proposal from your wife's solicitors. You appreciate how complicated it has been to produce a valuation of the marital assets; your business is difficult to value, there has been some dispute over the market value of your holiday home…'

'The sales manager at Greenacres is adamant that my Caravan is only worth £10,000,' I interrupt.

'Hmmm … your wife's solicitors are equally adamant that he sold one last week – the same model and age as yours – for £30,000.'

How the hell did they find out about that?

'In addition,' he continues, his expression unreadable, 'your wife's solicitors are challenging your accountant's valuation of your Optometric practice, which was £15,000. They have unearthed details of the sale of a similar practice in Cornwall for £35,000.'

'But that's ridiculous. You can't compare Scotland with England, the NHS set-up is totally different here.'

He cocks his head, and I swear there's a hint of a smirk on his bovine face.

'Quite so. In England the NHS pays an examination fee of just slightly more than £20. In Scotland, because of the extra responsibilities assumed by Scottish Optometrists, the fee is nearer £40. Your wife's solicitors therefore contend that your own practice is worth rather more than the one in Cornwall.'

This is not good. Who's she got working for her – MI5? And what's he looking so smug about?

'The third pension fund, which you neglected to declare, and the £10,000 of shares registered in your name, which also slipped your mind, well, I'm afraid they know about those.'

'I'm expected to remember every little detail...?'

Now he's leaning forward, elbows on the leather-writing pad of his walnut desk, peering at me through piles of cardboard-clad documents.

'I have already explained to you the prohibitive cost of going to court on this. Your wife's solicitors have intimated that, should you reject this proposal, they are instructed to commence court proceedings.'

She can afford court costs – she's on Legal Aid.

'Your wife's solicitors wish to simplify things, and I would advise that their offer is worth considering. They suggest that Mrs Rogers' interests could be satisfied by the transfer of the marital home to her name, together with an additional payment of £10,000. The outstanding mortgage would also become Mrs Rogers' sole responsibility. I really think...'

I'm on my feet, shouting; the air-conditioning is doing nothing to cool my burning face.

'The equity in that flat is worth £100,000. That's like giving her a salary of £20,000 a year for the time she was married to me. Over and above what she's already spent. Then she wants another £10,000 in cash? I'd have to sell my shares, my last liquid asset.'

I begin working through the different ways of expressing the word 'No.'

'No way.' 'Not a chance.' 'When Hell freezes over.' And so on…

Mr Diggins waves his hand back and forth; his expression suggests he's unimpressed by my angst. No doubt he's seen it all before.

'You'd be left with your pension funds, your business, and your holiday home. Taken together, these are worth considerably more than your wife is asking for.'

'But I'd also be left without a bean. Not a bloody bean. In fact, what I'd be left with is negative beans. Definitely not, this is ridiculous.'

Mr Diggins pushes his glasses back up his nose. He's making a show of reading the offer.

'One more thing – your ex-wife says that should you accept this offer, she will not consider pursuing custody of one of the pet dogs.'

Now I sit down. Mr Diggins winces when my chair scrapes noisily on his precious floor.

The dogs have never been mentioned before; they're my dogs, she's never wanted them. The fact that she'd even consider separating them shows how little they mean to her. If it came to handing over one of them, I'd have to give her both so they could stay together.

Now I feel the air conditioning. I'm cold all over.

…damn.

Finally I lift my face from my hands, causing Mr Diggins to twitch. He needn't worry, I'm calm. Unhappy, but calm.

'Accept the offer, Mr Diggins,' is all I say before standing up and walking out of his office.

Driving home, I'm trying without success to get my head round this new penniless situation. Oh, I've got my pensions - they'll come in handy in twenty years time. Got to keep my business too - whoopee. Not to mention the Caravan - nice of them to leave me with a roof over my head.

No cash though - just a twelve thousand pound credit card debt I've run up with Mr Diggins' legal fees.

So no cash for the foreseeable future.

I didn't foresee this particular scenario because I didn't expect Sally to be able to take over the mortgage on the flat. Presumably the new man in her life is bringing his income to the table.

When I turn off the main road onto the single track that leads down to Greenacres, the Town House Spire at the centre of Haddington sinks slowly out of sight. Greenacres is set in a valley; there are long grassy slopes on all sides which quarantine the outside world.

The sky tonight is rich orange, bringing the 'Shepherd's delight' connotation to mind. I tap the brakes, to give a rabbit time to survive its game of chicken.

Halfway down the potholed road an aerial view of Greenacres pops out of nothing. The Caravans form a green and white chequerboard, a couple of hundred squares of simple respite. There's no sirens or blue lights down here, no drunken singing on a Saturday night - well, except for Tom and Kathy - financially, the whole set-up is as big a con as Sally's acquisition of my biggest asset, but this is different. This is a swindle I can live with. What I get back transcends the financial insanity.

The dogs are surprised but uncomplaining when I drop to the floor and hug them for quite a long time.

The laptop screen's blinking, which means I've got email. No doubt the Area Optical Committee inviting me to something extremely boring.

Nope - it's Diane.

To: Mark.Rogers@yahoo.com

From: Diane.Wells@btinternet.com

Subject: Re: Dinner?

Hi Mark

Yes, that sounds lovely. It's awful posh though, isn't it? I'd be quite happy with a Chinese you know!

Work was a pain today, the other staff nurse was off sick, so I've been chasing my - em -self all day!!!!!!!!!!! Seems to be some sort of bug going around. Just about to settle down with a glass of wine and a bit of telly.

Hope your day was good. Let me know when you've booked our meal for Saturday, and the time, and I'll be there.

Looking forward to it.

Diane x

I'm smiling as I uncork a new bottle of Glenfiddich. There's things in life that are real, and...

...the rest don't matter.

FOUR

Tibetan Terriers are about to become extinct in East Lothian. Or at least the one that lives with me is. Molly is playing 'catch me if you can' - with my wallet in her jaws. Ziggy is sprawled on the sofa listening to what's going on; I can almost hear her tutting under her breath. I can't really win here - even assuming I could catch a dog that moves so fast it couldn't catch itself, the resulting tug of war would turn my wallet into a Braille notepad.

Having just come out of the shower I am naked, which puts me at a psychological disadvantage, even though Molly isn't wearing clothes either. Firm commands edged with pack-leader authority seem to be amusing her. I haven't got time for this.

The moment I open the treat drawer Molly materialises at my feet, ready to negotiate. Ziggy's right behind her; as co-counsel she expects to be paid too. Getting my wallet back costs me two dental chews.

I'm in a rush because I'm meeting Diane in town for dinner, and I've only got an hour and a quarter to get ready and make the trip into Edinburgh. This isn't as much time as it sounds. To avoid traffic problems I'm taking the train from Prestonpans, and although the train journey is only fifteen minutes I've still got to drive to the Railway Station and make the walk at the other end. That only leaves half an hour to get ready.

I was stupid enough to make a pile on the bed of the 'mustn't forgets' - wallet (with vital credit cards,) mobile phone, car keys, paper tissues for the inevitable embarrassing sneeze. (How did Molly miss those?) Still bare-skinned, I carefully load all these essentials into my new jacket, which is hanging over the back of a chair, before going to barter with Molly and Ziggy over the ransom for my socks and underpants.

It takes about fifteen minutes to get to Prestonpans, so I've allowed half an hour to be safe. Before leaving, I stash fifty pounds in my hip pocket. Most people carry their cash in their wallet, but I just use the wallet for my credit cards. That way, if I lose the wallet, I've still got some cash. If I lose the cash - well, you get the idea. I shout goodbye to the dogs, but they aren't interested. Ziggy's gone back to her beloved sofa, and Molly's in her basket chewing something.

When I turn the ignition key, the engine immediately turns over - and turns over - and turns over. It's not catching though.

DON'T DO THIS TO ME

My panic and despair are fused by disbelief. Slamming the door hard, hoping it hurts, I'm off at a run to B Field.

Tom is gardening; he's watering Kathy's fuchsias while Kathy herself is taking a supervisory role from a lounger on the verandah. Tom looks up when I shout his name, and he does that grin that scares small children.

'Thought you was away out with wotshername off the computer.'

'My car won't start. Come on Tom, you know about cars. I need you to look at it, I should have left by now.'

In the time it takes Tom to digest that, Kathy's down from the veranda and snatching the watering can out of his hand.

'Move, you big lunk. He's late for his date.'

A very important date, I'm tempted to amend; why does Tom remind me of a playing card with legs?

Five minutes later Tom announces his diagnosis.

'Sorry mate, you're screwed.'

'What's wrong with it?' Kathy asks.

'Fuel pump's gone.'

'Can't you fix it?' I ask.

'Nope.'

Oh, I'll extract more details later; that's all I need to know for now. Checking my watch I groan loudly.

'I'd ask for a lift to the Station, but we'd never make it in time.'

Tom nods absently; I think his mind's still back on B field with the fuchsias. He yelps when Kathy's hand slaps the back of his head.

'Don't worry luv,' she says to me. 'Tom's going to drive you into Edinburgh to see your wee girl.'

Tom's confused.

'Am I?'

Kathy's hand starts to gain altitude again.

'Oh right, course I am. Come on Mark...'

Barring traffic holdups there should still have been plenty of time to get to Edinburgh, but Tom doesn't like going over fifty miles an hour. Kathy calls him 'Tom Tailback.'

I'm watching the hands on my watch, which seem to be spinning faster than the wheels on Tom's boxy Peugot, when he clears his throat. That makes me cringe, since it usually precedes a 'Tom-ism.'

'Y'know, I'm not sure I understand this Internet dating thing Mark. How can you get to know somebody properly by writing them letters?'

'Well, you don't. When you meet them, they're never anything like the picture you've built up in your head from the letters.'

He thinks this over while our speed drops by another 5mph.

'So why bother with all that letter-writing then? Why don't you just meet up straight away?'

He doesn't actually say 'Like normal people.'

Deep breath - in - hold -

'The letter-writing's just to weed out people you definitely wouldn't want to meet up with.'

Inspiration makes me add:

'Imagine you were buying a new car. You wouldn't look at anything with over 50,000 on the clock, or too small an engine size, now would you? That doesn't mean you'll buy the first two year old 1500cc that you see in the paper, does it? You'd still want to test drive it, but you've saved yourself from wasting time looking at crawling old bangers.'

Tom's grin splits his face.

'NOW I get it.'

There she is, standing by Fleshmarket Close like we arranged, and we're ten minutes late. I texted her though, and she texted back that it was alright. She's wearing a short cream coat, and her nyloned legs don't need any encouragement to draw attention.

'That's great Tom, stop the car and I'll get out here.'

'Naw don't be daft, I'll take you right up - is that her standing over there?'

If only Kathy had come along. The fleshy slapping sound when her hand connects with some vulnerable part of Tom is a bubble of vacuum this moment doesn't need. I wonder if I should just fill that void myself, it's the best way to communicate with him…too late, we're drawing up right beside Diane and…Tom's getting out?

I wonder if he's intending to come to dinner with us?

'Hello Sweetheart.'

I don't believe this. He's kissing her on the cheek. Whose bloody date is she?

'I'm Tom, Mark's best friend.'

No you are not.

'He's told us all about you, lass.'

Oh, I bet she loved that.

Diane looks confused, standing there with Tom's beefy hands on her shoulders, taking the full force of his wrinkly grin. Me, I'm just mortified. I'm standing to the side, waiting in turn to greet my girl.

As suddenly as it erupted, the maelstrom disappears back into the Peugot and glides off at 10mph below the speed limit, inked birds on a bare arm flapping the air outside the driver's window.

'Well', says Diane, stepping in front of me.

Through the lingering smog of Tom's Brut I can smell honeysuckle and cinnamon.

'Well, that was Tom,' I apologise, stepping closer.

We're now almost nose-to-nose, and she's lifting her eyebrows. Oh, right… quickly I lean in and kiss her cheek. Well, that's what I meant to do, but suddenly her mouth is where her cheek should have been. A sensation of crushed velvet changes to a softly-abrasive scrape when she takes a step back and scrubs my mouth with a paper tissue.

'Nice shade of lippy there' she says, her eyes waltzing with mine.

While we're walking to the restaurant, our hands remember the Garden Centre and slip together. She's about five foot three, and I was five foot nine last time I checked, but it feels like I've grown since then.

The restaurant's on the Royal Mile, and it's called Terrapins.

'Think I'll pass on the fish course.'

She slaps my shoulder, reminding me of Tom and Kathy, and a waiter who looks like his cat just died leads us to our table.

Diane's reading the menu, and she looks worried.

'Have you seen the prices here?' she whispers.

'Don't be silly, this is a special night and it's my treat. No arguments. Now, what do you fancy for a starter?'

'Well, I love seafood, but look at the cost of that seafood cocktail...'

'Seafood cocktail it is then,' I tell her firmly. 'Don't worry, you can help me wash dishes afterwards to pay for it.'

That makes her smile, something I'm finding I enjoy, and then she excuses herself to visit the ladies room. While she's gone, I take a quick glance at the menu myself. Whew, she wasn't kidding. Never mind, I'm out to impress, and this is *the* place to eat in Edinburgh. I'll be lucky if the fifty pounds in my hip pocket covers the tip. This is one for the plastic, and I pat my wallet through my jacket. Then I pat again, a little harder. Now I yank open my jacket and shove my hand into the pocket where my wallet should be ... but isn't.

A cold chill condenses around every internal organ while my mind's eye watches the scene as though I had been there...

...my jacket hangs helpless over the back of the chair while I busy myself in the bathroom with body spray and mouthwash. Molly decides the wallet felt too good in her mouth to relinquish so easily; she springs onto the chair, nuzzles back the jacket-lapel and dips her snout into the inside pocket. Pulling the wallet out like a canine Artful Dodger, she slinks off to hide it in her basket, Ziggy trotting curiously behind...

I know the modern thing is to split the bill, but I've already made it plain that I'm picking up the tab tonight. Or did I? No, I did. Made a big thing of it in fact. So. Options.

Hide under the table and refuse to come out.

Wait a minute though, I've got fifty quid. Scribbling quickly on a paper napkin, referring to the menu, I can see that this is still workable. It'll take a little discreet stage direction when it comes to ordering, but yes – it can be done.

A cough makes me look up. Diane's standing behind her chair, watching me with a curious expression. Quickly I stuff the spreadsheet/napkin into my pocket.

'Just jotting down some work stuff,' I explain.

'Oh,' she replies, sitting down.

'Right, let's take a look at this menu. Now, while you were gone, I spotted one of those steak things going by, and it looks absolutely fabulous. What do you say we go for that?'

She traces her finger down the menu lying open between us, stopping at the steak-en-croute I'm talking about.

Clearly marked as 'For two people.'

In other words, the economy dish.

'Yes, that looks lovely.'

I'm on a roll.

'Now, when I saw that steak thing go by, I also saw that it's a huge portion. I mean, I think we'd be hard pressed to eat half of it. So I thought, maybe we should skip the starter...'

Her eyebrows have started a steep ascent...

'In fact…' and I hope I don't sound as hysterical as I feel, '…probably we'll have to skip dessert too, we'll be so full.'

Now I can't tell anything from her expression.

'That'll be fine.'

Her tone isn't really giving anything away, but I think she's okay with this.

When the waiter appears, I give him the order.

'No starter, sir?'

SHUT UP.

'No, I don't think so.'

I said that with a condescending 'what do you know you silly little man' inflection.

Now he's got it in for me. With a flourish, he produces another leather-bound menu. 'The wine list sir.'

HELL.

I'd forgotten about wine. It's not in the spreadsheet.

I make my choice, explaining to Diane that I've had this one before, it's too perfect to pass on, what a pity they only have it in half-bottles…

Finally we're left alone, no more awkward questions to field from the hired-help. The smile I beam at Diane projects warmth and confidence.

'So.'

'Yes.'

'Sorry about keeping you waiting, then unleashing neanderthal man on you.'

'Oh but Tom was sweet, it was so good of him to give you a lift. What are you going to do about your car?'

'I'd scrap the beggar if I could afford a new one.'

She's laughing. She probably thinks I'm joking – on both counts. Well, I am the first poor Optometrist I've known personally…

She's stopped laughing.

That's because the waiter's brought our meal. I had no idea they were into nouvelle cuisine here. Beautifully presented - a work of art really - but barely enough to feed a small gnat.

Diane's looking from her plate to me. I think maybe she's hungry.

'Looks like the dish I saw, the one that came in huge helpings, wasn't this one after all.'

'Obviously.'

The waiter's back, and he's pouring the wine. The glasses are like vases, so he barely half-fills each before the bottle runs dry. As he walks off he throws a parting shot:

'Let me know if you need another bottle, sir.'

Bastard.

I chuckle; it comes out like a pig being garrotted.

'Think this'll be enough, don't you? We don't want to get tipsy, do we?'

'Oh, I don't know.'

We start to chat over our meal, but there's barely time to confirm yesterday's weather before the food's all gone.'

'Well, that was nice', I say, tossing my napkin onto the plate, where it skids over the surface, and raising my hand for the bill.

Diane excuses herself to the ladies room again. I wonder if she's got a weak bladder? While she's gone, I turn over the bill.

£58 - how can it be £58? I've only got £50. Oh hell, there's a 20% service charge. I grab the menu and sure enough, there it is in the small print.

'20% service charge. Individual gratuities at diners' discretion.'

Individual gratuities? They'll be bloody lucky. I wonder how Diane would feel about doing a runner? I'm actually estimating the distance to the door when she returns, and the expression on her face brings me back to the real world. Has her cat died too?

'Look Mark, it's OK you know. No big deal.'

She's guessed.

'Really? I mean, you're alright with this? I've been feeling awful about it.'

She shakes her head; her smile seems weak.

'These things happen, Mark. Let's just pay the bill and leave, shall we?'

'OK - how much money have you got? I need at least eight pounds, but if you think we need to leave that waiter a tip, I'll need more.'

Her face has flushed a deeper shade than her lippy and she grabs the bill, scans it, then hoists her bag onto the table before ripping a couple of banknotes from her purse.

'Here, I can pay my share, thank you very much.'

Then she's gone, head high, marching past our smirking waiter, leaving two banknotes air-dancing in her wake.

Processing this latest development took me countable seconds, and I had to lift my chin back off the floor, but now I'm accelerating to a speed Einstein said was impossible, leaving two more banknotes airborne, only this time crumpled in a ball and bouncing off our waiter's smug face. Out on the street I look both ways, and for one panicked moment I can't see her. Then I spot the cream coat zipping towards Waverley Station, and I'm off like Tom to the bar at last orders. By the time I catch her I'm having trouble sucking in enough air to keep my blood oxygenated, and my heart's playing a military tattoo.

Somehow I muster enough breath to shout: 'Diane, wait - what's wrong?'

Diane stops and turns, and there must be a horrible slimy monster standing right behind me. Either that, or she's looking at me.

'Mark, just leave it. I understand, OK? I've been there too. It doesn't matter, just go home and I'll do the same.'

I'm missing something here.

She hasn't 'been there' - she can't have, she doesn't have a dog.
Following as she backs away from me, I'm desperately trying to explain my side of what just happened…

'…so I didn't have enough money to pay the bill. I thought you understood, but - now I don't know what you're thinking?'

Glory be, she's stopped walking backwards. There are tears running down her face, making my intestines twist painfully. She's making a strange noise, too - something halfway between a sob and something else? While I watch helplessly, my heart in stasis, she draws a deep breath…

'I thought you just wanted to get the meal over and get away from me … I thought you'd built me up in your mind, then got a disappointment when you saw me again…'

'Oh.'

My voice is cracking, even though I've recovered from the running.

'But you could never disappoint me, Diane…'

The chill air suddenly concedes to an airborne gulf stream when she steps forward and loops her arms round my neck. I start gabbling more apologies, until she places a finger over my lips. Her eyes are full of the softest light I've ever seen.

'Just once Mark,' she says, her stern expression not reaching her voice.

'Just once, would you please do what you're supposed to?'

So I do.

Discovering in the doing that the taste of Diane's lippy outclasses nouvelle cuisine. It's a while before my mouth's free to whisper in her ear. Then she's shaking with laughter, and her arms tighten round me before her lips move to my own ear and she whispers back:

'Yes, I'd love some fish and chips.'

FIVE

Monday evening, and carelessly I've let Tom and Kathy talk me into having a drink with them in their Caravan. Caravans are cosy places, with their low roofs and narrow rooms. They never feel cramped, even though they are.

Tom and I are sitting on the built-in sofa and Kathy's in a free-standing armchair, within striking distance of Tom.

To keep control of the situation I've brought my own bottle of Glenfiddich, rather than have Tom topping me up every ninety seconds. Only problem is that Tom's taken quite a fancy to Glenfiddich, and he's using my bottle to keep his own glass full. Still, at least this means I won't get drunk tonight.

Kathy of course wants to know all about Diane and our date.

'Tom says she's a right bonny lass, he was quite taken with her.'

Yes, I noticed. Oh I've forgiven him now, especially since he helped me get my car fixed today.

'I'm seeing her again on Wednesday night, we're going to a film.'

'What's the film?' Tom asks, which starts Kathy laughing.

'Oh Tommy, where's yer romance? They wont be watching the film.'

I'm playing at beetroot, and Tom's scratching his head.

'But what's the point of...'

Kathy cuts him off. 'Don't bother. You wouldn't understand.'

Tom huffs, and reaches over for my bottle of Glenfiddich. Why doesn't he just stick a straw in it?

'So what does she do?' Kathy asks, and I tell her that Diane's a nurse at the Royal Infirmary.

'So she'll understand all about what you've been through with your chemo and all?'

'Ah.'

Tom's not looking, so I'm able to retrieve the bottle of Glendfiddich.

'Well, I've not mentioned that to her yet. I mean, we've only had one proper date.'

Tom's back watching the Glenfiddich, waiting for me to put it down again, and he passes the time by commenting: 'It'll give you something to talk about, her being a nurse and all.'

'Tom, if she was a mechanic, I wouldn't spend the night telling her about my busted fuel pump. Anyway it's a bit personal, and you never know how people are going to react, nurse or not.'

Oh, Auntie Kathy's onto that one like a cat on a mouse.

'Now luv, it's nothing to be ashamed of. Quite the opposite, the way you've come through it.'

'Yeah, but…that's the problem. I'm not through it yet; it could come back any time. In fact, I've just had a letter from Doctor Gordon asking me to come for another blood test on Wednesday because of the anaemia. Clear scan or not, anaemia isn't a good sign. Nor is it exactly the best qualification for starting a long-term relationship.'

What's so funny?

'So it's a long-term relationship you're thinking about with Diane, is it?'

Did I say that? I really am drinking too much.

'You know, Mark…?'

Now it's Uncle Tom.

'…I think you were doing the right thing before, meeting all them different women. Playing the field, like. I mean after Sally, d'you really…'

Oh, I felt that. Kathy put her all into that one. He's probably got concussion.

'He wasn't playing the field, ye daft lump. He only ever saw any of them the once.'

I know. Pathetic, wasn't it? Ah, she's got the 'Auntie' face back on.

'Mark love, a relationship's got to be based on trust and mutual respect…'

She stops, looks at Tom for a moment, then shakes her head.

'…what I'm saying is, if you don't trust her to accept you as you are, then you're right back where you were with silly Sally.'

'Dilly dally,' Tom says happily, closing his eyes. My bottle of Glenfiddich is empty.

'Kathy, it's not as simple as that. If you're with somebody and this happens, then of course you stick with them. But we've only just met, so she's quite entitled to decide a partner with cancer isn't a risk she wants to take.'

Tom's snoring, and I'm making a tactical move for the door. Kathy's last shot follows me out.

'Maybe you should let her decide that for herself, Mark.'

Wednesday's a muddle of a day. I'm going to see 'The Time Traveller's Wife' with Diane this evening, I've got my blood test at the hospital this afternoon, and my morning includes Ted Danby.

Ted's 88, he's a retired miner from Yorkshire. Calls a pick a pick, but he's a big softie really. Dotes on his great-grandchildren; in fact he moved here to be near them.

The visit today falls into a category guaranteed to snatch the sun from the day for any Optometrist. A recheck. An 'I can't see with these glasses you've given me.'

'I persevered son, I really tried, but the telly's just not coming right.'

'Ted, I did tell you you've got a bit of early cataract in both eyes. I didn't think it was bad enough to send you for treatment, but it sounds like maybe we should think again about that...'

'NO. I'm not going to no hospitals at my age, once they get you in there they never let you out.'

'But Ted, it's such a simple procedure; it's done under local anaesthetic, so you get back out the same day. There's nothing...'

'My granny had a cataract done, and she went blind after. I'm no wanting that.'

They've all got a relative who got a cataract 'done' fifty years ago that went wrong. A lot of surgery, all over the body, routinely went wrong fifty years ago. Since then there's been one or two little advances in medicine - but try and get that over to them. However, I am reluctant to refer Ted if it's at all avoidable. He suffers with COPD, chronic obstructive pulmonary disease. A lifetime of mixing 40 cigarettes a day with coal dust has caught up with him, and he's permanently attached to an oxygen-nebuliser. COPD patients are fragile, and they get tired very quickly, so it would be an ordeal for him to go to hospital. Having to lie flat and still for up to thirty minutes could be another problem.

Cataracts can be challenging when it comes to prescribing spectacles. What we call cataract is a gradual loss of clarity in a biological lens just behind the iris. Sometimes this misting occurs in irregular little zones, with the result that the best corrective lens depends on which 'bit' of the cataract the patient is 'looking' through at any given moment. So I have to find a sort of average power lens that gives acceptable vision throughout the field.

The effect a cataract has on vision is not unlike looking through a lens clarted with hair lacquer; bit of a long shot as Ted is completely bald, but after Mrs Rutherford I checked his spectacles first. No, only one strike of lightning this month.

'H…A…Y…O…U…T'

Well, if he can see that line he shouldn't be having a problem with his television. Though some people are better than others at recognising distorted letters, so his vision could be worse than his reading of the chart suggests. I'm not coming up with a better correction; it's beginning to look like referral for cataract extraction is the only option.

Ted's started thumbing buttons on his TV remote to demonstrate his difficulty to me. A lot of them do things like this; it's as though they think I'll somehow be able to look through their eyes and see the difficulty first hand. There is a sense of the ridiculous about it. With a faintly audible click, Ted's wide-screen TV snaps into a swirl of form and colour.

'There, see what I mean, it's not clear at all.'

I have to agree with him.

'No Ted, it isn't. I can hardly make out the faces.'

Either cataract is contagious, which they never told me at university, or that picture's not right.

'Ted, there's something wrong with your TV.'

'Can't be. I've only had it a few months, same time my grandson got that satellite thing put in for me so I could get more channels.'

Now, two weeks ago when I delivered Ted's glasses, I remember there was one hell of a gale blowing. Unusually fierce for June; must be all this global warming stuff. A few people have told me since that they had slates blown off their roof...

'Just popping outside for a minute, Ted...'

When I come back in, Ted looks puzzled.

'Forget something from the car, did ye?'

'Ted, your satellite dish is pointing a different way to everyone else's.'

'But I only got it fitted a few...'

'It was that wind a couple of weeks ago, Ted. It's blown your dish out of position, you need to call them back to re-align it.'

A quick conversation on my mobile with Ted's grandson gets the repair process under way. Ted's not convinced. As I edge towards the door, he's still saying:

'But the telly was fine until I got them new glasses...'

Ted was in Grangemouth; now I'm back on the M9 heading for Edinburgh's Western General Hospital to submit yet another syringe-full of blood. Parking at the Western used to be difficult, but they're building a multi-storey car park which should solve that. While they're building it, parking has become impossible.

Not for me, though. A couple of months ago I found a little metered street about five minutes walk away that no one else seems to have discovered. My job has given me a knack for finding parking spots.

The Western General is the usual uneasy alliance of old and new architecture. It's set high off Crewe road, ten minutes from Princes Street. It's really a campus; it'd be hard to point to a 'main' building. It's become a special place for me over the last six months.

I am a little worried about this recall. My MRI scan is clean, but anaemia is an early sign of blood disease; since Lymphoma is essentially blood disease, Dr Gordon wants to repeat the test. She knows my eating habits are shameful, and frequently lectures me on the importance of eating properly. Recently I've been doing just that, except for Saturday night with Diane - which was balanced out by the fish and chips later.

Dr Gordon is my heroine. She's about my age, and dresses in wool cardigans and tweed skirts. She's every inch the professional, and she inspires confidence in her patients that borders on devotion. There's a little spark to her that suggests a different life outside, sans wool and tweed.

There are no out-patient clinics running this afternoon, but Dr Gordon told me to just go up to ward 8 and ask the staff nurse there to take the blood. I've no trouble finding ward 8; I had to spend a week there when I was first diagnosed, having every inch of my biology scrutinised and analysed.

The ward is made up of rooms which each house four patients. I can see a nurse in one of them making up an empty bed, so I wander in and wait for her to notice me. When she finally turns round I step back, my hands flying up.

'Mark.'

'Diane.'

Bloody Hell.

'But...you work at the Royal?'

'Oh, two of the staff nurses on this ward are off sick today, so I got sent over to help out. But what are you doing here? It's not visiting time.'

Good question. There must be an answer to it.

I could say I've come to see her, but then I'd look like a stalker. There's a man of about 60 sleeping in one of the other beds.

'I've come to see him,' I blurt, pointing. 'His eyes.'

Diane's head tilts a few degrees.

'But you haven't got your equipment with you.'

I look down to confirm that she's right about that, and remember the pen torch in my pocket. Pulling it out, I start clicking it on and off.

'No, it's just a quick neurological check Dr Gordon asked me to do. Pupils, ocular muscle field, that sort of stuff...'

'Oh, alright. I'll wake him up.'

'No, it's okay. I'll come back when he's awake.'

'Don't be silly, you can't do that. MR JOHNSTON – WAKE UP.'

Please don't. Oh dear, he has.

'Who're you?', he asks suspiciously.

'I'm Mark Rogers, your Optometrist.'

'No you're not.'

'Just for today I am.' Please. 'Now, look at my light – oh, that's a nice agile direct reflex – and yes, consensual also present. Now, follow the light as it moves – no, without moving your head, just your eyes. Great – now, keep looking at me, are you aware of my fingers moving at the side?'

I'm running out of tests.

'Look right up at the ceiling and keep looking there – keep looking.'

'What's that for?'

'To rule out myasthenia gravis.'

'I don't have that.'

DIANE, GO AWAY.

Oh, she's finding this little performance fascinating. The observations sheet – it's on a clipboard hooked to the bed rail. Grabbing it, I read intently about Mr Johnston's oxygen-saturation. Don't understand a word of it, but it's given me a breathing space.

'Do you ever have trouble with swallowing, Mr Johnston?'

'Yes, sometimes. But why are you doing all this for an in-growing toenail?'

Don't be awkward.

'Well you know, Mr Johnston, it's amazing how the body connects up inside. Everything affects everything else. Anyway, that's me finished with you now, so you can relax.'

He doesn't look any more relaxed than I feel.

I'm gently extricating myself, shuffling towards the door, dropping platitudes behind me. Diane's following and she looks impressed, maybe even a little respectful. Finally we're back in the corridor, and I've gotten away with it. My bedside manner works with real beds. I'll get the blood test another day when Diane's back at the Royal.

Just as I poise for flight, there's a flicker of wool and tweed in my peripheral vision.

'Ah Mr Rogers, you were able to come for that test. Good.'

NO...

'Yes Doctor Gordon, I was.'

'Well, I've got to see another patient just now, but I'd like a word if you could wait outside my office?'

'Of course, Doctor Gordon. Happy to.'

What about the blood test, though? What am I going to do about that? Now she's talking to Diane.

'Nurse, would you mind doing a blood test for Mr Rogers? And could you have the analysis prioritised, and send it straight to my office so I can discuss it with Mr Rogers.'

'Of course Doctor.'

Well, that's blown it. I wonder what Diane's thinking now. Doctor Gordon is vanishing through the swing doors, and I can't look Diane in the eye.

'Mark, have a seat over there while I get a blood tray.'

I do as I'm told; she doesn't seem too upset. Must be shock. She's probably looking forward to sticking a needle in my arm. Taking her a long time to get that tray - I wonder if she's having a moment to herself, trying to make some sense of all this?

Here she comes now - strange, no blood tray.

'All done Mark, and the results should be with Doctor Gordon in a few minutes. Do you need me to show you where her office is?'

Huh?

'But you haven't done the blood test yet...?'

'Of course I have. After - oh, let's not say how many years - it only takes me a sec to get a blood sample, and Mr Johnston's got good veins.'

Mr Johnston?

Oh, she thought...

Oh no.

'See you tonight Mark.'

She looks so lovely - so trusting...

'See you later, Diane.'

I remember as a teenager being called to the headmaster's office. This was over a little prank involving the deflation of a sociopathic French teacher's car tyres. I feel very much now as I did then. Doctor Gordon would make a wonderful headmistress. She's sitting behind her office desk looking from my notes, to me, and back to the notes.

'Well Mr Rogers, your anaemia has disappeared.'

I nod, throwing in a sick smile.

'In addition, your blood group has changed from O to A.'

'Really?'

'Yes, and you're rhesus negative now. You were rhesus positive a month ago.'

'Strange.'

'Isn't it? I would by now be unleashing the fires of hell at nurses and lab technicians, but on speaking to Nurse Wells I discovered that she took this blood sample at random from an innocent bystander – on your instructions?'

'Well no, it was your instructions actually...'

Her eyebrows just hit the ceiling, and if she was Superman there'd be burn holes through my head. I'd swear her lips twitched though...

'Semantics, Mr Rogers.' Her hands are doing aerial gymnastics. 'An unnecessary blood test was done because of you. Do you disagree?'

'No.'

Sorry...

'Why?'

So I tell her. Finishing with a passionate plea for lenience to Diane, since it really wasn't her fault.

Doctor Gordon is silent for long moments. She looks down at her desk, and starts to tap her pen lightly on the melamine top.

'Well, no harm done,' she finally says. 'So long as Mr Johnston doesn't sue us, but that's unlikely since he suspects nothing.'

She leans forward over the desk, and she's not being a headmistress any more.

'You know, Nurse Wells seems a very sensible person. She is a nurse after all. Why are you scared to tell her about your Lymphoma? Do you really think she's going to run at the mention of it?'

I explain as I did last night to Kathy, it's just so early to bring up things like that.

'Well.' She sits back. 'It's out of your hands now, because in the course of sorting out your apparent genetic mutation, and obviously before I realised there was a personal involvement, I told her about your condition.'

Oh.

'How did she take it?'

Doctor Gordon shrugs.

'I don't know her well enough to judge, but my impression was of two main reactions. The first was concern for you. The second, I think she wondered why you felt the need to keep it a secret from her. Actually, she wondered that quite loudly. I'd make a cautious approach next time you see her…'

A glance at my watch. In about three hours. If she turns up.

'Right.' She's pulling a metal trolley over to my side of the desk. 'I'll take that blood myself this time, just so I've got some idea of whose blood it is that I'm dealing with. Sleeve up, Mr Rogers. This may hurt, if I can make it.'

I'm still anaemic. She puts me on iron. Considers having my endoscopy and colonoscopy repeated. Decides that it's too soon for that to be useful. Frowns.

'Come back in a month and we'll have another look; if it's still the same I might send you for another MRI. Any - and I mean ANY - symptoms or signs before then, you phone my secretary straight away. In the meantime Mr Rogers, DO try to eat properly.'

Then she winks.

And good luck - she seems really nice, as are you, even if you are an idiot.'

I have to smile. Halfway through the door, I pause.

'Oh, Doctor Gordon. You might want to check Mr Johnston for myasthenia gravis - he has mild bilateral ptosis, his levator muscles fatigue easily, there's a Cogan's twitch sign, and he has difficulty swallowing sometimes.'

It's an ill wind…

SIX

I wonder what Diane's doing now – and what she's thinking…

DIANE

'Give me one of those.'

Jackie's mouth just dropped open. 'But you don't smoke, Diane.'

No, I don't, not since I gave up five years ago. Which is why, when the smoke hits my lungs, I start coughing and my head starts to swim. It feels good.

This so-called smoking shelter doesn't give much protection from the weather; it's function is to protect the enlightened masses by isolating the smokers. I didn't follow Jackie here with the idea of stealing one of her cigarettes; I simply needed to be out of the building while Mark's still in there. I am SO angry. I've told Jackie the gist of what happened.

'You know Diane, you can sort of understand it. After all, you haven't known each other very long…'

'That would be all fine and good if he just hadn't told me, but he went a lot further than that. He deliberately set out to conceal it from me, and caused chaos in the process. I mean, the whole thing turned into a sodding farce. He had me taking a blood test from a patient who didn't need one; he could have got me into serious trouble.'

'The Dragon Lady knows what went down, so she isn't going to blame you. Talking of which I'm a bit surprised she told you as much as she did, seeing as how you two are - well, you know, sort of involved. Seems a bit unethical, that.'

That has me shaking my head. Doctor Gordon is anything but unethical.

'When she told me about his condition she didn't know there was anything between us. She was just trying to find out why she had a blood analysis that obviously came from somebody else. She clammed up as soon as she twigged, but I'd got the picture by then, and when she went charging off to read the riot act to Mark I had a squint through his records on the computer.'

'Now that's definitely unethical.'

'What - and pretending to be doing a neurological examination isn't?

Jackie's got nothing to say to that.

'I thought we were getting on really well. Mark's no Tom Cruise, and he's a bit weird sometimes, but he tries hard and he can be a lot of fun. Thing is though, I can't stand liars. If he's lying about this, what else is he lying about?'

Jackie's thinking something, but she's hesitating...

Diane, have you given enough thought to your feelings about getting close to somebody with cancer? Do you not maybe think that's part of what's bothering you...?'

'NO. Well alright, it is a bit scary, especially coming out of the blue like this. He seems to have come through it though, and...no, I don't think I'm that shallow. It's just... after Matthew, I really hate being deceived.'

'You never really got over Matthew, did you Di?'

'Come on, it's only been nine months. Yes I thought Matthew and I were good together, but that's in the past now. Matthew's got nothing to do with this, he's history. Totally.'

What's that look supposed to mean?

'Right Di, we'd better get back. Fancy a coffee at the end of shift? You might have a better perspective on all this by then.'

'Can't, I'm meeting him at the cinema later, and that would make me late…if I still decide to go at all… oh, I suppose I need to talk to him, but wait - on second thoughts, yes to that coffee. Be good to bat it about a bit more with you first, and while he's waiting he can think about what he's done.'

Ocean Terminal is in Leith, and from the outside looks like a big warehouse. Inside, it's the same old glitzy mix of chain stores and fast food outlets. The cinema's on the second floor, and while I'm still on the escalator I can see Mark waiting outside.

He hasn't spotted me yet. He will in a moment though, his head's flitting about and he's shuffling like his shoes are too tight. I'm twenty minutes late – carefully worked out, just enough to frighten him without the risk of finding him gone.

'Diane!'

Running up, relief all over his face. When he tries to kiss me, a flick of my head tells him a cheek is all he's getting.

He's waiting for me to explain why I'm late. If he had a tail, he'd be wagging it.

'Mark, if we don't get into the cinema right away we're going to miss the beginning.'

'Sorry – right, let's go.'

He pauses by the goodie-counter.

'No Mark. I don't want popcorn, or juice, I just want to see the film.'

Tail's stopped wagging.

The credits roll. Mark tries to hold my hand.

'Don't – I'm watching the film.'

Actually, I am. All my friends told me this was a rotten film, but they were wrong. I think maybe it'd be hard to follow if you hadn't read the book. I actually haven't, but Mark has and he's told me enough to help me catch on quickly. Basically it's all about a man with a genetic condition that makes him jump without warning into the past or future. He makes friends with his future wife, Claire, while she's still a little girl, but when they meet again as adults that hasn't happened yet for him – so she knows him, but he doesn't know her. I'm just about following it, it's a stretch for me but not for Mark, he seems to have the type of mind that can bend round this sort of thing easily. Funny coincidence – Mark's first wife was called Claire.

The ending's sad – the Time Traveller knows when he's going to die, because he's outside the window watching himself when it happens. His wife knows too, because he's told her. There's nothing they can do to prevent it happening, and they're so much in love… I'm crying, though I'm not sure who it is I'm crying for.

Mark's got his arm round me, telling me it made him sad too. If I thought he was just saying that I'd throw the arm right back at him.

He's got a nice smell, reminds me of chestnuts, and I could easily stay like this for longer with my cheek against his neck and his fingers drawing on my back. The lights have come on though; we're sitting at the end of the row and people want past, so we have to move.

Back in the shopping centre we wander out to the observation area, a second-floor viewing platform overlooking the Port of Leith and the retired Royal Yacht Britannia. There's a bar just inside with the same views, and Mark suggests a drink. No, too many people milling about, I want to have a proper, private talk. That's why I left my car at home and came in by bus. Raising my wrist, I make a show of consulting my watch.

'I'm going to have to go now Mark, or I'll miss the last bus home.'

'Bus? What's wrong with your car?'

'Nothing, I just didn't feel like driving. I really need to...'

'Well I've got my car, I'll give you a lift. That means we can have that drink, too.'

'Okay, I'll take the lift, but let's not bother with the drink. I don't feel like one, and you'd have to stick to coke if you're driving.'

It takes about thirty minutes to drive from Leith to Gorebridge. Mark's car is a Subaru, the Impreza 4x4 model. It's pretty smart even though it's got a big mileage. He keeps claiming to be broke, but it doesn't show.

He says the four-wheel drive is necessary for his job – I think it's more a case of boys and their toys.

The first part of the journey's a bit awkward now that we're finally alone. At first we find ourselves talking quietly about the film, but what we aren't saying is louder. Mark's awful intent on his driving, even though the roads are fairly empty. Time to get this out in the open.

'You could have got me fired you know.'

He has the grace to look sheepish.

'I told Doctor Gordon it had nothing to do with you, I took full responsibility for what happened.'

'Yes, and so you should have. What did your blood test show? Yours I mean, not Mr Johnston's.'

'I'm still anaemic, so she's put me on iron. Now that you know about my wee problem…'

'Mark, you had cancer. It's not a 'wee' problem, but it's not something to be ashamed of either. Why was it such a big deal that I didn't find out?'

'It wasn't … well, it was, but only because I hadn't told you. I would probably have mentioned it tonight – or if not tonight, next time…'

'Next time? First I've heard about there being a next time.'

I'm back to seeing him with a tail and I just kicked him. This is not fair, why should I start feeling guilty?

'Okay, so tell me about it now.'

'But you already know.'

Men. Everything's a list of facts.

'I don't know how it made you feel, how you got through it, whether you're worried about the anaemia. I don't know anything because you aren't telling me.'

'Oh.'

That's going to take him a few minutes to digest, and we're turning into my street already. Weird not having to give directions; his satellite navigation's very impressive. It's certainly done more talking than he has.

'Over there, the white bungalow. Look, you'd better come in for a coffee. That's just because we haven't finished talking, clear?'

Oh, I sensed that smile being cancelled before it showed. Men just can't help themselves; it's all about points, and getting asked in for coffee's a bonus score. I hope he takes sugar, because I haven't got any.

'This is nice, Diane.'

'It's a bit of a come-down from where I used to live, before…oh, it's alright I suppose. Not very big, but I don't really need more room than this. You'll have to excuse the mess – I'm not the world's tidiest person.'

Marcus, my cat, is waiting in the hall. As soon as he sees Mark his back arches and he starts hissing like an angry snake. Hah – take that, Mr animal lover.

Mark doesn't seem bothered though; apart from a murmured 'Nice cat', it's like he doesn't see Marcus as we walk into the sitting room then through to the kitchen. Marcus is traipsing behind us, looking annoyed.

After switching the kettle on, I bring the cafetières out of the cupboard while Mark continues making the right noises about my house. He seems intrigued by my potted herbs. Back in the sitting room he settles himself at one end of the sofa, clutching his coffee against his chest, while I plump myself down on the other end. Now he's looking at the wall, and a picture of a Venetian gondola-park.

'What an unusual angle – did I tell you I went to Venice a few years ago…?'

Sip of coffee. Stare him down. Voice cold – think liquid nitrogen.

'I didn't ask you in to talk about Venice, Mark.'

'Alright … to be honest, I don't find talking – this sort of talking – comes naturally, it's not easy…'

'Mark, you've been married twice. Didn't you talk to your wives?'

'Maybe that was part of the problem.'

He said that quietly; for a moment he's looking into another place and time.

'I've always been pretty self-contained I suppose. I went out with someone else a while back, and she said I had shields up – that she didn't know who was really in there, and didn't think she'd ever be allowed to. I knew she was right, but I still couldn't talk to her.'

'Bet you talk to your dogs,' I can't help quipping.

'Yes…they don't say a lot back, though.'

I'm not sure if that's a joke or not. Long pause, which finally I have to break.

'Mark, I just want to know how you felt – how you feel about something so important. Otherwise how can I think I know you at all?'

He nods, and his eyes drift off again.'Well, I was bloody scared at first. I thought that was it, the end. Strange though, after a day or so I started to - accept it. I don't mean I gave in to it, I just sort of – adapted. That was how things were, so I lived with it, and life still went on – I realised it always goes on, if it ever doesn't I won't know about it.'

'Well, I was bloody scared at first. I thought that was it, the end. Strange though, after a day or so I started to - accept it. I don't mean I gave in to it, I just sort of – adapted. That was how things were, so I lived with it, and life still went on – I realised it always goes on, if it ever doesn't I won't know about it.'

'You're very philosophical.'

'I got into Zen a while back, after the split from Claire – it helped me a lot.'

Weird man.

'What was your worst moment?'

'That first night when I found out, I started thinking about all the things I hadn't done that I wanted to do, and I tried to imagine a world without me in it…I actually started crying…'

He looks startled, as though he's hearing this for the first time, before a wave of shame washes over him. Quickly I shake my head, no. He smiles, but only with his lips.

'The Tibetans didn't understand what was wrong, and they started pawing at me and whining. Snapped me out of it – I couldn't stand seeing them upset like that.'

Damn dogs. Soft bugger. Tears are slipping down his face, and mine too. I can't help myself; I've got his hand clutched in both of mine. This is a long sofa; I've no idea how we both ended up in the middle of it.

'What about now, are you worried about this anaemia thing?'

He's wiping his face, looking at the fingers of his free hand as though he's wondering why they're wet.

'A bit. Doctor Gordon doesn't seem too concerned though, more puzzled, and I've got a lot of confidence in her. So it's probably okay, but yes, it is on my mind.'

'Mark, you bottle things up too much. Don't you feel better for talking about it?'

He pulls my hands to his lips and speaks through my fingers.

'Yes, I do. I'd forgotten how much easier things can seem if you're not alone. By the way, there's something else I haven't told you...'

Oh Hell. What now?

'...I – em – I live in a Caravan. On a holiday park. I know it sounds strange, but...'

Blessed relief.

'Somebody I worked with lived on a Caravan Site. I don't think it's that big a deal these days, though you obviously do. Anything else?'

'What?'

'Any more surprises in store for me – you know, your hobby's serial killing, you were abducted by aliens – any little details like that still to come?'

'No, that's it. I promise.'

I believe him. His eyes are half-closed now; he's hiding again, but I think this has been so good for him.

For us.

Suddenly, I can see an us...

Now my face is pushing into his shoulder, both my arms are around him, and I'm crying for real. I'm crying for this daft man, for his loneliness when nobody should have been alone, and I'm crying because he trusts me...

I've just noticed that my cat is curled up behind him, snuggled into the small of his back.

SEVEN

Mark Rogers
Mobile Optician

Sight Tests at home for people who have difficulty getting out to high-street practices.

Local service from experienced Optometrist.

Examination is free to all; spectacles also can be free to patients on low incomes.

Tel: FREEFONE 0800 09 7723

I was busy all day Thursday and then most of this morning. Now that my divorce is settled, however disastrously, it's time for the phoenix to rise. I've put an advert in the local paper, printed up fifty reminder letters for patients who've ignored their recalls, sent another thirty current recalls, ordered a few thousand business cards to distribute, and done a nice chatty mail-shot to all the Optometrists who refer patients to me.

I've scraped together enough overdraft to order spectacle cases printed with my phone number. One of my more ill-advised budgetary measures a while back was to start using unprinted cases; I wonder how many patients have wanted to call me before their recall, and discovered they'd lost my telephone number.

In addition I've written a crawling letter to the chairman of the local Area Optical Committee, apologising for my absence from the last four meetings and re-affirming my commitment to our professional goals. Those meetings are good for reminding people to refer to me.

I've done some work in the past for The Royal National Institute for the Blind. RNIB. Contrary to popular belief they're quite involved with sighted people, particularly those with learning difficulties who might benefit from a sight test. When I phoned Craig, the local manager, he seemed to have some difficulty remembering who I was, but I think he was just being silly.

I feel focused; I'm determined to crawl out of the crater of my divorce.

I've even made an appointment with the bank, to see about a loan to pay off my credit card. The interest rate on a bank loan will only be a fraction of what I'm paying to the credit card company.

I actually feel excited, and I like the feeling; optimism has been a sorely missed companion this while back.

With Doctor Gordon's last instruction in mind I decide to break off for some cheese on toast. I didn't actually know Molly could jump that high, so the replacement batch gets put up high on top of the fridge to cool.

This afternoon I have a couple of patient visits, then an appointment at the Health Board; periodically I get called in to have my equipment inspected, just as high street practices receive regular visits for the same purpose. I'm on my way out when the phone goes.

Only a select few of my patients have their numbers permanently stored in the phone's memory to make their names come up on the Caller ID screen; just the ones I appreciate advance warning of.

'Mrs Forsyth, how are you today?'

'Oh, I'm simply fine Mr Rogers. Yourself?'

Such courage in the face of so much pain.

'How's the Blepharitis Mrs Forsyth? I presume that's what you're calling about?'

'No, it's not troubling me at all today Mr Rogers. It's my glasses that are the problem - they've gone very loose.'

Oh bugger. I adjust new spectacles very carefully when I deliver them, and as a result don't get many call-backs for adjustments. Still, it's aftercare, which the NHS insists is included in my initial fee. It seems to me that if I were really being paid for all the things the NHS claims it's paying me for, my fee should be double what I actually receive. However, I do appreciate that spectacles are not much good if they're hanging down on the end of the nose, below the line of sight.

'Don't worry Mrs Forsyth, I'll pop in next week sometime and fix them for you. Meantime, just keep pushing them back up your nose.'

'Pushing them...? Oh no, they're fine when they're on, nice and tight like you made them. No, it's when I take them off, the legs are just flapping about.'

Come on...

'Mrs Forsyth, if they're fine when they're on, I don't think this warrants a special visit. The sides are held on by little screws, granted they can get a little loose with wear, but your spectacles are not going to come apart.'

'Are you sure Mr Rogers? I've been awfully worried that they might.'

'Mrs Forsyth.' Firmer tone. 'If they fall to bits then so what? I'll just zip round and put them back together again. As for giving the screws a little tighten - well you know, as I seem to see you quite regularly, I really think that could wait until the next time I'm there about something else.'

She's not altogether happy, she looks forward to our little visits, but she gives in gracefully. Now I'm going to be late for my first appointment.

After putting the phone back down I stand and stare at it for a moment before muttering:

'How about if I start coming round first thing every morning and clean them for you...?'

Mr Inglis promises to be an interesting experience. He left a message on my phone a couple of weeks ago asking for an appointment; he also left his address, but forgot to leave his (unlisted) telephone number. I had to write to him to ask if he would ring me back. When I finally got to talk to him on the phone, I think all of Greenacres must have heard me trying to arrange the appointment.

Mr Inglis is very, very deaf.

The street outside his grey Council House in Armadale is a little cul-de-sac, and the front garden of the house opposite is both memorable and familiar. A river of pebbles raked with Zen-like precision, a little wooden wishing well, a wheelbarrow also made of red cedar and filled with pot plants. I've been to someone in this street before.

Mr Inglis's front door is wide open and I take this as an invitation, stepping inside before yelling:

'Mr Inglis – it's the Optician.'

'Through here son.'

The atmosphere is dark and dreary, like so many of my patient's domiciles. Mr Inglis has obviously given up on cleaning, or even putting things away. He's a small man, sharp featured, and his clothes are hanging off him. Maybe he's guilty of forgetting to eat too.

My throat soon starts to burn and I wish I had a megaphone to aid communication. I also begin to wonder if Mr Inglis is showing signs of early dementia. When I go to measure the strength of his old glasses on the Focimeter, he looks puzzled.

'You should already know what they are from last time.'

'NO, IT WASN'T ME WHO TESTED YOU LAST TIME.'

'What did you say, son?'

In a case like this, Retinoscopy is the best way to determine the spectacle prescription. By shining the Retinoscope beam through different powered lenses into the eye, I can work out the spec prescription very accurately. Except when there's a bit of 'smudgy' cataract, not bad enough to need referral, but sufficient to make the Retinoscope useless.

So I've got to do a subjective – 'better or worse?' – 'best with number one or number two?'

'IS THAT BETTER OR WORSE, MR INGLIS?'

' T...V...H...X...'

'NO, DON'T READ THE CHART, TELL ME IF THIS LENS LOOKS BETTER OR WORSE.'

'What? You'll have to speak up son.'

It's tedious and exhausting for us both, but eventually I've come up with the magic numbers. Now I need to find out if he pays for his glasses.

'DO YOU GET PENSION CREDIT?'

'I don't know, son.'

'WELL, IF YOU GET PENSION CREDIT, YOU CAN GET YOUR GLASSES FREE.'

He must get it, it's obvious he's on a low income, but I need him to declare it.

'DID YOU GET THEM FREE THE LAST TIME?'

'You should know that.'

'I KEEP TELLING YOU, IT WASN'T ME WHO SAW YOU LAST TIME. PENSION CREDIT, MR INGLIS. DO YOU GET IT?'

'Eee, I don't know. You'll have to ask my brother, he does all that stuff for me.'

'OKAY, WHAT'S HIS PHONE NUMBER?'

It takes Mr Inglis ten minutes to find his brother's phone number. Together we go through piles of junk mail and old hospital appointment-cards and finally unearth a battered old notepad which is Mr Inglis's address book. Keying the number into my mobile, I'm hoping the brother isn't deaf too.

Oh wonderful, he isn't.

'This is Mark Rogers, Mr Inglis. I'm your brother's Optician, and I'm with him just now. He's not sure if he gets pension credit, for free glasses, but he thinks you might know.'

I sound like that guy on "Who Wants To Be A Millionaire?"

Phone a brother.

'Yes, he gets pension credit. Thought you would have known that from last time.'

A horrible thought has occurred to me. I'm scared to ask this.

'Was it me who saw him last time?'

'Yes, of course it was. About three years ago.'

So that's why the street looked familiar. If I'd had the old record card, I wouldn't have had to measure his old glasses, I'd probably have known in advance about the cataract and not wasted my time trying to do retinoscopy; there's all sorts of things that I've just repeated needlessly. I could have been finished in half the time, and my throat would only be half as sore.

'IT WAS ME WHO SAW YOU LAST TIME MR INGLIS.'

'Aye, I told ye that already, son.'

The next patient is easy. She admitted to being a previous patient when she made the appointment, so I've got her old record to refer to. She can hear perfectly, and her eyes haven't changed. Incredibly, I make it to my inspection on time.

The Health Board offices have an abundance of polished glass and shiny aluminium in their structure. Mr Diggins would give a lot of my money for these sort of opulent surroundings. No wonder there's no cash left for actual healthcare.

One of the army of minions that swarm the place shows me into a so-called boardroom. It's filled by a big table with about twenty chairs round it - maybe that's why it's called a boardroom - and presumably, this is where I'm supposed to lay my equipment out. My frame stock isn't part of the inspection, so I only had to carry two cases in here - plus a visual field screener, a test a lot of my patients don't have the ability to perform, so it only gets fetched into their houses when it's needed.

Pretty soon I've set up a display worthy of our trade show, Optrafair. Not many domiciliary Optometrists use an air-puff Tonometer, since it's a heavy swine to carry around. The classical alternative however, the Perkins Applanation Tonometer, while no larger or heavier than an Ophthalmoscope, requires the use of topical anaesthetic. I don't believe in administering anaesthetic on a scattergun basis; sooner or later the statistics for inadvertent corneal damage have to catch up. There is another alternative, a clever little tonometer using a projectile principle, and it would be perfect, but it's too expensive to think about at the moment!

My major worry today is my Slit Lamp. A Slit Lamp is a biomicroscope; it consists of a binocular viewing piece attached to a slit-light source, and is used for viewing the eye in 3D at high magnification. Problem is mine stopped working a few months ago. The fault was fairly simple, a wire to the bulb had come loose, and since I can't afford either the expense or the time away of having it professionally repaired, I bought a soldering iron and fixed it myself. Because the solder I used was a little bulkier than it should have been, and displaced the bulb slightly, the slit of light now shines at a ten-degree angle. I haven't found this to be a problem; I simply tilt the instrument and myself by the same amount and it's straight again. I'm a bit worried the examiner might feel differently.

'Mark!'

'Tracy!'

What's she doing here? Tracy's an Optometrist too; physically she's one of the more interesting examples of the breed. Think Meg Ryan though make her a bit sterner and just a fraction heavier. We had a wee fling just before Sally, but I ended up making a run for it. Tracy is Meg Ryan with limpet suckers on short tentacles. It must be a couple of years since I've run into her.

'Oh, it's so good to see you Mark. I've left practice - I'm an Optometric Advisor now. In fact, I'm your examiner today.'

This is good news. She may have crossed over to the enemy but Tracy still seems to like me, and that could get me through this inspection. It quickly becomes apparent, however, that she's not going to let personal feelings interfere with her work. I should have expected that; Tracy has a mean streak that makes her perfect for this job.

She's pounced on my air-puff Tonometer.

'When did you last have your Pulsair calibrated, Mark?'

'Couple of months ago.'

Months – years – as Doctor Gordon would say, semantics.

'That's good. You'll have brought the paperwork with you?'

'Oh Tracy, do you know I never thought to do that.'

'That's OK, you can fax me a copy tomorrow.'

'You know what, Tracy? I'm not sure I could put my hands on it that easily – I'm so disorganised…'

'Mark, I have to see the paperwork. If you've lost it, I'm sure the company that did the calibration can supply you with a copy.'

Blast.

'Well, it might have been a fraction more than a couple of months, but be reasonable Tracy. Every time I refer a patient for glaucoma, I double-check their pressure with that...'

I'm pointing at my Perkins Applanation Tonometer, laid out on display beside the Pulsair.

'…and I know it's accurate because I regularly calibrate it myself with the kit that came with it, and the readings between the two Tonometers are never more than a couple of mercury-millimetres apart. Come on Tracy, the Pulsair gets its calibration checked every time I have a glaucoma referral. You know full well that to get the Pulsair professionally calibrated I've got to send it to the manufacturer in London, which would mean being without it for a week or more, never mind the expense – money that could be better spent on other improvements for my patients.'

I added that last hastily; the NHS skimps masterfully, but doesn't approve of anyone else doing the same.

She makes me demonstrate that I know how to calibrate the Perkins, and that it is reading accurately, before reluctantly accepting my logic. Now she's picking up my Slit Lamp.

'Oh, this is dinky. I've never had a shot of a portable one. Here, let me try it on you Mark.'

As she moves into position, I tilt a little so the slit will look straight to her. She must have sensed my movement, because now she's leaning over the same way. I lean a little further, and she follows me. We're both going to be on the floor in a minute…

'I don't think I've got the slit adjusted quite vertical, Mark.'

Hah. She thinks it's got a rotation control. Which it hasn't.

'Don't worry Tracy, I'll re-set it later. Here, look at all the filters it has.'

I'm beside her now, twisting a knob and holding up my other hand to demonstrate how the slit can be changed into an illuminated disc. The angle of the bulb doesn't make any difference to a round blob of light.

Now I'm flicking a lever through its range of stops, making the light turn red, then blue, then yellow.

'Incredible little machine, isn't it?'

Nonchalantly I take the Slit Lamp from her, and put it back on the table.

'Yes, marvellous. Now, could you plug your visual field screener in so I can see it working?'

Don't mind doing that, since I know the screener's working perfectly. Which it does. Along with everything else. I'm beginning to think I've got through this without any penalties when she asks about my complaints procedure.

'I don't think I understand the question, Tracy. I work alone, I don't have any staff, so if anybody's got a complaint they just tell me.'

'Mark.' A crimson fingernail taps the air in front of my nose. 'You must have a written complaints procedure, it's Health Board policy.'

'What would it say – if you've got a complaint, make it to me?'

'Yes, more or less. But you must have one. Now – I can help you here.' She passes me a sheet of paper. 'You can download this as a Word document from the Health Board website, then you just insert your name in the blanks.'

Scanning the document, I'm finding this unbelievable. After it's been customised, it'll read something like:

'If you have a complaint, please complain to ME. It will take me approximately X weeks to investigate your complaint; if you feel this is too long, then please re-submit your complaint instead to ME. If you are still not satisfied with the handling of your complaint, you should inform ME. Should you still be dissatisfied, you may appeal to ME. If you would like further information about this complaints procedure, please contact ME. Ultimately, you may take this complaint instead to your local Health Board, at INSERT ADDRESS.'

I certainly wont be *INSERTING ADDRESS.*

'Have you brought your public liability insurance policy, Mark?'

What?

'Public liability? Tracy, I visit patients in their own homes. What do you think I'm going to do, drop one of my cases on somebody's foot?'

She nods seriously. 'Yes, that could happen. Or you could knock a valuable ornament off a table; there are all sorts of possible scenarios. Are you telling me you have no public liability insurance?'

I really don't believe this. When I shake my head, she tuts loudly. 'I'm going to have to issue a notice on that, Mark. You'll have 30 days to arrange cover and produce the policy for inspection; if you don't, we'll have to suspend your List Number.'

Suspend my List Number – that means they'd stop paying me. I capitulate. Suppose I've gotten off fairly lightly, it could have been worse.

'Now, where's your nametag that tells your patients who they're dealing with?'

'In the car.'

I am NOT wearing one of those.

'Oh alright, but you do know you must wear one. Last thing Mark, the regulations require you to display notices informing patients of their rights to NHS services and the provision for help on low-income grounds. How do you comply with that?'

'Tracy, I'm a mobile practice. I inform my patients verbally of all those things. I can't believe you're going to make me stick notices on my cases.'

She actually has to think about that before nodding. 'I'll accept that you use appropriate means to convey the necessary information. There now, that wasn't so bad, was it?'

I'll tell you when I find out how much this damned insurance is going to cost me.

'No Tracy, you made it very easy, thank you so much.'

She goes off to fetch my enforcement notice while I pack my equipment away. By the time she comes back, I'm ready to leave. She's wearing an outdoor coat now.

'Here, I'll help you down with those cases Mark. In fact, you could be an absolute love and give me a lift home. I take the bus to work to avoid the rush-hour traffic, and I know I'm on your way.'

No you're not - you live off Ferry Road, that's not on my way at all. Oh bugger, my List Number probably depends on this.

'Of course,Tracy. Happy to...'

Tracy lives in an expensive flat that overlooks the playing fields of Stewart Melville College. After I've parked next to her sporty two-seater Lexus, she insists I come up for coffee. I immediately, politely and firmly, decline - but I'm talking to empty air; Tracy's already out of the car and halfway to the main door.

I need that List Number...

Tracy's flat is still familiar from my previous visits, which were made under very different circumstances. The walls are covered with metal geometrical shapes that I take to be modern art. The furniture must have earned her an Ikea loyalty card, and an array of hanging spotlight tracks project a strangely relaxing mix of coloured lights. The sound system is state-of-the-art Sony, and together with the lighting it switches on automatically as soon as we walk into the living room. Sweet melodies and psychedelic light – no wonder I lost my head the first time I came here.

I'm becoming aware of Tracy in a way I don't want. Her blonde hair cries out to be touched, and she has this knack of catching your eye, then looking away, but you know she's still got you in the corner of her vision.

'Oh Mark, coffee's boring. Let's have a glass of wine, it's been ages since I've seen you.'

'Can't Tracy, I'm driving.'

'One wouldn't hurt. Mark, do take that stupid jacket off. And this…'

Before I can react she's in front of me, manicured fingers unknotting my tie and sliding it ever so slowly off my neck.

'Really Mark love, who wears these things nowadays?'

I do, though only at work. Older people expect the old fashioned look. It makes them feel safe; they appreciate a tie much more than a stupid NHS nametag.

Tracy flicks the end of the tie at my face, then tosses it onto the floor. Is it the coloured lights, or has her face flushed pink?

'You know Mark, it's really warm in here. Maybe I should take something off too…'

She's wearing a red one-piece dress that buttons up the front. Well, it was buttoned up the front until a moment ago…

'Tracy, look, this isn't…'

Her finger's on my lips. 'Shush silly.' Then her mouth seals itself tightly over mine and her tongue starts playing cricket with my tonsils. As for her hands…they shouldn't be doing that, but the feeling is…

I've been living like a monk since long before Sally and I actually split up, and my body's about to take over the decision-making here; buried needs are rising to the surface faster than the geyser at a Texas wildcat oil strike.

Tracy is trouble with a capital 'T', I know that, but it would be so easy to go along with this…

Except for one thing. When she put her finger over my lips, it reminded me of Diane after the meal at Terrapins.

Diane's capital 'D' is bigger than Tracy's capital 'T.'

When I yank my mouth free it sounds like a cork being pulled from a bottle, and a part of me is screaming silent frustration. Doesn't matter, another part shouts back - I am bigger than my animal needs.

Quickly I step back, my hands held out defensively in front of me…

…a mistake, because Tracy followed me back, and my palms are now in contact with lace-clad things they shouldn't be touching. Tracy's eyes have gripped onto mine; there's no coy breaking of gaze as she slowly moves sideways, first one way, then the other. I hear breathy moans. Hers I think.

Or are they mine?

No, definitely hers.

I want to curl my fingers, fit them around – but instead I snatch both hands away, moving rapidly backwards at the same time. My palms are tingling.

'Tracy, no. NO. This is no good. We've been here, and it didn't work – right, I'm going. I'm going now.'

Feet, did you hear what I said? We're leaving.

What I told Mr Johnston must actually be true; everything must be connected up inside, because my feet are listening to the wrong part of me.

Manual Override.

Move, move, MOVE…

I'm actually running through the door; Tracy's voice is chasing me.

'Oh Mark, you silly, silly…'

I'm out.

Taking the stairs two at a time, car keys at the ready, finger on the unlock button.

Tweet.

Slam.

Wheelspin.

Just about gave that bus-driver a heart attack, but I'm back on Ferry Road, and heading safely for home.

Feeling guilty as hell.

Back at the Caravan, Molly and Ziggy give their usual frantic welcome. As I always do when I come in, I give them each a treat. The treats go down faster than Tracy's tongue went down my throat, after which Ziggy goes back to the sofa and Molly trots off to her basket. Within moments they're both fast asleep.

Sometimes I wonder…

Grabbing the bottle of Glenfiddich, I'm off to 'B' field.

I'm spilling it all out to Tom and Kathy. Tom's eyes are wide, and he's wearing his happy face. Malt whisky and sex – Tom couldn't ask for more.

When I finish my confession Kathy comes over to where I'm sitting and pulls my face into her chest with one hand, pats my back with the other.

What is it with me and bosoms today?

I know she means well, it's supposed to be comforting, but I can't breathe. I squint sideways, frantically, at Tom, but the telepathic message I get back is:

'You're on your own, mate.'

Finally Kathy lets go; my face is burning, and sucking in a fresh lungful of air is producing a gurgling noise. Kathy's features crease with concern.

'He's having a panic attack. Quick Tommy, pour him a drink.'

Tom grudgingly pours a finger or so of my whisky into a glass. Sharply, I jog his elbow.

'Y'know Mark, you're a jammy beggar. I just don't understand why you didn't ...OW.'

Kathy turns her attention to me.

'I don't see what the problem is, Mark luv. You did the right thing, what are you worrying about?'

'Thing is Kathy, I wanted to do the wrong thing. I really wanted to do the wrong thing. I wanted to cheat on Diane practically before we've even started. To be honest, I'm not feeling too good about myself.'

'Oh Mark, if thought was deed, he'd be - well - deid.'

Tom looks annoyed, though I'm not sure he understood that well enough to know why he's annoyed.

'Doesn't thought lead to deed, Kathy?'

'It didn't though, ye daftie. Anyway, you can't say no to something unless you've thought about it first.'

Makes sense I suppose.

'It doesn't matter a hoot what you thought or felt - it's what you did that counts. You didn't do anything wrong Mark, and I bet Diane would say the same.'

'No she wouldn't because she's not going to hear anything about this. Clear?'

That last directed at Tom, who nods sheepishly.

'Not a word Mark, promise.'

I hope he means that, because Diane's coming down here for the Greenacres fun day tomorrow.

A thinly disguised excuse to try to sell Caravans to innocent visitors, the fun day is an annual event each June. There's a barbecue and beer tent, sideshows, a car boot sale, and ten percent off all holiday homes.

We experienced holiday home owners have noticed that the usual one year waiver of Site fees is missing from tomorrow's deals, which makes the sale prices one or two percent dearer than the normal prices...

I need to double-check that Tom's clear on this.

'So really folks - you wont let anything slip to Diane tomorrow, will you? Her husband cheated on her, that was how they broke up, so she's a bit sensitive about this sort of thing.'

They're both shaking their heads solemnly.

'I'm really looking forward to meeting her,' Kathy says.

My smile feels a tad forced. I'm a bit scared about that, but they are my best friends.

Back home, I suddenly remember that I haven't checked the phone for messages. There's just one.

'Mr Rogers, it's Mrs Forsyth. I don't think I'm seeing properly, everything seems a bit blurry. Could you pop in and take a wee look?'

Translation: My screws are loose and I want them tightened.

I should have known she wouldn't let me off that easily.

EIGHT

Saturday afternoon and the sun is shining. I've spent all morning giving the Caravan a bit of a clean, and Diane's due at any moment. All the windows are open for airing, letting in the sound of mallets thumping pegs as the Site workers set up stalls and tents for the Fun Day.

Molly and Ziggy have started a cacophony of barking and they're throwing themselves at the door - Diane must be here.

On the balcony I find Diane standing on the top step, still on the other side of the gate, and looking worried. Ziggy's growling and woofing, and she's standing on her hind legs like a miniature polar bear. She knows someone's there, but can't see where, so she's pirouetting to make sure her pre-emptive strike hits home. Molly on the other hand seems to like what she sees; she's got her head stuck through the bars, waiting patiently for the expected pat.

'Mark, I'm actually a bit scared of dogs. Uh - do they bite?'

I can't help laughing.

'Them, bite? No, they'd be too scared you'd bite back. Wait a minute…'

Scooping Ziggy up in both hands I dangle her over the railing where she can catch Diane's scent.

'Give her a pat on the head, Diane.'

Diane reaches out and taps Ziggy's head, looking like she expects to get her fingers burnt, but Ziggy quietens as soon as she feels Diane's hand, then stretches her neck for more.

'Molly, sit.'

No response.

'Molly, if you sit, I'll give you a treat.'

Molly smacks her bottom on the balcony, sitting like the canine equivalent of an infantryman on a parade ground. Slowly I open the gate, holding Molly's eyes while Diane steps cautiously onto the balcony. Molly leans over and sniffs curiously, then very daintily lifts a front-paw into the air. That does it; Diane's lost all her fear, and while she's shaking Molly's paw I can see smiles appearing on both their faces. Lowering Ziggy back to the ground, I watch closely as she trots over to Diane and Molly. After locating Diane's ankles with a probing paw, Ziggy slowly walks herself upright against Diane's leg, then moves her head from side to side in an obvious invitation to pet.

Molly's now glaring at me. Okay, a deal's a deal, so I fetch a couple of treats and make the payoff. Unfortunately this means I have lost all control of Molly who suddenly hurls herself at Diane, sending Ziggy spinning, and wraps her front paws around Diane's white cotton skirt.

Good thing I gave them both a bath this morning.

I'm expecting Diane to scream in terror, but she seems to have got the measure of my four-legged friends. She's actually laughing while Molly burrows her head affectionately into the waistline of a baggy lilac sweatshirt.

Lucky Molly.

After switching on the kettle I take Diane on the grand tour. She's fascinated; she says she's never been in a Static Caravan before.

Opposite the front door is the kitchen area; all the appliances are against the wall, and a big 'island' work surface serves as a divider from the living space, which has a long built-in couch and two freestanding armchairs. I have a big plasma TV on the wall which I use mainly to watch DVDs; I'm not a great fan of live television. Unlike Sally; she had the thing on night and day, and the quiet after we split up was a heavenly contrast.

Off the kitchen a door opens into a narrow hallway, which in turn leads to the bedrooms and the bathroom. Well, bedroom and workroom in my case. Diane's particularly impressed by the en-suite off the bedroom. Molly draws her attention by leaping onto the bed to retrieve a chew.

'Do the dogs sleep in your bed?' she asks.

'Well, they both used to, but after Ziggy became blind she kept falling off, so now she sticks to her basket. Molly spends half the night on the bed, and the other half down beside Ziggy.'

I wonder, with a little surge of optimism, what prompted that question?

After our coffee, Diane and I go out to investigate the fun day. The stalls are set up on a big grassy area at the rear of the Club, but our first stop's the visitors' car park, and the car boot sale. It's fun browsing but there's nothing we really want to buy, so we walk back to the Club to try our luck at the sideshows.

Diane wants a coconut. I offer to buy her one next time I'm in Tesco, but she insists I throw beanbags at triangles of tin cans. All three shots miss. Now I'm on a mission - I nearly succeed at the darts stall where I spear two cards out of three. Hoopla is just embarrassing. We're passing the beer tent, which is more of a beer awning, when I hear my name being called. Of course, where else would you expect to come across Tom and Kathy?

Tom's dispatched to fetch refreshments while Kathy introduces herself to Diane with a trademark hug. The two women seem to hit it off straight away, not that Kathy gives anyone much choice. Diane makes a joke about having given up on her coconut just as Tom returns with the drinks. Kathy takes Tom's drink in her other hand, and motions with her head.

'Tom - coconut.'

Tom pads off obediently to the 'beat the goalie' stall. Wow, the goalie never stood a chance. Back he plods and hands Diane a coconut.

'He tried out for Rangers when he was young,' Kathy says proudly.

There's a swarm of picnic benches set at the side of the beer enclosure, and we manage to find one that's free. Diane asks me how the inspection went yesterday. I tell her fine, bit of red tape, but the examiner was a decent enough bloke. I can feel Tom and Kathy giving me a look, but I ignore them.

Diane's curious about the birds tattooed on Tom's arms. So am I - I've always wanted to ask, but was scared to… It's Kathy who answers.

'He was about twenty, and his best mate said he was going to get a picture of a bird tattooed on his arm. Tommy decided to go along and get one too.'

Tom takes up the story, looking a little sad as he recounts the betrayal. #

'When we come back out I saw he must have changed his mind, because he'd gone and got a picture of a lassie done instead...'

A thin spray of lager shandy hits the side of my face, and Diane starts to choke. I pat her on the back until she can breathe again. She's mortified and starts to mop my face with paper hankies. Giving her a wink, I ask:

"Payback time?"

While Tom's distracted, watching people milling around the stalls, Diane mouths to Kathy:

'Haven't you ever told him?'

Kathy shakes her head and silently says back: 'Naw. He's happy with the world the way he thinks it is.'

'Mark.'

It's a loud female trill. When I look round shock envelops me. Tracy's at my shoulder. She bends over and plasters a wet kiss on my mouth.

This is not good.

'I thought I'd find you here. I've got something that belongs to you...oh.'

The fact that I'm holding Diane's hand has drawn Tracy's attention.

'Who's this?'

She's glaring at Diane; Diane's not looking happy either.

'This is Diane, she's my...'

Heck, what is she? Can I say she's my girlfriend, or is that presumptive? I finish lamely with

'...friend.'

'WELL. You certainly never mentioned her last night. By the way, you left this in my flat.'

Pulling my tie from her bag she tosses it onto the picnic bench.

Diane's like a statue, Tom's mouth is hanging open, and Kathy's getting to her feet.

Tracy's tone is wheedling. 'I'm really disappointed Mark. I thought...'

What she thought is lost in a scream. Kathy just poured a pint of lager over Tracy's head.

'Oh...oh...why did you do that, you horrible woman? Oh...'

Well, it's had the desired effect. Tracy's off at a run for the Club, strings of wet hair flapping against her back, presumably to find a ladies room to dry off in. Only trouble is, Diane's shot off just as fast. Hell. Oh, and security's on it's way over to check out the trouble. Wait a minute, that's Eric; he must be doubling as the bouncer today. That's okay; Tom and Kathy can handle him. I make a dash after Diane, but I've lost her in the crowd. I've got a good idea where she's headed though, so I 'excuse me' myself through the bustle then go straight to the car park. When I get past the area cordoned off for the car boot sale, there's no sign of Diane's Mazda.

Blast.

I've got to go after her.

A couple of minutes lost going back to the Caravan for my car and then I'm in pursuit, roaring up the dirt track in third gear, onto the A1 and off towards Gorebridge. I'm well over the speed limit, but there's still no sign of Diane's car. She must be going like the clappers. I have to slow down when I come into the village; finally I turn into Diane's street but - still no Diane's car.

Where's she gone?

Parking outside Diane's house, I try to think. Surely she'd come straight home; is there another way here I don't know about? Nothing else for it, I'll just have to wait.

So I wait - and wait.

An hour later, still no sign of Diane. I'm on the point of giving up; if only I had my mobile phone I could check with Tom and Kathy in case she went back to Greenacres. Maybe she realised it had to be a misunderstanding.

I'll go back and see.

I'm just about to start the car when there's a tap on the window, and I lower it to two big East Lothian policemen.

'Would you remove the ignition key and step out of the car please, sir.'

What the hell? I do as I'm instructed, and one of the policemen takes my car keys from me.

'Could you tell us what you're doing here, sir? We've had a report that you've been sitting watching this house for over an hour. Do you live here?'

Sodding Neighbourhood Watch areas. Impatiently I explain that I'm waiting for my girlfriend, deciding this is no time to be pedantic about our relationship, assuming we still have one. One of the policemen nods knowingly.

'So you had a disagreement, and now you're waiting for her - and presumably she's scared to come home?'

'No, no, no. It's not like that at all. Look, I have to go and find her.'

I'm becoming more and more agitated; I don't have time for this. Without thinking I make a grab for my car keys. Next thing I'm face down over the car bonnet feeling cold steel circle both my wrists.

'I'm charging you with attempting to assault a police officer in the performance of his duty. You are not obliged to say anything...'

I've been in this little room at the Police Station for over an hour now. The walls are dirty-white, there's a table that looks like it came from a flea market, and I'm sitting in one of two wooden chairs that don't stand flat on the floor. One of the policemen who brought me here is standing with his back to the door, glaring at me.

My world is falling around me. Diane hates me, and when the General Optical Council gets to hear that I've been charged with assault, they'll suspend my licence to practice.

I've had better days.

The door opens and another huge policeman strides in; this one's got Sergeant's stripes on his arms. He sits down opposite and pushes a cup of coffee towards me. There's something vaguely familiar about him.

'Thought it was you, Mr Rogers. How've you been?'

Now I remember. Mr Jameson. Or as it turns out, Sergeant Jameson.

'I've been fine Mr Jameson – until a couple of hours ago. How's your mum?'

Sergeant Jameson turns to the officer by the door. 'This bloke saved my mum's sight. She had a tumour on her ... where was it?'

'Pituitary gland,' I answer.

'That's it. Anyway, her surgeon said she could have gone blind if this bloke hadn't picked it up so early when he was testing her eyes. Now...'

He turns back to me.

'I've had a word with the lad that arrested you, and we've agreed to drop the assault charge. It was really just an excuse to bring you in, they were worried you were out to do your girlfriend some harm. Want to tell me what's really happening, Mr Rogers?'

So I tell him, starting with Tracy. His eyes widen.

'You must have something, lad. Can't quite see it, no offence like, but I wish I had problems like that.'

We share a manly chuckle, and the police force decides I am no longer a threat to the public at large.

'Um – will there be any sort of record on a computer anywhere of my being charged? Only our disciplinary committee gets a bit excited about stuff like that...'

'Naw, it's all a misunderstanding and it'll get written up as one. We'll give you a lift back to your car, Mr Rogers.'

Then he wags a finger at me.

'Now just you behave yourself in future, understand? My mum'd be really upset if she had to get somebody else to come and test her eyes because you were locked up in the slammer.'

He laughs loudly at his own joke, and I feel it politic to do the same. Finally I'm back at my car, waving goodbye to my new friends in blue (although they seem to wear black these days) and noting that Diane's car is still not outside her house.

It's dusk by the time I get back to Greenacres. A little part of me that still believes in optimism is hoping to see Diane's car in the car park, but of course it isn't. Leaving the car outside my own Caravan I don't even take time to check on the dogs; instead I walk straight over to 'B' field, and knock on Tom and Kathy's door.

'Where the 'ell did you go.'

'Long story, Tom.'

Pushing past him I encounter Kathy, who's glaring at me from her armchair. Diane's not here, not that I really thought she would be. Now Kathy's on her feet.

'How do you do it, Mark? Just how do you manage to screw up everything good that comes your way?'

I was hoping for sympathy, maybe a large scotch...

'It seems to be an inborn talent.'

I wonder if my tone is as full of self-disgust as the rest of me. 'What happened to Diane? Have you seen her since she ran off?'

'Yes, and let me tell you, she was NOT a happy bunny. Took a lot of persuasion from Tom and me before she agreed to wait for you to come back and explain what had happened - but just how long did you expect her to wait? Where have you been?'

'Well, I went after Diane, I tried looking for her in Gorebridge, then I got arrested…oh, it's a long story. Later…'

Wearily, I make for the nearest armchair. Kathy takes my arm and turns me around. It's not the first time I've noticed how strong she is. Before I know where I am, she has me out the door.

What's this?

'Just you go and get yourself a good night's sleep. You can sort all this out tomorrow.'

Tom's shrugging his shoulders, as if to say: 'You know what she's like.'

Well I do, but she's never been like this before. I'm plodding through a quagmire of confusion on the way back to my own Caravan. Kathy must be really annoyed with me.

It's dark enough for the Site lights to have come on; they'd be streetlights if this pothole-scarred track was a street. The main light in my Caravan's on too – I have it on a sensor so that if I'm out when night falls, Molly isn't left in the dark. Ziggy, understandably, isn't too concerned.

When I open the door Molly hurls herself at me, gives me a doggie hug, then vanishes back into the Caravan. Strange, there's no sign of Ziggy. Stepping inside I see why. Ziggy's on the couch purring like a cat, being stroked by Diane who's holding a glass of Glenfiddich in her other hand. Molly's on the opposite side, snuggling in. I'm standing gaping, trying to make sense of my constantly shifting world, when Diane speaks.

'Where the hell have you been?'

This reminds me of being married. Reaching out for the glass of whisky, on the presumption that she's poured it for me, I'm taken further aback when she whisks it away.

'Get your own, Rogers.'

Swimming through another sea of bewilderment I fetch myself a very large drink and sit down on one of the armchairs – there's no room for me on the sofa – and take a very large sip.

'I've been looking for you for hours, Diane. Then I got arrested…'

She seems riveted by my story, until she breaks into a huge grin. Why is she grinning?

'I thought you were mad at me? And how are you here?'

'Tom and Kathy told me all about your encounter with Mata Hari last night, and about the history that went before. That rotten bitch is obviously off her head. Would have been nice if you'd trusted me with the truth though - haven't we had this conversation before? Anyway, I was worried when you didn't come back, but Kathy insisted you'd just have gotten yourself into some other scrape - she says it happens all the time. Eventually though she got worried too, so we phoned the police to see if there'd been an accident. Tom got talking to a Sergeant Jameson, turns out they support the same football team, and the Sergeant told him they'd just let you go and we could expect you in a half hour or so.'

'Wait a minute - where did you go?'

'I didn't go anywhere. I wandered around for a bit, then decided it was better to come back and have it out with you. Of course, by that time you'd done your disappearing trick.'

'But your car - it wasn't in the car park...'

'No, when I first got here today the car park was already full with the car boot sale being there, so a man in a fluorescent jacket - Eric I think he said his name was - directed me to a field round the back they were using as overflow parking.'

Rubbing my eyes first, I take another sip of whisky. My glass is almost empty.

'But how did you get in here?'

'Ah.' A wee sparkle has appeared in her eyes. 'That was Kathy's idea. She reckoned it'd be best if we got some time to ourselves, so they let me in with the spare key you gave them. Tom showed me where the Glendfiddich was - talking of which...'

She's waving her empty glass in the air.

'I think we're both ready for a refill.'

Getting up to fetch the bottle, something stops me.

'But you can't have any more if you're driving – in fact, you've probably already had too much.'

She's looking me straight in the eye, but I can't read a thing from her expression. Then she breaks the silence.

'Who said I was driving?'

NINE

Monday morning, and this week's scheduling is going smoothly. I'm in such a good mood the patients are probably wondering if I've been in the drugs cupboard.

'Yes Mr Smith, see you then. SO looking forward to it...'

'No problem Mrs Purves. I'll take pleasure in sorting that out for you...'

Once I've finished, I pop into the Site shop and buy a big bunch of flowers from Eric.

Kathy's delighted with them, and I give her a big hug too. The table's covered with sheets of newspaper, and Tom's fiddling with a bit of his car. He raises a hand in greeting.

'Where were you yesterday, Mark? We didn't see you all day...Ouch.'

On the way back, I make a detour to pick up my post. Our post is delivered to the Site office, where the office-staff sort it into pigeonholes to await collection. Amongst the usual optical stuff there's a letter from Greenacres. Wonder what they've found to charge me for now?

After giving Molly and Ziggy a treat each, I make a coffee and sit down with the mail. The one from the Caravan Site turns out to be more worrying than just another bill. A few months ago Greenacres changed ownership; this is the first communication we've had from the new owners. I'm sufficiently concerned to go and find Alf, the general manager of Greenacres. Alf doubles as sales manager; that's his real job, he used to be a second-hand car salesman in a back street before Greenacres headhunted him.

When I track him down, Alf's busy sticking bright pink notices on Caravans that are taking too long to sell. According to the blurb on the posters, these have become real bargains. Ten per cent off, free Site fees for two years, half price gas for six months. What they don't say is that to enjoy all these philanthropic presents, you have to take finance through the Site at interest rates that would make my credit card company weep with envy. Waving the letter at him, I ask:

'What's all this about, Alf?'

Alf holds his arms up, an 'it's nothing' gesture. If Alf had been in Kansas when the twister hit, he would have taken credit for the weather and started selling tickets to the yellow brick road.

'Mark, Mark, it's just the new owners dotting their 'i's – the Site only has a holiday licence, so they've got to make a show of discouraging people from living here.'

'But when I moved in you told me it wasn't a problem so long as I registered for Council Tax.'

'It still isn't, Mark. All they're saying is that you have to have another address separate from the Caravan Site.' He taps his finger on the side of his nose. He's a small man, and his nose is as plump as the rest of him. 'Any address will do – a friend's, an auntie's - it's just a formality. Any mail from the Site will go to the new address, but you can still have all the rest of your post coming here.'

'Alf, there's about a dozen of us living here. Why don't the owners just get a residential licence?'

Alf shakes his head in a show of sadness. 'Oh Mark, it's not as easy as that. You see, it costs a fortune to get a residential licence. There's all sorts of things they'd have to spend money on to comply with, for example, residential fire regulations. There'd need to be a night watchman, and it'd cost you too - you'd have to upgrade your Caravan to residential standards.'

Bollocks. Alf makes it up as he goes along. I've checked into this before; what they're really scared of is the extra legal rights that residential owners have, like security of tenure on their pitches, and the power to elect a residents' committee who have to be listened to.

'So what you're telling me Alf is that this is just a wee front - that nothing's going to change as long as I give the office an address where they can send Site correspondence?'

Alf's nodding eagerly.

'Okay, I suppose I could use my accountant's address as a post box.'

Alf could easily make a living as a professional poker player, lying comes naturally to him - I've heard him selling Caravans.

Hell, he sold me mine.

But there's a definite 'tell' in the hurried way he winds up our conversation then rushes off. He hasn't reassured me.

I never see patients on a Monday, but I'm making an exception today. This patient is in East Kilbride, beside Glasgow; it comes under Lanarkshire, and that isn't one of the Health Board areas that I'm registered with, so I wont be getting paid for my time.

East Kilbride was the first 'New' town built to house the overspill from Glasgow, a problem dating back to the industrial revolution and the consequent relocation of much of the rural population to the cities.

East Kilbride sits high on the landscape, and many of its inhabitants live higher still in concrete towers that reach for the sky. My patient however has her feet firmly on the ground. She's in a new, purpose-built nursing home. Under the shadow of a towering stack of human rabbit-hutches, Oasis stands haven-like in a sea of manicured grass. Red brickwork and picture windows form a one-storey complex of interconnecting modules. The reception desk is like check-in at the Hilton.

When I go to nursing homes now, it's to see individual patients. Ten years ago I started off in domiciliary work with a national company who dealt exclusively with nursing and residential homes. I was expected to see twenty or more patients in a day, albeit I was given a dispensing assistant to do the vital flogging of specs to my mass-produced prescriptions. I became a regular item on the nurses' end-of-shift handover reports, and the night-staff used to bring me cocoa. The dispensing assistants assigned to me complained bitterly, despite the overtime hours I was generating for them.

Freda's room is huge, with its own separate bathroom and a massive picture window that looks out on a maze of bushes and a menagerie of stone woodland animals. Freda sold her house in Glasgow at the height of the property boom, finally giving in to the rheumatoid arthritis and chronic heart-condition that mean she can only enjoy the gardens here from a wheelchair. She's a small stick of a woman, she wears her white hair short, and she dresses simply but elegantly. In her mid-eighties, she has the sharpest mind I've ever known; it must howl with frustration over the broken body that imprisons it.

'Hello mum.'

'Mark darling, I've been so looking forward to seeing you.'

My own mum passed away eight years ago, shortly after my dad. Freda adopted me, in spirit at least, when I got together with Sally.

Freda is Sally's mum. This is the first time I've seen her since the break-up.

Kissing her cheek, I'm careful to make the cuddle very gentle.

'I hope you didn't mind me ringing you Mark, but I don't trust anybody else to do my eyes - certainly not the bunch of clowns they have coming in here. Do you know, on 'eye test' days there's a long line of wheelchairs outside the day room, and it's no more than an hour before the staff are busy wheeling the next lot round.'

Sounds familiar.

'Course I didn't mind, I was really glad when you called. I've missed you, but I felt a bit awkward getting in touch after Sally and I...'

Her hand waves dismissively.

'Don't you ever feel awkward around me, Mark Rogers. I know exactly what Sally's like - by the way, she told me about the so-called settlement. I am sorry. Sally's my daughter and I love her dearly, but I'm not on her side about that, it was scandalously unfair. I can't believe she's reduced you to living in a Caravan.'

'Oh, things are not so bad.'

Well, they are, but I'm not telling Freda that. Instead I emphasise the idyllic side of life at Greenacres, and explain about what I'm doing to get my business back on track. She asks about Molly and Ziggy; I wish I could have brought them to see her, but Oasis has a strict no-pets policy.

'Anyway.'

Down to business as I pop drops in her eyes, then unpack my kit. The news isn't good. Freda had some age-related macular degeneration the last time I tested her, but it's gotten much worse since then. I can't get her more than a couple of lines down the chart, so her telly's not going to be much use to her, and reading, which is so vital to a woman of her intelligence, just isn't practical any more with ordinary glasses. The best I can do is a powerful magnifier with its own light source, which has to be held in contact with the print, and Freda then has to move her best eye close to the other side of it. Because of the magnification the field of view is small, only a few words are visible at once, so she has to keep sliding the magnifier along the page. Freda's arthritis makes all this problematic; I suggest trying telescopic lenses mounted in a spectacle frame, but as I suspected might be the case, Freda refuses to look like a Borg from Star Trek.

I manage to rig an adjustable table so she doesn't have to bend so far, but I'm not feeling hopeful - re-learning to read a few words at a time is a lot to ask of an octogenarian. Still, Freda's a determined lady. I gently suggest that 'talking books' could be worth a try, and point out the alternative to television of radio programmes.

'If that's the best that can be done I'll just have to learn to cope with it. Is there nothing else I can try, Mark? - what about these new expensive drugs that they inject straight into the eye? I've still got a bit of money laid by, I could afford to go privately.'

'No Freda, what you're talking about is a treatment for wet macular degeneration. You have the dry type, and I'm sorry, but there's no treatment for that.'

'Hmmm.' She absorbs this. 'So what is it, are my eyes just wearing out? Is that why they call it 'age-related macular degeneration?'

She's the type of lady who finds things easier to accept if she understands them properly.

'Sort of, Freda. The bit that's stopped working properly is the part of your retina which removes waste products. These waste products then build up under the retina causing inflammation, that's the main problem though they also push the retina away from the blood vessels that feed it. It's simple enough in concept, no doubt one day there'll be a chemical or even a genetic treatment that removes the waste before it causes problems, but anything like that's still a long way off.'

I've had a hand on her bony shoulder while I was talking and now she places her own hand, which has knuckles like marbles, over mine.

'Thank you dear, for taking the time to explain all that. Now, how much do I owe you? I've got a chequebook here, and I absolutely insist…'

We fight that one out. I allow her to pay for the Eschenbach magnifier, but I wont take anything for my time. I don't charge family. I feel obliged to ask:

'How's Sally?'

Freda's face saddens. 'How should I know? I hardly see her. Her new man works in banking, did you know that? When she does come to visit, she's forever going on at me to let him manage my money. Hah - my daughter she may be, but I wouldn't trust her near what's left of my cash.'

That made me laugh, though I don't think Freda was joking. Strange, despite everything that's happened, being reminded that Sally's with someone else made me feel strange for a moment.

A very short moment.

Back at Greenacres, I look at the telephone for a long time before finally lifting it and dialling Sally's number. She's the last person on the planet I want to speak to, but I feel duty-bound to bring her up to date with Freda's visual problems. A very precise, very smarmy male voice (am I being catty?) answers.

'Good afternoon.'

'Yeah. Is Sally there?'

'Who should I say is calling?' The voice has a newly-honed edge of suspicion. He must be getting to know Sally quite well.

I wonder how he likes living in my flat?

'Mark Rogers.'

'Oh, you're...one moment, I'll see if she's available.'

When Sally's voice comes on the line, I feel disorientated for a moment. Familiarity and its antithesis – bit like a first meeting with an Internet date.

'I wasn't expecting to hear from you.'

'Yes well, it's about Freda. I went to see her this afternoon...'

'Mark, I'm a bit puzzled why you should feel the need to continue a relationship with the mother of your ex-wife.'

'Apart from the fact that I like Freda, I went to look at her eyes. That's why I'm phoning – I feel you should know that her vision's getting very bad, in fact she practically qualifies for the blind register. I've given the staff at Oasis a report on her condition, and now I'm doing the same for you. You know Sally, if you could spare some time, I think she'd really love to see you. It would help her through this.'

Pause.

'Oasis has a perfectly good domiciliary company to provide their residents with eyecare, Mark. I really don't understand why you should insist on forcing yourself on my mother. I mean really, is business that bad?'

Oh Sally sweetheart, you haven't changed one little bit.

'Look, I've done what I felt obliged to do. If you've got any questions about Freda's condition I'll be happy to answer them, otherwise I'm hanging up.'

'That's your answer to everything, isn't it? Hang up. Go for a walk. You've spent your life running away…'

CLICK.

Well, I did warn her.

It's nine o' clock in the evening, and I'm sitting on the sofa nursing a Glenfiddich. My day starts early tomorrow, so I can only have the one. Allowing my mind to wander is generating a strange mix of feelings. I'm still on a high about Diane, but I'm depressed about Freda. Talking to Sally brought back a lot of stuff that I wanted to keep buried.

There's a lot of frustration in my job; too often I find myself helpless in the face of my patients' problems. Medical science has advanced so much, yet it's still primitive in many ways.

We're told not to get personally involved, and specifically that we shouldn't take on as patients people with whom we have personal involvement. Staying detached, however, removes the incentive to try and do the impossible. Detachment is just one step away from not caring, and I believe caring is essential – it's the driving force to finding some way of helping your patient. Even when the situation's hopeless people can still tell whether you care. Knowing you do reassures them that everything possible has been done.

Sally – how could I ever have been in love with that woman? I don't think I was, in retrospect what I felt was infatuation, but it seemed like love at the time. Trying to reconcile the Sally I spoke to today with the Sally I met five years ago is making my head hurt. Some things are better blocked out.

Back to the present, and Diane. Just thinking about her produces a fuzzy glow. It's been thirteen hours since she left this morning, and I miss her already. But an undercurrent of worry is starting to tug…

Are things moving too fast? We've only known each other for - well, how long? Can you count the time we spent emailing, or does the clock start from our first meeting at the garden centre? If the latter, then it's been only slightly more than two weeks.

I'm wondering if I should call her, but I'm scared of setting a precedent. I know how this goes. Next thing we'll start feeling obliged to make contact every day. The fun will all go out of it, and we'll start to get uptight about imagined slights. We'll become frustrated by a lack of time for all the things we're used to doing, because we're spending so much (too much?) with each other.

'Oh Diane,' I say out loud, and both dogs swivel their heads at the door.

'No, no, she's not coming tonight…'

I know, I'll compromise by sending her a text. Then she'll know I'm thinking about her, but we wont get into the habit of phoning each other every two minutes.

To: Diane
Message: Hi had a wonderful time this weekend hope ur day went well speak soon Mark x

Then I press 'send' and the grammatical nightmare that is a text zooms off through the ether to find Diane's phone.

Picking up 'The Girl Who Kicked The Hornet's Nest' and using Ziggy's head as a book-rest, I settle down to read. Before I've finished the first paragraph my phone rings.

'Hiya Mark. Why are you texting? Isn't it easier to pick up the phone…?'

After chatting for an hour that felt like a minute, I find myself relaxing about the whole relationship thing. Diane isn't like any woman I've ever known before.

What's that warning you see about stock market investments?

Something like: 'Past performance is no guide to future events.'

TEN

Wednesday morning and I'm in Dunfermline. This is a new patient, who reminds me a little of Freda. Mrs Wilson is small and bony, and her cheekbones overhang shadows of stretched skin. She recently had a stroke, is on oxygen constantly, and her arthritis is so bad she lives in one room of her terraced Council House. There's a commode tucked discreetly in the corner, and a big hospital-style bed occupies the space adjoining the whole of one wall.

It's warm out today, but she's got her gas fire on full.

Usual routine - drops in first, then set up the equipment. Mrs Wilson's sitting at the opposite side of the room, so I pop the chart on top of the bed; that puts it at a perfect height and distance.

Mrs Wilson has a bit of cataract, but there's no way she's well enough to even consider treatment. There's also a bit of macular degeneration, so I don't know how much I'm going to be able to do for her. With her old specs she can't even see the top letter on the chart, but after I've discovered that the cataract has made her short sighted, her face brightens in a mix of amazement and delight when I pop a pair of minus-fours into the trial frame.

'That's much better. I can see some of the letters now.'

'Great - read down to let me see how far you get.'

She manages the first four lines. I'm winning.

Mrs Wilson's a bit deaf but her mind's clear; so long as I speak loudly enough she's giving me competent answers, allowing me to go on and assess how much astigmatism she has.

'Does it look best with number one, or number two?'

CRASH.

My chart just fell off the bed. I'm on my knees beside Mrs Wilson's chair, it's the best position for flipping lenses in and out of the trial frame and I do most of my subjective tests like this. My poor chart's still in mid-bounce when I start crawling towards it, probably looking like an oversized toddler.

The power lead is lying separate from the chart unit; two little prongs which plug into a socket at the back are both bent at oblique angles.

Beggar, things were going so well up until now.

I start trying to straighten the one centimetre metal prongs, speaking through my teeth as the hard metal digs into the flesh of my fingers.

'I don't understand it, Mrs Wilson. I put it well back from the edge - you don't have a poltergeist in here, do you?'

Her hand flies to her mouth. What, the place is haunted?

'Mr Rogers, I'm so sorry, I should have thought. After the stroke, I developed a bedsore.'

I wait, nodding encouragingly. I can't quite see the connection; maybe she's not as lucid as I thought.

'That's when they gave me the bed. It's a vibrating bed, to stop me getting any more bedsores.'

Ah. Right. Gosh, you'd never know - no sound, no obvious movement - but it vibrated my chart into oblivion. Automatically telling Mrs Wilson not to worry, it's not her fault, I give the prongs on the plug connector a last painful twist and - yes - now they're lined up with the holes on the socket.

Connected.

Flick the switches and the little spotlight at the top comes on - so the power's flowing again - but the chart stays dark.

'Is it broken?'

'It must be the fluorescent tube inside that's cracked. Now don't worry, it was me that was stupid enough to put it there. It's easily fixed.'

Well, actually it isn't. The whole casing's got to be taken apart to replace a tube, and anyway it might not be that at all, it could be one of the little circuit boards that's damaged. I wont know until I get it home. Last time I had a problem with my chart, it took me two hours to fix it. I need it for tomorrow, and I'm going out for a meal with Diane tonight.

Bugger.

Can't think about that now, though. I carry a little clip-on spotlight for demonstrating to doubters the dramatic difference a proper reading lamp can make. Taking temporary possession of a little table, I set the chart on top and clip the spotlight to the edge of the table. The effect is practically as good as when the chart is working. Reminds me of the bad old days when visiting Optometrists pressed a drawing pin into the wall and hung a paper chart from it.

Actually, I've heard there are still some people doing that...

My improvisation produces a happy conclusion to the examination. Despite the cataract and macula problems, Mrs Wilson gets down to the sixth line. She's delighted at the prospect of being able to see again, but she's still worried about my broken chart.

'Can I pay for the damage?'

'No, not necessary. I'm insured for that, you see.'

I'm not. Now, if it had been the bed that got broken, I've got brand new, very expensive, public liability insurance...

My next patient is an old friend; I've been going to him for years. He lives in Culross, a little village near Kincardine. Culross is a step back into a past world; the side-streets are steep, narrow, and heavily-cobbled, and the mostly terraced houses evoke the word 'Gingerbread.'

'Hello Ronnie, I'll just pop your drops in and then get my equipment set up.'

The tranquil atmosphere of the village shatters abruptly at Ronnie's reaction to the drops. He should be used to them by now. His memory isn't very good, though. Ignoring a dwindling series of waily moans, I start unpacking my equipment.

'You know Mark, you could make some money there.'

My ears do a Jodrell Bank; this is a subject guaranteed to grab my attention.

'How's that then, Ronnie?'

'Well, see that chart of yours. If you could figure out a way to put a light inside it, instead of having to shine that spotlight at it, I bet all the other Opticians that do home-visits would be queuing up to buy one...'

Back home, I lug my case into the Caravan ready to do battle with my damaged chart. First though I have to answer my phone messages, walk the dogs, then write out my spectacle orders and fax them to the prescription lab. The rest of the paperwork can wait until tomorrow.

It's frustrating. I want to get on with fixing the chart before Diane arrives, but if I don't get the orders in promptly, the specs take longer to come back. Then if everything gets out of synchrony, I can too easily end up having to test in Falkirk and deliver to Dunfermline on the same day. Or vice versa.

By the time I've finished the orders it's after four, and Diane's due at five. I need a shower – and decide it's safer to have the shower first, in case she arrives while I'm still working on the chart.

Finally, I'm ready to make my first incision. Just as I lift the screwdriver, the dogs erupt at the door. Oh no, she's early.

Ah, it's just Tom. Molly grabs her pull toy and waves it at him. Tom takes the other end and starts pulling. I'm not sure who's enjoying the game more.

'Kathy's away out with the girls, so I thought you might fancy a few pints at the Club?'

'Sorry Tom, no can do. Diane's due to arrive soon, and we're going to Dunbar for a meal. Well, we were, but I've got to fix this stinking chart first – took me hours last time.'

'What happened to it?'

His eyes widen when I describe how my chart took a dive for the floor.

'Wow, a vibrating bed? I haven't heard of one of them – hey, I thought you only went to old people?'

'She was old, Tom. The bed's for bedsores, not what you're thinking.'

'Huh. Sounds to me like that'd be more likely to *give* you bedsores. Anyway, move aside, let the dog see the rabbit.'

He plucks the screwdriver out of my hand, and in less time than it takes Molly to swallow a treat he's got it open, and starts raking through bunches of thin coloured wires.

'Right – got a spare tube there?'

With equal measures of doubt and hope blooming within me, I relinquish the fluorescent tube. He has it in place before my hand's made it back to me, then he flicks the power switch. Nothing. Tom prods a finger at a circuit board while I smack my forehead.

'This is what I was scared of. It must be something complicated in the electronics that's…how did you do that?'

The tube's glowing bright. Tom shrugs.

'Just a bad connection I think – looks like it took one hell of a wallop. Not to worry – it'll be fine now.'

By the time he's said that the casing's reassembled and my chart's standing upright, beaming brightly. I've seen him do things like this before.

'Tom – how do you do that?'

He shrugs.

'Dunno – just got a knack for fixing things. Anyways, I'd best get off if Diane's coming.'

A thought has occurred to me.

Diane is turning out to be something special, and I don't want things to go wrong between us. I'm still worried that we're getting too close too quick – we need time to get to know each other before any sort of routine settles in and makes things stale, or worse.

'Tom – would you do me a big favour? Come back round at about nine, sit yourself down and start drinking my Glenfiddich. And don't, no matter what I say, don't leave until Diane's gone.'

Tom's scratching his head.

'But wont I be in the way … you know…?'

'That's the whole point, Tom. I want to slow things down a little with Diane, give us time to build a proper foundation. I sort of think we need to walk a bit more before we get too used to running…'

Oh, I've lost him. Doesn't matter, he's user-friendly when it comes to programming.

'Look Tom, just do what I said – park your bum, drink as much whisky as you want, and don't on any account leave before Diane. Got it?'

'Okay, if that's what you want. I guess…'

Dunbar is a considerable distance to go for a Chinese meal, but I'm hoping Diane will find the journey worthwhile. There are loads of Chinese restaurants much nearer, but the one on Dunbar high street is special. The main dining area is spacious enough, but above it is a narrow mezzanine floor and there's something cosy and special about sitting up there looking down. The décor is stylistically simple; a wooden cabin of a bar adds atmosphere, and the food is always delicious. Unlike the zombie in Terrapins, the staff are cheerful and friendly.

The bubbly owner laughs at Diane's suggestion that going up to the mezzanine is unfair on the staff when there are seats downstairs. She practically pushes us up the stairs, provides us with menus, and dashes off to fill our drinks order.

Diane's wearing a grey trouser suit and a white blouse; she has her hair tied back tonight, which focuses deserved attention on the bone-structure of her face, all the symbiotic little asymmetries that add delight to beauty…get a grip, Mark.

Initially we were both a little restrained. Being together all weekend, then not seeing each other for a couple of days – well, it skews the senses a bit. It was like we were both wondering: are things still the same as we left them?

Telling the story about the test chart, and Tom's timely intervention, dispels the last of any awkwardness.

'I've been meaning to ask you, what does he do? And Kathy – does she work?'

'Kathy's easy, she works part-time as a carer in a residential home. Matter of fact she's got me quite a few patients from there. Tom – now that's more complicated.'

'Why doesn't that surprise me?'

'I've never really got a straight answer from either of them about what Tom does, I've had to put it together from scraps of conversation. I know he does people's gardens, and I know he works in a garage sometimes fixing cars; a few months ago he was fitting kitchens. He's talked about plumbing jobs too, and building walls. What I don't know is whether he's self-employed, or whether he just takes work where he can get it.'

'He seems to be really good with his hands, then.'

'Yep – his hands make up for his head. Seriously, he seems to have this amazing, instinctive talent for fixing things. You should have seen him with that test chart – I got the impression that he didn't have a clue what he was doing, yet he had it apart and back together and working like a flash.'

Diane takes a sip of her coke, swallows thoughtfully.

'I thought at first they must live on the Site. The way you talk they seem to be there all the time.'

'They live on the East side of Edinburgh, but yes, somehow they manage to split their time so they always seem to be around.'

'I like them, they're honest and open and – just nice.'

I'm glad she likes them; before Saturday that was a worry. Not everybody takes to Tom and Kathy. Sally certainly didn't.

When the main course arrives Diane jokes that it's cordon bleu, but not nouvelle cuisine. I tell her not to remind me

Over coffee, Diane catches my eye; she's got her serious look on.

'Mark, about the weekend, you know…'

A sense of foreboding grips me. She scowls.

'Mark, don't do that.'

'Don't do what?'

'The minute I start to talk about anything to do with us, your eyes cloud over and you're gone … I don't know where you go, but all I get is the answerphone.'

'Am I really that bad?'

'Yes - and welcome back by the way. Try to stick around for a while, huh? Long enough to tell me what your thoughts are.'

'Thoughts on what?'

'The weekend, what happened on Saturday night...'

'Don't forget Sunday morning...and...'

'You're not funny. You're just doing it again, hiding behind adolescent humour.'

'Sorry. Well, actually, I've been thinking about it quite a lot.'

'That sounds promising. Any chance of you telling me what you've been thinking?'

She was born out of her time; she would have been great in the Gestapo.

'Well, if you must know, I've been a bit worried that maybe we're going too fast. I mean, I really like you, there's nothing not to like, but I wouldn't want to get - you know - too quick...'

'I think the word you're looking for is trapped, or smothered. No...'

She raises a hand as I try to take it back.

'...no, I understand. To be honest, I've been feeling a bit the same.'

'You have?'

'Yes. Mark, we've both been on our own for a good while, we've got our own way of doing things, our own little eccentricities...'

She pauses for a moment, and a little smile flits over her lips.

'...you more than me on that last one. Thing is though, we've each got our own worlds, we had to go through hell to rebuild them, and the thought of putting all that at risk - well, frankly it terrifies me.'

I'm nodding vigorously.

'Yes, that's exactly how I feel. Trouble is, it would be so easy to… never mind easy, I want to. That's what scares me, because I've done it before, and I'm worried…'

She interrupts by reaching over to clasp my hand.

'Exactly. We don't trust our own judgement. That doesn't mean there wont be a time when we will?'

When I add my other hand to the pair in play, Diane's free hand joins the party. Love snap. I like this talking thing when we're both on the same wavelength.

I think I'm getting the hang of it.

'We just need to keep the fire door unlocked until we're sure we don't need it,' I clarify.

'Oh, I'm so glad you feel the same. Don't you think that in itself is a good sign for us?'

I do. Whoops. That was a bit Freudian…

Back at the Caravan Park, Diane gets into her car. As a result of our talk, we've decided staying over isn't to be taken for granted. Next weekend's booked, but not tonight. I kiss her one last time, then she pulls her door shut and turns the ignition key. There's a loud click, but that's all. I can see her twisting the key again. Another loud click. She gets back out.

'My car's not starting.'

What is this, an engine epidemic? Something in the air at Greenacres has been distinctly car-unfriendly these past few weeks. At least this time I'm familiar with the symptoms, as I tell Diane.

'I know what's wrong, it once happened to me. The starter motor's gone.'

'Oh – so what do I do about it?'

'Well, there's not enough space to push-start it here, and beyond the car park's all uphill, so it'll have to be towed to a garage to get a new starter. Don't worry, I'll give you a lift home and tomorrow I'll…'

She's tugging strands of hair loose; it gives her a sort of urchin look.

'But how will I get to work tomorrow? We're so short-staffed already, I have to be there – oh, I suppose I'll just have to get up at the crack of dawn and take two buses…'

I'm thinking.

'Listen Diane, we've established the ground rules, and we both know what the other's thinking, so really – is there anything to stop you staying tonight just seeing as how this has happened? It would mean I could take you to work tomorrow.'

Now it's her turn to cogitate, but it's only a second before she links her arm through mine and leans in close. I love that cheeky glint in her eyes.

'Just don't expect this to be habit-forming, Rogers.'

Trying to unlock the Caravan door, I realise it isn't locked. Tom's sitting with a big glass of Glenfiddich, watching a football match on TV. Molly and Ziggy look bored.

Merrily, but carefully, Tom waves his glass in the air.

'Hi Mark. Hi Diane.'

Diane whispers: 'Does he do this a lot?'

Catching Tom's eye, I jerk my head at the door. He does the same.

He thinks it's some kind of greeting.

'Wont Kathy be looking for you?' Diane hints.

'Naw, she's out with the girls. She wont be home for ages yet. Want a drink love – oh no, you can't, can you? You're driving.'

He slips an exaggeratedly sly wink at me, causing Diane to throw her hands over her head.

'Oh, you deal with it. I'm going to the loo.'

Quietly, I explain to Tom how things have changed. I don't need his help anymore. He grins and shakes his head.

'Now Mark, you was very firm that no matter what you said, I wasn't to go before Diane. I promised, and I'm not going to let you down.'

He needs a reset. Trouble is, Kathy's the only one who knows where the reboot button is.

A deliberate cough makes me look round. Diane's back and she heard that.

'Can I have a word?' she says, pointing at the corridor.

'Sure love.'

I push him back onto his chair.

'She means me, you idiot.'

Conference in the corridor. Molly and Ziggy have joined us. They're sitting on the carpet, looking serious. So's Diane. Well, she's not sitting on the carpet...

'What's this all about, Mark?'

'Oh, you heard. I asked him to play gooseberry so we wouldn't slip into any sort of routine tonight. I'd forgotten all about it – I mean, we've already talked that through, and it's fine, and I want you to stay tonight. Thing is, Tom means well, but I just can't budge him.'

'You really have to make everything so complicated, don't you?'

I think it's okay; she looks like she's trying not to laugh.

'Can't you just explain to him...?'

'I've tried, but I told him earlier he wasn't to leave before you, and he's sort of fixed on that.'

'Hmmm. What about if I pretend to leave, then come back after he goes?'

'You'd be sitting in your car for hours – there's still more than half a bottle of whisky left.'

Diane points at the closed door.

'Molly, Ziggy. Kill.'

Molly cocks her head. Ziggy starts scratching her ear.

'Oh, I can see I'm on my own with this one. You're useless, the lot of you.'

Following her back through I watch while she rummages in her bag, takes out her mobile phone. Then she marches back into the corridor. I can hear her voice, but I can't make out what she's saying. Tom's oblivious; it's 2-2 and they're in extra time.

Diane re-appears holding the phone to her ear.

'Right, so more or less between the ears. Sounds like the occipital region – uh huh, I'd agree that's probably where he does most of his thinking.'

She's behind Tom now, and he's looking round warily.

'How hard, Kathy? Really – as hard as that?'

Tom's out of his chair, backing towards the door.

'Uh – you're talking to Kathy?'

Diane smiles sweetly. She's still listening intently.

'Right – yes he's on his feet now – kick him where? You're not serious…?'

Tom's opening the door.

'Uh, sorry mate, but … got to go now. Sorry…'

Then he's gone.

Diane ends her call, and breaks into a fit of the giggles. A thought occurs to me.

'Where did you get Kathy's mobile number? Did she give you it on Saturday?'

Diane flops onto the sofa and starts petting Ziggy. Her head's pointing down, so I can barely hear her reply.

'I don't actually have Kathy's mobile number…'

ELEVEN

Mr Chalmers and his wife live in Corstorphine, over on the west side of Edinburgh. They're quite near to the zoo, and tell me they can hear the seals barking when the wind blows the right way. Their bungalow is a modest two-bedroom affair, with small gardens to front and rear. In this location, its value will be astronomically out of proportion with its size.

This is the first time I've seen Mr Chalmers. He's got a very sore eye.

'About two weeks now. The doctor gave me some cream, that helped a little, but it's still giving me jip.'

'Did the doctor come out to see you, Mr Chalmers?'

'No, I rang the surgery to say I had a sore eye, so he sent a prescription for cream to the chemist, then they brought it round.'

Thought so. Even a GP couldn't have missed this. Not that I mean to malign GPs; the human body's a big complex structure and they've got responsibility for the entire organism - all told, they do a great job. I just wish they could get over the notion that all eye-problems are treated by a tube of chloramphenicol ointment.

Mr Chalmers has a right lower lid Entropion. This means his eyelid is curling inwards, and the eyelashes are scratching at the cornea. Imagine someone flicking a mascara brush over your eye every five seconds or so and you've got some notion of what Mr Chalmers is going through. The only reason the ointment has given a little relief is because it forms a greasy coating over the cornea, cushioning the impact of the lashes.

With my thumb I gently pull down on the eyelid then hold it against the underlying bone, and Mr Chalmers immediately announces how much better that feels.

'I've been trying to keep it closed, I never thought of pulling it open.'

Experimentally I move my thumb from side to side, investigating the dynamics of this particular case. Next I cut a thin strip of micropore tape and apply one end to the skin underneath his eyelid, pull gently sideways, then press the rest of the tape in place while maintaining the tension. Mr Chalmers is ecstatic. Blessed relief.

A drop of fluorosceine stain reveals multiple track-marks over his cornea but they're all superficial, and the chloramphenicol the GP prescribed will protect him from infection while they heal.

Mrs Chalmers used to be a nurse, so I show her how to apply the tape.

'You'll have to change it at least once a day to be sure the tension is kept up; the important thing to realise is that the tape has to pull mainly sideways, not down like you might expect. That's because the weak muscle also runs sideways, and the tape's replacing its pull.'

Mr Chalmers is looking worried.

'So will I always have to wear tape on my face now, or will it get better with time?'

'No, no, I'm coming to that. You need a little operation to tighten the loose muscle, but I don't know how long you'll have to wait. This is just a stop-gap until the hospital sends for you.'

I have to categorise my referrals as 'Urgent,' 'Soon,' or 'Routine.' According to the guidelines, Entropion is classified as 'Routine.'

Bit strange, since apart from extreme discomfort, there's a danger of secondary infection which could result in a sight-threatening corneal ulcer. The longer it's left, the more chance of that happening.

I have to be careful though. If I veer too far and too often from the guidelines, there's a risk that the hospital may get annoyed and start giving my patients less priority. I'll compromise by labelling it as 'Soon.'

With a note in the comments section saying that I consider it fairly urgent.

The tape may cause some skin irritation, but Mrs Chalmers' nursing skills will be able to deal with that. She's got a question.

'What about his glasses? He's had those ones for a few years, and I've noticed him peering at the telly.'

'We'll leave that until after the operation. The sore eye's too irritated to test right now, and the ointment in it would distort the result anyway. Give me a ring a few weeks after it's been fixed, and I'll come back then.'

Next stop Balerno, on the south side, to make a delivery. It's only eleven am but I'm yawning. We had to leave pretty early since Diane's shift started at seven; by the time we got to sleep last night it was hardly worth bothering.

I wont have any problems with doorbells at Mrs Stein's house. She suffers from early dementia, and she's fixated on security. Her carers go in three times a day, and as soon as they leave, Mrs Stein locks the door and then, just to be safe, hides the key. Trouble is, she forgets where she hid it.

Her son solved the problem by fitting a key-safe to the outside wall. The carers just have to tap in a four-digit code, and that gives them access to a spare front door key. Thoughtfully, Mrs Stein's son has given me the key-safe code.

While I'm still walking up the crazy-paved path to the door of Mrs Stein's cottage, I can see her through an old-fashioned sash window. She's watching daytime television.

I often indulge in self-debate regarding the role of daytime television in the lives of older people with dementia; is it a soothing distraction to the confused mind, or could it be the root cause of the condition?

8 – 3 – 6 – 2. Open the little panel, and – no key.

Bugger.

Nothing else for it, have to try ringing the doorbell. So I do – and as usual, prepare myself for a long wait.

'Oi.'

The voice sounds as though it's right beside me; recovering my balance, I nervously look around for the source.

Mrs Stein's head is poking through a twelve-inch gap at the bottom of the front window. Bringing with me what little dignity I have left, I stroll across the front lawn.

'Good morning Mrs Stein. I'm afraid the key isn't in the key safe.'

The head rotates to meet my gaze.

'It's that stupid Amanda. She's new, ye know. And lazy. She keeps putting it in her pocket and going off with it.'

'Ah – I don't suppose you've got your own key – no, I thought not. Well, maybe I'd better come back with your new glasses another day…?'

'Oh no, I want me glasses.'

The head retracts back into the living room, and a pink chubby palm takes its place.

'Ye can give me them through the window.'

'But I need to see them on, to check they're fitting properly…'

'Aye, ye can see through the glass, can't ye. It was only cleaned yesterday.'

Sometimes it's easier to just give in gracefully. Dropping the new glasses into her waiting hand, I see them vanish quicker than a punter's life savings in Alf's sales office.

I watch her through the window as she tries them on.

'Naw – they're a bit loose.'

The disembodied limb returns the spectacles to me. The frames are plastic, they're quite fine, and they're expensive. Opening my dispensing case I extract a frame-heater, then set it down on the windowsill.

'Could you plug this in for me, Mrs Stein?'

The plug disappears through the gap, and a moment later the power light on my heater lights up. This is a first – I've never altered specs in a front garden before.

Once the plastic has softened I tweak the earpieces and bow the sides a little, then let them cool before sending them back through the window.

'That's better – yep, that 'll do.'

When I pass through a mirror, she looks pleased. They are nice specs, red and black, a modern shallow shape, and open sides with a fine mesh pattern in the gaps.

'Okay, bye.'

She goes to close the window.

'Hang on, Mrs Stein. There's still just the little matter of your bill.'

Mrs Stein's nose spreads over the glass in front of me, like a trodden-on marshmallow, and her voice is shrill.

'Don't ye try that with me, my lad. I paid ye when ye was here last. Would ye credit it – trying to rob an old lady. Shame on ye.'

I'm looking all around, feeling unwarrantedly guilty. A chap walking by with his dog has stopped by the front gate.

'No, really Mrs Stein, you didn't ... yes, alright. Whatever you say. Have a nice day, now.'

'Thief', she shrieks at my back.

The man with the dog is glaring at me. He's quite big, too.

'What's going on here,' he demands.

I raise my hands placatingly.

'Misunderstanding. I'll sort it out with Mrs Stein's son.'

He's not appeased.

'That's an old lady on her own, you know – you shouldn't be bothering her.'

'I'm her Optician.'

'Hah. Opticians don't go out to people's houses.'

By now I'm through the gate, edging past him. His dog's a boxer; it looks like it's just waiting for the attack command. It doesn't look half as dangerous as its owner though. Luckily, they both seem satisfied simply to see me leave. Opening my car door, I hear a loud mutter:

'Bloody door to door salesmen.'

To avoid having an audience, I drive a couple of streets away before stopping to phone Mrs Stein's son on my mobile. He has the cheek to laugh when I tell him what happened.

'Ee, she's getting worse, isn't she? Don't worry Mr Rogers, if you send the bill to me, I'll send you back a cheque. I wouldn't care, she made me go and get the cash out of the bank a week ago so she was sure to have it when you came.'

He's not chuffed about the carer taking the key away with her, and says he'll be looking into that. The neighbours all around have the key-safe code in case of emergency, such as a fire, but that strategy depends on there being a key in the box.

He knows who the man with the boxer was:

'I'll explain it all to Charlie when I see him, in case you run into him next time you're there.'

As I start the car back up, I'm thinking it could have been a lot worse.

Imagine if she'd made me do her eye test from the other side of the window.

My last patient brings me back to home territory, to Haddington. After this I've got that appointment with the bank.

Mr McKenzie is another new patient. His house is a small one-bedroom terrace in a sheltered housing complex. When he answers the door, his demeanour is challenging.

'What?'

'Optician, Mr McKenzie.'

Long pause.

'Oh, aye, right. Come in.'

The house is clean and the coffee table is empty; no weeks-old mail or yesterday's newspaper. The kitchen is just off the living room, and I notice that the draining board is empty. He either has daily carers coming in, or an attentive family.

Looking through my Ophthalmoscope I immediately see flakes of black pigment in the central retina, punctuated by round yellow dots of drusen; the cause of his symptoms is obvious.

'I'm afraid you have macular degeneration, Mr McKenzie.It's a sort of wearing out of a bit at the back of the eye. There's really not much I can do to improve the television, but I might be able to make your reading a little better…'

'Why can't you make the telly better? Can't you just give me stronger glasses?'

'No, that wouldn't help. In fact, it would make it more blurred. Your glasses are already the right strength for TV…'

'But I can't see it properly, so how can they be the right strength?'

This goes round for some time, and at the end I'm still not sure he's convinced. I try to explain about using a stronger light when he's reading, but he's not buying that either. Patients like Freda understand and, most importantly, accept their problem. They're willing to try anything to get a bit of improvement.

The larger group, patients like Mr McKenzie, want their vision back the way it was. No compromises. They aren't interested in the best that can be done; it's all or nothing. Sometimes this is a by-product of dementia, sometimes it's a lack of intelligence; in all cases it's a refusal to accept reality.

Mr McKenzie agrees to try stronger reading glasses, but I'm worried that when I bring them back they wont match his expectations.

I've just finished loading my cases into the car when a yellow Volkswagen Beetle roars up. An attractive lass in her twenties jumps out, dark hair billowing behind her. She trots up to me.

'Are you the Optician?'

I admit that I am.

'Oh, I'm so sorry, I got held up. That's my grandfather you've just been in to see.'

'No problem, I'll give you a wee summary of what I found and…'

'No, you don't understand. He had somebody out to test his eyes six weeks ago.'

'Six weeks ago? ' I repeat, feeling my spirits sink in synchrony with my cash flow.

'Yes, and somebody else a few months ago. It's his dementia, you see. They all tell him his vision can't be helped, but he forgets, then he phones another one of you.'

Hell! This means I don't get paid.

The Health Board has decreed patients over sixty can have one sight test a year, and one only. Any problem arising between tests is to be dealt with by the Optometrist who performed the primary examination.

Because I'm now aware that Mr McKenzie's last test was less than a year ago, and that there's nothing to prevent him accessing the previous practitioner, I can't submit a claim form.

If only the granddaughter had been held up a little longer…

She's looking worried.

'I'm really sorry your time's been wasted. Em – will he have to pay something because of this?'

Technically yes, I could bill him privately. However, hounding old people for money they probably haven't got isn't part of my job description.

'Forget it. Nobody's fault, just one of those things.'

As I turn away to my own car, she calls after me…

'Oh, thanks ever so. You're much more understanding than that Chiropodist was yesterday…'

My bank is in Haddington too, and the Loan Advisor is called Jane; she's wearing a jacket and skirt in the bank's marketing colours, neither of which succeeds in concealing some interesting geometry. Jane's a redhead, her hair drapes her shoulders like a shawl, and she spends a lot of time flicking her fringe out of her line of vision. I'd imagine her sales figures with male clients are better than average.

After greeting me like a long lost brother she ushers me into a little room made bright by orange pile on the floor and crimson rag on the walls. Hanging down from the acoustic ceiling-tiles, an array of cold spotlights adds glare to ostentation.

The seating is heavily-padded bucket-style chairs, and we face each other across a desk made of standard-issue teak. There's a strange sense of sensory deprivation; it's just me, her, and the computer.

I accept a coffee; it's free here. I feel a bit bad when she disappears through a second door, then returns five minutes later with two cups and a plate of biscuits. While she was away, I could hear the kettle coming to the boil.

'Now Mark, I believe you're looking for a personal loan?'

'Yes, I have a credit card debt and I want to pay it off with a loan at a more reasonable rate of interest.'

'Very sensible. Credit cards are only realistic for short-term finance. How much are we talking about?'

'Twelve thousand pounds. I also want to make some preliminary inquiries about the possibility of mortgage finance in the future.'

I've been giving this a lot of thought.

I love living at Greenacres, but it isn't going to be feasible in the long term. Holiday Parks have a nasty little clause in their pitch agreements which artificially limits the life of holiday homes. At Greenacres that limit is set at fifteen years. In twelve years time I will be told to remove my Caravan from the Park, which in practical terms means giving it to the Site for nothing then buying a new one from them.

I do of course have the option to take my Caravan somewhere else. The contract specifies that I would then owe Greenacres one thousand pounds for disconnecting the services and dumping my van at the front gate, after which I would need to pay a haulage company the same again to move it to ... where? A lay by?

There are Parks prepared to take fifteen year old vans but they either have next to no facilities, or they're in very unsought-after locations. Often both.

So I'm living in a depreciating asset, and in twelve years time I would have to buy another depreciating asset just to maintain the status quo.

At some point I will have to move back to bricks and mortar.

Jane looks quite excited by the prospect of selling me a mortgage. I emphasise that it's early days.

'Now, you're self-employed, aren't you? Have you brought your Accounts for the last three years?' She takes a quick look. 'There shouldn't be any problem here.'

This is another factor in the timing of my return to mortgage-land. Business-Accounts are historic documents; the recent downturn in my profits wont show until the next set, the preparation of which I can delay for up to another six months. After that, the amount the bank might be prepared to lend me will shrink dramatically until future Accounts hopefully restore my credit status.

For the time being though, I'm still a valued customer.

'Well Mark, the loan certainly wont be any problem. We'll sort out the details for that in a moment. Shall we take a little look at what we could offer you in terms of a mortgage? How much do you expect to spend on a property?'

'Let's say £150,000, although it might be less.'

She starts tapping keys.

'And how much of that would you be looking for from the bank?'

'All of it.'

The tapping stops abruptly. Her head snaps up, and she's playing goldfish with her mouth.

'But…surely you have some equity in your current property?'

'Ah, well, my current property is a Static Caravan. I was divorced recently, you see.'

Understanding floods her face, and her mouth resumes normal service.

'Oh, I'm SO sorry. Such a painful time. I went through it myself a couple of years ago. The bad news is, though, that banks don't do 100% loans since the credit crunch set in. You can exceptionally get up to 95%, but the interest rates are very high. Practically speaking, you do need at least a 20% deposit.'

Bloody credit crunch. Now the Economy's conspiring against me.

'Alright - well, how would it work if I borrow the deposit as another personal loan?'

'Hmmm...people do that, though the bank can't officially condone it. If you've got the income to support the repayments however, well, there are home improvement loans...'

'Oh, I'd definitely need to make improvements. At least 20% worth...'

She looks torn between official condemnation of my intended skulduggery, and admiration for my cheek.

'Tell you what, let's run a dummy mortgage-application through and see what the system offers you, then we'll look at the question of loans...

Tap. Tap. Tap. Beeeeeep.

Jane's gone back to being a goldfish. Her hands are out over the desk, palms up.

'I'm very sorry Mark, but the system has refused your application.'

'It's turned me down? How can that be? I've never been refused a mortgage before.'

I can see a hint of suspicion in her returning gaze.

'Your credit score isn't high enough. In fact...it's quite low. It indicates that you're a poor risk.'

Now I'm really indignant.

'I've never defaulted on a loan, or even missed a payment. What's it saying I've done?'

'We don't get those sort of details, you'll have to check your credit report yourself. You can do it online. I'm afraid though, until you can sort out whatever the problem is, the bank wouldn't be able to offer you any sort of finance.'

'Not even the credit card loan?'

Sad shake of the head. Her downcast eyes are fixed on what's left of the plate of biscuits; I think she's regretting bringing them out.

Perhaps she has to buy them herself.

'Go and find out what's wrong with your credit report Mark, it may be something you can fix, and if so, come back and we'll take another look at things.'

I have no patients booked for the next day, Friday, and I was intending to use the time to continue marketing. As it happens, it takes until Friday afternoon to get the promised 'instant access' to my credit report through one of the online agencies. The problem seems to be that my address doesn't exist, because my mail goes to the Site office.

Greenacres is on Royal Mail's register of delivery addresses, but I'm not.

Greenacres exists, but I don't.

It seems to be assumed that I sleep on the third park bench on the right.

The credit agency insists I prove my identity by faxing them my driver's licence, my passport, and some recent phone and credit card bills. Finally they accept I'm who I say I am, but because my case is 'not straightforward', I can't have online access. They want to post the credit report to my non-existent address. By now I know their telephone menu by heart.

'Press 1 to join a queue, 2 to talk to a computer, 3 for someone in Asia who wont understand what you're saying, nor you them.'

I also have the digital version of 'Greensleaves' buzzing in my head long after I put the phone down.

The credit agency's representative in Timbuctoo is finally swayed by the logic of my suggestion that they look up my non-existent address on BTs online directory, then fax the report to the number listed there. They accept that this is no different from posting the report to the same address. Finally I have the damning document in my hand.

Ziggy probably has a better credit score than I do.

I have no outstanding court judgements or unpaid loans. No slur of any kind on my financial history.

I am also of no fixed abode, compounded by a non-appearance on the Council's Electoral Roll.

This is strange, since I pay Council Tax and remember filling in the form for electoral registration.

Another hour wasted pressing 1 and 2 on the Council's system; they play Star Wars while they keep you waiting. I then discover that the Council is happy to charge Council Tax on a non-existent address, but they're not going to sully their Electoral Roll by listing it there. I try contacting Royal Mail, to have my address registered.

Button 1 ... Button 2 ... Beethoven symphony number 5 ...

'No sir, we can't register any address that the postman doesn't deliver directly to.'

'Fine – tell him to bring the mail along to my Caravan instead of dropping it off at the office.'

'No sir, we can't do that. Mail for Greenacres gets delivered to the Site office...'

So I'm screwed. Totally. For the rest of time my income is going to be split between credit card interest payments, and saving for new Caravans to replace the ones that Greenacres remove every fifteen years.

At some point in the future, I'm going to be hit with an unexpected and major expense. A costly piece of equipment is going to reach the end of its useful life, or the car's going to develop an acute problem.

(What's that thing Tom talks about that means a car's defunct? Cylinder head gasket? Tom used to call that car cancer, until the time he said it in front of Kathy...)

To replace a Slit Lamp or a car, I'd need a bank loan. Since I can't get one, my business will fail and when the Caravan comes to the end of its fifteen-year cycle I wont be able to buy a new one, and I'll be homeless.

Unless I can find a way out of this mess, I really am going to be living on the third park bench on the right.

TWELVE

It's Saturday afternoon. My financial woes can wait until after the weekend, I've got enough to think about right now.

Diane and I have decided that I should be going to Gorebridge more, rather than her coming to Greenacres all the time. Since our visits increasingly last overnight, I have to be able to bring the dogs. Which means the dogs have to meet Marcus.

I want them on their leads for this first meeting. Ziggy hates wearing a lead; as soon as I snap the collar in place, she proceeds to shake her head violently. Two floppy ears merging into a single propeller reminds me of Dumbo in the old Disney cartoon. I have to wait until Ziggy gives up on her attempt at flight before I can walk them up to Diane's door and ring the bell. At least I know this one works.

When Diane opens the door her face reflects my own trepidation. Dogs and cats are not natural friends. Molly and Ziggy are vying for Diane's attention, but even while she's doing her kangaroo impersonation I can see Molly's nose is twitching. She smells something…alien?

'Where is he?' I whisper.

'In the kitchen. Come on.'

At the kitchen door Molly freezes, Ziggy sniffs noisily, and Marcus's jaw drops wide. He glares accusingly at Diane before arching his back and spitting like an air-puff Tonometer on overdrive. That's too much for Molly who begins barking and growling, surging forward to the full length of her lead.

Ziggy calmly sits down; she reckons Molly's got the situation in hand.

The joints in my arm are stretching under the strain of keeping Molly a foot or so short of Marcus. Very deliberately, Marcus raises a paw and swipes the air in front of Molly. Bark stifled in her throat, Molly's eyes follow Marcus's talons as they zip by. Molly then cocks her head and thinks for a moment, before lifting her own paw and clunking Marcus on the side of the head.

Now Marcus is staring in pure disbelief; after a moment, he re-animates and slashes for Molly's nose. Molly's ready though, when her head floats back it's like watching a cobra dance to the flute.

Thwarted, Marcus first spits dispiritedly, then turns abruptly and swaggers over to his food dish. Molly's eyes shift with her focus. Food?

While I nervously let the lead out behind her Molly creeps up behind Marcus, and lies down on her tummy. Marcus throws a quick look over his shoulder before making a show of crunching dried cat food. Eventually he sidles off, leaving a couple of scraps in the bowl. Molly carefully raises herself, leans forward, and clears the bowl with one sweep of her tongue.

Marcus by now is at another dish, lapping milk. There's a separate water bowl, and Molly carefully moves over to have a drink. Hoping I'm doing the right thing, I reach down and unclip Molly's lead...

Cat and dog finish drinking at the same time, turn to glare at each other, then lope off in opposite directions. Some sort of accommodation seems to have been reached, causing Diane and I to exhale in unison.

Ziggy hears Molly drinking, and ambles over to slake her own thirst. On the way, she and Marcus pass within inches of each other. Ziggy cocks her head, sniffs, then continues on her way. Marcus simply gives her a sidelong glance; his pace doesn't falter.

'Do you think they'll be okay now?' Diane asks me

'No idea. We'll have to wait and see, I guess.'

A layer of peace hangs over Diane's living room; it has the solidity of damp tissue-paper. Molly is in one corner, playing staring games with Marcus across the room. Occasionally Molly's gaze becomes recriminatory when it shifts to Ziggy, who has settled herself comfortably beside Marcus. I think she's decided he's just some strange variation of dog, or at least is using this theory to justify sharing his woolly blanket.

I'm watching them from the kitchen doorway, warily, and chatting to Diane at the same time. She's making a special meal for us, involving pan-fried pork and a lot of cream. There's a large bowl of spinach standing ready, too.

'That's really not necessary you know, I'm taking the iron tablets.'

'Mark, the iron tablets are a stopgap. You've got to start eating green stuff to balance your diet.'

When I start singing the theme from 'Popeye the sailor man' Diane throws me a look so reminiscent of Kathy it stalls the song in my throat. Just then my mobile goes off. A glance at the display tells me it's my younger daughter, Zoe.

'Hi love, how are ... you're where? What?...oh, for goodness sake. Yes ok, right, no I don't know, could be anything up to half an hour.'

Snapping the phone shut, I'm trying to control the irritation welling within me.

'What was that all about?'

'It's Zoe, she's at Prestonpans Railway Station. Seems she's fallen out with her mother, and come to live with me.'

I lift my arms, a 'What can you do?' gesture. Diane covers a flicker of disappointment with a smile. She gestures at the food she's preparing.

'Plenty here for three.'

I offer to take the dogs with me to the Station, but Diane reckons she can cope. She's keeping a big jug of cold water handy.

Zoe's fifteen, which is a difficult age. Years one through fourteen were also difficult ages. Zoe has inherited her mother's feisty nature; she shoots first and asks questions later. Her older sister Kara, nineteen, is her mirror image in personality. They're both tall like their mother, wear their blonde hair to their shoulders, and neither has an ounce of weight to spare, again reminiscent of their mother. Kara has come out of herself since starting to train as a vet in Glasgow, but she's still quiet by comparison. Zoe is not quiet, and neither is her mother.

'I'm never going back. She's a dictator.'

'Yeah, I know…I mean, look, be reasonable Zoe – if your books were lying all over the living room, she had every right to clear them away…'

'She just chucked them into my room. Anyway, it wasn't only books – all the drawings for my art project are crumpled, I'll have to do them again from scratch. Have you any idea how long that's going to take me?'

'But you know what your mother's like – okay, she's a bit obsessive-compulsive about having the house tidy, but it's always been like that. I used to get it in the neck too, you know.'

'Exactly. You understand. That's why I'm coming to live with you.'

'Zoe, it's not that easy. Do you really want to change schools at this stage? What about all your friends? Anyway I don't have a spare room. Well I do, but it's a workroom.'

'You could get an office unit in your bedroom, Dad. Or you could get Tom to pull out the plumbing in the en-suite and use that as an office.'

Simple. Why didn't I think of that? Oh bugger.

We're pulling up at Diane's, so that discussion will have to continue later. This wasn't how I'd envisaged introducing my progeny to my new girlfriend.

The dogs give Zoe a manic welcome, at which point Marcus decides he's had enough. He marches into the kitchen, and a moment later the click of the cat door resonates like an indignant whiplash.

'Think he needs some space' I murmur unnecessarily. Diane shrugs.

'He'll be back when he's hungry. Talking of which I hope you are Zoe, 'cos dinner's ready.'

The pork is just how I like it, lean and cooked-through; strawberries and cream round it off nicely. Amidst the small talk, Zoe and Diane are carefully sounding each other out. From my vantage, it appears I am territory having my jurisdictions established. It's not until coffee that the subject of Zoe's living-arrangements rears again.

'Honey, it's going to be tough enough finding some private space for you tonight, never mind on a permanent basis.'

Diane chimes in. 'What do you usually do when she visits?'

'I sleep at Kathy and Tom's. Why can't I do that tonight, Dad?'

'Because they aren't there. Tom and Kathy have finally remembered they have a house in Edinburgh. You'll just have to take my bed, and I'll doss on the sofa.'

Zoe wrinkles her nose. 'Do you have a change of sheets.'

She does a teenage 'Yeeugh' when I shake my head. Diane comes to my rescue.

'I've got a spare room Zoe, and the sheets are fresh. Do you want to stay here?'

'Cool.'

Thanks, daughter of mine.

'Oh, dad.' She winks. 'I realise you'll be staying too, don't get yourself in a lather about it. I'm not a kid.'

Diane seems to think that's funny. Well, no way am I staying here tonight. It just wouldn't seem...I wouldn't be relaxed. Diane's smile changes to a frown when I explain that.

'No, I'll be going back to Greenacres to sleep. I've no desire to be part of a female pillow party, and anyway I think Marcus has had his fill of the dogs for one day.'

When the time comes, and I call goodbye, all I get back is a muffled pair of:

'See ya's.

Best I can gather, there's some sort of makeover session going on through there. I've got a feeling my joke about a pillow party wasn't so wide of the mark.

Back at the Caravan Molly's relaxing for the first time since meeting Marcus. The giveaway is that all her legs are sticking up in the air. After a little thought, I decide it's not too late to make a phone call. Having dealings with both ex-wives in the space of one week has to be some sort of record.

'Claire? It's Mark. I just...'

'You can keep the little madam, I've had her up to here. Do you know what she said to me? Cheeky little...'

'CLAIRE. All I know is that my little girl is sobbing her heart out here because she misses her mum.'

Silence. Then: 'Right, sure. Are we talking about the same teenager here?'

'Claire, I'm not kidding. The poor kid's hysterical, she sees how badly she treated you, she sees the life she knows, all the security she needs so much slipping away from her…'

'Alright, alright. Put her on.'

'I'll get her to call you in a few minutes; she'll need time to compose herself.'

After disconnecting, I dial Zoe's mobile.

'Hi Dad.'

'Hi Zoe. Listen love, I've just had your mum on the phone, she's in a terrible state. She feels she's driven you away, and ...'

'Dad, are we talking about the same mum here?'

'Zoe, I've never heard her so down. Give her a ring love, she really needs…'

'NOT a chance. If she wants to ring me she can. If she does that, then I promise I'll be nice to her. '

Hell.

'Okay sweetie, I'll tell her. Could you put Diane on for a sec?'

'Mark?'

'Diane, listen. Don't say anything, just do what I tell you. Walk out of the room as though you want to talk privately with me - okay, you out of earshot of Zoe? Good. I want you to find Zoe's mum's number on that phone, let it ring a couple of times, and hang up. Then get the phone back to Zoe fast.'

I'm fairly confident Claire will take the bait; she always had a thing about ringing back missed calls. Another of her OCD tendencies.

Meantime, I need a drink...

Next day I collect Zoe from Gorebridge and take her to the Station. Long shot, but it worked. Both she and her mother thought the other was making the first move, so they've successfully reconciled. I'm just hoping neither of them works it out too quick once they get together.

Zoe's a bit quiet in the car.

'You nervous love? It'll be fine, she'll be so glad to see you...'

'No, I'm not worried about that. Everything's cool Dad.'

Is it?

'Did you enjoy staying with Diane last night?'

'Oh sure, she's a lot of fun. We had a great time.'

That sounded honest, but there's something nagging at her.

'So – you don't mind me seeing her then?'

'Dad, you're a big boy, you can see whoever you want. You don't need my approval just like I don't need yours – no, you can take that look off your face, you don't get to vet my friends either.'

'Hmm. Well, I'm glad you liked her.'

'I did, it's just – oh, never mind.'

'What?'

Tying knots in her hair, never a good sign.

'Well, you know, I just think she's maybe still a bit hung up on Matthew, her ex. Just what she said when we were chatting, not even what she said, just a feeling I got.'

Oh. Well, she was married to him for a long time, and it's only been a few months since they split up, so it's quite natural she'd still feel a bit funny about it. Kids don't understand grown up relationships. I try to explain this to Zoe.

'Yeah, I'm sure you're right dad. Just, you know, don't get in too deep too quick...'

'Zoe, when have I ever...? Alright, it's not that funny.'

'Will you say hello to auntie Freda from me?'

'Of course I will.'

After putting Zoe on the train, and watching it leave the Station so I know she didn't get off again, I head for the Bypass before taking the M8 to East Kilbride.

Freda took delight in playing surrogate granny to both my daughters, and Zoe wanted to come with me to see her. Unfortunately Freda's going downhill fast. Oasis phoned me on Friday, presumably at Freda's behest, to tell me she's had two more strokes since last Monday. Because of this, I told Zoe, more than one visitor would be too stressful.

In actual fact, my real concern is that I don't want Zoe's happy memories of Freda sullied. It's becoming plain that soon, memories will be all we have.

On arriving at Oasis, I'm immediately taken to one side by a nurse in starched white.

'Freda didn't have a very good night, Mr Rogers. We're having to restrict visitors to close family only. I'm afraid time is becoming short.'

Although I've been expecting this, that doesn't make it any easier.

'Of course. I'll be on my way…'

'Oh no Mr Rogers, that's not what I meant. Freda's been quite adamant that we're to treat you as very close family, I just wanted to help you understand what's happening. Come on, I'll take you in, but do be careful not to tire her.'

The nurse leaves me with a sleeping Freda, who's now surrounded by an array of beeping monitors. Freda has a transparent tube coming out of her nose, and intravenous lines in both her arms. Her face is gray, and her mouth has sunk into her head. After gently gathering her shrunken hand in my own, I stroke thin folds of skin with my thumb. I can feel a solitary tear trickling down my cheek. Freda has always been one of the most alive people I've known; to see her like this is a travesty of universal law. She must have felt the contact because her eyes flicker, open, then focus on me.

'Mark, I'm so glad to see you son. I've been worried that I might not get the chance to say goodbye properly.'

I have to swallow before I reply.

'Don't talk like that, Freda. This is just a little setback...'

She's smiling, and shaking her head. 'I've had a good life Mark, and you know, this isn't what I thought it would be. I'm not at all scared - more curious about what comes next. I wish I'd always known how natural death would seem - I've spent too much time thinking about dying when I should have been concentrating on living. Anyway, you've still got it all to come - don't waste it. I see a lot of myself in you, Mark, and you've got a lot of living to do yet.'

Her eyes slip shut; she's exhausted herself. Such a wise woman, and so compassionate - I can't imagine a world without her in it. No sooner have I completed that thought than the steady beep of the monitoring machines changes to a piercing monotone. The hills and valleys of her ECG trace have become a flat and empty plain.

Freda has gone into cardiac arrest.

My own voice is screaming in my ears:

'I need help NOW.'

A part of me knows that was unnecessary; help will already be on its way. But I can't wait. Raising and unhooking the metal side from Freda's bed, I send it spinning across the room. My meagre CPR training was on rubber dummies, but I know the basic principles. Nipping Freda's nostrils closed with my fingers, I tilt back her head and fasten my lips over her mouth, trying to breathe life back into a woman who has been my inspiration. The plastic tube is preventing me from sealing one nostril properly, but I can see her chest rising. Pressing the life-giving air back out of her lungs, I start compressing her ribcage, willing her heart to start beating again.

ONE. TWO. THREE.

Sweat is running down my face in straight tracks that mimic the horizontal lines on the ECG screen.

Nothing's happening.

Freda's not breathing.

Raising my fist I clench it into a hammer, ready to pound activity back into Freda's cardiac muscle. Then hands close gently around my shoulders, drawing me back, and a voice speaks softly in my ear.

The nurse in the starched white uniform.

'You have to stop now, Mark. It's pointless, and anyway, it's not what Freda wants.'

Not what Freda wants?

'What are you talking about?'

Where's the crash team, the doctors, the electric paddles?

The nurse has unhooked a clipboard from the end of the bed, and now she's holding it up for me to see. The letters 'DNR' are stamped on the top sheet, big and bright red.

'Do Not Resuscitate.'

The nurse's hands haven't moved from my shoulders, and she's still speaking; slowly, softly…

'You see Mark, Freda understood what was happening to her – what the likely outcome would be if she suffered another incident like this and we brought her back. She'd already lost so much physical control, she couldn't stand to lose more or, worse, to find her mental faculties affected. She made the decision that something like this would be her signal to go.

Mark – it was a sensible, informed decision made by a very determined and intelligent lady...'

My body slumps, causing the nurse to tighten her grip. My mind is numbed by the unreality of the last few minutes.

After a moment I gather myself, stand straight, and the nurse tentatively lets go of my shoulders. I'm surprised to realise how young she is.

Drawing a deep breath I turn back to Freda, lying still and, yes, peaceful. Her features are relaxed, she looks younger, there might even be the hint of a smile on her lips. How typical of Freda to maintain control of her destiny even this far down the road.

'Do you want a moment alone with her?'

I shake my head.

'No, we had lots of moments when she was alive. I don't need to say goodbye to her, because she'll always be there somewhere in my head.'

The tears are flowing freely now as I make my way, unsteadily, out of the room. Just when I reach for the handle the door flies open, and Sally rushes in. The nurse meanwhile is gently lowering the bed sheet over Freda's face, and that brings Sally to an abrupt stop. Her mouth falls open. Suddenly our differences mean nothing; I turn to her, ready to offer comfort, and to receive it too. She takes a step towards me, strangling a sob.

'This is your fault, you bastard. What are you doing here? She wasn't well enough to deal with the likes of you. You've killed her.'

Quickly I move past her and out into the corridor, Sally's hysterical accusations still bouncing off my back. I need to put some distance between us, and fast, because I'm about to explode with laughter.

I'm in shock, I know that, but nonetheless there really is something terribly humorous about the fact that Sally is holding me responsible for her Mother's death.

I always said she could blame me for the weather, and now she's proved it.

THIRTEEN

The girls took Freda's death badly; it was like losing a Gran. I worry about Kara in particular; she's always been such a sensitive soul…

KARA

Chapel 2 at the crematorium is pretty gloomy, like you'd expect. It's awful hard getting my head round the idea that auntie Freda is in that wooden box at the front. My dad, my sister, and I are sitting as far back as we could get. Dad's trying to keep a low profile since Sally Cirrhosis accused him of being responsible for her mother's death. What a bitch. And how typical of Sally to insist her dead mother make the effort to come to a crematorium near Sally's home in Edinburgh.

'Do you know anyone here?' Zoe whispers to me.

'No,' I reply, 'but then we never really knew any of Sally's family apart from Freda.'

Dad is on the other side of Zoe, and he looks so sad. He and Freda were close; I remember the long chats they used to have. A couple of times I tried to listen in, but most of it was over my head. I remember thinking he'd have been better off marrying Freda than her nutty daughter. Leaning past Zoe, I put my hand on his knee.

'You ok, Dad?'

He nods absently. 'I guess. Still struggling a bit with the idea that she's gone.'

I give him a quick squeeze before taking my hand back. I still haven't met his new girlfriend, Diane, though I've heard plenty about her from Zoe.

'Why isn't Diane here with him?' I said that softly into Zoe's ear so that Dad didn't hear. Zoe leans in close.

'She never met Freda, plus Dad was worried that Sharky Sally would make an excuse to have a go at her.'

I have to nod; she probably would.

'How the hell did he ever get himself mixed up with somebody like Sally? Makes me worry about the new one – if she's not right for him, you can bet he'll be the last to see it.'

'Oh she's nothing like Sally, she's really cool. We had a great laugh the night I stayed with her. My only worry is that she's still a bit hung up on her ex – it isn't really that long since they split up. I tried warning him about that, but I don't think he listened.'

'Never does, does he? You think that might be a problem then?'

Zoe's shaking her head thoughtfully. 'No, not really. I think she's still a bit shell-shocked because the ex went off with some bit of stuff, but I can't see her going back to him. Besides, he's got the bit of stuff now, so she hasn't really got a choice there. Mm – what's that all about?'

I follow Zoe's eyes to Dad. He's leaning forward to glare at the backs of some heads belonging to people in front. Despite the surroundings they're not making any effort to keep their voices down, and although it's only three in the afternoon, they sound like they've had a few.

'I'll miss her, but she was a nasty old bitch. All airs and graces she was, but everybody knew she was common as muck.'

Doesn't sound like the Freda I knew. Oh no, my usually non-confrontational Dad just saddled up his high horse.

'Excuse me, but do you really think that sort of comment is appropriate?'

Two large red noses swivel round and scrutinise my father.

'What's yer problem mate?'

Dad's face has gone red; he's intent on meeting the guy's eye, which isn't that simple. First there's the dilemma of which eye to meet; having made that decision, there's then the difficulty of keeping up with an eye that's zig-zagging about with the rest of its owner.

'Freda was a lovely lady. I couldn't hear anything said against her at the best of times, but during her funeral it's just a bit much.'

The red noses turn to apposition, then swing back to Dad.

'I'm sure she was, whoever she is, but we're talking about big Edna. It's her that's in the box up there man, not no Freda.'

Dad's lost his power of speech, so I take over.

'Isn't this Chapel 2? Freda Warrington?'

'It's chapel 2 hen, but this here's Edna Evans's do.'

The red noses lose interest and return to face front, while Dad looks helplessly at us.

'Sally definitely said Chapel 2…'

Bloody Sally. She's sent us to the wrong flaming funeral. Dad's realised the same, he's on his feet and moving for the exit. As Zoe and I follow, I can hear the red noses getting excited.

'Yup, going to be a right old knees up at the Dog and Duck after. Pity Edna wont be there, she loved a good party.'

Outside we immediately run into Sally, who's about to get into a funeral limo. She stops short when Dad calls her name, and I'm sure I saw a nasty little smirk flash across her face.

'Did I say 2 at 3? I'm SO sorry Mark, it was 2 at 3, but then it got changed to 1 at 2.30. You'll HAVE to forgive me, I should have let you know of course, but I'm sure you can imagine how distraught I am. I have just lost my mother, after all.'

Dad's just looking at her, not saying a word. Sally turns away and closes the limo door without getting in.

'Need to pop to the ladies room. Wait here,' she tells the driver in her best imperious tone.

Before she can re-enter the building Sally gets intercepted by an emerging mourner. A woman in Chanel black, basically mutton dressed as lamb – looks just Sally's type.

'Sally darling, where is the reception to be held again?'

Reception? It's not a bleeding wedding. Sally's air-kissing the woman's cheeks, and replying in the same la de da voice.

'This must sound so silly, but I really don't know. George made all the arrangements, but now he's had to dash off on business. The driver will know though, you can ask him. Excuse me dear, I must pop back in to the loo.'

While she was talking to lamb chops I was edging my way behind them, so when Sally turns back to the crematorium entrance she finds herself facing me. Taking a step forward, not really trying to control my temper, I pin her eyes with mine.

'You really are one class A fucking bitch, Sally.'

'Dearie me, such language from Miss Prissy-Knickers. Go screw yourself, darling.'

Water off a mutton back.

Still fuming I return to Dad, who's too upset to have even noticed that little interplay. His lips are pressed together so hard they're white. When he speaks, I can see he's fighting to keep his voice level.

'Well girls, I'm afraid it looks like we missed the funeral. We obviously are not invited to the 'Reception' but that's ok because I wouldn't have gone anyway. I think we should go and find ourselves somewhere to have a quiet meal. Then we can talk about Freda, remember her properly, which is what today's supposed to be about.'

He and Zoe both look like they're ready to burst into tears; they're already moving towards the car park. I call after them 'I'll just be a minute,' and Dad turns and nods before walking on. Sally's disappeared inside, and her hoity-toity friend has got what she wanted from the driver of the funeral limo, so she's vanished too. The driver is standing beside the car, waiting to open the door for Sally when she deigns to re-appear. Casual-like I stroll up to him, smiling innocently. He nods politely.

'Hello, I'm Mrs Roger's stepdaughter. Mrs Rogers is too upset to deal with any of this herself, so she asked me to instruct you that there's been a change of venue for the funeral tea. Do you know the Dog and Duck?'

He nods but looks a bit puzzled, so I quickly add:

'It may seem strange, but this was a place that had special meaning for her mother. Salvation Army, you know? Anyway, don't bother Mrs Rogers with this, just drop her off there.'

His face breaks out with genuine concern.

'But I've just told that other lady to go to the Civic Hotel.'

'Oh' I purr. 'You mean cousin Dinah? Don't worry, I'll catch her up and put her right.'

I start to turn for the car park, but the driver has one more question.

'Am I still to wait and take Mrs Rogers home afterwards?'

Pirouetting back to him, a smile is welling unseen within me.

'I'm so glad you reminded me. No, we'll see that Mrs Rogers gets home safely. You're to wait until she's safely inside, then you can go.'

He touches his hat. 'Yes Ma'am,' he says, and I hightail it after Dad and Zoe, holding back the giggles until I'm well out of earshot.

Dad's brought us back to a country pub near Haddington. A jungle of plant-life clings to the outside walls, and inside is all polished oak.The food's good, and dad's already on his third Glenfiddich.

Zoe and I decided he was in need of some medicinal whisky, so we've worked out a plan whereby I'll drive him home, then use his car to get Zoe and me to the Station to catch our trains. Predictably dad moaned about what it'll cost him for a taxi tomorrow to retrieve his car from Prestonpans.

He's broke but he drinks Glenfiddich.

Sure.

Dad's on his mobile; when he hangs up, his face is the lightest it's been all day.

'That was Diane, she's just finished her shift and she's on her way to join us. I asked her if she could give me a lift home after; that'll give us a bit longer here, then you two can go straight to the Station.'

Uh-huh; and I'll just bet she'll be giving him a lift to Prestonpans tomorrow as well, even if she doesn't know it yet. When I put that to him, he just brandishes his innocent look. Yep, the taxi fare is sorted. Still, this is going to be interesting, finally meeting the famous Diane.

She times her arrival well; we've just finished dessert when she comes through the door. First impression? Nice. Looks comfortable, certainly attractive, not overbearing like Sally thank goodness. There's a touch of shyness about her, especially when dad introduces her to me.

'Have you eaten, Sweetheart?' he asks her.

Zoe's eyes catch mine; it's been years since our parents divorced, but it still feels weird to hear him talk like that to another woman.

Deciding the mood needs lightening, I confess to my little prank with Sally. Dad reacts with alarm, but I'm not fooled.

'You do realise it's me that's going to get it in the neck while you're safe back in Glasgow?'

Diane's laughing. 'You don't seem too worried,' she comments, before turning to me. 'You really shouldn't have though. She has lost her mother after all.'

'You obviously don't know her that well,' I reply. 'Sally doesn't give a damn about anybody except herself.'

I think I like Diane. She's certainly not pushing herself on my dad, and she doesn't seem the type to beat him into submission like mum and Sally did.

'How did you and Freda get so close?' she asks dad. 'And manage to stay so close after everything that happened with Sally?'

Dad closes his eyes for a moment; when you ask dad a question like that, he needs time to think the answer through.

'Mainly we connected on an intellectual level. Freda was an unusually talented and knowledgeable person, not somebody you'd want to take on at Trivial Pursuit. But the thing that sticks with me was how clearly she could think. She seemed to be able to cut through the side-issues and get straight to the heart of any problem.'

'I know what you mean,' Zoe chimes in. 'We used to talk about stuff - you know, boys, booze, all the heavy stuff - and she seemed to understand everything so well. Like, she told me not to try to decide what to do when I leave school, she said to wait until what I was going to do decided on me.'

Dad's studying a big picture on the wall; a group of horses with red-clad riders and hordes of dogs swarming around.

'She gave me a lot of advice about a lot of things,' he murmurs. 'Her thinking could be very fatalistic, she believed in cause and effect ... karma.'

'What goes round comes around,' Diane offers. 'I think there's a lot of truth in that.'

Dad's tearing up again, and excuses himself to the loo. Diane watches him until he disappears, looking sad for him. Yes, I think I like her. A loud electronic trill shatters the mood. Dad's left his phone on the table. Picking it up I glance at the display. Aha. It's for me.

Diane and Zoe look puzzled when I press the answer button.

'Hi Sally, how was the knees up?'

Oh dear, that didn't go down too well. Dad can probably hear her in the gents; maybe that's why there's no sign of him coming back. When Sally pauses for breath, I speak very softly into the phone.

'Sally, take those twisted knickers and put them round your neck. And don't mess with me or mine again, because next time I'll do a lot worse. Yeah, yeah ... go swivel on it, bitch.'

Then I hang up. The other two are showing their tonsils. Zoe speaks first.

'Where the hell did you learn to be such a hard-ass, Kara?'

I turn on a look of mock-confusion before I answer.

'Hey, you've got the same mother as me, sis.'

That's when I wink at Diane.

'We learned from a master.'

FOURTEEN

Back at Greenacres, where Diane's nursing a glass of red wine and I've poured myself another large Glenfiddich.

'So what did you think of Kara?' I ask her.

'She's a gem, just like her sister.'

'Kara's more like me. She's quiet as a mouse compared to Zoe…'

Breaking off in mid-word, I quickly clap Diane hard on the back. Looks like that last sip of wine went down the wrong way. No sooner has she recovered than my mobile starts to scream. Caller ID tells me who it is, causing me to put the phone back down on the coffee table.

'Sally – again. I don't much feel like talking to her just now.'

'I don't blame you, that was a rotten trick she pulled. Still, you don't think Kara went a bit far, do you? I mean, Sally must be feeling pretty down, it was her mother…'

'Well, the time and chapel were changed, so it wasn't outright deceit. The question is whether Sally forgot to tell me, or just didn't bother. I'm leaning towards Kara's opinion on that; lately I've been realising more and more just how self-centred Sally really is.

'Hmm. I do wish I could have seen her face when she gate-crashed big Edna's send-off.'

The laughter's infectious, and for a moment I manage to lose myself in shared hilarity. Funerals are funny things, you spend the day grieving and facing your own mortality, then your mood lightens. I've seen it happen before, when suddenly a sombre funeral tea turns into a party. Maybe it's to do with everybody feeling relieved they're not the star of the show; grief transposing into that curious sense of immortality that derives from our inability to comprehend death.

It's not long before I feel my eyelids droop; Diane puts down her wine and stands up.

'Come on, you need to sleep,' she tells me.

She's right; I barely make it into bed before the world slips soundlessly away.

Don't know if it's all the emotion I expended today or one too many Glenfiddichs, but I'm having the weirdest dream. I'm walking into Jane's office at the bank, pushing a supermarket trolley in front of me. Molly and Ziggy are curled up in the trolley, surrounded by piles of empty tin cans. The clothes I'm wearing are filthy, and they smell.

Jane is behind her desk; she stoops and lifts a small box of banknotes onto her desk. She looks embarrassed.

'I'm sorry Mark, but this is all we can let you have.'

Then the door behind her flies open and Mr Diggins lumbers in. He grabs the box of cash, a gleeful smirk playing over his porcine face.

'I'll take this,' he snaps, and lurches back out the way he came in.

Feeling a too-familiar sense of defeat I turn to leave, and that's when I see Freda. She's standing in the doorway, and she's smiling.

'Oh Mark, you just keep letting it all slip away from you. But you never give up, do you? Just remember, there's always a way. It might not seem like it, but the solution to your problems could be just round the corner. No matter how hard things get, you've got to keep on turning those corners.

It is going to get easier – I promise.'

Then I wake up.

Diane's snoring softly, Ziggy's snoring loudly, and Molly's standing on the bed, head cocked, looking at me curiously. That dream was unusually vivid; Freda in particular was so real. Her voice is echoing in my ears.

It's a while before I can get back to sleep.

Since Freda's death I've fallen behind with work, so when Diane drops me off at my car in Prestonpans I'm going to head straight off to Falkirk. Diane's gone a bit quiet; I don't know if it's morning blues, or whether there's something on her mind, so I ask her.

'There is, but it's nothing important. We're almost at the Station – I'll pop over tonight and tell you about it then.'

'Tell me about what?'

'It doesn't matter, and anyway there isn't time – look, we're here. Go on, you'll be late for your first appointment. I'll see you later.'

Watching as her Mazda disappears out of the Station car park, I wonder-

what was that all about?

By ten I'm outside Mrs Ponder's building, where I discover that she lives on the second floor of a tenement-style house. No lift of course.

Two flights of stairs are broken by mid-way landings, and getting three cases up them feels like scaling Everest. Two cases to the first landing, back for the third, pick up a second at the landing, leave two cases at the top of the first flight and go back for the other one. Then do it all again. By the time I reach Mrs Ponder's door it's getting hard to breathe. I don't think it's the altitude.

I could use a minute to compose myself but I had to buzz Mrs Ponder on the intercom before I could get in, so she's already waiting in her open doorway. She's a small lady, whose zimmer frame seems to dwarf her further.

'Are you all right son? You look a bit flushed.'

'I'm … fine, Mrs Ponder. Just … need to catch my breath.'

Mrs Ponder fusses away as we traverse her hallway into a big room with bay windows. She manoeuvres her zimmer with one hand while constantly checking with the other that her kirby grips are doing their job. After dissuading her from making me a cup of tea, or calling an ambulance, I proceed to ruin her day by instilling eyedrops.

Once she's stopped shrieking, I unpack my equipment. There's plenty of space for me to work in Mrs Ponder's living room, and chairs and tables aplenty to lay out my kit. It turns out that Mrs Ponder is the helpful type – to the point of obsession. A lot of my patients are like this.

'I'll get you that little table.'

'No, I don't need it...'

'It's alright, I'll get it for you.'

'Please don't…'

'There you are, that's better.'

'Do you mind if I put it back? It's sort of in my way...'

'I'll sit in that other chair, it's higher, that'll be better for you.'

'No really, the one you're in is fine, and I've set everything up around it...'

'I think I'd better move, you're going to need me higher than this.'

'No I don't, I need you where you are - no, stop - I don't want you to move…'

It takes some time to find a compromise between what I need, and what Mrs Ponder thinks I need. This type of patient's obsession with sorting out my ergonomics often develops into a competitive predilection to score points on the vision tests. In Mrs Ponder's case this manifests while I'm testing her for reading glasses using a standard Near Test Type.

'The camp stood where until quite lately…'

Good, she can read it. But can it be made more comfortable? I slip a couple of extra lenses into the trial frame.

'Is that better or worse?'

'…had been pasture and ploughland; the farmhouse still stood…'

'Better or worse than before, Mrs Ponder?'

'…in a fold of the hill that had served…'

'No, stop reading and watch as I change the lenses … like this … now is that better or worse?'

'…half an acre of mutilated old trees…'

Well, unless she knows the intro to 'Brideshead Revisited' by heart, I can't be too far out.

She turns out to be quite decisive when it comes to frame selection, and amazingly I'm ahead on time as I repack my bags. I've got my cases as far as the hall, contemplating tactics for the descent to ground level, when she calls me back.

'I need to ask you about my foot,' she says, handing me a little cardboard box. The box contains padded plasters. I must look as mystified as I feel, so she elucidates.

'I've got a sore bit on my foot, and the Chiropodist gave me those last week. They work a treat, but I'm worried about what it says on the packet.'

She taps a ragged fingernail on the relevant paragraph in the blurb on the back of the box, and with a sense of unreality I read it aloud.

'If you are diabetic, consult your health professional before using this product.'

'I'm diabetic,' she announces ominously.

'Yes, I know. Mrs Ponder, feet really aren't my thing. I'm pretty good on eyes, but feet are a long way out of my area of expertise...'

Her face sinks in on itself while her eyes moisten.

'But I've got nobody else to ask...'

Oh hell.

'Don't fret Mrs Ponder, I'll help if I can. But I'm a bit confused, what precisely is worrying you?'

'Well, I need one of them health professional people to ask. Do you know where I can find one?'

Ah.

'Mrs Ponder, the Chiropodist IS the health professional for feet. He prescribed these for you, so there's nothing to worry about.'

'Oh. It was a she by the way, and I didn't really trust her. She's too young to know much about anything and I don't want to do my foot any more harm, I've enough trouble walking as it is. Would you just take a quick look at it for me? You seem like a health professional person.'

Without waiting for an answer she flops onto a green-velour settee and pulls off her slipper, then hoists her leg onto the glass-topped coffee table. Feeling a little inadequate, I crouch and inspect a red patch on her sole.

'Yes,' I find myself saying authoritatively. 'That needs cushioning. It's quite all right to use the plasters as long as there's no open wound. If any sort of sore develops, then you must consult your GP or nurse straight away.'

She's so grateful.

I've no idea if that was the right advice or not, I'm simply relying on the Chiropodist's expertise and trying to put an old lady's mind at rest. Housebound people who live alone have too much time to dream up imaginary problems. Hopefully, if her foot falls off, it wont be a complaint the General Optical Council will feel inclined to take action on.

Between patients I pop in to see Mrs Duffy. She got her new glasses a couple of weeks ago, and she's having some sort of problem with the tint I gave her. Strange, she suffers with migraine, is very light sensitive, and raved about the specs when I delivered them.

'You see, my sister was in the other night, and she says I'm squinting through the tint. She says it's too dark under the room lights, and that I should have Reactolites like she's got. Can I get these made into Reactolites?'

'Ah. Well, you can't add a photochromic tint, you would have to buy new lenses, and that's expensive.'

'How much?'

She got those glasses free under the NHS, so she's not going to like this.

'The NHS wouldn't give you any more help, so it would cost around eighty pounds.'

'Hmmm.'

She doesn't seem too fazed.

'So if I got them, my lenses would go really dark when it's sunny, and be clear at night.'

'Well yes, they would, but I'm a bit puzzled Mrs Duffy. Firstly you never go out, so as long as the roof doesn't fall in, you're never exposed to strong sunlight. Second, I thought you found the TV very glary at night, and that the tint was helping that.'

She thinks for a moment.

'That's right. I mean, I'm really happy with them, they're the best glasses I've ever had, it was just my sister that said…'

'No offence to your sister Mrs Duffy, but if you're happy with the glasses, why pay a lot of money to change them? They would go really clear under artificial light, but doesn't that mean the telly will be too bright again?'

She nods thoughtfully...

'My son said I was daft to take any notice of my sister, and you've just confirmed it. She's nothing but an old busybody. Thanks Mr Rogers, I'm sorry if I've wasted your time.'

Oh, I shouldn't worry. Nobody else seems to.

Despite a full day I'm back at Greenacres in time to catch Alf in his office. I want to ask him something.

Alf's office is neat, mainly because it's fairly empty. A desk, a chair on each side of the desk, and a shelf unit loaded with files. Bare walls, wooden floor, a window wearing venetian blinds. The portakabin look.

Alf himself makes me think of a poker-playing gnome. As usual he's all false smiles.

'How are you today Mark?'

'Fine. Alf, I've been thinking about this business with the new owners, I'm feeling a bit insecure about their attitude towards residents here. PLUS…'

I hold up my hand to stay the usual waterfall of reassurance.

'…in the long term, I really need to get back to bricks and mortar. I'm wondering how much the Site would offer me for my Caravan if I decided to sell.'

It's one of the many unbelievable conditions of living here that you can only sell your van to the Site; you're not allowed to sell it privately. Publicly the reasoning is that this allows the Site to vet prospective owners for the sake of all; everyone knows though that it's just another dodge to make money for Greenacres.

Alf carefully extracts a black-covered book from his desk-drawer and lays it reverently on the desk in front of him. He opens it slowly, turning the pages as though he were handling a priceless historical document, like the Magna Carta. This is Alf's bible, the Caravan-Trade's guide to prices.

'Let me see Mark, you've got an Aspen, and it's three years old, right?'

I indicate agreement. Alf sucks the end of a pencil, then reaches for a calculator and starts pressing buttons.

'I paid over £40,000 for it,' I put in hopefully.

Alf looks like he's going to cry.

'Oh Mark, things are so bad around here just now. We're not selling Caravans at all; nobody's got the money to buy them. I'm up to my neck in stock – now if you wanted to trade up to, say, a nice pine lodge, I could do you a real deal…'

'Alf, I don't want to buy another holiday home, I want cash to put a deposit on a house.'

'Ah. Well…I suppose I could offer you twenty-three thousand…'

'WHAT?'

'…but I couldn't give you the cash until I sold it, and you would have to move out in the meantime. I can't sell a van if I can't show it empty and at its best.'

'Let me get this straight. You want to give me a pittance for my van, and you need me to move out for however long it takes you to sell it. I've got nowhere to go, Alf.'

'Sorry Mark, best I can do. Way things are, it wouldn't sell very quick either. Now, if you insist on cash on the nose, well...you know, the new owners are watching me like a hawk, so I've got to be careful here...but I might be able to get you eighteen thousand.'

Sometimes I think all the people I deal with should just peg me out in the sun and let the crows pull my flesh off bit by painful bit.

Actually, that's what it feels like they all do already.

'Alf, that's more than twenty two thousand less than I paid for it three years ago. How can you possibly justify that kind of robbery, especially since you're the only one I can sell it to? Anyway...'

My last meeting with Mr Diggins just came back to mind.

'...I have it on good authority that you sold one just like mine fairly recently for thirty thousand.'

Again Alf seems on the verge of bursting into tears.

'But Mark, we've got to make a little profit somewhere. If it was up to me ... but it isn't, I've got to answer to the powers that be. That really is the best I can offer you, and it would give you a deposit.'

My head's spinning. I knew they'd want to fleece me, but I didn't anticipate this. Eighteen thousand as a twenty per cent deposit – that makes my budget for a house ninety thousand without allowing for all the other costs involved.

I'll be lucky to get the freehold on a park bench for that.

After telling Alf that I'll think about it, adding that he shouldn't hold his breath in the meanwhile, I go straight from the office to the Club. I've taken a sudden craving for a portion of Eric's home-made steak pie.

As always, it's delicious; I can see the pride in Eric's face when he brings it to my table. We race each other back to the bar, since I want (need?) another pint.

Refreshed, but still in financial shreds, I return to the Caravan and take Molly and Ziggy for their walk.

A little sunshine still lingers, and it feels good to be out after all the driving. The dogs are off their leads and some distance away from me when a huge Rottweiler appears from nowhere, and takes an aggressive stance in front of Molly. I've never seen the beast before; it must belong to a renter.

My heart's bumping off my ribs as I shout 'OI' and start running to cover the distance separating us. Both the dogs' eyes are locked now, and I know I'm not going to be in time. I'm not even sure what I can do since the brute's nearly as big as me.

Then a short, sharp 'YIP' rings out from under the Rottweiler, who quickly ducks his head to look between his front paws. Ziggy's standing directly under his undercarriage, eyes popping, teeth bared. Next thing, the Rottweiler's a fast-moving dot in the distance.

Well, I can't blame him.

Think I'd have reacted the same way...

'It was either retreat, or castration without anaesthetic.'

Diane's laughing, Ziggy's strutting about with her best 'Don't mess with me' look, and Molly's looking a little huffed at not being the centre of attention.

'Anyway, what did you want to talk about this morning?'

I've been wondering about that all day...

Her mood just quietened.

'It's nothing really, it's just that I've had a few emails from Matthew, and he wants to meet for a chat. Seems…my replacement has taken off, and suddenly I don't look so bad again.'

She's trying to be light-hearted about this, but I can see she's not. Zoe's warning comes thundering back at me

Out comes the Glenfiddich.

'No, not for me, I need to drive back. Early shift tomorrow.'

Well, I bloody need one.

'So – how do you feel about this?' I ask carefully.

'I don't know, Mark. I'm trying to keep everything above board, Matthew and I were married for a long time – it seems like a lifetime – but things have changed, and I don't appreciate being his first reserve. Still … I feel I owe it to him to just talk things over, can you understand that?'

No.

'Yes, of course I can. When are you meeting him?'

'Don't know yet, I wanted to speak to you first so you wouldn't think I was doing anything underhand.'

Oh great, yes, lets do it all out in the open. That'll make me feel much better.

'I appreciate that, Diane. Well, I suppose we'll just have to wait and see what happens.'

Gosh, that first glass of whisky went down fast.

Time for the second.

'Mark, don't be silly. I'm just being up-front with you, and I'm only going to talk to him. Stop slurping whisky like it's water.'

I can't think of anything else to say, so I slurp some more whisky.

'Right, I need to get off. That early start – look, I'll let you know when I'm meeting him, and I'll speak to you after and tell you how it went. This is difficult for me too, you know.'

I've thought of something to say.

'Once a cheater, always a cheater I reckon. Do you really think you could ever trust him again?'

She looks sad as she answers:

'You don't know that.'

'Yes I do – I know it because I couldn't cheat.'

When she tries to say goodnight, my only response is to wave my glass in her direction. Ziggy yelps indignantly when a spot of Glenfiddich hits her face, then sniffs curiously before stretching her tongue to catch a taste.

Diane leaves without saying anything else.

So let me get this straight. I'm on a one-way road to being homeless, my best friend's dead, and my girlfriend looks like she's going back to her cheating ex. I'm also in remission from cancer, and Tom's appeared to watch the football and drink the rest of my Glenfiddich.

'Where you going, Mark?'

'To the Club to get another bottle.'

'Don't think they've got Glenfiddich in the Club.

'Tom, I don't really care what Eric gives me so long as it's got alcohol in it. Way I feel, a bottle of turps would do.'

Yep, I'm going to be right at home on that park bench.

FIFTEEN

Saturday morning – I can't decide if I'm looking forward to today or not. In just over an hour I'm due in Glasgow for a CET session.

Continuing Education and Training.

To retain my licence to practice I have to make regular submissions to the General Optical Council of evidence that I am keeping my knowledge up to date. The furtherance of my understanding of these little round things we look through is measured in points, and I need at least 12 a year. I can get half the points I need by reading papers in the comic (professional journal) then completing on-line tests to prove I've really read them. These multiple-choice quizzes are each worth one or, at the most, two points.

The other half however has to be 'interactive'. This means there has to be a practical element to the points, or a degree of discussion with other Optometrists. It's generally a huge pain in the neck, (except for the time we managed to arrange collaborative discussion in a bar, but we've been banned from doing that again because we never got round to talking about eyes), so I try to use events that provide a whole bushel of points in a oner

Today I'm set to grab a whopping six at once by attending a clinical training seminar at the University in Glasgow. I had hoped to meet-up with Kara afterwards, but she's spending the weekend at her mother's in Falkirk.

Points apart, today's activities will keep my mind off the mess that I call my life.

Diane phoned to say she was meeting Matthew tonight for their little tete-a-tete; I haven't seen her since she threw that particular stick of dynamite at me the day after Freda's funeral, and until the forthcoming summit meeting is over, I wouldn't really know what to say to her. Well, I would, but it's probably best that I don't.

I leave the dogs eating their cornflakes, ignoring the looks of betrayal being flicked my way for deserting them on a Saturday morning. Traffic's light, and I'm soon sitting in a small lecture theatre appraising my fellow inmates as they drift in.

I don't have many close friends in the Optometric community. To be brutally honest, I don't particularly like most Optometrists. There used to be a lot of wanna-be doctors who couldn't make the medical grade. That's become less common as, over the years, competition to get on our course has rocketed. Back in the day, I got in with an A and two Bs. Now they're looking for four As.

On the whole my colleagues tend to be an arrogant bunch; a favourite pastime is to flout an apparently encyclopaedic knowledge of our rather narrow field, and none of them are ever wrong about anything. Paradoxically, there's a lot of manic insecurity about too. We practice in an age of litigation; one mistake can mean the end of a career.

'Mark!'

'Oh no, who let you in?'

This is Bruce, a lanky six feet of creased clothes and flailing limbs. His whiskered, long-haired head, in particular the mouthy bit, is as restless as the rest of him. We trained together a very long time ago; we also drank together, went hunting for female company together, and caused chaos together during rag week – on one memorable occasion we brought the country's mainline rail services to a halt for two hours. Bruce is certifiably nuts, and possibly the most brilliant Optometrist I've ever known. His slender fingers, made agile by years of keyboard playing, are now tapping out a rhythm on my scalp.

'Aren't you in the wrong building? Hair replacement's next door.'

'Yeah, which building's the psychiatric ward in, and how did you get out?'

'You still going door to door then? How is the brush-sale trade?'

'Ha. Ha. Better than hiding out in the ivory tower, Rapunzel.'

Bruce also answers to Dr Dixon, and is a senior lecturer in a University down south. So what's he doing here? A horrible thought occurs to me.

'Bruce, you're not involved with the teaching today are you? Please tell me you're not.'

Bruce flicks a long strand of greying hair back behind his ear before answering.

'Yep, moved here from Manchester a couple of months ago. I'm your host for the games today, Marky boy. Be nice, or I'll send you to stand in the naughty corner. Talking of which…' He scrutinises my chest. 'Where's your security badge, didn't they give you one at the front desk?'

I hate name badges; they make me feel uncomfortable.

'In my coat pocket.'

I point to my raincoat on the seat beside me, then look up sharply when Bruce whistles quietly.

'Whoa, feast your peepers on that.'

Bruce has never married; he doesn't feel it would be fair to deny the rest of womanhood his proven charms. His attention has been caught by a shapely, blonde-capped figure wearing jeans so tight they leave the imagination redundant. She's talking to another participant; it isn't until she turns around that my eyes close in horror.

'Oh no.'

Bruce is delighted by my discomfort.

'Who is it then? One of your harem of ex-wives?'

'Worse, her name's Tracy. She's an Optometric Adviser in Edinburgh, and she hates me.'

When Bruce grins, it's like a shark spotting a bad swimmer.

'Go on then, what's the story? Is the problem what you did, or what you didn't manage to do?'

'Don't judge others by your own inadequacies, Bruce.'

Which makes him laugh; Bruce has no feelings of insecurity in that department.

'We did have a bit of a fling,' I continue, ignoring his exaggerated hilarity. 'Somehow she saw it as a bit more, then there was a little misunderstanding that ended up with a friend of mine pouring a pint of lager over her head, and, well...'

Bruce is still laughing, a very snorty sort of sound.

'You always took things too seriously, Mark. Must say though, I'm impressed – bit better than the double-baggers you used to pull in the old days.'

'Double baggers?'

'Yeah – means you need to take two bags to bed. One to put over her head, the other to put over your own in case her's comes off.'

When I stop to think about it, I really do have the strangest set of friends.

The program today is all about emergency situations involving ocular trauma. I very much doubt that the average victim would take a bus to the nearest Optometrist if they got acid splashed in their eye, but since the course has been approved for CET points, details like that don't matter. Bruce is an entertaining lecturer; he's currently emphasising the different degrees of trauma between having acid and alkali come into contact with the ocular surface. Most people would guess acid to be the biggest threat, but Bruce is demonstrating the severity of an alkali burn by rolling around on the floor. For acid, he simply jumped up and down and screamed.

After the introductory lecture, Bruce leads a crocodile of ten or so ageing Optometrists to the student clinics to try out our new knowledge. I'm careful to keep well away from Tracy who, as usual, is at the front of the queue. The entrance to the clinics is guarded by an electronic keypad, and I'm not too far down the line to be able to note the numbers Bruce punches in to gain access. I automatically memorise these; I can't help myself. Most nursing homes use the same system, and before developing this habit I wasted a lot of time searching for a member of staff to let me out of those places.

The first workshop is on Gonioscopy, and we pair up in little cubicles to practice on each other.

Acute glaucoma, a massive rise in the internal pressure of the eye, results from blockage of the eye's drainage system. A fluid called aqueous humour is constantly produced just behind the iris, and when the stuff suddenly has nowhere to go, the pressure goes up like a student's bladder during a night in the Union bar. This is very painful, and can cause blindness if it's left too long.

So can glaucoma.

Our role here is preventative; by looking through a special viewing device, shaped like a watchmaker's eyeglass and called a Gonioscope, we can spot any anatomical predisposition to the condition before it manifests. The Gonioscope has to be held in contact with the eye, necessitating the instillation of topical anaesthetic. Then we can see the 'angle,' the meeting of the cornea and sclera where special veins carry aqueous humour out of the eye. It's as much like plumbing as biology.

I consider it very fortunate that this test can't be done in the domiciliary situation, a non-portable Slit Lamp being an essential part of the set-up. I've never been able to make any sense of the appearance of the drainage angle; it reminds me of the picture my father got on our first black and white television when he had the aerial pointing the wrong way. Bruce tries to help me interpret the fuzzy bands, but soon gives up and sends me to sit on the other side of the examination table so my partner can have a go. While that's happening, he sidles off to Tracy's cubicle. Despite my warnings she's caught his eye, and I can hear Bruce trying to talk like his namesake with the surname Willis.

'Excellent Tracy, you're doing very well there.'

'I HAVE done this before, you know. Excuse me, but could you take your beard out of my ear? You might think about washing it sometime, too.'

Catching Bruce's eye, he gets my best 'Told you so' look; I get the finger back. Bruce doesn't take rejection well.

Finally it's lunchtime, and Bruce and I are walking down to the cafeteria.

'What's up next?' I ask.

'Taking embedded foreign bodies out of sheep's eyes.'

'I should have brought Kara, she's the vet in our family.'

Bruce wobbles his head.

'The eyes aren't attached to the sheep any more, Mark.'

'Wow,' I exclaim. 'That was pretty radical treatment for a foreign body.'

The cafeteria's in another building, and we're about to step outside when I see that it's started to pour with rain.

'Damn, I've left my coat upstairs in the clinic. You go on Bruce, I'll catch you up.'

'You'll need the code to get in - oh, alright clever clogs.'

After explaining how I was able to recite the keypad number, I set off back up the stairs.

7 - 2 - 5 - 1 ... and I'm in. Now, our room was just down here ... no it wasn't, so it must be down there...or was it over here?

The student clinics are a warren of corridors and doors that all look the same, and I'm wandering around helplessly trying to remember the route we took earlier. I'm concentrating so hard that I jump when a voice speaks just behind me.

'Can we help you sir?'

Two black-suited security men, very big, very intimidating. Very suspicious.

'I'm just going back for my coat, I'm here for the seminar on ocular emergencies.'

The older of the two, whose head has been shaved to a black fuzz, is glaring at my shirt-front.

'Where's your security pass, sir? Weren't you told you must wear it at all times?'

'Well, yes, but I thought it'd be okay if I had it in my pocket...'

'That's fine sir. If you could just bring it out and let us have a look at it...'

'Ah, well you see, the pocket it's in is part of the coat I'm on my way to fetch. Look, just come with me to the clinic, and I'll get the coat and show you the stupid pass.'

'There's nothing stupid about a security pass, sir. Anyway, all the clinics are locked, and we don't have any authority to enter them.'

'I know the keypad number,' I suggest helpfully.

He draws in a sharp breath. 'YOU certainly don't have any authority to enter a locked clinic ... sir. I think you'd better come with us.'

Here I go again. What is it with me and uniforms lately? I'm being practically frogmarched to the security office when I spot Tracy coming along the corridor in the opposite direction. She's wearing her security pass.

'Tracy – listen, I know her, she'll vouch for me. Tracy, would you tell these guys who I am.'

Skinhead melts visibly in Tracy's presence. 'Good afternoon, miss. Could you just confirm that you know this gentleman?'

Tracy bathes Skinhead in a brilliant smile, making his whole bulk sag noticeably. Then her face tightens, and she slowly looks me up and down. No smiles now.

'I've never seen this man in my life before,' she says. 'I can only presume he read my name off my badge.'

'Right,' says my escort, placing a huge hairy hand on my shoulder. 'Let's go, sunshine. You've got some explaining to do.'

Luckily Bruce appears before I get locked away in a dungeon. He must have realised I was taking too long and come looking for me. We go through the routine again.

'Do you know this man, sir?'

Bruce looks puzzled. 'Nah, never seen him in my tot.'

My face falls, and Bruce crumples into helpless hysterics.

'Oh your face, Marky boy.'

Skinhead leans in to examine Bruce's badge.

'Is that your badge, sir?' he inquires nastily. Bruce sobers up, hilarity displaced by indignation.

'Of course it is. What d'you think I did, mugged the real Dr Dixon and stole his ID?'

'Well sir, you're not exactly behaving like a doctor, now are you?' He exchanges glances with his partner, a younger man who's shaking his head ominously, and who now speaks for the first time.

'I don't like the look of this, Guv.'

'No,' Skinhead agrees. 'I think we'd better take them both back to the office and do a little checking. This way please, gentlemen.'

I feel a sense of deja-vue when Tracy re-appears, again walking towards us. Bruce brightens.

'Tracy. She'll vouch for us. Tracy, just tell these…'

Tracy eyes do a dance with Skinhead's. 'Oh dear, you are being kept busy today, aren't you? Sorry, don't know this one either…'

Bruce and I are half an hour late for the foreign body removal clinic. His department head was not chuffed at being called in on a Saturday afternoon to identify the new senior lecturer. Bruce is even less chuffed about missing his lunch. Watching him angrily rolling the corneas of disembodied sheep eyes in little heaps of sharp metal fragments, I find myself thinking it would be unwise for either Skinhead or his partner to consult Bruce in the staff eye clinic anytime soon. Listening to him rant on the way back, it became obvious that Tracy too has made an enemy.

Embedding a hail of foreign bodies in 10 sheep eyes takes a little time, then Bruce still has to dab a spot of red stain on each with a fine brush. This is to simulate a rust stain, the result of waiting too long to have a metallic foreign body removed. We'll practice removing those with a small battery operated burr. To remove the bits of metal, we all have a tray of tools to choose from. There's the traditional fine needle, handles with different-sized loops of wire or plastic and, for anything superficial, sterile tissue-paper to screw up and dampen with similarly sterile saline.

Bruce attaches the eyes to clamps on the Slit Lamp chinrests, and we're ready to begin. Most of us have never attempted these procedures before, and the thing that impresses itself quickly on my mind is how tough a cornea actually is. I'm stabbing away at a particularly stubborn chunk of tin, and each time I miss the sharp needle just bounces back off the cornea. Through the Slit Lamp eyepieces, I see a giant hand descend and grab my wrist before twisting it sharply. Bruce's voice is beside my ear.

'NEVER – EVER – approach an eye with a needle front-on, Mark. Look, you come from the side, like this, that way you wont accidentally blind your patient and get sued and struck off.'

He says it softly, which I appreciate, since I'm feeling pretty stupid.

Bruce has moved on to Tracy. This time he's practically shouting.

'Tracy, you're not doing a cataract extraction here. For goodness sake, you're picking lumps out of that cornea.'

Tracy's voice has a catch, and her eyes are saucers of bewilderment.

'I don't understand it. I've done this before and I've never had this problem.'

THWUCK. Every head turns as a piece of metal attached to a large lump of corneal tissue flies across the room. Bruce's head is in his hands.

'Tracy, if I ever get something stuck in my eye, I really hope you're not in the same county. I've never seen such a mess.' He pauses, looking around him. 'Everyone else seems to be managing alright. Have you always been this ham-handed?'

Tracy throws down the needle and jumps to her feet. Her cheeks are fiery and wet as she rushes her humiliation out of the room, leaving behind little gurgling sobs. I wander over to stand next to Bruce for a look.

'Wow –she really ripped that eye to pieces, didn't she.'

Bruce nods sadly, and answers in a loud voice. 'Yes, she'd make a wonderful butcher's apprentice, but I don't think she's safe to be around human eyes. Rather lucky for her potential victims that she's become a pen-pusher now – easy to see why she made that career move.'

Everyone looks smug; nothing to boost the morale like somebody making a bigger mess of something than you are.

Bruce winks at me then flips his head down. Following the gesture to his closed hand, I watch as his fingers uncurl to reveal a small tube of superglue. Closing his hand, Bruce glances meaningfully at the open door.

'Nobody messes with me,' he whispers.

Tracy doesn't return; after the last clinic, Bruce takes me for a nostalgic pint in the Students' Union before I set off back home. We exchange telephone numbers, home and email addresses, and declare that we will keep in touch. Every so often we meet up accidentally, and each time we go through this charade, but I know I wont see him again until our next random intersection in the optical community. I always enjoy my encounters with Bruce; he makes me feel like the young student I once was.

Time to face the real world again now.

When I get back to Greenacres the dogs make a show of being huffed by my absence - until I say the magic 'dinner' word. Then we're pals again, and I go to check the phone. One message – from Mrs Forsyth. She sounds worried –what's new? Feeling the usual trepidation, I dial her number.

'Mr Rogers, thank goodness you're back. This is a real emergency.'

Obviously I am just in time to stop a helicopter from being scrambled.

'Calm down now Mrs Forsyth, and tell me what's wrong.'

'My eye is BLEEDING. I think it's burst, oh Mr Rogers, do you think I'm going to lose it?'

You lost it a long time ago, love. Bleeding? Hey, we covered this today.

'Now take it slowly, Mrs Forsyth. Is there any blood actually coming out of your eye? And have you had any sort of injury, like a fall, in the last twenty four hours?'

'No, I haven't fallen or anything, and the blood is ON the eyeball. Mr Rogers, my eye is COVERED in blood – what's wrong – will it go blind?'

'Mrs Forsyth, it's all right, really. What you have is a sub-conjunctival haemorrhage.'

She loves terms like that; I can hear a pen scratching as she jots it down for future use.

'See, there's a thin membrane that covers the white of the eye, sort of like clingfilm. Now, if one of the tiny blood vessels in it bursts, just a drop of blood gets out, but the clingfilm spreads it flat as though it was on a microscope slide. So you've got this big bright red patch, but it's only a tiny speck of blood, and quite harmless.'

'So what do I do now, Mr Rogers? Do I have to go to a hospital and have it operated on?'

You wish.

'No, I already told you it's of no consequence. It'll disappear over a week or two, really it's just a special sort of bruise, so before it vanishes it'll turn all the colours a bruise does.'

'But how did it happen. I haven't knocked my eye, I'm so careful with my eyes, you only get…'

'…one set of eyes, yes I know. You could have knocked it without knowing, say in your sleep, or it can result from a fit of coughing…'

'Oh, that's it. I've been coughing a lot Mr Rogers, you're so clever to know about that. I think I've got a virus - I've told the doctor, but he wont give me any antibiotics for it. Now look what's happened - I'm going to have words with Doctor Davidson, if he'd treated my virus properly, this would never have happened.'

Poor Doctor Davidson. His problem, though. She's still talking at a rate of knots, and I interrupt.

'No, don't bathe it, don't do anything to it. Just wait for it to go away, Mrs Forsyth. I promise it will soon disappear if you leave it alone.'

Finally she rings off; I'd guess it's Doctor Davidson's turn now. It might be the weekend, but I'd bet good money she's got the poor bugger's home number.

A walk with the dogs, two sandwiches and a pint with Tom, then in the middle of a large Glenfiddich with the X Factor the phone rings. I'm not really up to talking Mrs Forsyth down again, so I don't answer it. It doesn't take long before guilt compels me to check the message.

It's not Mrs Forsyth.

It's Diane.

'Hi Mark, I guess you're out with Tom or something. Anyway, just wanted to tell you that Matthew and I have had a long talk, and it's obvious to both of us that things are best left the way they are. I'm sorry, I know this must have all seemed a bit weird, but I had to do it this way. Matthew and I have a lot of history, and I'm really hoping we can stay friends, but that's all. Anyway – maybe see you tomorrow? Give me a ring, but not tonight – I'm knackered after all this, and I need to sleep. I've to be in work for eight tomorrow, but I'm off at four, so you can get me after that – if you feel like it? Hope to hear from you …oh beggar, that's the doorbell. Got to go. Night.'

As tension drains from my muscles, I actually feel my shoulders dropping. I hadn't realised how much this was bothering me.

After throwing the dogs a biscuit each, I pour myself another drink – a celebratory one. I've still got plenty to worry about, but right now I don't care.

Suddenly none of my other concerns seem that important.

SIXTEEN

DIANE & MATTHEW

'You really hurt me, Matthew. You hurt me so much.'

'I know, and I'm sorry - how many times do I need to say it? Look, Veronica was a mistake. I see that now. You've got to understand...'

'No Matthew, I haven't GOT to do anything. You can't just discard me like that, then come along here and say 'Hey Diane, let's forget what happened and just carry on like before.' Something did happen, something I never dreamed would happen, something I still haven't gotten over...'

'All I'm asking for is another chance, is that so much...'

'Yes. Yes, it's far too bloody much. Do you really think I could ever forget what you did, ever stop seeing you with that top-heavy airhead that you chose over me? Do you?'

'I never meant to hurt you like that Di, really I didn't. Things just got out of control, but I realise now...'

'IT'S TOO LATE NOW. How the hell you can ... ohhhh ... look, sorry, I didn't mean to do this. Here, let me top up your wine, and let's talk about this like adults.'

'Well, that's what I've been trying...'

'Don't push it, Matthew. I'm being far nicer to you than you deserve, that's why I'm putting this wine in your glass rather than over the top of your head while it's still in the bottle. Look, I'm glad we're having this talk, really I am. We were together for a long time, most of it was really good, and I can't just block that out. But …no, let me finish…I can NEVER block out what I felt when you went off with Veronica. I can NEVER trust you again. And – another little complication is that there's someone else in my life now.'

'Oh. I see. Twenty years of marriage and the minute you're on your own, you're off with…'

'DON'T you dare. Don't you even try to suggest that I've done anything wrong. I had no-one to cheat on, remember? Anyway… look, let's be calm about this.'

'I'm calm. It's you that…'

'Oh shut up. The long and short is that meeting tonight has helped me realise two things. First is I could never feel the same about you again. Second is how I feel about – well, the new person I've met. He's not perfect, there are snags, one big one in particular…but that's by the by, I still want to be with him. I'm sorry Matthew, I'd like us to stay friends if possible, but that's all I'm offering.'

'Can I have some more wine?'

'Here. Better watch though, you're driving.'

'Sure, sure. Is there nothing I can say to change your mind?'

'No, there isn't. If you're honest with yourself Matt, isn't a lot of this tonight about wounded male pride? Veronica's done to you what you did to me, and surprise surprise – here you come back on the rebound, back to what you see as safe. Good thing or bad we've both moved on, and we can't go back Matt, we really can't.'

'Well, if you're mind's set, there's not a lot I can do. Never was when I think back. Like that rusty Volkswagen you insisted on buying – oh that's good, it is nice to see that smile again.'

'Okay, that time you were right. It was just such a nice shade of orange…'

'Do you still choose cars by the colour of their paintwork?'

'Very funny. You didn't do so well choosing my replacement on her bodywork.'

'Hey, I thought we were gonna be nice. I still think you're wrong about this, but I can see I'm not going to shift you, so I suppose I just have to live with it – or rather, without you. I'm going to miss you, Di – a lot.'

'I already know what it's like to miss you, Matt. I mean it about being friends – I really want to know what's happening with you. Promise we can keep in touch, just as mates?'

'Promise – I guess. Anyway, time to go.'

'Goodnight, Matt. Take care.'

'…I'm off at four, so you can get me after that – if you feel like it? Hope to hear from you …oh beggar, that's the doorbell. Got to go. Night.'

Now who can that be this late? Matt – what are you doing back?'

'Car wont start.'

'Oh no. Well, it's too late to do anything tonight, you'll just have to stay over – in the spare room, Matt, let's be clear on that. Come on, I'll make you a coffee before bed. You look like you could do with one.'

'Don't really want a coffee, Di….'

'Matt, don't do that. Really, I mean it…'

'No you don't…'

'…Matt, I really do mean it…

…Matt…?'

…Matt…this isn't the spare room…'

SEVENTEEN

It's a long time since I've been out on a Sunday morning at this hour. It wasn't that I couldn't sleep; I slept like a baby. Maybe that's why I woke before six, had the dogs walked by six thirty, and then took this daft notion.

The roads are empty, and the houses I'm passing are closed and dark. No one else who doesn't have to be, and is in their right mind, is up at this time on a Sunday. But I'm not in my right mind. Or maybe I am. I didn't realise until last night how important Diane has become to me. The thought of losing her…well, that doesn't matter now. The threat has passed, the storm has rescinded to clear skies, and once again roses are blooming in my world.

Okay, I've got one or two other things to sort out, but when you're floating ten feet above the ground feeling like Hercules, those other things suddenly don't seem like such a big deal.

In my new Action Man persona, I've decided to join Diane for breakfast. If she's starting at eight she'll be leaving the house around seven thirty, so seven should be just right to surprise her at the kitchen table. By my calculations she'll be sitting there in her dressing gown, fresh from her shower, sipping her second coffee of the day.

Diane's street is as lifeless as the rest of Midlothian when I arrive; I can't get stopped right outside her house because of a blue Ford Mondeo. I've got a vague feeling I've seen it around here before, and I think parking square-outside Diane's house is a bit rude of whichever neighbour it belongs to.

Passing Marcus at the gate, I stoop to give him a quick stroke. Then I'm off down the path and round the side of the house. The back door opens into the kitchen, and since that's where Diane will be, it seems more sensible to go straight round rather than make her leave her reviving coffee to answer the front door bell. A quick knock on the back door so I don't give her a fright, then I open it and walk in, and…

Stop.

Dead.

While my world comes crashing down around me...

I'm frozen in total disbelief; for a moment I'm sure I'm still asleep and having a nightmare.

Diane's sitting at the little bistro table in the kitchen, as expected. She's wearing her white cotton dressing gown, and her steaming cup of freshly made coffee is in front of her, again as expected. Not as expected, there's also some ponce with a stupid moustache sitting at the same table, wearing the blue dressing gown I left hanging on Diane's bedroom door the last time I was here.

I take it this is Matthew.

Diane's on her feet, blood draining from her face faster than water from an un-lagged pipe in December; her coffee's splashing on the table top...

'Mark … what are you … I mean, this isn't…'

The ponce is smiling. Smiling! His voice is as smarmy as the bristles on his upper lip.

'Ah, you must be him.'

I have this unreal premonition of him getting to his feet and holding out his hand to shake. If he does that, I think I'll hit him. With the mental image of my fist crashing into his jaw, and him flying back to splatter against the kitchen wall, adrenaline starts to flow, stoking a sudden, wild excitement. Then it comes back to me that the last time I hit someone was in the playground, and most of that memory is of a direct view of the sky, and quite a lot of pain. The ponce isn't very big, but there's something about him that suggests Bannatynes and barbells.

Diane's mouth is moving, and I can hear her voice, but I can't make out the words. The buzz in my head is drowning her out; for a moment I feel myself sway, and without conscious thought I turn and walk back out the door. Something stops me, some primeval need to express my hostility, so I turn and stick my head back in.

'By the way, moustaches like that went out around the time of Charlie Chaplin.'

As I make my way back round the house, Diane's voice ringing senselessly in my ears, I regret saying that. It was no substitute for punching his lights out; it was just pathetic. But then that word describes me so perfectly.

Pathetic.

That's what I am. Forty five years old. Cuckolded. Again. A failure in every way it's possible to fail.

Pathetic.

I stop at the blue Mondeo. Well, if pathetic is my new watchword, I need to live up to it. Crouching, I unscrew the cap from the valve on the tyre and press my fingernail against the stem until the hiss of escaping air stops. Then I do the same with the other three tyres.

Climbing into my own car, it almost makes me laugh when I find myself wondering whether Matthew has ever been a French teacher.

Almost.

I need to get out of here fast because when I do release an emotion, it's not going to be laughter. The last thing I need is for Charlie Chaplin to see the tears currently struggling for release beneath my lower eyelids.

Resting in one's own consciousness is like sitting at the bottom of the ocean. The tides above are the swirling thoughts of the ego; on the sandy floor there is only the gentle sway of the current. I am aware of the carpet beneath me, the Jack Vettriano print on the wall of my Caravan, my dogs resting quietly by my side. I hear the ticking of the red clock over the kitchen area, the hum of the refrigerator; outside a sparrow is chirping. I feel the stretch of muscles in my crossed legs, and from the open window a breeze wafts gently over my face.

I see, I hear, I feel – but I am removed. Removed in reality - a paradox perhaps? - but who can explain the workings of Zen meditation?

I found Zen during my break-up from Claire; after Sally, I went back to the haven it offered. Now it's time to take respite again, and I am not disappointed. My breath flows easily, my sense of being is amplified, and the horror of my pain is exposed. Before Zen I reacted to pain like most people; by resisting it, trying to push it away, down to a place where it couldn't hurt me. That's myopic behaviour; repressed pain festers, expands, and eventually overwhelms. Better to embrace it, allow it to burn, recognise it for the reality it is, and wait for the hot fire to settle into a manageable glow.

Reality isn't always pretty, but it's all we've got. Good or bad, it's what it is. The path of life is a one-way street; the sidetracks we think we see are illusion, they lead only to madness. Sometimes we get to stroll the path, sometimes we have to march, and sometimes we just have to lie down and rest for a while until we're strong enough to carry on.

In my mind I see Freda, just after I discovered that Sally was having an affair. Her voice is as clear now as it was that day.

'Move on, Mark. You deserve better than this. I know it's hard, but you have to let go.'

As the memory fades, her voice continues.

'Know when to move on, and when to make a stand. Weigh the pros and cons – don't be too quick to run, think about what you might be losing.'

My eyes snap open. Freda never said that.

She's still speaking. I can hear her.

'…I just popped in to see if you wanted anything from the shop, but you seem pretty deep in whatever it is that you're doing…'

That's not Freda. It's Kathy. She's standing just inside the door, with the dogs swarming round her.

While my consciousness struggles its way back from wherever it's been I drag my legs out from under me and, feeling a little shaky, get to my feet. Kathy's watching me curiously, concern flicking over her slightly over-sized face.

'You okay Mark?'

Said warily; I guess it must look a bit weird.

'Fine, I was just meditating. Needed to de-stress a bit, and thanks, but no, I don't need anything out of the shop.'

She's studying me now, her expression unreadable. Then she turns to the kitchen area, flips the switch on the kettle.

'Sit,' she commands. 'I'm going to make some tea, then you can tell me about it. No…' Emphasised by a raised hand, palm out. 'Don't bother, I can read you like a book. We're going to talk about it, whatever it is, because even if it's not something I can do anything about, it always helps to talk it through.'

She gets it out of me, the whole sordid story. The Spanish Inquisition would have gone much faster if Kathy had been around then.

'You know, there could be an innocent explanation.'

'Kathy, I'd love to hear one, but I'm having a bit of trouble imagining what it could be.'

'Well...oh, there's no point in making up theories without knowing the facts. Diane's the one you need to be talking to, sooner the better.'

'Not today.'

'Don't be stupid.'

'Kathy, it really wouldn't be a good idea. Too much chance I'd start shouting at her, or she'd start shouting at me...and where would that get us?'

'Mmm.' She heaves herself up and moves towards the door. 'The longer you leave it though, the harder it's going to get. Why don't you just give her a call?'

I shake my head.

'She's working until four o'clock anyway.'

Kathy pauses on her way out.

'Well, if you need some company, you know where we are.'

She looks at me for a long moment, and I can see a film of moisture forming over her eyes. Then she's gone.

At half past four, the phone rings. Diane. I don't answer it. Not then, nor any of the other times. At six, there's a knock at the door. Then another. Then the handle turns - but I locked it earlier. Her voice cuts like a hail of razor blades.

'Mark. Mark, I know you're in there. Please open the door - we need to talk.'

Eventually she gives up, and it's quiet again. The dogs settle and go to lie down in their respective spaces; they look confused.

Not as confused as I am.

I'm trying to occupy my mind by thinking about my other problems, but it's not working. Homelessness and financial ruin seem remote concepts at the moment. Even health, or lack of it, fails to gain a foothold.

Giving up, I just sit and stare at the wall opposite.

This activity seems to suit me best at the moment.

At seven, the door handle turns again. This time it's followed by the scratch of a key and the click of the lock. The door opens, and Tom and Kathy march in.

By themselves, thank goodness.

Tom's carrying a tin tray, and three pints are rocking gently on its battered surface. He would make a great waiter; probably he's been one at some time in the past.

'What's this?'

Kathy answers.

'Well, he said: 'I bet Mark could do with a pint,' and I said, 'Mark wont come in here tonight.' So off he goes to the bar, orders three pints, pops them on Eric's tray and marches out. I think I can still hear Eric yelling blue murder.'

I wouldn't have believed it, but she's made me smile.

'Yes, I've heard he has to pay for breakages out of his wages.'

Tom sets the pint mugs on the coffee table.

'Thought you'd have been well into the Glenfiddich by now.'

I shrug.

'Funny, but I don't really feel like any. That pint looks good, though.'

Tom agrees, and picks his up. Before he drinks, he muses: 'Diane wasn't drinking either, but maybe that was because she was driving.'

'Diane?'

Kathy's glaring at Tom, but he's too busy draining off half his pint to notice.

'She came looking for us in the Club, seeing as how you were playing silly buggers and pretending to be out.'

'I was not pretending anything, I just didn't feel like answering the door.'

'Yes well, she reckoned talking to us, so we could pass it on to you, was the best she could do under those circumstances.'

I glance nervously at the door.

'She has gone though, hasn't she?'

'Yup,' Tom chimes in. 'Left ten minutes ago. I walked her to her car, so I saw her drive away.'

Kathy wipes her lips with the back of her hand.

'Mark, she says nothing happened last night. Matthew's car broke down, so he had to stay – that's all.'

I think for a moment, then turn to Tom.

'Tom, what's the odds of my, Diane's and Matthew's cars all breaking down in the same month?'

Tom rubs his head.

'Well, three breaking down can't be that much more strange than two breaking down, can it?'

He's got as much comprehension of mathematics as I have of Hebrew. Kathy's speaking again.

'She did say he tried it on, but she wasn't having any of it, so he slept in the spare room.'

'Right, after he tried it on she still let him stay?'

'Oh Mark, what was she supposed to do? Turf him out to walk the streets all night?'

'Ah, right. There's no hotels in Gorebridge, is there?'

'Actually, I don't think there are ...'

Ignoring Tom, I look Kathy straight in the eye.

'Did you believe her?'

Kathy glances to one side; after a moment her eyes return slowly. She shrugs.

'I don't know, Mark. I honestly don't know.'

Tom's been acquiring a faraway look. When he finally speaks, it sounds like his mouth hurts.

'You know, I've been thinking.'

Kathy groans loudly, but for once he ignores her.

'Technically, like – if you've been married to somebody, does it count properly? I mean, how can you be unfaithful with somebody you've been married to?'

Kathy's face is indescribable; I don't know whether it's the inanity of Tom's convoluted logic, or disbelief that he could come up with an original thought. A few lines of response run through my mind before I decide it'd be best to just ignore that. When I scythe my hands in front of me the meaning's clear, and they both shut up.

'Okay look, I'm glad she's denying it because at worst that means I must have meant something to her. Maybe it was all a misunderstanding, though frankly that doesn't jive with the pictures in my head from this morning. I will speak to her, when I'm ready, but unless she said anything else that I really need to hear, I don't want to talk about it any more tonight.'

After that the conversation becomes a bit stilted, and it doesn't take them long to finish their pints and leave.

Leaving me to resume my study of the wall…

EIGHTEEN

Monday morning; I'm up early, though not as early as yesterday. By one I've finished the week's scheduling, prepared all the NHS forms, and taken care of my 'do on Monday' list, which included ordering a few frames and sending out some 'your sight test is due' letters.

Business has picked up well. It's still a little sporadic, but it's coming back. A regular, dependable income assumes new importance in the light of my planned foray back to the world of property – and mortgages.

Jane at the bank took my case to higher management, and they've decided to risk giving me an eighty per cent mortgage. Not a penny more; I suppose I was lucky to get that, all things considered. If I take Alf's derisory offer for the Caravan, I can go shopping for any property up to eighty five thousand. I don't have high expectations about what's going to be available within that sort of budget, but I've got an appointment to view something that looks interesting at two o'clock today.

There's time for a coffee before I leave, and just as I sit down with it the door opens and Kathy wanders in. Uh oh, no Tom – that means she has an 'Aunty Kathy' talk planned. She sets about producing another cup of coffee, starting the counselling session as she works.

'So – have you spoken to her yet?'

'No.'

'Mark, you can't run away from this. Diane's made an effort to talk to you, how long do you think you can just play at being an ostrich?'

'I'm not burying my head in the sand. Well, maybe I am a little, but that's only because I don't know how to handle this. I'm tired, Kathy. It's been a long life, and I'm sick of trying to fix things that just wont mend.'

'How do you know it wont mend?' Said snappily.

'It never does. I tried with Claire, I tried with Sally…'

'Mark, this is somebody different. And you're just not giving her a chance…why are you scratching your leg like that?'

'Don't know, it's just been itchy…top cupboard.'

She finds the dog biscuits and feeds a couple to Molly and Ziggy. Not a spontaneous gesture; my dogs are gifted when it comes to extorting food.

I know Kathy's right in what she's saying, but I don't want to deal with it right now. I've got too much else to sort out.

'No you haven't, Mark. You're using everything else to keep your mind off what's really important.'

'Look Kathy, I honestly WILL talk to her. Soon. Don't know what the hell I'm supposed to say to her, though. She's hasn't done anything wrong; whatever the truth is, she's got every right to do anything she wants…just like I've got every right to decide I don't want to see her any more.'

There's silence for a moment; Kathy tilts her head to one side, and waits for me to stop avoiding her eyes before she speaks.

'First – you don't need to say anything to her, what you have to do is listen to what she wants to say to you. Second – don't pre-judge the situation until you've heard what she's got to say. Doesn't she deserve that much?'

I nod. Good advice, I know. I'd still rather go back to not thinking about it for a while. To steer her off her one-woman daytime-therapy show, I tell Kathy about the house I'm going to see in Prestonpans.

'Offers around eighty thousand? You wont get much for that.'

'Thanks Kathy, I'd sort of figured that out. This might be a compromise though; it's terraced, just one big room downstairs and a converted attic. It's big enough, well, just, and it's even got a little garden for the dogs.'

Kathy looks dubious. 'Why are you so hell-bent on moving all of a sudden. You love it here.'

'You've heard the rumblings, Kathy. The new owners are making it plain they don't want residents on the Site. I was talking to Sam across the way earlier, and the latest is that Greenacres has started to charge parking fees for any extra cars.'

'What?'

'Their logic is that families coming down for a holiday just bring one car, and they're right – all the second cars belong to people who stay here all the time. Sam's just had a bill for thirty quid for his wife's car –for one month. No Kathy, I'd rather move while I can still do it at my own pace, and anyway, it's not viable in the long term to stay here. I need an appreciating asset, not a depreciating one that needs replacing every fifteen years.'

'Couldn't you save up for a while, get something a bit better?'

'What, while I'm paying Site fees, and inflated insurance premiums, and buying bottles of calor gas at sixty quid a time, and...?'

Kathy pulls a face. 'Okay, okay, don't remind me...'

'Anyway,' I continue. 'Apart from all that, the longer I wait, the less I'll get for the Caravan. I don't see I've got a choice really.'

Kathy looks sad now.

'Everything you say is true. To be honest, I don't know how much longer Tom and me can hold onto our van. Tom's not been getting much work lately, and the nursing home's been giving me fewer and fewer shifts.'

That's the first I've heard about this.

'Kathy, I'm sorry. I didn't know. I couldn't imagine this place without you two around.'

Kathy smiles, but it's forced.

'We couldn't imagine it without you either, Mark. If you go then, to be honest, that'll make it easier for us if we have to give our van up.'

I'm stuck for words. Kathy saves me by getting up and rinsing her mug before placing it on the draining board. She stops at the door. Tosses her parting shot.

'Talk to her, Mark.'

The house viewing in Prestonpans doesn't go well. The stair to the attic conversion is little more than a ladder; Ziggy would break her neck trying to go up and down that. The open-plan ground floor is attractive enough the way the current owner has it, but I'd have to substitute the dining space with my office. Not only would I be reduced to eating with a plate on my knees, my growing pile of undone clerical work would be staring me in the face and ruining my appetite. As for the garden, how they've got the cheek to call a twelve-inch strip of clearance around the front and side of the property a 'garden' is beyond me. If my girls were boys, there'd barely be space for them to cock their legs. I tell the anxious seller that 'I'll think about it;' from the sag of his shoulders it's obvious he knows what that means.

I don't usually see patients on a Monday, but Mrs Dawson lives in North Berwick, and all my other patients this week are in Edinburgh and West Lothian, so she was proving hard to schedule. Seeing her after the house viewing seemed the easiest alternative to keeping her waiting for another week. Or maybe I just want to keep myself busy at the moment.

Mrs Dawson has a cosy ground floor flat. Her building's all dark sandstone, and a salty tang in the air confirms it's not far from the sea. It's an impressive structure, modern but with a used look about it. Big too. The door-entry panel has thirty buttons; it's sited under a projecting wooden awning that reminds me of a beach hut.

I've seen Mrs Dawson a couple of times before, and I've always admired her flat and its location. My Grandfather was a trawler skipper in the far North, and I think he's passed some seawater into my blood.

Mrs Dawson spends most of the day attached to her oxygen machine so as a rule she leaves her own front door unlocked, relying on the intercom at the main door for security. After she's buzzed me in, I open the inner door to her flat and shout down the hallway.

'Mrs Dawson, it's the Optician.'

'Come away in dearie.'

Her sitting room's big and bright, the walls a neutral pastel emulsion that set off a rich red carpet. Merry, her cockatiel, starts jumping around his cage while chattering excitedly.

'Is he talking? I can't quite make out...'

She's laughing.

'Yes he is, and it's just as well he's not a clear talker. Mr Dawson taught him a few naughty words before he passed away.'

Ah, right. I thought he was saying 'buckaroo.' Mrs Dawson's barely five feet tall, but she likes her sweeties; if she didn't already qualify for a visit on the grounds of her respiratory condition, morbid obesity would be going in the 'reason' box on the NHS form. She's also diabetic, big surprise, but she's happy. Strangely, much more so than in the days when Mr Dawson was still shuffling this mortal coil.

'So how is your vision?' I ask, to distract her from the drops I'm putting in.

'Oh it's ... ouch ... fine, Mark ...oh hell, that stings!'

'It's...getting...better...' I say slowly, using the power of suggestion.

'No it f****** isn't, laddie. It's getting worse.'

Doesn't always work

I spend a little time studying her cataracts. They've advanced since last year - quite a bit.

'How's your vision watching telly, Mrs D?'

'No bother, Mark. I can see it fine.'

Hmm. With the trial frame on, one eye occluded, and trial lenses of the same power as her last prescription slotted in, I ask her to read the chart.

'T.'

'Yes...go on.'

'Well, I can't really see the ones under that too plainly. I think that light you were shining in my eye has left me a bit dazzled...'

Her other eye's no better. She gives good, accurate responses to my 'better or worse,' 'better with one or two' questions, but the best I can get her to is four lines down the chart - 6/18, a big improvement, but still not great. When it comes to near vision she can barely read her TV magazine, even with some extra magnification. Removing the trial frame from a nose that stretched the width-adjustment knob, and ignoring Merry's obscene suggestions, I sit myself down on the carpet in front of her chair. Time for counselling.

'Mrs D, your cataracts are a lot worse. I really think it's time we thought about getting them fixed. The procedure itself is quite minor...'

'Don't be silly Mark, I can see fine. There's no need for that...really.'

Well, she said that when I came in, she seems very definite about it, and the new glasses I'm going to give her will improve the vision she's currently happy with to a quite significant degree. Plus, she'd find lying flat for twenty or thirty minutes very uncomfortable because of her respiratory condition, and that's assuming she'd fit on the operating table in the first place.

She's happy, she's going to be even happier, so...who am I to argue?

Patient needs vary widely; so long as those needs are being met, arbitrary criteria lose importance. It's very easy to take the professional high-ground in a case like this; your vision could be better, so I need to make it better. I have to remember, though, it's the patient's needs that matter, not mine.

'Okay, if you're happy, I'm happy...for now. But if your vision becomes a problem before your next test, you only have to call me...'

A dismissive wave from a hand that I wouldn't like to be in the way of.

'It wont, dearie. Now, let's see some of your bonny frames. I fancy something really swish this time...'

While she admires herself in my best 'bingo-player' diamante-encrusted frames, she's also chattering about a recent problem with her neighbours.

'...terrible it was. Music blasting until all hours, funny looking folk coming and going.' Her voice lowers. 'They say there was drugs going on, so they do.'

Solemnly, I make the right noises of commiseration.

'But they're gone now? You must be relieved.'

'Oh, I am that. Not that it would have been a problem for long – I'm going into that big Nursing Home down by the shore next month. My son's arranged it all for me.'

'I didn't realise things had become that difficult for you; you always seem to be coping so well.'

'Och, I manage, but I'm getting a bit fed up with it all – 'specially being on my own. At least I'll have company down there – and all my meals cooked, they do say the food's really good...'

'Well, I'm happy for you if it's going to make things better, but I'll miss you. I know the place you mean – they use one of the big national eyecare companies, so I suppose...'

'Oh, beggar that. I'm still having you to do my eyes. You don't mind coming there, do you?'

'Delighted.'

Give me a chance to market the matron – with any luck...

'Don't know when they'll manage to sell that flat next-door though. Seems it's in a terrible mess – no kitchen left so I heard, and needs doing up from top to bottom. It's the bank that's doing the selling of course – they defecated on their mortgage.'

'Defaulted,' I correct automatically, my ears doing a Ziggy while Mrs D talks on.

A Repossession, in a lovely building, in a great location, left in a state, and being sold by a bank that just wants to break even?

Going for a song perhaps?

Maybe even as little as eighty-five thousand?

It does sound like it needs a lot of work – but that's something Tom's short of at the moment...

At five fifteen I'm back in North Berwick. The selling agent was very accommodating when I phoned her, which must be a good sign. She agreed to meet me for a viewing on her way home; that gave me time to find Tom and hustle him back here.

They want offers over ninety thousand.

I'm hoping that, given the circumstances, there might be a little leeway there.

Delia is over sixty, but she isn't submitting easily to the march of time. It's apparent that she has an intimate relationship with Max Factor, and her clothes look like they were bought in the trendiest teen-age retail stores.

Actually, her bubbly personality carries it all very well.

'This is SUCH an opportunity for the right person. A little tidying up and you'll have a beautiful little nest at an absolute steal of a price. Did you notice how close the sea is…?'

'A little tidying up?'

My heart's gone into free-fall. This place is a wreck.

There's green-yellow blotches on the tar-layered walls and they look biological in origin. The only uncontaminated areas are several gaping holes.

The carpet's riddled with cigarette-burns; it'd be hard to say what its original colour was.

The wooden windowsills look as though someone's been trying to kill spiders with a machete, and the bathroom's - well, let's not go into that.

As for the kitchen - a worktop covered in goo sits atop a wooden framework that once carried doors and shelves and drawers. The mixer tap over the dented sink is bent at an angle five times the deviation in my Slit Lamp's illumination system.

Tom's wandering around like a kid in a sweetie shop, prodding and pressing. I think Delia has sensed my reaction, because she says she's going to step outside for a cigarette and leave us to 'talk amongst ourselves about what we could do with this little treasure.'

If it wasn't a flat, my best suggestion would be to demolish it and start again.

'Y'know, it's not as bad as it looks, Mark.'

'How can you say that? I've never seen such a mess.'

'No, see…it's all on the surface. Them holes would fill quick enough, and some heavy paper would hide the patching; couple of tins of plastic wood would fix the sills and skirtings. The carpet goes in a skip, the bathroom really just needs a good clean…'

'Tom, you're forgetting the kitchen. Or the lack of one.'

'Nah, c'mere...'

He leads me through to the kitchen, chattering on as we go.

'The worktop's okay, just needs some powerful cleaning – look, I can scrape through this stuff with my fingernail, the surface is okay underneath. The carcass is all intact, it's just a case of putting cupboard doors on, fitting drawers and shelves, bit of matching veneer – I can get everything I need in B&Q, it's all standard size gaps.'

'But the sink…and the tap…'

'Poo – new sink doesn't cost much, have one fitted in a jiff, and the tap'll mend. See, folk don't fix things enough these days, they're too quick to yank everything out and start from scratch. I could have this beautiful for a fraction of the cost of a new kitchen.'

Hmm. He knows what he's talking about when it comes to this sort of stuff. Suddenly I'm getting excited.

'You're sure – we could fix it up on the cheap, and it'd look alright?'

Tom nods confidently.

'No danger. I could price it out roughly for you tonight if you want?'

Just then Delia arrives back from her smoke break; she's subdued, and I can hear the fear in her voice.

'So Mark, what are you thinking?'

Carefully, I put on my saddest face.

'Oh Delia, this is so much worse than I'd imagined. It's going to cost a fortune to put right, it needs a new kitchen, new bathroom, new floors, new ceilings…'

Tom nudges me. Don't overdo it. I catch myself.

'…there's so much work involved, not just the cost, but the organising – it'll need whole teams of tradesmen working for weeks...'

Tom nudges me again, harder, but I don't know - Delia's looking pretty sick.

'…I'd need to get loads of estimates before I could say anything for sure, but if I was to consider taking on this…this…'

I wave my arm helplessly.

'…well, I can't see us talking more than eighty thousand.'

I checked on the Internet before we came back; another flat in this block sold for a hundred and twenty thousand a few months ago.

Delia isn't looking just as sceptical as I'd anticipated.

'That sounds a little on the low side Mark, but…'

She sidles up to me, speaks quietly, sharing secrets.

'…I do know that the man at the bank who's dealing with this is very anxious to get …um…achieve completion on this particular project. Just between you and me, he has indicated that he'd be very open to offers...'

It takes less than an hour for Tom to draw up a costing of the necessary renovation works to make No.5 Seaview habitable again. He seems to have B & Q's catalogue stored in his head. According to his figures we could have it back in pristine condition for around fifteen thousand pounds, including his labour; that means if I offered eighty thousand, my potential profit is twenty five thousand pounds. Well, since I need to live there the profit would be in equity rather than cash – but equity's easy enough to get at, via a secured loan, then I can invest in something else…

The dogs were used to living in a flat before the Caravan, but I don't know how they'll feel now after experiencing the wide-open spaces of Greenacres. There again we'll be near the beach, and they'd love that.

I'm starting to buzz.

I'm going to have Mr Diggins put in an offer tomorrow. Meantime, I take Tom to the Club to go over his figures. Can't shake him; he seems to have everything worked out precisely. He's even costed Kathy in, for a cleaning role. I feel it prudent to double-check on this, especially remembering those worktops.

'Have you asked her?'

'Oh sure, she's fine about it. Kathy likes cleaning, not that she'd admit it, but this'll give her a kick. Uncovering those worktop surfaces'll be like anthropology.'

That leaves me gaping stupidly; Tom and a big word like that? He must have looked it up before we came out.

'You know, like people digging for fossils and things,' he explains helpfully, then winks. 'I used to have a metal detector, you see.'

Ah. That explains it. I think.

I leave after the second drink; I've got a few more figures to work on before I'll be satisfied I'm doing the right thing. Specifically cash flow; how to source the deficit, and make the repayments. I'm walking up to my gate on automatic pilot, oblivious to my surroundings, when a familiar voice cuts through the numeric haze.

'You didn't seem to be in, so I thought I'd just wait…'

Diane. Sitting on the verandah steps. Wearing a blue aertex jacket, and still shivering a little against the night breeze. Looking lost … as lost as I suddenly feel.

It takes a moment for me to change gear. Then:

'You'd better come on in.'

She nods, and follows me.

I make coffee; reminds me of the night in Gorebridge when we talked properly for the first time. That seemed hard, but it was a dawdle compared to tonight. I don't know what to say to her; I don't know if I want to know.

She speaks first.

'Look Mark, I know how it looked on Sunday morning, but it wasn't like it seemed. Really. His car broke down, so I let him stay in the spare room. Simple as that; end of story.'

Her eyes have fixed on mine, and they're still as stone.

'Do you believe me?'

Trying to keep my own eyes from ducking is almost making me shake.

'So…nothing happened?'

'No.'

That was vehement, but I saw her eyes slip a fraction.

'No,' she repeats; is it my imagination, or did that second 'no' lose momentum. Barely perceptible if it did…

'I want to believe you. I really do. But I don't want you to lie to me either, however good your intentions. You were right before – honesty is more important than anything. Without honesty, we don't have anything.'

She studies me with her lips pursed.

I mean it; I don't want a relationship based on lies. But how will I handle honesty if it isn't what I want to hear?

Is the whole issue really so important anyway? It's not like Matthew was somebody new, throwing up issues of whether she was dissatisfied with me. Matthew was a part of her life for twenty years before we met.

Tom's attempt at moral philosophy comes back – can it really be called cheating when an ex-spouse is involved? Maybe he had more of a point than Kathy or I gave him credit for.

When Diane speaks again, it's to the light diffuser on the ceiling.

'Nothing happened. He stayed the night in the spare room because his car broke down. Do you really want to throw away everything we had for the sake of that?'

'No, I don't. I don't think. Oh Diane, I'm really confused with all this. I don't know what I'm thinking any more.'

Now she's looking at me again, and her lower lip is trembling.

A pulse of something – excitement? relief? – surges through me when suddenly, slowly, she reaches out to touch my cheek with her fingertips - trails them down to my neck. My skin's tingling where the tips of her fingers just raked softly through bristles of night-time shadow. My reluctance is on a see-saw with desire.

When her fingers reach my jawbone she pauses, pressing gently against the underside, and it's then that my own hand decides by itself to touch her hair. She doesn't seem to notice; suddenly she's become lost in her own thoughts.

Finally she speaks, but not in the tone I was expecting.

'Mark...your lymph nodes are swollen.

NINETEEN

It's looking like I'm going to have to stay overnight at the Western.

Diane came with me, but she starts work soon, so she's gone to ask Tom and Kathy if they'll bring some things in for me.

I do hope they behave themselves - especially if Doctor Gordon's around...

KATHY

There's five or six cars ambling along behind us on Ferry Road. They haven't got a lot of choice, not with my Tom at the wheel. Luckily, at seven pm, the traffic's fairly light.

Could just be word's gotten out that Tom's on the road.

'Rum do,' he mutters.

Mark's been kept in overnight at the Western General; it sounds like his cancer's come back.

'I feel sorry for Diane, she'd obviously been crying before she came to tell us about it.'

Tom's slowed to a crawl in case the green light we're passing turns red.

'Reckon it's all this upset with her ex, made it worse sort of.'

He's right; it sounds like they were starting to work through their problems just as this happened. I think Diane's confused about where she stands now; she wants to be there for him, but she's not sure about her place. Maybe just as well she's gone to work tonight and left us to bring Mark's stuff to him, though I could see she was on the point of cancelling her shift to do it herself.

When Tom eventually gets us to the hospital, Mark's waiting for us in a four-bed ward. There's only one other patient in the room, and he's got a couple of visitors too. Mark's sitting in a chair by the side of his bed, fully clothed. Tom, of course, is taken aback.

'Shouldn't you be in bed?'

'Tom, I feel fine, there's no need for me to lie in bed. I'm only here because Doctor Gordon wants me on hand when my test results come back tomorrow, in case I have to start treatment.'

'More chemotherapy? Bummer.'

Luckily I'm wearing heels, and I jab Tom's ankle just hard enough to make him grunt. Mark realises what I did and smiles; good, that's what I was hoping for.

'Here, we brought you some grapes.'

He scowls. 'Is that meant to be a joke?'

Tom's grinning; it was his idea. His sense of humour developed when he was a kid, but it never got much further. He reaches into my bag for his other idea.

'Ginger beer? Gee thanks Tom, don't know how I could have gotten through the night without...'

Tom's up and moving to the water dispenser at the door of the ward; minute later he's back with a paper cup, which he half-fills from the ginger beer bottle and holds out to Mark.

'Try some.' He winks. 'I think you'll like it.'

Looking pretty reluctant, Mark raises the cup to his lips.

'Ginger beer isn't really…oh. Bloody hell. Oh, well done Tom.'

Tom tops him up. 'Thought you'd be ready for a wee Glenfiddich, Mark.'

'Cheers. Tom, why do you keep winking at me?'

'He's had a sore eye since last night,' I answer for Tom.

Talk about holding a magnet to a pin. Mark's on his feet like there's a spring in his backside, specs off and dangling from his hand as he bends over Tom. Seems because he's short sighted, he sees things close-to bigger without his glasses. He's totally absorbed, pulling Tom's eyelids down and sideways, peering intently all the time. I think if the fire alarm went off he wouldn't even notice. Now he's talking to me.

'Kathy, have you got any tweezers in your bag?'

After a rummage I hand him a pair.

'They're eyebrow tweezers, is that alright?'

He nods absently.

'That'll do fine. Keep still Tom; look down for a moment…there. Don't be a baby, it didn't hurt that much.'

Don't know what he just did, but everybody's looking round to see why Tom yelped like that. I think he was just taken by surprise though, because he's back to his trademark Cheshire-cat already.

'Hey, how'd you do that, Mark? It's been prickling at me all day, but it feels fine now.'

Mark's already sat back down on his chair; he looks much more himself than when we came in.

'It was an in-growing eyelash, I just pulled it out. Quite common, should be okay now. There's just a chance it'll grow back in the same way, but if it does you'll know straight away what it is, and we'll just do the same again.'

'MR Rogers.'

The stern voice belongs to a middle-aged woman standing at the end of the bed. She's dressed in a long skirt that looks stiff enough to stand up by itself, and a billowy blue cardigan. She sounds fierce, but her eyes are twinkling.

'Do you think you could refrain from holding eye clinics in my wards, and try to accept the concept that, for the moment, it is you who is the patient?'

Mark obviously knows her; his voice is humble, but I can see the smile he's holding back.

'Sorry Doctor Gordon, if anybody else gets a problem tonight I'll just let them go blind.'

'Hmm.'

She's a gruff woman, yet she makes me think of a teddy bear. Bonnie lassie too, when you look past the camouflage. I'm thinking she's a lot younger than she seemed at first glance. She's talking again:

'Nothing to tell you yet, but we'll have all the test results in by morning. Why are you scratching your leg, Mr Rogers?'

I answer for him; when you live with Tom, you sort of get into the habit.

'He's got some sort of rash, been there for days.'

'Has it indeed.' She motions sharply with her hand. 'Up on the bed please, roll the trouser leg up.'

Mark does as he's told; I'd reckon most people do. She peers at his leg with the same kind of intensity that he used on Tom's eye, then steps back.

'Interesting. Alright, trouser leg down, you can go back to the chair.'

She'd be great in a circus, training the tigers.

'I'm going off duty now Mr Rogers, but I'll see you in the morning...oh, is that ginger beer? Would you mind if I had a taste? I'm absolutely parched...'

Without waiting for an answer, she's off to fetch a paper cup. Mark's looking helplessly at us; I can feel his terror. Boy, that woman can move. She's back before Tom's managed to close his mouth, pouring a generous measure of 'ginger beer' into her cup.

She raises it to drink, then stops and sniffs. Looks at the ceiling. Sniffs again. Then takes a careful sip. Looks at Mark. He's wriggling, like he's trying to burrow through the back of the chair.

He doesn't say anything. She doesn't say anything.

She sniffs her drink again. Then sips. Then tilts the cup, and drains it. Rolls her eyes towards the ceiling.

'It's been a long day. I needed that.'

Then she picks up the bottle and strides off to the sink. Crouching so she's at eye level, she starts pouring the contents away. When she comes back, the bottle's only about a quarter-full. She sets it down on top of Mark's locker with a sharp click.

'I think that should be a sufficient dose of ...er...medicine to see you through the night Mr Rogers. I'll be back in the morning.'

With that she's gone, and Mark's pulling in big breaths, huffing them out. Tom's taken that familiar glazed look, but then he chuckles.

'Don't think she twigged what it really was in the bottle, eh?'

As usual, Mark's coping well. On the surface at least. Hard to know exactly what's going on underneath. It took Tom and me a long time to really get to know him. One thing with Mark though – once you break through the barbed wire, you've got the most loyal, dependable friend anyone could want.

I think he's feeling better than when we arrived, but I'm hoping we can give him another little boost before we go. I've agonised over this; I hope I'm doing the right thing...

'You know, Diane's really worried about you. You, as in yourself, and you as in both of you.'

'It was her who spotted the swollen lymph gland in my neck. I hadn't noticed anything - maybe been a bit more tired than usual lately, but I was putting that down to...'

'Yes, about that.'

I look meaningfully at Tom. For once he's on the same wavelength, and gives me a little nod. I take a deep breath.

'I've got a wee story to tell you, Mark. You may be angry that I haven't told you before now, but I gave my word... anyway, last Saturday night, when Matthew's car broke down, Diane phoned us to see if Tom would come and have a look at it.'

He looks like Molly and Ziggy being shown a couple of steaks. Tom pipes up on cue:

'Yeah, it really was broken down Mark. Couldn't do nothing about it without a part.

Mark's head swung to Tom when he spoke, now it's on its way back to me. Reminds me of Wimbledon.

'So.' I take up the story. 'This is the bit you'll find hard Mark, but Diane was worried about having Matthew stay the night. The wee nyaff had already made a pass at her, and she wasn't sure she could hold out if he tried it again. I mean, remember all the time they were together, she's over him, but in that kind of situation...anyway, she told me all this, and asked me to stay, sort of be a chaperone like. So I did - I slept on a put-u-up in her room - that's how I know nothing happened that shouldn't have. When you arrived in the morning, I was in the bathroom having a shower.'

Oh boy, if that doctor had wanted to examine the inside of Mark's throat she should have stuck around a bit longer.

'Why didn't you tell me any of this before?'

'I promised Diane I wouldn't. She couldn't get past the fact that she'd be admitting she wasn't confident enough to be in the house alone with him, and she didn't want you to know that. She thought you'd just believe her that nothing happened, but I know you're not finding that easy, and I don't want it hanging over you while this is going on. I'll have to tell Diane tomorrow what I've done, but I think she'll agree I was right.'

'I don't know what to say, Kathy. It just gets more and more confusing. Still, thanks – that has helped, really.'

'Good. C'mon Tom, time we made a move.'

Tom drags his eyes away from the ginger beer bottle and stands up. Poor luv. I'll take him into the Club for a pint when we get back.

Tom's being quiet.

'You okay?'

'Just worried we did the right thing back there. I mean, we don't really know what happened with Diane and Matthew on Sunday, do we?'

'Does it matter, really? You've seen her and Mark together, and the effect she was having on him before all this nonsense about Matthew. He deserves a bit of happiness. More than that, with this happening, his cancer coming back and all, he needs her. You know what he was like last time; we were all he had, and he hardly let us do anything to help, wouldn't talk to us about how it was affecting him. I'm not having him go through that alone a second time.

Diane's a lovely girl. If she made a wee mistake, well, so what? Doesn't change anything from where I'm standing.'

'You know best about this stuff I guess.' He still looks worried. Then he brightens. 'Fancy some fish and chips and a few cans?'

'I was going to take you to the Club, but that sounds better. We'll get the dogs some battered sausages while we're at it. They need cheering up too.'

'Can we afford it?'

He's joking, but he's not. I punch him on the shoulder.

'Ouch.'

Oops. Maybe that was a bit hard.

You sound like Mark, dopey.'

'Yeah - but WE really are broke.'

'Oh, who cares. Forget about it for tonight - chip shop, then offy. Right?'

The grin's back where it should be. I just said three of his favourite words.

He's a doll - he's so easy to please.

TWENTY

While the Déjà vu is chilling in its implications I've reached a plateau of acceptance, just like last time. The big difference between then and now is a deep-flowing angst of frustration. I was getting my life back together in so many ways before this chasm re-opened under me.

The CT scanner this morning held out a sinister familiarity, and again I'm accustomed to being milked for blood samples; I've already stopped flinching when the needles go in.

Scarily, I'm back in what I call 'institution mode.' This is when life begins to revolve around mundane landmarks, specifically meals and coffee trolleys. I'm sitting here listening intently for the trundling sounds that will soon herald the WRVS lady, and despite being aware of the morbidity, I'm getting quite excited.

Such is life on the ward.

I'm alone in the four-bedded room; my roommate has wandered off to watch football in the patient's lounge. I'm lost in the dilemma of which type of biscuit to have with my coffee today when light fingers touch my shoulder.

'Hey – you were miles away.'

'Diane – I thought you'd still be sleeping after working last night.'

'Couldn't sleep for thinking about you, so I decided to just come and see you. What were you thinking so hard about then.'

'I'm torn between a digestive or a hob-nob with my coffee.'

She looks a bit blank; obviously doesn't understand the deeper behavioural implications of institutionalisation. Just then the trolley arrives, and she solves my problem by fetching one of each type of biscuit and setting the plate on my lap. I study them for a moment, then lift the plate and put it down on my locker.

'No, you don't understand. I have to decide between them; it's important.'

She looks at me strangely for a moment, then sips her own coffee before changing the subject.

'So – any news?'

'No, none. I'm hoping to hear something today, but Doctor Gordon warned me she might need more tests before she can say.'

'How do you feel?'

'Fine. That's the worst of it in a way. I'm stuck in here, and I don't feel any reason for it. It's a bit disorientating.'

There's sympathy in her nod. 'Maybe it's a false alarm.'

I nod back, but I'm not interested in platitudes; they don't work. The only way I can cope with this is to glide the space between optimism and pessimism. What was developing into an uncomfortable silence is broken by a flurry of angora as Doctor Gordon explodes into the room.

'Mr Rogers…ah, Nurse Wells too. Good to see you again.'

Diane shifts in her chair. 'I'd better go…'

Doctor Gordon flaps her hand.

'No, assuming Mr Rogers is agreeable, you might as well stay. Save you having to use your computer privileges to read my notes.'

I bob my head in agreement to the idea of Diane staying; don't know what that last was about, but Diane's face has turned pink. Doctor Gordon plonks herself down on the bed, facing us. She's still looking at Diane.

'I know, MRSA, I'm not supposed to sit on patients' beds. Frankly however my feet are killing me, and I know you're sympathetic to the breaking of rules now and again.'

If Diane's face goes any redder it's going to ignite.

'In any case, it's a moot point - MRSA contamination - since the bedding will be laundered before anyone else uses it.'

Does that mean what I think it means?

'Yes Mr Rogers, I'm setting you free. You wont be needing any more chemotherapy.'

'So the tests were…?'

I'm scared to embrace this before I've heard all the details…

'Quite clear as far as Lymphoma is concerned, you're still in remission. Your anaemia is better too.'

My hands wander to my neck.

'But the swollen lymph nodes…'

'Have you heard of a condition called Systemic Lupus Erythematosus?'

I have as it happens; it can have some ocular implications, but rarely, so I need to dig deep for details.

'Um…disorder of the immune system, usually characterised by a distinctive facial rash, or the rash can be elsewhere on the…'

My eyes drop to my leg.

'Precisely. Quite common for the rash to be on the leg, and another sign of this condition is swelling of the lymph nodes.'

Diane's breathing hard; her words are unsteady when they come.

'Is this …Lupus…serious?'

'Like many conditions, it comes in varying degrees of severity. This case…' she inclines her head in my direction '…is a very mild manifestation. I am expecting it to resolve without the need for any treatment.'

She studies me for a moment.

'It is more usual for an episode of Lupus to precede Lymphoma rather than follow it, but I have become accustomed to things happening back to front where you're concerned.'

My breath flows out in a rush; Doctor Gordon is still watching me closely. I inhale, slowly, deeply. Exhale. Feel the fear and helplessness float out of me.

'Doctor Gordon, you're a marvel.'

She does a mock recoil, but there really is a smile on her lips – a small smile, but it's the first one I've seen making it to the outside world.

'I, Mr Rogers, am merely the messenger. I am very pleased, though, to be bringing this particular message.'

I'm tempted to hug her, but she probably knows judo. Diane turns and throws her arms around me, squeezes tight. I'm dimly aware of Doctor Gordon's voice somewhere in the background, her Scholl sandals clicking as she makes for the door.

'I'll give you some privacy. I've already signed your discharge Mr Rogers, you can leave whenever you're ready.'

'I'm ready now,' I mean to announce, when Diane's tongue slips between my lips.

Okay, maybe in a couple of minutes...

Diane drops me off at the Caravan Site, with my little suitcase. She'd like to stay a while, and I'd like her to stay, but she needs to get some sleep before her shift starts. After quite a tender goodbye, I stand and watch as her car disappears up the track. So many feelings ploughing through me; relief, the joy of de-institutionalisation, desire for Diane, fear that I'm going down the wrong road again, especially after this Matthew thing...

…I head straight over to B field, don't even bother to drop off my case...

Molly and Ziggy explode from Tom and Kathy's van like bees from a bumped nest. Unlike the bees, they're happy. Ecstatic even.

Molly's just hurling herself at me, again and again. Ziggy's got a grip on my leg with her two front paws, and she's rubbing her head against me … I'm home.

Tom wants to pour me a celebratory drink but it's too early, and I have a lot to do, so Kathy makes coffee instead.

While she's setting out mugs, Tom asks about my latest diagnosis.

'So is this Droopus thing going to be a problem for you?'

'Lupus. No, I don't think so. It can be serious, but I've only got a very mild dose, and Doctor Gordon thinks it'll clear itself quite quick. I've to go for a check up in three weeks, but really everything's looking fine.'

'Did you speak to Diane about what I told you last night?' Kathy asks. She looks worried.

'No, she had to go home and get some sleep before work, and before that we were - well, we didn't do much talking as such.'

I can't hold back a little smile. Kathy sighs.

'Oh good, I want to talk to her first. Explain about breaking her confidence, you know?'

Funny - the thought of Kathy breaking a confidence doesn't ring true.

After bringing the dogs home I spend an hour reinstating my patient schedules for the week. The old ones sound confused; a couple of them insist on being re-booked for next week. Old people worry about other people's illnesses, specifically about whether they're contagious. There's just time to catch Mr Diggins about the flat in North Berwick; luckily his secretary tells me the last appointment's free, so I jump in the car and race off up the bypass.

With the conclusion of my dealings with Sally, I hadn't expected to be coming back to the lush pasture of Mr Diggins' working environment. I did think about trying another solicitor this time, a less expensive one, but despite my low opinion of his professional abilities I've become used to Diggins. It's that 'devil you know' thing. Maybe another solicitor would be even worse - hard to imagine, but must be possible.

Mr Diggins is as talkative as ever when I sit down on the other side of his desk. He nods as I explain why I'm here, holds his hand out for the property details, studies them intently. Finally his head rolls up, causing wattles of flesh to undulate towards his collar.

'Why would you want something that's in such a mess?'

Funny how you can be dead sure about something, yet feel uncomfortable about explaining it to an authority figure like a lawyer.

'Well, I have a friend who's going to help me do it up. He's very good with his hands, and if I can get it for the right price, I think I stand to do rather well out of it.'

'Mmm.' He goes back to the details for a moment, then asks: 'Where are you going to get the deposit?'

Disconcerting, his intimate knowledge of my financial situation.

'I'm going to sell my Caravan back to the Site. I'm only getting eighteen thousand for it by the way, despite all that nonsense my ex-wife's solicitors were talking about its value.'

That gets his attention. He sighs loudly.

'Pity you hadn't done this a couple of months ago, we'd have been in a much stronger negotiating position having the value of your Caravan established like this.'

Yes, rub it in why don't you? He's not finished.

'So how much do you want to offer?'

I bite my lip. I'm not sure what his reaction to this will be.

'Well, I want to try going in at eighty thousand. It is in a terrible state, no kitchen…'

My words trail off; his meaty palm's come up like a stop sign.

'With a bank repossession we'll be unable to establish warranties on, for example, the central heating system. It's very much a case of 'sold as seen' with essentially no comeback. No, I'd be more inclined to make an initial offer of seventy thousand.'

My mouth's moving, but there's no words forming.

They'll never accept that.

Finding my voice again, I tell him so. He places his elbows on the desk, drops his chins onto cupped hands.

'You have to understand that in a situation like this, banks are anxious to move on. This isn't their business; they only want to recoup what money they can, and get rid of what is essentially a nuisance.

No, they wont laugh at seventy thousand - they may want more, but still we'll have set the tone of the negotiation to our advantage.'

He's good at this. I'm dumbfounded. A sneaking suspicion is forming in my mind.

'Do you do a lot of property work Mr Diggins?'

When he nods I feel the breeze generated by flapping folds of greasy tissue.

'Yes, that's what I spend most of my time on.'

'So … how much of your time is taken up with family law - like divorces?'

He has the decency to flush pinker than normal before he replies.

'As a matter of fact, you were my first. I was quite pleased with the outcome, as, I hope, were you.'

I can almost feel my fingers squeezing his throat; the thick, sweaty feel of that skin would be repulsive, but the sound of his last breath wheezing it's way past the constriction would be music. As would be the crack of that thick law book on his shiny skull.

I think he's read my reaction; he's sitting way back in his chair and his pebbly eyes are darting all around, looking for an escape route.

However, that was then, this is now. I hadn't even considered going as low as seventy thousand; what I said to Delia was pure bluff. In my current financial state, an extra ten thousand represents riches beyond belief.

I decide to let him live.

'Okay,' I say, a little stiffly. 'Put in an offer for seventy thousand, I don't suppose there's much chance of it being accepted, but as you say…'

I get back to Greenacres just before six; at five past Diane arrives, swinging a carrier bag adorned with a picture of something between a goldfish and a shark.

'I thought you were working.'

'My shift starts at seven. We've just time to eat these fish and chips, if you fancy.'

Fish and chips. My mind jerks back to Edinburgh, and our first date at Terrapins. Maybe that was the idea.

The chippie's delicious, but neither of us has the appetite we thought we had, so the dogs end up with most of the food. When they've finished, Ziggy staggers off towards the couch. I think she'll need a stepladder to get up there. Molly meanwhile lowers her head, and burps loudly.

'You know,' I say. 'When Arabs do that, it's considered good manners. Something to do with showing appreciation for the food.'

I don't think she even heard me - or Molly.

'Kathy phoned me earlier - she told me about that chat she had with you last night - about the weekend.'

I nod slowly.

'She feels bad about breaking your confidence, but she was...'

'Mark. None of that happened, she was making it up.'

'What? But why would she...?'

'She was trying to help, but I wish she'd spoken to me first. Look Mark, this has gone on long enough. I'm going to tell you what really happened on Saturday night. You might not like some of it, but I can't stop thinking about what you said about honesty, and I agree. The truth might hurt, but hiding things would hurt more in the end.'

We're sitting on high stools, on opposite sides of the kitchen worktop. I reach across for her hand, capture her clear blue eyes.

'No. I don't agree. The past isn't real, neither's the future. All we have is the present moment, what we see, hear, smell. Feel. The past's only important for what it bodes for the future, for its value as a warning. Whatever happened last weekend I don't see it as a warning, or as something that's likely to leak into the future - or the present.

So I don't want to know.'

I'm on my feet now, moving round to her side.

'I'm happy with now. I'm happy with you. Let's move on.'

Tears are splashing on her cheeks.

'But wont you wonder - wont it always be in the way, between us...?'

'No.'

Emphatic.

'I've told you about some of this Zen stuff I find so helpful. First principle is we're reborn in every moment, because the moment is all we have. It's not mysticism, it's simple sense. It's how I've lived my life, even before I was able to verbalise it. Everything starts here, Diane. There isn't any before.'

When she comes into my arms, my world feels complete again. I want to keep her there forever, but she's pulling back.

'I have to go - I'm going to be late. Mark...' A kiss. Then another.

Then she's gone.

Life is what we make it. We can choose to make it how we want. I've made my choice. Maybe I'm not just as sure as I made out, but I'm sure enough.

I think.

I need to clear my head. The dogs need their walk. Our needs coincide.

Adjacent to the Caravans is a huge expanse of wild greenery. The land is owned by Greenacres, so no doubt one day it will be full of Caravans and lodges. For the moment though, it's one of the features that makes this place perfect for dog-owners.

Every so often the groundsman drives his grass cutter over the whole area, and there are well-beaten paths reflecting the favourite ambles of various walkers. While we're threading our way through the Caravans I've got Ziggy on her lead, which isn't pleasing her. She does know her way around pretty well but there's always the risk that she'll walk into an unexpected obstruction, like a newly-sited firebox. Before we're halfway through the maze of holiday homes Tom and Kathy appear, on their way to the Club. It's a nice night, so they decide to join us for our walk.

Kathy looks troubled.

'Mark - about that business with Diane, you know, what we told you…'

Tom interrupts.

'Never mind the 'We,' It was your idea.' He turns to me. 'She didn't half get it in the neck from Diane on the phone.'

Kathy - getting it - taking it - in the neck? Diane must have hidden depths that even I haven't plumbed yet.

'Anyway luv, I'm sorry if I upset anybody. I was just trying to do what I thought was best.'

I slip the dogs' leads into one hand, and put the other round Kathy's shoulder.

'I know. Don't worry, no harm done. In fact, I think Diane and I have got all that sorted out now, so let's forget about the whole thing.'

She looks surprised, but before she can delve deeper someone calls her name.

'Oh, it's Marjorie. I just need to go and speak to her about my catalogue order. Here…'

She holds out her hand.

'…let me take Ziggy, she gets on well with Marjie's poodle. I'll catch you up in a minute.'

Kathy strides off with Ziggy, and Tom and I resume a leisurely stroll towards the open space. Good; I've been wanting to get him on his own.

'Tom, these money problems you and Kathy are having – how bad is it?'

His face sags.

'Oh, she's told you has she? Problem is, the nursing home's getting bigger, and they're taking on more full-time staff, so Kathy's not getting anything like the days she used to. Then all the folk I job for are feeling the crunch; they're not getting the work, so neither am I.'

'So you're struggling?'

'We could manage if it wasn't for the cost of this place. It's starting to look like we'll have to give the Van back to Alf for two balloons and a birler, like you're doing.'

'But you spend more time here than you do at home.'

'Maybe that's a bit of the problem. Maybe if we're not enjoying ourselves down here so much, we'll be able to find more work than we're doing.'

Before I can say anything else, Molly growls softly. The fur at the back of her neck springs to attention, and Tom and I both follow the vector of her nose. It's the Rottweiler – the one we had the run-in with before.

This time it's with it's owner, on the lead; they're a couple of Caravan-lengths away from us, and on a collision course.

The owner's a youngish bloke in a leather jacket who seems tall but it's all long legs; bit wimpish, the Rotty's obviously his badge of manhood.

The Rottweiler's seen Molly too, and it's going crazy.

His owner's got the lead in two hands, pulling sharply, but the dog's lost it. He's a kaleidoscope of teeth and spit and raucous barking. Ducking down quickly I snap Molly's lead into place, then nudge Tom.

'We'll turn round, nip between the Caravans, and come back another way.'

Tom nods, transfixed by the menace emanating from the big dog.

'Needs a boot up the arse if you ask me,' he mutters, but shows no sign of trying to carry out that plan.

Kathy's voice booms.

'You need to keep that thing under control.'

She's emerged from a gap in the vans just ahead, between us and the Rottweiler and his struggling owner. She's holding a rolled-up lead in her hand – she must have let Ziggy off to play with the poodle. Hurriedly I scan the ground all around.

So where's Ziggy?

The air suddenly splits to a fearsome, agonised howl. The Rottweiler's started screaming, again and again, a series of short bursts that sound like a demented police siren.

The ropey lead rips free from the owner's hands and the Rottweiler's off like an exocet missile, back the way they came. The owner gapes stupidly for a moment before running in pursuit, big loping steps that seem to carry him sideways as much as forwards. He shouts after his dog, which he has no chance of catching until it decides to let him.

'Horace, stop. Come back right now. Horace…'

Horace?

My eyes flick back to the spot the Rottweiler fled from, drawn by a blip of white on the edge of my vision

There stands Ziggy, paws planted firmly, head up, smacking her lips…

TWENTY-ONE

After all the excitement and trauma of the last couple of days, it's back to the grindstone this morning. A new patient, a Mrs Tomkins, awaits me in East Linton. Only fifteen minutes away, so I got a bit longer in bed.

It was Mrs Tomkins' daughter, Susan, who made the appointment, and when I park outside her mother's cottage I see her coming to meet me.

East Linton is pretty, and Mrs Tomkins' home is no exception to the rule. Roses ravage the front garden, and leafy snakes of ivy scale the dark brickwork of the cottage. There's a wooden arch halfway down the front path, made from wood that looks like it was recycled from the ark.

Susan offers to help me with my cases but I tell her no, they're too heavy. Besides, my public liability premiums would go up if she injured her back with them. Susan's painfully thin, and quite prim. She's chattering away nervously as we make our way down the stone-pavers and under the wooden arch; I get the impression she's trying to pave a different path, to prepare me for her mum. When we arrive in a small, dull-lit parlour, I see a sweet little old lady sitting in a tight-woven basket chair. Her hair is done in a neat grey bun, and she's wearing a flowery dress and a navy cardigan. She exchanges greetings quite pleasantly, and I wonder what Susan was on about.

As usual, it's drops in first. I take care to relax the old lady, and prepare her a little, then I pop the tropicamide into each eye. There. It's over before she knew it.

SLAP.

I was aware of a blur of movement in my peripheral vision just before Mrs Tomkins' hand connected hard with the side of my head. I'm stargazing, and my face is stinging. Susan's voice rings out, a bit tremulous.

'Mother, behave. You promised.'

'Sodding drops. Wont hurt he said. Bloody liar. What bit of me's he going to fiddle with next, that's what I want to know.'

I make a mental note; no need to ask, the Dom reason is obviously dementia.

'Where do you come from, son?'

The voice is soft, relaxed. She probably doesn't remember she just clonked me one. I pick up the Tonometer.

'Just near Haddington. Now, this machine blows a puff of air into your eye to measure the pressure. It may make you jump a little, but it doesn't hurt.'

PUFF.

SQUISH.

The squish was the Tonometer flattening my nose under the impact of Mrs Tomkins' palm. For eighty nine, the old woman's strong - and fast.

'Mother. We talked about this. Now behave - PLEASE.'

I don't think my nose is bleeding, at least nothing's showing on the tissue I'm holding to it. I might be breathing through my mouth for a while though.

'I'm so sorry Mr Rogers. She's so naughty. She promised to be good today, but you see what she's like.'

I do. The pressure in her right eye was fine; I'm not going to attempt the left. I'll compare the appearance of her optic discs; if they look the same in both eyes, it'll be fairly safe to assume the pressures are the same too. Next thing is to check the strength of her old glasses on the Focimeter - I can do that on the other side of the room.

They're strong - plus eights.

'Does she wear these all the time?'

'I'm right here you know. Don't talk about me as though I were somewhere else.'

'Mother, behave. Yes, she never has them off.'

Ophthalmoscopy is scary; I'm right up close, looking at the back of her eye through the instrument, which means I can't watch her hands. A few times I think I sense something coming and jerk back, but she's sitting quiet as a lamb. When I finish and start writing a description of her eyes on the record card, she pipes up:

'Do you drink, laddie?'

'I will be tonight,' I answer absently. Susan's laugh is nervous. In fact, the old dear's eyes are in lovely shape. She's obviously had cataracts operated on at some time in the past, so her media is clear, and her retinae look fine, including identical and healthy discs. I ask her to read the chart.

'Tevuhixooaa.'

'No, it's not a word...oh look, what's this one here.'

'A.'

'Good, and this one...'

'Can't see it.'

Hmm, her glasses must be well out. Retinoscopy, to find out what strength her glasses should be, is performed at a distance of two thirds of a metre. This is the first test I've done where I feel relatively safe.

'Bet you get a cheap do at the hairdresser, son.'

'Mother, behave, please.'

Touching my head self-consciously, I scribble down the Ret results. I think I know what's happening here.

'Does she have another pair of glasses?'

'Don't talk about me...'

'Shut up mother. She used to have reading glasses, but I haven't seen them for ages. She doesn't read any more, so I haven't bothered too much.'

'Those are her reading glasses she's wearing. That's why she can't get very far down the distance chart. They're the wrong glasses.'

'Nothing wrong with my glasses. I can see everything I need to. Don't you touch my glasses, you piece of...'

'MOTHER.'

'Right.' I set up the trial frame with the proper distance correction, and gingerly place it on her face, at arm's length. 'Now what's this letter...good, and this one...and that? ' I turn to Susan. 'She's reading the third line from the bottom, that's really good.'

'Don't talk about me...'

'Behave, Mother. So her eyes have changed, then?'

'No, not really. She's just wearing the wrong glasses.'

'Nothing wrong with my glasses.'

Unlike the other day with Mrs Dawson in North Berwick, this is a case where I know better.

'I'm just going to try some frames on you, so you can decide which ones you like best...'

'I like my own. Where are they. Give them back, ye wee thieving...'

I hastily hand over the old glasses. 'Look, you hold onto those, and I'll just try this other pair on you...'

Then I duck quickly as an airborne spectacle frame parts what little hair I have left before bouncing off the opposite wall. Quietly I beckon to Susan, taking her into the kitchen for a confab.

'Don't talk about me as though...'

'Susan, I think the best thing I could do would be to make up a pair of glasses in a frame that looks like her own one. I'll guess at the fitting as best I can, then I'll send them to you, and maybe you could swap them with the old ones...hopefully she wont notice, except she'll see much better than she's doing at the moment.'

Susan nods. 'Sounds like a good plan. I'm really so sorry Mr Rogers...'

'No problem, it's not her fault.'

When I say goodbye to Mrs Tomkins, she beckons with her index finger.

'Come here son.'

'Um.'

I look helplessly to Susan, but she just shrugs. Tentatively I approach the basket chair, my hands level with my chest and ready to block.

'Closer.'

Oh dear. I don't like this. I lean in slowly, nerves tight as drumskin. Then she grabs me in a bearhug, squeezes. She's going to wrestle now?

'Thanks for coming son. I've had a rare time. You're a good lad.'

Aw. I hug her back; we stay like that for a few moments, then she releases me and waves at the door.

'Right, off with you.'

Well, it was different. My face is still burning, and my nose hurts, but I'm smiling. Despite everything, I quite enjoyed that.

All the other patients are tame compared to Mrs Tomkins, so by three o'clock I'm on my way home. This is a normal time for me to finish my visits; the likes of Tom thinks I've got it easy, working 'half a day.' What he doesn't realise is the back-room work involved when you're a one-man show. When I get in I'll give the dogs a treat (mandatory) answer my phone messages, go through my post, write up the NHS forms and orders for today, put the deliveries through the computer so they get a letter when their next test is due, prepare the paperwork for tomorrow's patients, check any completed glasses that have come in – and that's just the routine stuff, there's always something extra, like writing a referral letter, or updating my complaints procedure. (Yeah, right)

The dogs insist on two treats rather than just one, and I haven't got time to argue, so I break all the training-rules and comply. Amongst my phone messages there's one from Mr Diggins. Must be something about the flat. I play it, feeling a strange tingle in my belly as I wait for the robot to start its announcement.

'MESSAGE RECEIVED WEDNESDAY, 27th JUNE, AT 2.46PM.'
'Ah, Mr Rogers. Diggins here. I have received a verbal acceptance of your offer for number five Sea-View in North Berwick. The sellers are prepared to accept your initial offer, that was for seventy thousand pounds if you recall. I shall proceed to formalise the matter, and will be in touch if there are any queries, but it all looks very straightforward.'

They accepted it. Seventy thousand pounds. For a flat that's going to be worth one hundred and twenty. No wonder the old bastard sounds so smug. Things are really turning around now. I smile, tightly. Finally, I'm back in the game.

I phone Jane at the bank; she doesn't anticipate any problems with the mortgage, especially since the Home Report is valuing the flat at ninety thousand in its current state. After arranging a time to go in and sign the paperwork, I head off to the Site office. Alf is an essential pivot in my plan.

He's sitting behind his desk, sipping tea and munching on chocolate digestives. Reminds me of my recent return to the ward. He waves me to the plastic seat facing him, swallows, and grins.

'Thought you'd be back. Take it you've found somewhere to buy?'

'About this eighteen thousand, it's monstrously low Alf…'

'Problem is,' he interrupts, 'I was speaking to one of the new owners about it, and he reckons I went over the top a bit. He says fifteen thousand is all the Site can really afford at the moment.'

'WHAT?'

'I know, I know, it's just the times Mark, they're very hard for all of us. If you're interested in the fifteen thou though…'

He leans across the desk, lowers his voice.

'…I would move quick on it, because I don't know how long they'll keep the offer open for.'

As my body slumps I feel the stubby back of the chair dig into my spine. Why is everybody out to shaft me? Fifteen thousand is downright insulting, but…there's no other way I can get the flat. I'm going to have to accept.

Alf nods sympathetically at the language I accept in, and offers me a chocolate digestive. I refuse. He slides a piece of paper across the desk; how convenient he had it to hand.

'Need you to sign this, Mark. Just routine, so everybody knows where they stand.'

I speed-read the document. Basically it says that, by adding my signature, I have committed to sell to the Site, and cannot sell to anyone else.

There is one exception to the rule that we must sell our vans back to the Site, which I'd forgotten about until now. It's worded to say that we can actually sell to anyone we please, so long as the Site approves them. This little clause is probably only there to avoid an Office of Fair Trading investigation, and it's well known that the Site will find fault with any outside buyer, so it's mostly useless.

Except if the buyer is someone who already has a van here, and wants to upgrade. Under those circumstances, the Site can hardly turn them down. If they're already here, then they must be already approved.

My brain's going full speed now; the reason Alf wants this signed is because he doesn't want to be gazumped. He expects to get around thirty thousand for my van; I could make a serious profit over the deal he's offering me by selling it for as little as twenty. I might even get twenty-five.

This warrants further investigation.

'Let me take this away and read it, Alf. I'll bring it back tomorrow.'

Or the next day. Or the next.   His face crumples.

'Mark, you're taking a big risk. Even tomorrow, things might have changed. I can't guarantee that offer until you've signed.'

For a moment he almost has me. The thought of losing the North Berwick flat would be too much to bear. But common sense takes over.

'Alf, I need to read this properly before I can sign it. I can't see twenty-four hours making that much difference. If it does, well…'

I shrug my shoulders, draining all expression from my eyes.

I can play poker too.

When I make a fast, tactical exit, Alf's predictions of doom follow me all the way out. Fear blooms inside me; what if I come back and they renege? I'm on the point of turning round, but stubbornly keep moving.

I'm sick of being taken for a mug.

It's Saturday before I see Diane again. While she's working late shifts it's difficult to find any worthwhile overlap in our days. I think though we both might have found the time apart useful, for reflection on where we are, how we stand with each other. I know I did.

In the meantime I've been asking around to find out if anyone's interested in upgrading to my van at a bargain price. Tom and Kathy have been canvassing for me too. So far no takers. A couple of people showed interest at first, but then they started to worry about what Alf might offer them for their own van, in retaliation. Still, I haven't given up yet.

Diane's night duty finished last night, she'll be getting up around noon, and I've arranged to collect her at two so we can go over to North Berwick for a viewing of my new home. Parking outside her gate I get out of the car and – freeze.

Parked right behind me is a very familiar blue Mondeo. My heart does a drumbeat solo while I absorb the shock – I thought we were done with all this.

Can't be any subterfuge involved though, she knew to expect me right about now. Should I wait until he leaves? Oh beggar that, I'm going in – but I'll ring the front door bell and wait for her to answer it this time.

'OI. I want a word with you.'

Big chap, about my age, face like a bulldozer shovel – what's his problem? He marches up to me and pushes my shoulder quite roughly, making me stagger back a step. I'm torn between angry outrage and blind terror.

'Hey, what's the problem? I don't even know you.'

I hope that wasn't as squeaky as it sounded.

'What the hell you think you were doing, letting all my tyres down?'

Oops. I point to the Mondeo.

'Um…is that yours, then?'

'Course it's sodding mine. Who the ****'s did you think it were?'

'Ah … you see, that's just it. I thought it was someone else's, obviously I was wrong, and I can only…'

'Who the hell are you anyway? You don't live here, do you?'

'No.'

Indicating Diane's house, I have to think for a moment. I'm back to being confused about to how to label our relationship.

'That's my – friend – who lives in there, I'm just going to see her.'

Shovel-face thinks for a moment; I can tell by the noise of crashing gears. Then his belligerence gives way to a cheesy look of comprehension.

'Oh, now I get it. So you and her…'

He waves towards Diane's house.

'…and then that bloke with the stupid moustache stays the night, then you let all my tyres down...'

Now he's snickering. Bloody neighbourhood watch areas – they must train with SAS surveillance squads.

'Look, I'm really sorry about your tyres. It was a stupid thing to do, and I'll be glad to compensate you for any expense it might have…'

That's caught his attention.

'Garage charged me twenty quid to come up on Monday morning.'

Silently, I hand him a twenty-pound note.

'Then they charged me another ten to blow the tyres up.'

I pass over a ten-pound note.

'And me and the missus was going somewhere on Sunday, and we couldn't, because…'

I've got one twenty left. Well, I had…

'You can stop now, you've cleaned me out.'

His hand goes to my shoulder again, but this time it's a matey clap.

'Cheers pal, you're a gent.'

He jerks his thumb towards Diane's house.

'Hey, if you need that geezer with the moustache sorting out, me and my brother...'

To my shame, I actually consider that for a moment.

'No, that's alright. It was just a misunderstanding, all history now. Eh...nice meeting you.'

'You too, Guv.'

Oh well, if Diane wants a coffee in North Berwick, it's going to have to be on her. Still, after Terrapins, she should be used to that.

Diane's poking her finger through the holes in my living room wall.

'Needs new walls.'

'Ha. Ha. Tom reckons he can fill them easy enough...'

'Mark, are you sure Tom knows what he's doing? There's an awful lot needs doing here - oh, and what's this?'

She's pulling an exaggerated 'yeeugh' face while prodding warily at the semi-solid substances on the kitchen worktops.

'Tom's great at this stuff, it's because he's so clued up on fixing things that there's no room for anything else in his brain. Have a bit of vision, Diane – I can see this place transformed into a little palace. Okay, well a really nice flat anyway.'

Her nose is twitching now.

'How are you going to get rid of the smell?'

'That's Kathy's job, she says it'll be fine. Diane, this is going to solve all my problems. I'm going to have a huge chunk of equity once it's done, and that'll let me...'

'What?'

'Well, I don't know exactly yet, but it doesn't stop here. Never mind back on my feet, I want back to the top of the tree.'

'Oh Mark, you're such a dreamer. I can see this going horribly wrong – look, let's get out of here and go for a coffee. I want to talk to you.'

I cringe. I haven't told her about the Shovel-face incident.

'Em, I don't actually have any cash on me…'

'Quite the Richard Branson, aren't you? Come on, I'll spring for coffee.

She does. In a very nice tearoom on the narrow main street. She goes one further, and orders cakes from the home-baking stand. Once we're seated by the window on hard spindly chairs, and my mouth is full of strawberry gateaux, she gets straight to the point.

'I know you need to move out of the Caravan, but I'm not sure you're doing the right thing selling it for pennies to buy a slum – no, I know how you think it's going to be once Tom's waved his magic wand, but right now it's a slum. So I've been thinking – why don't you move in with me, at least for a while?'

My jaws have stopped chewing. I'm about to try and answer when I remember the mass of cake in my mouth, so I quickly help it down with a gulp of coffee.

'Diane, we talked about moving things along too fast. I mean, it's really great of you to offer, but I'm not sure…'

'Why not? It's the perfect solution all round. Don't forget, if you move to North Berwick, we'll be a lot further apart. An extra twenty minutes might not seem like much, but it rules out any casual popping-over.'

I stare into my coffee cup, the half-eaten gateaux now forlorn and forgotten. I didn't see this coming; I'm not sure how I feel.

'Look Diane, I'm really grateful for the offer, but I don't think it would work – not yet, anyway. I need to get myself sorted properly, financially, before I could think about anything like that. I'd feel like a sponger, living in your house...'

'Nonsense. You could pay your share of all the running costs, there'd be no need to feel that way. Hell, it's not necessary, but if it made you feel better you could pay rent. It's not just that though, is it?'

A tear appears, moving slowly beneath her eye.

'We're still not right, are we?'

Pouncing on her hand I try again to explain.

'It's nothing to do with that. It's me; I need to climb out of the mess I got myself into. Once I've done that...and anyway, this is too good an investment to pass up.'

'So why not go ahead and buy it, do it up, then sell it? You don't need to move into it to do that.'

Oops. She's got me there.

'I just think...we need more time before...'

'Have you finished? I want to go now.'

The ride home is polite. Neither of us mentions the chat in the coffee house. When we get near Haddington, Diane says:

'I think these nights I've been working are catching up with me. Would you mind just taking me straight home? I fancy having a wee nap.'

That took me aback; I'd assumed we'd be going back to Greenacres, maybe picking up a takeaway and a bottle of wine or two on the way. I wanted the chance to smooth things over. Carefully I say, trying to keep my voice unconcerned:

'If that's what you want...'

'I'm not in the huff or anything Mark, I really am tired. But yes, I think it might not be a bad thing if we both take some time out – I did spring that on you a bit. It's just ... I really do think we get on awful well, and it simply seems the obvious thing...but it's your decision. How about I bring a curry down later, maybe about seven, and we can have a bottle of wine...and talk if you want to, or not if you don't.'

Whew.

'That sounds good, yes, that's what we'll do.'

When I pull up outside Diane's house, her lips curl and she jerks a thumb backwards.

'See those two we just passed? That's my neighbours – right pair of wasters. I try not to have anything to do with them.'

A glance in the rear-view mirror confirms it's Shovel-face, plodding along beside a female sumo-wrestler. When they come abreast of the car, Shovel-face slaps the roof loudly. Diane jumps, and I open the window.

'Wotcher mate. Okay?'

I nod, stretching a plastic smile over my mouth.

'Fine. You?'

'Yeah, just been down the bookies with the missus.'

He bends, sticks his head halfway through the window.

'Wotcher, hen.'

Diane's face is a glacier on fire.

'Hello.'

Shovel-face is satisfied with that, his head withdraws to the street and he ambles off, the 'missus' testing the tensile strength of the pavement as she sumo-walks alongside him. I turn to Diane, who's obviously waiting to hear what I've got to say.

'Don't ask,' is the best I can come up with.

I pretend I've wandered over to Tom and Kathy's van to ask Tom something about the flat renovation, but it's counselling I'm really after. I feel out of my depth; I wish I could talk to Freda about this. With typical insight, and despite the obvious awkwardness of the situation, Freda tried to warn me about rushing into things with Sally. Auntie Kathy, though, is a pretty strong second string.

Tom's not there, there's a football match being shown live on the Club's satellite-linked television. Good; it's a one to one chat I want.

Kathy quickly twigs my real reason for coming over; she makes coffee and a little small talk; then she hands me a mug, sits down, and waits expectantly

'What? Can't I just come over for a coffee and a chat?'

'That's what you're getting. I'm just waiting to see what the chat's going to be about – Diane, presumably?'

'She's asked me to move in with her.'

I'd meant to lead up to that slowly, but it just blurts out. Kathy's surprised, but she recovers quickly.

'Seems a bit soon after all the...you know...'

'Diane's sort of taking a practical view of things. I need somewhere to live, she's got somewhere, we're getting back to where we were...'

'But you're not keen?'

I shake my head, feeling guilty.

'I don't know, Kathy. That's the problem. Diane's not like anyone I've ever known, I want to be with her – but I'm scared, I admit it. Both because of my history, and because of the way things suddenly went pear-shaped last week.'

'Only possible answer is wait until you're sure. Not fair on either of you to push things before you're ready.'

'Yeah – but I can understand how she must be feeling when I didn't just accept outright, I only have to put myself in her place. It's humiliating, and it says out loud that I'm not sure enough about us – which I'm not, and I suppose that's the real problem.'

'Diane must feel pretty sure to have asked you. Either that, or she's over-compensating for last week.'

'I hadn't thought of that – she could be doing this for the wrong reasons.'

Kathy tilts her head; her eyes are warm, her lips twisting in sympathy.

'You can't go rushing into anything when you're not sure, luv. You're going to have to find a way to put her off without making her feel rejected.'

Hmm. That's a good idea.

Diane's fanning her mouth.

'How can you eat curry that hot? Just a taste of yours is setting my mouth on fire.'

I grin. I've heard this before, many times.

'I worked in Birmingham for a couple of years when I first qualified. Now THEY know how to make curry; your typical brummie curry would make this one look like a korma.'

'Pooh.' She flaps her fingers disgustedly. 'I'll stick to my biryani, thank you.'

After we've finished eating, and I've encouraged her through a couple of glasses of white wine, I decide to implement my master strategy.

'About this moving-in thing, now that I've had time to think about it, I see it's a great idea. I'm sorry if I was a bit freaked-out before, it just took me by surprise, but now that I've thought it through properly…'

She looks pleased. Good. I top up her wine inconspicuously before continuing.

'Been thinking it through in practical terms too, though. While I'm doing up the flat in North Berwick, I'm better staying there rather than zooming back and forth from Gorebridge all the time. Same when I'm selling it …I'd forever be shooting across for viewing, so we really need to wait until the flat's done and sold before we can…'

She nods; she looks thoughtful, but placid.

'Okay, that sounds fine. You let me know when you think the time's right.'

She's holding out her glass for a refill.

Great. I think she bought it.

Which buys me a breathing space.

TWENTY-TWO

My Tuesday patients have been straightforward so far. No big hold-ups, which is good, since I've got an appointment with Jane at the bank this afternoon to sign the mortgage papers for the North Berwick flat.

My last patient, Mrs Chiswick, lives in Cockenzie under the twin shadows of the power station's giant smoke-stacks. This will be the first time I've seen her. I'm relying on my Sat-Nav which is taking me along the main street, now through a maze of twisty side streets, and finally to the iron gates of a big Victorian house. The house must have been grand at one time, but today it's a mess of discoloured stonework and hanging gutters. The paint on the window frames is peeling, and the roof is a patchwork of missing slates. It's an overcast day; all the windows are as gloomy as the sky above, and I feel a little chill going through me that has nothing to do with the cool breeze.

The place is spooky.

There's no doubt about whether this doorbell is working; its booming chime sounds like four Big Bens striking on the hour. As the massive timber front door slowly creaks open, I'm half-expecting to see a seven-foot man with a square face and a bolt through his neck. Instead, I'm greeted by a small dark-haired woman of about thirty, wearing white jeans and a yellow T shirt printed with bold red letters that proclaim 'LOOK, BUT DON'T TOUCH.' For some reason, this reminds me of Tracy.

'Hello Mr Rogers, I'm Naomi. Gran's all ready for you.'

Obediently I follow Naomi into a hall like an aeroplane hangar, bumping my wheelie-cases over folds in a carpet so worn that its canvas backing has assumed the role of whatever pattern was originally displayed. 'Gran' is in the lounge, sitting in one corner, on an oversized faded-leather armchair. Like Naomi she's small, but her dress sense is more demure; a dark paisley-pattern dress sits loosely under a faded-green cardigan.

Her white-framed face looks sad.

After introducing myself I try to get her talking about her visual problems, but she's strangely reticent. Naomi has settled herself on a huge grey footstool beside her granny; she reaches over for the old lady's hand, and speaks gently to her.

'Would you like me to explain to him, Gran?'

Gran nods shyly, and Naomi turns to me, keeping hold of the small, wizened fingers.

'Gran's vision has got a lot worse over the last few months, but the real problem is that she's ...well...seeing ghosts.'

I can see Naomi's face turning hard while she awaits my reaction; a readiness to fight has emerged, no doubt in anticipation of a derogatory response from me. I concentrate on keeping my expression neutral, and my voice respectful.

'How long has she been seeing the ghosts for?'

'A few months now. I only got it out of her a couple of weeks ago, she was too embarrassed to talk about it. She's scared that she's losing her mind, but honestly Mr Rogers, she's sharp as a needle. If she says she's seeing ghosts, then she's seeing ghosts. It's as simple as that.'

'Does she recognise the ghosts? Are they people she's known?'

'Yes, they're all folk from her past.'

There's still suspicion coming my way; she's not sure whether I'm just playing along here.

'Mr Rogers, I don't know if you can help. Probably not I'd guess, but in that case my next step's going to be to get some sort of clairvoyant person in.'

'No, I think I'm the right person to deal with this.'

The theme from 'Ghostbusters' has started up in my head, but I'm trying to ignore it. I establish a little more history, pinning down the onset of serious vision loss to the same time as the ghosts began appearing.

'Do the ghosts say anything?' I ask, lifting my Ophthalmoscope.

It's the old lady herself who answers this time.

'No, they look like they want to, but they've never made a sound. They just…float there…then they slip away.'

Her macular areas are a mass of scar tissue. The macular degeneration's been developing for a long time; possibly she didn't notice that one eye was already blind until the other began to bleed. Wet macular degeneration is treatable in some cases, but it's too late to consider that here. Maybe if they'd got me in sooner – a lot sooner.

It's no surprise that she can't see even the top letter on the test chart. Dropping a knee onto the floor, I crouch in front of both the women. I find this the best position for counselling; I think it encourages a relaxed, unthreatening atmosphere.

Quietly I explain about the damaged retinae, how spectacles wont help, nor even magnifying aids, and talk about sensory substitution, radio instead of television, talking books on CD.

The old lady takes it well; I don't think I'm telling her anything she didn't already know. Naomi's surprised at how bad her Gran's vision actually is, and says so.

'Well, at least we know what's what now,' she adds, then puzzlement steals over her face…

'But if her sight's that bad, how can she see the ghosts so clearly?'

'Exactly. She isn't seeing them with her eyes…'

Naomi's instantly on her feet.

'Don't you dare suggest that she's imagining it...'

I hold up a placating hand.

'I know she isn't. Have you heard of 'Charles Bonnet Syndrome'?'

I take the silence to be a 'no.'

'Although Bonnet described the phenomenon way back in the eighteenth century it didn't hit the textbooks here until the 1980s, and it's still not widely recognised.'

I have their attention; they're both locked on to me, one with eyes, the other with ears.

'When we suffer serious loss of sight, our brain takes a bit of getting used to that. It's like the part of the brain which processes our visual images suddenly has nothing to do, but instead of sitting idle, it starts making things up. Nothing to do with mental processes,' I add hastily. 'It's an unthinking area of the brain, its function is to pass pictures sent from the eyes to the thinking area, so when suddenly there are no clear images coming up to pass on, it like keeps its hand in by sending stuff from the archives - memory - often likenesses of people we've known in our lives.'

Reaching out, I take Granny's other hand.

'Your 'ghosts' are just old memories being projected into the gap your loss of sight has left. This is in fact very common - I've seen it often - and I know that you're terrified of sounding as though you're going crazy. Everyone this happens to feels the same. The good news is it'll happen less and less, and I'm going to teach you some distraction techniques that will help you cope better with it.'

In fact, just having the phenomenon explained will probably hasten its resolution more than anything. I leave a couple of RNIB leaflets, highlighting useful gadgets like stick-on touch-markers for the washing machine dial and spoons that 'beep' to avoid overflow when a teacup is being filled. After loading my cases into the car, I snatch a last glance back at the towering obelisk Mrs Chiswick lives in. My mind's eye can see bolts of lightning clashing around the jagged roof-ridges. While Charles Bonnet Syndrome isn't in any way considered to be a psychiatric condition, I can't imagine a more powerful predisposing environment for its manifestation.

Jane is in a cheerful mood. Must be the commission from the mortgage she's selling me; my plate of biscuits is piled high.

'Just sign here, Mark…and here…'

I never sign anything without at least giving it a skim over. I've already caught a clerical error.

'Hang on Jane, this is wrong. See, it says the deposit is £18,000. Twenty per cent of £70,000 is £14,000.'

'No no, Mark. The deposit is based on the value as per the Home Report, not what you're paying for it. Twenty per cent of £90,000 is £18,000. What a wonderful bargain you've managed…'

Her voice has drifted to one side; the deposit is £18,000? This is a disaster. Spreadsheets from my laptop materialise, as real as Mrs Chiswick's ghosts. My available funds consist of the Caravan proceeds, which have shrunk from £18,000 to £15,000. I've got £2,000 of credit left on my card, so available funds equals £17,000.

That's one thousand pounds short for the deposit, and I've still got Diggins to pay. He wants his money up front, as usual, and his bill's going to come to around two thousand pounds including all the mysterious outlays, land registrations and so forth. Instead of having one thousand pounds to start the renovation off, I'm now three thousand pounds short without even thinking about making the place habitable, and I've got no idea where to find it.

'I'd really rather stick to the smaller deposit Jane. I'm pushing things a bit as it is...'

'There's no way round that, Mark. The deposit has to be twenty per cent of the value...is this going to be a problem?'

Her eyes flick to the plate of biscuits, and her fingers start twitching, as though they're considering snatching it back. Hastily, I scrawl my signature in all the places she's indicated.

'Problem? No, of course not. Don't worry Jane, I've got it covered.'

How?

On the way home, I have to force myself to concentrate on the driving as my mind reels with this new setback. I'm three thousand pounds short to complete the deal on the flat, without a dicky bird of where I'm going to find it. On arrival at Greenacres I accede easily to the dogs' demands for walkies; I need the space to think.

We're in the big expanse of barren land adjacent to Greenacres; the dogs are both off the lead, roaming happily. This is so good for Ziggy's confidence since there's nothing for her to bump into, other than soft undergrowth. That's just one of many things that's been making the thought of moving so scary, but I'm counting on the beach to be an equally safe walk for my blind dog.

I'm deep in thought, still chasing that elusive three thousand pounds, when I hear a polite:

'Woof.'

Dropping my eyes, my leg muscles spasm at the sight of the Rottweiler standing a few feet away. He's got a rubber ring in his mouth, and he's waving it at Molly, who's looking at him with a baffled expression. I can't believe it when the Rottweiler drops his front end, splaying his forelegs in an invitation to play. He snaps his head sideways, and the rubber ring flies off a few feet. Molly only hesitates for a second before she darts after it, picks it up, watches the Rottweiler for a moment, then tosses the ring back into the air. The Rottweiler lunges forward, grabs the ring while it's still in flight, and sends it whirling off again ... and away goes Molly to retrieve it.

I'm spellbound; the dogs are having a great time. The Rottweiler's owner comes waddling over. I'd hardly noticed he was there; from his expression, he's as awestruck as I am.

'Hi – our dogs seem to have made friends.'

I nod absently; it's all a bit weird. The Rottweiler's owner is scratching his head too.

'He's been acting really strange lately, went sort of nervous all of a sudden just a few days ago. Now this – I mean, he's a love, but he's never really been one to make friends with other dogs...'

An absurd thought slips into my head. Is Horace trying to buy insurance by making friends with the partner of his nemesis? As though to answer that question Ziggy, who's been padding about in some bushes and therefore invisible, suddenly reappears. She stops, sniffs the air suspiciously, then her face crinkles and she utters that familiar short, sharp 'YIP.'

The Rottweiler's head snaps round; momentarily he's a statue, then he's gone. His owner heaves a long-suffering sigh.

'Oh no, not again.'

Now he's off in pursuit, his legs doing a Russian dance as he careers after his fleeing hound.

'Horace – what's wrong with you, Horace…?'

I can't help a cruel smile when the thought floats into my mind.

I reckon Horace just doesn't have the balls for it anymore…

On impulse, I phoned Mrs Dawson in North Berwick. Her new specs are back; I don't often make deliveries after five o'clock, but I have a hankering to visit Sea-View again. Mrs Dawson is pretty free and easy, so she's not put out by the time.

The drive to North Berwick is something of a joy in itself. The quiet roads with their scenic beauty make me think of my veterinary counterpart, James Herriot, in his beloved Yorkshire. I have all his books, and suspect they were a strong influence in Kara's decision to become a Vet.

Yorkshire is beautiful in it's bleak expansiveness, but East Lothian can be just as emotive with its lush warmth. East Lothian is very green.

A weathered wooden sign points the way to East Fortune, where the Air Museum is the final resting place of a retired Concorde. East Fortune is also the home of the famous Sunday market, which to me means freshly made doughnuts and hundreds of cheap second-hand books. I haven't been there with Diane yet, but I must mention it to her; the market is one of my favourite weekend destinations.

Soon Berwick Law rises out of the scenery, a bing-shaped hill with a whale's jawbone perched precariously on its summit. The original osteo-attraction rotted into collapse in 2005, and was replaced in 2008 by a fibreglass replica. From here, it looks like a matchstick model.

The road into North Berwick is a gradual transition from countryside to seaside town. There are a lot of lovely old buildings, many of them converted to flats. Sea-View is a 'new' development, since the four-storey building is only about thirty years old. It lies to the North-East of the town; my only regret is that my ground-floor flat has no 'sea-view.'

My flat. I'm already thinking of it in the possessive.

Mrs Dawson is delighted with her new, sparkly frames; I don't think she could be happier if the paste adornments were real South African diamonds. Einstein was right, everything is relative; I'm worried about her deteriorating vision and the low standard I ended up giving her, she's raving about how good it is to 'see properly' again.

When I announce my plans to become her neighbour, at least until she moves to the Nursing Home, she's ecstatic about that too. She also makes a point which, surprisingly, hadn't occurred to me.

'There's a few like me in here, Mark. You'll get a bit of extra business right on your doorstep after you move in.'

Cool.

Like most of my patients, Mrs Dawson assumes I'm as well off as most of my colleagues in optometry.

'Thought you'd have wanted something a bit grander than this to live in, though. When you started telling me about it, I thought you meant you were buying it for an investment, to rent out. Or holiday let, there's a few like that here.'

'Really? Doesn't that bother the regular residents?'

'Not at all. It's not like it's groups of teenagers or anything, they're family folk or even older, all of them so happy about being here on holiday. They were always a joy to run into, back in the days when I was walking around the place.'

Mrs Dawson pays me, then thrusts an extra ten-pound note at me.

'Here, dearie. That's for your petrol, and maybe get a wee drink tonight out of what's left.'

I go through the motions of 'You don't have to do that,' then accept graciously and gratefully. This may seem a little unethical; I started out thinking so. I used to outright refuse to accept gratuities, until I realised how upsetting that was to the patient. They were embarrassed by the rejection, and disappointed because I wasn't allowing them to show their appreciation.

It doesn't happen often, maybe once every couple of months, but I quite enjoy accepting my 'tips.' It's a great compliment, and the warm feeling lasts through the spending of the cash, however little it may be

On leaving Sea-View I decide to have a stroll around the surrounding area, which leads me first to the sea itself, then on to the piers. I pass the famous Seabird Centre, where visitors can use high-powered binoculars to look at Puffins and Kittiwakes, and if they're lucky possibly seals or even dolphins.

In the distance, over the Firth of Forth, the Bass Rock climbs out of the sea, an extinct volcano with a tiny white lighthouse tucked beneath a huge crag. Well, it looks tiny from this distance.

By the time I've had a saunter along the main shopping street, it's gone seven. The pavements are narrow and the closed shops are Aladdin's caves of private endeavour with windows full of carefully selected treasures, many locally produced.

Although there's nothing arranged I have a notion to see Diane. When I ring her on my mobile she tells me yes, come on over, and bring some fish and chips. Fish and chips seems to have become something of a theme for us. Of course, fish and chips from the seaside are extra-special.

Opposite the fish and chip shop there's a big car park with, unusually these days, public toilets. These are maintained to standards a barracks-sergeant would be unable to fault, and have always been a reason to rejoice when I've been working in North Berwick. One of the drawbacks of domiciliary work is a critical shortage of public loos.

By the time I get to Gorebridge, a salty tang of vinegar now filling the car, it's nearly half past eight. Diane had actually already eaten; she just couldn't resist the opportunity of such a tasty nibble. It means Marcus is also in luck, as will be the dogs when I get back to Greenacres.

Diane jumps on the time, to further her argument about the location of my flat.

'It really wouldn't work, your living there permanently. I mean, that's taken you nearly an hour to get here tonight. Then there's your work-travelling, wouldn't it add about half an hour to most of the places you go?'

'Twenty minutes on average, actually…'

'You know what you're like already in the morning. Do you really see yourself getting up twenty minutes earlier every day?'

I shrug; it isn't a happy thought, but nothing comes for free. I'm not defending the point too vigorously though, remembering that as things stand, living in the flat is supposed to be a temporary arrangement.

Maybe.

Whole thing could be moot anyway, as I explain to Diane, telling her about the bombshell Jane at the bank has dropped on me.

'Three thousand pounds doesn't sound like such a lot…'

'Diane, when you haven't got it, believe me it's a lot. I've used what little cash I had with marketing the business – things are picking up, but not quickly enough to help with this. '

'So what are you going to do?'

'Don't know yet, but I'll think of something…'

She looks away, studies the doorway to the kitchen, her lips pursing. Then she turns back, takes one of my hands in each of hers.

'Look Mark, I've got a bit put by. I could lend you…'

'NO.'

Dropping my hands she draws back, looking stunned. Shame envelops me, at such an uncontrolled and selfish reaction to a selfless offer. Quickly I scoop her hands back in mine, but her arms feel stiff.

'Diane, I'm sorry. I didn't mean to be so…this whole money thing just gets to me so much.'

Her arms are loosening; her fingers starting to answer mine. Her eyes are saying: 'Go on.'

'It's just … I've worked my butt off for more than twenty years, and it's like I've got nothing to show for it. I'm supposed to be well off, everybody else I know in this business is, but not me. Funny thing is, I should have been more worried about the money implications of getting involved with somebody like Sally – who ended up taking the little Claire left me with. But I'm actually finding it harder to live with financial imbalance when it's the other way round. No…'

I shake my head in unison.

'…it's true. I probably earn a little more than you, but you've got this…'

My hand does a figurative encompass of Diane's house.

'...you don't have a mortgage, you're reasonably comfortable, and I'm terrified of finding myself scrounging from you in any way. I'm very...independent,' I finish lamely.

Now she's squeezing my fingers hard.

'I do understand. Mark, you've had some bad luck, but you're still young. There's plenty of time to get back where you want to be, and I know you can do it. The very thought of you scrounging...'

She smiles, and it's a big warm one that makes my skin tingle.

'...well, that's just laughable. If you want my help, it's there...look on it as letting me in on a good investment if you like, but I don't want to cause any...'

I can hear her consider the word 'more' in her mind, then reject it.

'...friction between us. I wont mention it again, but the offer's there.'

Having run out of words I give her a cuddle instead, and that quickly turns into a serious snog. It does feel good to be trusted so unconditionally, but I've got no intention of taking her up on that offer.

Absolutely none.

I wish I'd picked the dogs up and brought them along, but since I didn't I have to go home. Regretfully. I'm opening my car door when something hits my back, sends me sprawling into the drivers seat.

I'm being mugged?

'Wotcher mate.'

No, I'm not being mugged. It's just Shovel-face, on his way home from the pub and desperate to demonstrate bonhomie.

'Hi Shov...er, what is your name, anyway?'

'Albert. Put it here, me old china.'

Albert? Horace? Life is getting weirder and weirder I reflect, then groan painfully while Albert/Shovel-face tries to mash my fingers into vermicelli.

'I'm Mark, er... Albert. Look, nice seeing you, got to go now though...'

Obviously so does he; he lunges off, orbits an inconveniently-sited lamp-post a couple of times, nearly falls through his gate, then disappears down the garden path zig-zagging from stone to lawn in equal measures.

I hope his 'missus' has a tolerant disposition, or he could end the evening with his arms and legs knotted together.

TWENTY-THREE

Well, it was worth a try. Doesn't seem so unlikely to me that I might want to buy a portable Retinal Camera, but my business manager at the Bank is finding that difficult to comprehend. I have a suspicion his computer has told him I'm in the process of taking out a mortgage, and that he's somehow got it into his head that I'm trying to get extra cash through the back door.

The upshot is he agrees to lend me nine thousand pounds for this essential piece of equipment, but insists that I have the retailer send an invoice directly to him for payment. Which is a fat lot of good, since I have no intention of purchasing a Retinal Camera.

I'm tempted to buy a lottery ticket, but I can't really afford one at the moment.

My only realistic option seems to be taking 'high-risk' finance, at a high-high rate of interest; problem with that is I then wont be able to afford to make my flat habitable. Still, I suppose I could always pitch a tent in the living room...

I've wasted a chunk of Thursday morning talking to the business manager on the telephone, and as soon as I put the phone down it rings again. Mr Diggins' secretary, wanting to arrange an urgent meeting. What now?

Do I care?

On my way out to see today's patients, just two sight tests and a delivery, I stop the car outside Tom and Kathy's and pop in for a quick word. I'm hoping they'll have found somebody on-Site who wants to buy my Caravan, but Tom's response is preceded by a forlorn look.

'Reckon we've been round everybody on the Site by now Mark, and none of them's biting.'

Kathy jumps in to back him up.

'They're all too scared of what they'll get from Alf for their own van after he realises they've taken yours away from him. Sorry luv, I think you're stuck with the Site's offer. It's disgraceful, really it is.'

Tom's bereft tone changes to a growl.

'We should write to the newspapers, expose the money-grabbing beggars. It's not fair how they treat us.'

'I know Tom, you don't need to tell me. Do me a favour though and hold back on the media attack until after I've got my cash.'

Kathy frowns.

'What about the three thousand you're short, what are you going to do about that?'

I'd only meant to stay a moment, but instead I flop down in an armchair and cross my legs. Suddenly I feel very tired.

'It's looking like I'm going to have to raise some cash through the high-risk people. It'll cost me an arm and a leg of course, but I can't see any other way, and the flat's too good a deal to pass on.'

Kathy sits down too; Tom prefers to pace, he's still thinking about his letter to the Sunday papers.

'But how are you going to afford those kind of repayments?'

'Well, I've been thinking about trying to find some locum work. One day a week would probably cover the extra monthly payments. Course it'd mean working in a practice again, which will be really weird after all this time, getting things out of drawers instead of reaching into cases.'

Now Tom's scratching his head. He must be working on a thought.

'But surely you wont make as much cash working for somebody else?'

'No, I wont,' I agree. 'Plus the extra hours will be a killer. But I can't just conjure extra Dom-patients out of thin air – I've been going all out lately to get more business, and I've used up every marketing trick I can think of.'

'Hmmm...have you thought about putting cards in newsagent's windows?'

Tom the marketing guru. It's actually not a bad idea, but I don't think it's going to boost my turnover quickly or drastically enough to make the locum work idea redundant. Hauling myself up, I move to the door.

'I'm going to phone a couple of locum agencies tomorrow and see if I can get something in Edinburgh, ideally a nice busy practice that pays by the patient. Meantime, I need to get going and see my Doms.'

Both the sight tests and the delivery are in the North side of Edinburgh, which is fortuitous since I'm now booked in with Diggins, in nearby Leith Walk, for four thirty.

The second sight test is a bit different from the norm; he's in his thirties, and multiple sclerosis has confined him to an electric wheelchair.

Paul lives in an exclusive little sheltered housing complex, where he's probably the youngest resident. An obviously intelligent man, he used to be an executive for one of the big retail chains. Money clearly isn't a problem for him. This is obvious from the furnishings and adornments in his tiny flat; the walls are crammed with oil paintings, not a print in sight.

Although MS is associated with vision problems, that isn't the cause of Paul's current difficulty. His condition is unusual.

'It was March 2007, before I was stuck in this thing.'

He tilts his head at the control panel on the arm of the wheelchair, his face a battleground of disgust and anger.

'I was on holiday in Africa, and thought I was so lucky to be able to watch the eclipse. I stared at it for nearly an hour, it fascinated me – astronomy's been a hobby of mine since I was a teenager, you see...'

After making sympathetic noises, I have to add:

'Didn't you hear any of the warnings about the danger of looking at an eclipse?'

'I suppose I did, but I didn't take much notice – I mean, who'd believe that looking at an eclipse could damage your eyes?'

Unfortunately it can, and happens to people like Paul every time the moon moves in front of the sun. The intense visible light that functions as an ocular safety-guard for our eyes is blocked, but tons of invisible, harmful radiation are still creeping round the edges of the shadow.

Shining the light from my Ophthalmoscope into Paul's eyes I can immediately see pale rings around each macula, the sign of solar burns.

'V – U – A – X –T ...M? no, A..no...'

'That's not bad, Paul. 6/12. You'd probably make the driving standard ... not that I'd want to advise...'

He spreads both arms out and glares down at his wheeled metal cage.

'Like I could…no, I know my vision's not that bad, but it's hellish trying to read small print, and the books I want to read aren't available in large type. Astronomy, archaeology, art…and now that I'm stuck in this thing, being able to read has become critical to me.'

If Paul wasn't so weakened by MS I could probably fix his problems with simple magnifying spectacles, but then he would have to hold things closer, and he doesn't have the strength in his arms to hold heavy books up to his eyes. I have to go back out to the car to fetch what I hope will be the solution; I don't dispense many Low Visual Aids, so they're in a separate case.

Grabbing the LVA set, I find myself humming the theme tune from Gerry Anderson's 'Thunderbirds,' one of my childhood favourites. Thunderbird 2 was the equipment transporter in that innovative program, a bit like my Impreza.

Back in Paul's flat I rummage through the case until I find what I'm looking for, then hold it up for his inspection.

The solution to producing magnification without the necessity of holding things closer is a telescope. Unfortunately, telescopes comprise two separate lenses (four if both your eyes are intact) that must have a gap between them, a tricky arrangement to mount in a spectacle frame. There are designs that can be custom made at huge expense, but Paul doesn't need that sort of sophistication; his condition isn't bad enough, and luckily he has virtually no short- or long- sightedness to complicate matters.

COIL make a dinky pair of 'binocular-specs' in 'off-the-shelf' form. Though their very nature makes telescopic devices bulky, this one is relatively compact.

It's basically two spectacle-frame fronts separated by flat plastic dividers at each side. The dividers incorporate focusing knobs which change the separation between the two lens holders, allowing variable focusing. The magnification that results is only 1.5 times, but I reckon that should be enough.

Paul now looks like he's wearing something reminiscent of old-fashioned motorcycle-goggles, but he's not caring about aesthetics.

'These are wonderful. I can see everything so much better, even way down there on the table. Brilliant Mark, this is just what I've been looking for.'

Paul pays me in cash, from a thick wad of notes he extracts from an intricately carved wooden box on the coffee table. He says he brought the box back from another holiday in India. Job done, usually my cue to make an exit. I don't know if it's his age, or his intelligence, or maybe a combination, but I've enjoyed meeting Paul and I find myself hanging back for a little more chat.

Paul asks where I live, and there's the usual comedy reaction to that. To salvage my credibility, I tell him about the flat in North Berwick and the circumstances surrounding its sale. He's leaning forward in his wheelchair, a wistful look appearing in his eyes.

'Nice deal that, you'll do alright out of it. Oh, this takes me back.'

His eyes roam the room, stopping on various treasures.

'I had a good job with M & S, but it was property development that paid for all this.'

'What? You were a property developer - part-time?'

The answering nod is slow and sad.

'Weekends finding the properties, and evenings getting everything organised - that's what it's all about really, organisation. So long as you can finance everything that needs done, and show a profit when you sell, the cash just mounts up. Before I knew it I'd made enough to put down a deposit on two properties at a time, then three…I was seriously considering giving up work to do it full-time, then all my damn nerves started short-circuiting.'

'But surely there aren't enough bargains around - and what about the recession, nobody can afford to buy property any more…?'

That makes him laugh.

'The recession just means there's loads of bargains coming up as people default on their mortgages. So far as selling them goes, well, if you can pick them up cheap enough, you can sell them at a price that'll guarantee you a queue of buyers. Trick is to find properties that need just enough work to put the average house buyer off, but not enough to be a problem to somebody set up for it. Modernisation rather than structural re-building. No, if you ask me, this is the best time for small property developers – I just wish I was still in the game.'

Tempting though it is to chat longer with Paul, I decline his offer of a coffee…I've still got Diggins to see. Driving off along Ferry road, Paul's words are repeating in my head. It makes sense; this *is* the best time to get into the property game, and I've got a feeling I'd be good at it. If I did sell the North Berwick flat, I could use the profit to do the same again, only with something bigger for a bigger profit. And so on. Plus I've got Tom, house-fitter-extraordinaire. If I could give Tom regular work, it would solve his and Kathy's problems too. My excitement builds until I see the big flaw – if I sell the flat, I've got nowhere to live.

Or do I? What about Diane's offer?

I instantly feel ashamed; wouldn't that be using her?

No, I answer myself. Not if it's what we both want to do anyway.

But…isn't there a danger of wanting this so much that I allow it to influence my feelings – decide I want to move in with Diane, when what I really want is to make a heap of cash out of property development?

I'm nearly at Leith Walk, which is good, since my head's at bursting point. No doubt Mr Diggins will manage to distract me with whatever crisis has come up. Pessimistically, it occurs to me that my mental wrestling may already be redundant – Diggins is probably about to tell me that, for whatever reason, the whole deal is off.

That sounds more like my usual luck.

The receptionist at Mr Diggin's office looks like her last job was modelling for 'Vogue'. I'm surprised she can open her eyes against the weight of that mascara. The hairdo is exquisite but it doesn't move when she does, not that she moves much –

'Mr Diggins will see you now.'

Thinking back, that's all I've ever heard her say. That and 'Take a seat please.' Mr Diggins must run his staff training on a tight budget.

As usual, he's busy poring over some document or other when I enter his sanctum. I always worry that I'm disturbing him.

'Mr Rogers, thank you for coming in at such short notice. This is a matter with which I felt you would wish to be acquainted immediately.'

The flat purchase has fallen through.

He holds up whatever it is that he's reading.

'I have received a letter, concerning you, from Messrs Wallace and Wightfield…'

Sally's solicitors.

There's just so much the human psyche can take…

'Mr Diggins, you told me that my separation agreement was settled. You said I would hear nothing more from Wallace and Grommet…'

His expression grows pained.

'Wallace and Wightfield…'

'I don't bloody care if it's Laurel and Hardy. What the hell went wrong this time, eh? Did they suddenly realise they'd left me with the price of lunch in my pocket? Didn't you read the sodding contract properly? Well, that's it...I've had it, do you hear? I've had it with you, I've had it with Sally's bloodsuckers, I've had it with Morticia herself...'

Calmly, irritatingly so, Mr Diggins prods a pudgy finger at the intercom on his desk.

'Miss Donovan, would you please bring Mr Rogers a small brandy? Um ... and one for me too, please.'

Brandy? I can't afford to drink brandy in here. It would cost more than at Gleneagles.

'Mr Diggins...' I start to shout, but he simply holds up a pink palm while the door opens and Miss Donovan enters holding a silver tray. It looks like real silver, and the brandy glasses are monogrammed with a flourishing 'DD.' That distracts me. Dickie Diggins? Digby Diggins? Dudley Diggins? I've never wondered before about his forename – he's always just been *Mister* Diggins.

Our debutante barmaid sets the tray on the desk and leaves as silently as she entered. Mr Diggins takes advantage of my theorising on his given name; he talks quickly, if still precisely.

'This is nothing to do with your divorce, Mr Rogers. Um...do try the brandy, it's an excellent year...'

I'm feeling childish. Lifting the brandy glass and pointing at it exaggeratedly with my other hand, I interrupt belligerently.

'HOW much is this brandy going to cost me? Because I don't have any money left...'

Mr Diggins smiles. I've never seen him smile; I didn't know he could. I'm frozen. He jumps into the silence.

'Not a penny, old boy. It's on me. Now, as I was saying, or trying to say, Wallace and Wightfield have other clients besides your ex-wife.'

I cover my eyes with a shaking hand.

'Oh boy. So who's suing me?'

Another view of his expensive dental work. This is getting creepy.

'Among those other clients are your ex-wife's recently deceased mother, Mrs Freda Warrington.'

My head's spinning. Freda's suing me? Taking a gulp of Mr Diggins' vintage brandy I find myself, despite everything, savouring the smooth rich flavour. Somewhere in my head there's appeared an impression of Freda smiling. It's odd, there's no image, no sound, just this...very real...concept? Diggins is still talking, and I'm struggling to focus on his words.

'Mrs Warrington's solicitors were understandably concerned about writing on such an important issue to a Holiday Caravan. Since they obviously know that I have been acting for you they chose to address this communication to me, in order that I might acquaint you with its terms.'

Do they teach them to speak like that in law school?

'The crux of the matter, Mr Rogers, is that Mrs Warrington chose to name you as a beneficiary in her will. She has left you the sum of one hundred thousand pounds, along with a personal communication written before her death.'

He hands me a small, pale-blue envelope. I take it from him robotically; my brain's still trying to make sense of that last bit. Freda left me a hundred grand? There must be some mistake.

'No mistake, Mr Rogers. No doubt the letter from Mrs Warrington will make everything clearer, but the one hundred thousand pounds is already in my client account, awaiting your instructions to be transferred to a destination of your choosing. Now, might I take this opportunity to acquaint you with my firm's encyclopaedic knowledge of the investment market, and perhaps offer some advice...'

Everything seems to be in black and white and from the patter in my chest, I deduce I'm in shock. Vaguely I'm aware that Diggins is already chasing whatever percentage of my legacy he would rip-off to invest it in Government Stock, and the yelping laughter precipitated by this realisation is just further proof of my diagnosis.

The rest of Napoleon's brandy goes down my throat like a pint down Tom's, making Mr Diggins wince. Then I'm on my feet, shaking his hand.

'Thank you, Mr Diggins. I do apologise for my initial reaction, thank you also for the brandy, and now I need to go and think about this.'

The words come out in a rush; I plonk the brandy glass down on the silver tray (the resultant clang still manages to be perfectly harmonic) and head out the door. Miss Donovan follows me with her eyes as I leave the office, heading for the noisy anonymity of Edinburgh city centre.

I'm going to walk for a while; let my mind catch up with recent events. Get my head round this news.

My life just changed forever.

In Princes Street gardens, I'm basking in a nostalgic mix of sunshine and chilly breeze. The gardens are a strange horticultural refuge, sited as they are so close to the shops and the chaos ensuing from the Scottish Parliament's innovative brainwave to put trams back on Princes Street. Very forward thinking, our Scottish Parliament.

I have to duck, narrowly avoiding a mid-air collision with a pigeon who is obviously myopic. The near-miss hurls me back to childhood when my parents would dump me on a wooden bench down here, leaving me with a bag of peanuts to feed the pigeons while they went shopping. Sadly, you couldn't do that now. Maybe you couldn't do it then.

ONE - HUNDRED - THOUSAND - POUNDS.

I'm back where I was a year ago. Magically restored. Farcically, a parody of words form in my mind: 'Diggins taketh away, and Diggins giveth back.' I'm not sure my father, who was a Church of Scotland minister, would approve of that pseudo-theological twist.

Freda had a strong sense of justice and fair play. Things became awkward for us during my dispute with Sally, when Freda found herself playing piggy-in-the-middle. As a matter of principle she was on my side, but Sally is her daughter... now, ultimately, she has solved the dilemma, reversing what she saw as a wrong by leaving me more or less what Sally took from me, which of course will come out of Sally's inheritance. The beauty of Freda's strategy is that she isn't around to take the ballistic flack that Sally's going to be throwing. Which of course leaves me playing target, but I'll worry about that later.

The pale-blue envelope containing Freda's last message is screaming in my pocket, but it's too precious to scan on a wooden bench. Turning my eyes up to grey-white clouds illustrated on a sharp blue sky, I mouth the words:

'Thank you Freda.'

'You're very welcome.'

Imagination? Doesn't matter - it's what she would have said.

A plethora of feelings are chasing one another around my endocrine system. Foremost is relief. This last year has been unreal, and humiliating; I've felt so helpless, vulnerable even. I've never harboured any desire to be a millionaire; wouldn't mind of course, but what's always mattered most is having enough money to guarantee my independence.

Maybe, at root, my safety.

So what does this windfall mean? Well, I don't need a mortgage any more. Neither do I have to sell my Caravan – a revelation which releases fresh currents of warm contentment. Greenacres management are a bunch of modern day Dick Turpins, but I love being on the Caravan Site, and I love my Caravan. I adore the illusion of a simpler existence, the bonhomie and security of being part of a unique little community. If truth be known, I quite like the sheer eccentricity of living in a Caravan. It gives me a kick to watch people's reactions when I tell them.

Thanks to Freda, I can keep on living there.

With another flash of insight, I realise that the flat in North Berwick can now be the first seed of a venture into property development. Maybe I'll still take the mortgage after all, leaving me ready to buy the next property when I find it…then something Mrs Dawson said comes back to me, and a new idea is spawned…

It's getting colder and I want to read Freda's letter, so I climb the steps to Princes Street and wander along to Jenners.

Jenners is the Harrods of Edinburgh – or as they would say in this part of the world, Harrods is the Jenners of London.

Jenners is no longer privately owned but House of Fraser, conglomerate though they've become, are themselves an integral part of Scottish city-centre tradition.

I know it's imagined, but walking through Jenners I always think I can smell sawdust. The musty scent lingers in the ancient aesthetics of this grand old place.

An escalator takes me up, and up – my destination is the tearoom, overlooking the hub of Edinburgh, under the shadow of the gigantic Scott monument, basking in the regal grace of the Castle high on the battered rocks at the end of the Royal Mile.

The tearoom claws at remnants of Victorian austerity. Little groups of stone-faced ladies occupy many of the tables. Once they were the belles of Edinburgh society; it probably seems like yesterday to them.

After carrying my coffee to a window-table and removing the blue envelope from my pocket, I gently set it down in front of me. What will the letter say, I wonder?

Thoughtfully, I pour a little salt from a silver-plated shaker onto the table-top, then slowly run my finger through the grains, back and forth, and round and round. Soon the tiny particles, which started off in contact with each other, are all separate, yet together they form an intricate pattern. They're apart, and yet they still interact.

Freda's letter is an unexpected bonus. I didn't anticipate having this last exchange with her, one-sided though it will be. We still have our little imaginary conversations of course – well, I think they're imaginary – but this is different. In a strange way this letter is just as important as the money she left me. Part of me wants to go on savouring the anticipation of this unexpected gift, and another part is nervous about what it might say.

Abruptly, I pick up the envelope and replace it carefully in my jacket pocket.

I'm not ready to read it yet.

TWENTY-FOUR

Next day I'm up early to do something I've never done before. By nine, I've cancelled all my appointments for the day. It's a pretty easy thing to do, I soon discover, simply involving an exploitation of the psychology of the elderly patient.

'Good morning Mrs Jones. I'm terribly sorry, but I need to cancel our appointment today. I think I may have caught a bug...'

'GOODNESS ME, much better to leave it until next week then. Or maybe the week after, just to be safe? You can let me know...

...oh, I hope you feel better soon...'

Translation: I don't want your bugs, thank you.

I couldn't do any sight tests today; I'm too wired. So far I've only shared the news with Molly and Ziggy (who find the whole thing somewhat conceptual) and a bottle of Glenfiddich. My head is a little fuzzy this morning; another reason for cancelling the day's work. As soon as I've served the dogs with their cornflakes, I'm out of the Caravan and walking briskly along the track. I'm looking forward to this.

Alf is in his office, a cup of tea and a plate of toast fighting a bunch of documents for space on his desk. If the Site provides his tea, it's probably the same cup he was drinking on Wednesday. I doubt if they sprung for the toast.

A closer look reveals that the documents are in fact several new-owner agreements. I thought business was in the doldrums...?

'I've got your contract here, Alf,' I tell him breezily, plonking myself down on the seat opposite and pulling the paper from my pocket. Alf's face clouds; he puts down his toast, steeples his fingers.

'Mark, Mark. I did warn you that if you left it too long…'

I grin, and it's a big one.

'So what's the offer down to now, Alf? Ten thousand? Five?'

From the look on his face, this is not going the way he expected.

'Well, I could probably persuade the owners…'

I interrupt-

'Tell you what, Alf. Why don't you give this to the owners…'

Slowly, deliberately, I shred the contract into small pieces.

'…and advise them, from me, to stick it where the sun don't shine.'

Alf goggles. There's no better word to describe his reaction. Then he takes control of his befuddlement, and the poker face creeps back.

Now Mark, let's not be too hasty here…'

Standing, I lean over his desk and dribble the bits of paper over his toast where they start soaking up the melted butter.

'Changed my mind, Alf. I'm staying, but I'm buying a flat too, which makes me a holiday owner again. Which in turn means I don't have to rely on your worthless assurances to stay in my Caravan any time I want.'

Strolling to the door, I make a private bet with myself on whether Alf's mouth will have closed by the time I make my theatrical turn.

I win.

'Oh, and just thought I'd let you know - you might want to pass this on to the owners - that my solicitor – my very high-powered solicitor in Edinburgh – was quite disturbed to hear about the restrictive practices in operation here. He's checking into the legality of it all, and just in case you lot have covered yourselves there, he's also planning to mention it to a couple of members of the Scottish Parliament over dinner next week. If what you're doing is legal, they're the ones that can change that.'

Alf doesn't look very well; I do hope he hasn't caught my bug.

All bluff of course. Diggins may well dine with MPs, but if he does he hasn't told me about it, just as I haven't mentioned the Caravan Site's various forays into extortion. Be nice if it gave certain people a few sleepless nights though.

From Alf's office I go straight to 'B' field. During last night's bottle of Glenfiddich, I came up with a few ideas. Perhaps surprisingly, these still look viable in the sober light of morning.

Tom and Kathy are eating toast too; convention is a wonderful thing. Surreptitiously I lift a slice; hangovers always make me peckish. Then I tell them my news.

'That's wonderful, luv,' Kathy croons, planting a big kiss on my cheek while simultaneously setting a mug of coffee in front of me. 'Drink that while it's hot,' she adds meaningfully. 'You look like you need it.'

Tom gives me a slapping high five, which I return with vigour. Then I tell them about my conversation with Alf, and that reduces them both to tears of mirth.

'You two are so great. I know you've got problems of your own, yet you're being so happy for me. I just don't know what I would have done without you over this last year.'

Kathy waves dismissal of that.

'We always knew it wouldn't take you long to get yourself back together, didn't we, Tom?'

Tom nods; it's hard to speak when your mouth's full of toast. I hold my hands up.

'Listen folks, I've been doing a bit of thinking. Now that I don't have to move away from here, I need you to stay as well. I mean, where would I be without you keeping an eye on me, and pulling me out of the messes I get into.'

Kathy's face has turned sad.

'Mark we'd love to stay, but we've already decided we can't – in fact, we spoke to Alf yesterday. I'm not going to tell you what he offered us for the van, it galls me too much to even think about it, but we've reached the point where there really isn't any choice…'

'You haven't signed anything?' I interject, so violently that Kathy jumps.

'No,' she answers after a moment. 'We were going to, but Perry Mason over there wanted to read it first…'

Tom's between bites of toast.

'Only makes sense to read something like that properly, don't it Mark? I knew that was what you would have done.'

'Not that either of us can make head nor tail of it…' Kathy adds. 'Maybe you could take a quick look at it for us, Mark?'

'Hold on a minute. I'm still going ahead with the flat in North Berwick, and I need you to help me put it right. Then…'

Pause for effect. '

…when it's done, I'm going to keep living here and holiday-let it.'

Silence. Then Tom asks:

'But how can you let it to yourself? Anyway, with all that money you've come into, couldn't you manage a holiday somewhere a bit better than North Berwick?'

More silence. Then:

'Tom, I mean I'm going to advertise it as a holiday flat. People will come and stay there for a holiday, and pay me for the privilege. I've been looking into this on the Net, it's easier than ordinary renting-out because you don't have to worry about getting sitting-tenants out, and although it's a seasonal business, it rakes in the cash during the summer – for example, I found another flat in Sea-View advertising itself for holidays, and they're asking four hundred pounds a week in August.'

Tom's eyes pop, but Kathy's unmoved.

'That's about the same as the Site here charges for their rental vans.'

'Exactly,' I exclaim triumphantly. 'If you can't beat them, then join them. I've worked it all out – the income from the holiday lets will pay the running costs of the flat, including the mortgage, and still give me a profit that I can put away towards the deposit on the next flat...and so on.'

Kathy rolls her eyes skywards, but Tom's looking at me the way the dogs sometimes do, when they realise I'm all that stands between them and starvation.

'So if you buy more flats that need done up, you'll want me to help put them right?'

'You bet. But there's more to it than that. I need help with the holiday-let business itself. I mean, every week when one set of holidaymakers move out and the next lot move in, the flat will have to be cleaned from top to bottom. Then there's laundering, meeting older ones at the Station and getting them some shopping in – at an extra charge of course – I haven't got time for all that.'

Kathy nods thoughtfully.

'We could do all that for you, right enough. But don't get me wrong Mark, the extra money would come in handy, but it's not going to be enough to let us keep the Caravan, now is it?'

Exactly; now we're getting down to it.

'You've said you don't have much of a mortgage left on your house in Edinburgh, haven't you?'

I don't wait for an answer.

'...I've seen your house, it must have soared in value during the boom, and the recession wont have pulled it down so much that you couldn't sell it and clear your mortgage then probably still have enough left over to buy a flat in Sea-View. Now...'

Touching my nose...

'...I happen to know that the flat next door to mine is coming up for sale soon.'

Tom's eyes are chasing invisible flies.

'So what you're saying is we sell up in Edinburgh and buy a flat in North Berwick outright, then we wont have any mortgage payments to make?'

Kathy's frowning.

'No, it's a nice idea, and maybe we should do something like that somewhere else, but I'm not moving to North Berwick. We don't know anybody there, and it's too out of the way.'

'Ah...'

Time for my masterstroke.

'...see Kathy, you don't live in the new flat, you move into Greenacres like me, and come into partnership with me in the holiday-letting business.

It's perfect – you get your overheads cut, and the work you need, which you get paid for before we split the profits; I get the help I need – we start the business with two flats instead of one – and we've both got the security of owning bricks and mortar. As far as the Site's concerned we're holiday-owners, so no hassle there.

You get to stay down here, which you practically do anyway – and I get to keep you as neighbours.'

I'm rotating both hands in a flourishing 'Howzat', but Kathy still looks doubtful.

'I don't know, Tom and me haven't got any experience in business stuff, I think I'd be scared…'

'We're doing it.'

Was that Tom who spoke? Kathy's staring at him.

'Tom luv, I don't think you understand just what…'

Tom's face is granite; I've never seen him like this.

'I understand perfectly, Kath. We get to live here, we get regular work, hell we get a partnership in a business, and if Mark says it's going to work, I trust him. He knows about these things. No, no arguments. We're doing it.'

He folds his arms. I wait for Kathy to clout him. Strangely, she doesn't. Instead she looks down at the carpet for what seems a long time; when her eyes go back to Tom, they've taken on a new look. Acquiescence – respect, even.

'Alright love, if you say we're doing it, then we're doing it.'

Then her focus shifts to me, causing my backbone to start imitating a tuning fork.

'It better work though, Mark. Know what I'm saying?'

Of course it'll work. It'll definitely work.

I'm sure it'll work…

My new business partners and I convene our first board meeting. Kathy's sharp, and Tom's full of enthusiasm. It is going to work – I know it is. Truth be told, the best way for me would have been to hire someone to do all my Optical paperwork, giving me time to handle the holiday letting by myself. I did consider that scenario last night, but the problem is that there's no way I'd find someone experienced in Optical paperwork to come and do it in a Caravan a couple of days a week.

Plus I need to help my friends; I owe them so much. One thing's for sure; it's going to be a lot more fun doing it this way. We're discussing the best way to sell a house in Edinburgh when loud voices intrude from outside the Caravan, and I glance through the window to see who owns them. Abruptly, I stop talking in mid-sentence. What the hell is he doing here?

Tom follows my gaze and grins. He stands and waves to Shovel-face, who waves back. Tom senses my interrogatory look.

'That's Bert and his brother. Been on a few jobs with them, they're a handy pair. Good at decorating, even better at knocking walls down.' He grins. 'If a wall needs taking down, all you need to do is get them two to walk through it.'

'What're they doing at Greenacres?'

'The brother just bought a van here, that'll be them off to the Club. Boy, you want to see how those two can put it away.'

Coming from Tom, that's a frightening thought.

Between us we've drunk a lot of coffee by teatime, at which point I need to go and feed the dogs. I'm halfway back to my Caravan when a red two-seater Ferrari appears around the bend in front of me, its shiny wheels kicking up clouds of dust. The car slows as it passes, then comes to an abrupt stop. Leaping from low-slung seats, both driver and passenger come striding back towards me.

Sally doesn't look happy.

Sally always looked out of place on the Holiday Park. Today she's wearing green velour trousers and swimming through some kind of multi-coloured linen blanket that loops over her shoulder before metamorphosing into a fringed scarf.

Her companion is a rugby player. He must be, built like that. I smell money mixed with expensive cologne; his designer jeans probably cost five times what I paid for my M&S pair, and the pseudo tough-guy leather flying-jacket is as smooth as a 747's hull. This presumably is George, her new banking beau.

'You conniving bastard.'

No, she isn't happy.

She's in my face, prodding a finger dangerously near my eye.

'You took advantage of my mother, her mind was going when she signed that money over to you. It's illegal, unethical, criminal...you're not getting away with this.'

I just got angry.

'Freda's mind was never anything less than clarity itself,' I hear myself shouting back. 'Unlike that wet sponge you pretend to think with.'

zzip. She just raked her half-inch fingernails down the side of my face. Touching my cheek carefully, it feels wet. Now her Italian leather bag is in play; she's swinging it wildly, and it's battering my head. This is bringing back memories I've tried hard to suppress. A little flash of light in my right peripheral field warns me how dangerous this is becoming; if she keeps that up, I'm in danger of a detached retina. Without thinking I lunge out with the flat of my hand, catching her square in the chest.

'Ooooff.'

She staggers back before her velour seat descends at speed to the dusty track. Then she wails:

'He HIT me.'

'Don't be stupid,' I begin. 'I didn't...'

My words are lost in a rush of air as my lungs empty. I'm doubled over, clutching my stomach; the pain is incredible, and I'm expecting to see that slice of toast re-appear at any moment.

George's hand fumbles at the top of my head then he gives up trying to find a grip there and reaches under my chin instead. When my head is jerked up, I'm looking into a pair of eyes that are cold like marbles.

'You are going to be so sorry for that,' he grates.

I already am. Can't we leave it there?

Obviously not. George draws back a huge fist, the same one he hit me in the solar plexus with, and takes aim at my face. This guy is unbelievably strong; I'm completely helpless. At the back of my mind runs a single consoling thought; at least I can afford the dental reconstruction bill.

It isn't that consoling.

That the shock and fear of the last few moments are now causing me to hallucinate becomes apparent when George suddenly releases my chin, floats a few inches into the air, and flies off in a backward direction. He spins slowly in the air until suddenly his power of flight rescinds and he drops back to the ground.

Landing on his head.

Then something fastens crushingly on my shoulder and yanks me upright.

'Are y'alright, Mark?' says Shovel-face in a slurred voice.

'I will be when you let go of my shoulder,' I reply through my mercifully still-intact teeth. I thought George was strong…

'Sorry mate.'

He releases me, brushes my jacket perfunctorily before turning his head in response to a shout.

'Whaddya wanna do with this?'

Brother Bulldozer has hoisted George up by the collar of his now not-so immaculate leather jacket; George is dazed and dangling, his toes gently brushing the ground. Shovel-face looks at me.

'What we'll do, we'll take him over to that field back there and give him a good kicking. Y'wanna come and give him a couple?'

Good idea.

Fortunately the band of pain in my midsection has now settled a little; just enough to allow my mind to start functioning again.

Apart from the fact that I am a civilised human being who abhors violence (although exceptions could be made) up to this point neither I, nor Shovel-face, are at fault. Self-defence and intervention to prevent a serious assault are both perfectly legal. On the other hand, three guys kicking the stuffing out of another, whatever the provocation, is likely to be frowned upon by agents of the law.

And the General Optical Council.

Plus, news of the ruckus has spread and curious Caravanners are appearing from all directions. Still some way off, I can even see the unmistakable forms of Tom and Kathy.

Witnesses all.

I shake my head; try to correct my voice down an octave or two.

'Just let him go, okay? I'd say the score's about even.'

Shovel-face makes an expression of disgust, and turns to his brother.

'You heard the man.'

Bulldozer simply lets go his grip, and George crumples to the ground with a satisfying thump. He seems to have developed a sudden interest in nephrology.

Time slowed down so much that this whole thing seems to have gone on for hours, but Sally is only now hoisting her derriere off the track. In a moment she's back in my face; Shovel-face hovers nervously, suddenly unsure of how to intervene.

'I need that money, do you hear? George had a nice little investment lined up for me, I need the whole four hundred thousand to give to him.'

Freda left four hundred thousand? Blimey. I knew she was comfortable, but…and this explains George's interest a bit better. Looks like Sally's found a kindred spirit this time.

Her verbal attack's building up steam again, but happily the Taiuti shoulder-bag is still on the ground. I catch a glimpse of Kathy looming before suddenly Sally is spun around, still in mid-rant. Kathy raises her other hand, and…whew. John Conteh would have been proud of that one. Now Sally's back on the ground, blood oozing from her mouth. Between squeals she reaches for her bag, but not to use it as a weapon. She wants her mobile phone out of it.

She's calling the police.

Strangely it's the younger policeman who's attempting to take charge of the situation. His slightly grizzled colleague looks bored; he's seen it all before.

'Right, quiet please. So it all started when you struck her…?'

'I didn't strike her…'

'Yes he did…'

'QUIET. So then you punched him in the stomach, and then YOU beat the living daylights out of HIM…'

'Naw Guv, just pulled him off me mate was all…'

'…then YOU started throwing HIM about…'

'Nah, just helped him up like, dusted him down a bit…'

'…so then she hit her…'

'Unprovoked officer. Totally unprovoked. She's a lunatic, always has been…'

'You stuck-up little…'

Tom and Kathy's neighbours are chirping in now; they didn't see any of it, but that isn't stopping them from testifying that Kathy was simply defending herself.

'RIGHT. Seems to me like I've got two choices here. I either arrest the whole bloody lot of you, or we decide everybody gave as good as they got and leave it at that. I don't reckon a breach of the peace charge is worth the paperwork, do you Doug?'

Doug grunts something that's probably agreement; his thoughts are elsewhere.

Raising my hand respectfully, I check that there isn't going to be a formal caution issued. Even a caution would mean a GOC investigation for me. The young policeman's becoming as bored as his partner; he simply shakes his head.

'But if I see any of you again in the near future – especially you two…'

He looks piercingly at Shovel-face and Bulldozer, with whom he's obviously acquainted…

'I'm going to throw the book at you – hell, I'm going to throw the whole ruddy bookshop. Do I make myself clear?'

Nods all round; to say the heat has gone out of the situation is like describing the formation of floes in the Antarctic winter. The policemen return to their car and switch off their blue lights before making a tedious three-point turn on the narrow track. Sally and George stagger back to the Ferrari, and the crowd of gawkers heads for the Club. I hand Shovel-face a twenty.

'Get a drink on me,' I tell him.

Tom immediately decides it would be opportune to follow.

'Told you they were handy,' he calls over his shoulder.

I give Kathy a quick hug as she passes.

'You're not related to those two, are you?' I ask innocently.

I decide not to join the post-brawl party. I feel the need for a little quiet time with my bottle of Glenfiddich. There being a strong desire to get to said bottle as quickly as possible, I turn off the track and cut through the Caravans. I'm passing a big Atlas, one of the Site's rental fleet, when I stop abruptly and circle round to the verandah side, drawn by a series of low, distressed sobs.

It's the Rottweiler and his owner. The owner is sitting on a sun-chair, his head is in his hands, and he's weeping. The dog is on the deck in front of him, gazing at his master with the most miserable look I've ever seen on a dog. They haven't even noticed me.

Mounting the metal steps I cautiously open the verandah gate, all the time watching Horace carefully for signs of aggression, but he simply glances my way then turns back to his distraught owner. When I clear my throat loudly, it starts my stomach hurting again.

'What's wrong?'

Horace's owner looks up; his face is streaked and his voice is riding a tremor.

'Oh, it's just so unbearable.'

'What is?'

When I sit down on the sun-chair beside him the dog still doesn't react, thank goodness. Horace's owner takes a deep breath, then it all comes out in a rush.

'I'm moving abroad to be with my new partner, that's why I've been staying here these last few weeks since my house sold, just been tying up the details. The problem is Horace.'

He stops to pat the dog's head.

'He's a lovely dog, really he is, but he gives people the wrong impression – just like he did with you. He acts all macho, but he's a teddy bear really.'

Horace lies down, dropping his head on his paws as though embarrassed to have his secret revealed.

'I still don't see...'

'I haven't been able to find a home for him. I can't take him to Hong Kong, the flat's on the sixteenth floor and he'd hate it there. Anyway my new partner is allergic to dogs. My last hope was the rescue centres, but Horace acted up a bit, and they refused to take him.'

'Does your new partner live in Hong Kong?'

He nods, wipes at a fresh stream of tears.

'How did you meet her?'

I'm trying to distract him, calm him down a little. The look he throws my way is sharp.

'We met through the Internet ... Thomas is waiting for me, I have to go to him, so the only option I have left...'

He stops, stares sightlessly.

Cocking my head, I prompt:

'Is?'

'I have to have Horace put to sleep.'

He glances at a shiny gold watch.

'We're due at the Vet in half an hour.'

Then he crumples into a series of quiet wails.

'But surely…there must be another way. I mean – you just can't do that.'

That last might have come out a little louder than I intended, but I'm appalled.

'Don't you think I haven't tried everything I can think of? If there's another way, you tell me what it is. I'd love to know.'

He's angry now; I think he's projecting his anger with himself onto me.

I have the greatest respect for canine instinct. I don't know how much Horace has intuited about his current situation, but he's slid-crawled his way over to my feet, and has started looking at me with new interest. He smells a softy.

Carefully he rests his head on my moccasin, and stares into my eyes with a look of mute-appeal. Absently, I reach down and begin fondling his head. His owner's still ranting in-between sobs.

'It's all very well for you to take the moral high ground, but I've finally got the chance of a life, and I have to take it. What else can I do…?'

I shake my head. This whole concept is alien to me. I could never understand the decision he's come to, and I can't let it happen. It's barbaric. When I speak, it's without thought. Listening to the words, my mind reels and my stomach clenches, which is painful.

'Look, I'll take him. I'll find him a home somehow, but I can't stand by…'

Horace's owner is on his feet, stooping to throw his arms round my neck.

'Oh thank you, thank you, you wonderful, wonderful man. This is so – providential – the first time I saw you, I thought you had such a kind face. I even remarked on that to Thomas on the phone… although he was a little strange about it… you really don't know what this means to me…'

Gently I unknot his arms, put a little airspace between us. He's unperturbed, now he's rushing off to get Horace's lead, pack his toys…

What have I just done?

TWENTY-FIVE

Molly and Ziggy were a little surprised when I brought Horace back to our Caravan. That's putting it mildly. However, over the course of the evening an understanding seems to have been reached. This basically consists of Horace being confined to the bedroom, allowed out only for a drink, or to stand by the door to signal a need to complete the drinking cycle.

These rules were not imposed by me. Ziggy has taken charge of Horace, and Horace is being amazingly compliant. Molly is wisely keeping out of it.

My lower abdominal area feels much better now. Glenfiddich is a potent anaesthetic, though I'm still trying to avoid sharp movements.

Horace is a problem I could do without. There's no way I can keep him here permanently; he takes up half the Caravan, and anyway he can't spend the rest of his life in the bedroom.

I've started to see him in a new light though. He's smart, and when he's not acting the tough guy he can be quite affectionate - cuddly even. He seems to realise that he's had a narrow escape, and is on his best behaviour. He could easily grow on me...

I feel a little guilty that I haven't yet shared the news of Freda's legacy with Diane. I would have gone to see her tonight, or rather, after Horace's unexpected arrival, asked her to come here rather than leave the pack to their own devices. However, Diane's off on a girl's night out with some other nurses and she wont be back until late. Then tomorrow she's going to Perth to see her parents, so the earliest I can get together with her is tomorrow night. I've left a message on her phone, asking her to come here about six.

I'm surprised to be able to contact both my daughters on a Friday evening, but Kara's stayed in to study for a test and Zoe's broke again. They're both understandably curious about the reason behind my insistence that we all meet for lunch tomorrow, but I'm giving nothing away. Since Zoe doesn't even have the train fare left, and is maxed-out with her mother as far as loans are concerned, I agree to pick her up in Falkirk and drive her to Glasgow where we'll join-up with Kara.

I'm still worried about leaving my newly- expanded canine family unsupervised, but when morning arrives the situation remains quiet. Horace joins the other two for cornflakes, then takes the hint from Ziggy and retires to the bedroom. He shouldn't be quite as bored with the bedroom as might have been the case, since Ziggy turfed him out to the living room when she decided to go to bed last night.

Driving along this particular road on the outskirts of Falkirk still feels weird, even after all these years. The bungalow I used to share with my family is both familiar and alien; it looks the same, though the trees in the front garden have grown a little taller.

Two sharp blasts on the horn bring Zoe skipping down the path to the front gate. Movement in a front window draws my attention, then suddenly my eyes lock with Claire's. It's been a while since I've seen her, and the feeling is visceral. Unlike the explosive break-up with Sally, my parting from Claire was quiet and relatively dignified. There are always a lot of factors in play, but Claire's explanation was that she 'needed to get out of my shadow.'

We married too quick, and too young; I think that was the real problem. Since our divorce Claire has found a string of new partners, and made several courageous career changes. She even opened a small business, although she had to close it shortly after. We're very alike in many ways; perhaps that was also our undoing.

When Zoe throws open the passenger door I'm snapped out of my reverie, and by the time I look back at the window Claire has gone.

All the way to Glasgow Zoe chatters incessantly; I think her weekend was looking dull before I issued my surprise summons to paternal conference. I'm giving nothing away yet, to her frustration.

Kara's already waiting when we arrive at the Four Seasons, one of the new high-rise conference hotels that have sprung up in Glasgow city-centre. I continue to keep the girls in suspense throughout an excellent (and pricey) lunch in the bright 'Garden Room' restaurant attached to the hotel. It's like being in a huge conservatory. Plastic greenery fills the airspace above our heads, and the furniture is beech with big flowery cushions on the chairs.

Finally, over coffee, I get to the point.

When I tell them about Freda's last gift to me, they're exultant. Just like Tom and Kathy were.

Sometimes they make me very proud.

Taking an envelope from my pocket, I flap it in front of my face.

'You two were the grandchildren Freda would have liked to have had. She loved you both dearly, and I've given a lot of thought to what she would have wanted – expected, even.'

I hand the envelope to Kara. When she opens it and scans the cheque inside, her colour evaporates.

'DAD. Ten thousand pounds? What is this?'

Reaching over I gently clasp her hand.

'That's your share of Freda's inheritance, love. You haven't asked for much since you started Uni, and I haven't been able to give you much, so I hope this makes life a bit easier.'

She's up and out of her chair; her arms are tight around my shoulders. I can feel her shaking.

'Dad,' she whispers. 'You have no idea…'

She stays like that for a long moment; when she goes back to her seat, Zoe's looking at me. Pulling another envelope from the same pocket as the first, I hand it to her.

'No, I haven't forgotten you Munchkin.'

Zoe's less restrained than her sister when it comes to opening the envelope; she practically shreds it in her haste to get the cheque inside. When she reads it she goes still, and speaks slowly:

'Five hundred quid? I mean, I don't want to seem ungrateful, and I know she's the older sister, but isn't this a bit…'

Now I take Zoe's hand, fasten on her eyes and carefully hold them.

'You're right, Kara's older, and don't take this the wrong way sweetie, but she's also a lot wiser. You're both getting the same, but the rest of yours is going into a joint bank account with me. It's yours – I wont be able to get at it without your signature – but neither can you without mine. That…'

I point to the cheque, discarded on the table in front of her.

'...that's just fun money. The rest is for something special, like the damage deposit on your first flat...'

'Wont be enough for that,' Kara quips cheekily.

'...or your first car, or maybe some travelling...'

I feel Zoe's fingers start coming back to life.

'Yeah, okay.'

Her eyes snap back to the cheque and a little smile creeps in. She's started spending the five hundred quid already.

Kara looks worried.

'Dad, it's too much. I mean, I know you've been in trouble financially, even if you do exaggerate...'

I do not.

'...and anyway, if auntie Freda had wanted us to have this sort of money, she would have left it to us...'

'Freda liked to keep things straightforward, uncomplicated. I've thought long and hard about this, and I'm absolutely sure she expected me to see you two alright. I even wonder if it was a last little test she set me...'

I'm hardly conscious of my voice drifting off while once again I experience an interaction with Freda; she looks happy, approving, even though there's no image of any kind on which to build that perception.

The girls have gone quiet; they seem content to finish their coffee and give me a few moments in an internal world.

My girls...

My special girls.

When I get back to the Caravan, it's still in one piece. Molly and Ziggy are in the living room, and presumably Horace is in the bedroom. Wandering through to check, I stop long enough to give him a bit of a clap and a couple of treats.

He's absurdly grateful. If he's going to be staying for any length of time, I really need to have a quiet word with Ziggy… although he's not totally isolated, I have seen Molly sneaking through here a few times, usually when Ziggy's been asleep on her couch…

There's a message on the phone from Diane, confirming she'll be here at six. The other message was from a new patient in Gorseburn, a town I haven't heard of but which my mapping software tells me is in the Scottish Borders, off the A68 before Lauder. A Mr Anderson.

When I ring him back, he sounds young. Well, young by the standards of my patient list - maybe in his forties? I work through the Dom form I use for new patients, and when we come to date of birth it turns out he's thirty nine.

'Now, I need a medical condition for the visit box on the NHS form, whatever it is that makes you housebound?'

'Ahm…well, I don't know exactly…'

A lot of patients have difficulty with this one. They have so much wrong with them, it's hard to choose a particular condition. They think it's enough to say 'I can't walk,' or even 'I'm in a wheelchair,' but if I put that on the form, the Health Board will send it back marked 'Invalid Reason.' They insist on a medical condition. I try to explain this, and prompt him.

'What about arthritis? Or do you have a respiratory condition?'

He sounds relieved. 'I have asthma, does that count?'

'Of course it does Mr Anderson.'

Poor beggar probably can't walk his length without invoking a paralysing attack of wheezing.

'That's fine, that's all I need. I'll get back to you on Monday to make a day and time.'

'Thanks so much. I really need my eyes done.'

Work taken care of, I set about preparing for Diane. By the time she arrives the Champagne's chilled (well, Cava, but with a towel draped around the bottle she'll never know) and a couple of fillet steaks are primed ready for the grill.

Diane's first words to me are:

'What happened to your face?'

Gingerly I finger the raised weals left by Sally's fingernails; I'd forgotten about them, their memory displaced by the subsequent punch in the stomach.

'Run-in with Sally – never mind that now.'

I hold up a hand to block the indignation rising from her.

'I've got something much more important to talk to you about.'

Diane's eyes pop in unison with the cork from the bottle of bubbly I just produced. Accepting the glass I'm handing her she manages to caress my fingers, her eyes now probing mine.

'You've obviously got something to say,' she murmurs as we clink glasses.

Boy, do I ever. Strangely, her first reaction isn't what I expected. She seems confused, but quickly recovers and hugs me – I guess it's a lot to take in all at once. Strange – I'm catching a whiff of tobacco from her, but Diane doesn't smoke.

After a toast I tell her about the rest of my plans, the holiday letting partnership with Tom and Kathy. She laughs.

'I love seeing you like this. It's like something that's been clamouring to get out from inside you has finally found the light.'

'I've been floating for so long, going nowhere, I can't tell you how good it is to have plans again – and the means to carry them out.'

She's thoughtful for a moment.

'You know, the bug is catching. If you're so sure you can get the lets, how would you feel about starting the new business with three flats instead of just two?'

Huh? I don't understand, and tell her so.

'Well, it sounds so good I'm thinking I could join this fledgling company too. If I sell my house that would finance another property, and I'd be in as a full partner on the ground floor.'

She obviously hasn't thought this through.

'Problem is, Diane, you'd have nowhere to stay…'

She tuts loudly.

'Oh, you can be so slow. We'd already agreed you were moving in with me…'

Had we? Oh yes…

'…so now you're staying here we can just turn it around, and I'll move in with you.'

Silence.

I'm thinking, but my brain's stalled. When it finally starts whirring, the first thought out is a practical one; there's no room here, not with a Rottweiler in residence. Oh, but she doesn't know about that yet…

That's when Ziggy jumps off the couch, sniffs the air and, as though on cue, Horace pokes his head round the door. Diane screams. Since she's gotten so used to Molly and Ziggy, I'd forgotten her fear of dogs.

Horace stops, waits meekly. Ziggy tosses her head in the air, then jumps back on the couch. This must indicate a pass to the water bowl, and Horace carefully eases his way through the door. Diane's becoming hysterical...

'How did it get in…?'

'Shhh...relax.'

I try stroking her hand but she doesn't even notice, she's riveted on the spectacle of Horace filling up the kitchen space.

'That's Horace. He's very friendly, and he's …ah …staying for a while. Just temporarily…'

She's calming down a little.

'What, you're looking after him for someone?'

My head bobs up and down…

'Yes, that's it, I'm just looking after him…'

'That's a relief. For a moment I thought…I mean, sorry, but it isn't hard to imagine you being hapless enough to get another dog, and a completely unsuitable one at that. Anyway, he seems quiet enough. How long have you got him for?'

'Well, there's not a set date as such…'

Her head swings round slowly; helplessly, I watch blue-ringed pupils take aim...

'In other words, he's yours. How the hell could you…?'

I explain very quickly, adding that I have no intention of keeping Horace, I'm just going to find a good home for him…

'How do you expect to manage that when his owner couldn't find anybody mug enough to take him…oh sorry, I forgot, he did…'

'Diane, I couldn't let him be put down, he's lovely when you get to know him. It'll be fine, you'll see…'

'I can't move in with him here – I mean, there's not enough space, we'd be falling over each other…'

Yeah, that's right, isn't it. Good old Horace. Right Mark, tact…

'Di look, it's going to take you months to sell your house, assuming you go ahead with this after you've had time to think it through…I think it's a great idea though,' I add hastily. 'By the time we need the space, Horace will be gone. Really.'

Horace looks over at me, long and hard, an accusation of betrayal emanating silently from him. Then he pads slowly off, back to the bedroom.

Why does life have to be so complicated?

Diane stays over; we leave the big questions in abeyance, and instead concentrate on celebrating my good fortune. In other words, we party.

On Sunday morning I wake up to an over-whelming need for coffee, only to discover we're out of milk. Quick trip to the shop solves that; when I come back the scene in the living area freezes me in the doorway.

Diane's sitting on the couch with Horace at her feet, stroking his head. Horace looks extremely happy. Molly looks worried.

Ziggy's nowhere to be seen.

'You can't let this go on, poor thing's bored on his own through there, and he's quite sweet really…'

Mobility restored, I carry on into the kitchen and put the milk down on a counter, then flick the kettle switch while trying to hide the full extent of my delight.

'How did you get him past Ziggy?'

'Well, she wasn't too pleased, but I just told her this was how it was going to be and that was that.'

I look around.

'Where is Ziggy, anyway?'

'She's gone off in the huff. I think she's in the bedroom…'

Diane doesn't leave until Monday morning. By then, all three dogs are getting used to being in the same room, at the same time. Ziggy quickly became bored with the bedroom, so she and Horace have settled into a reasonably amiable truce. Molly's delighted since Horace loves to play, especially Molly's favourite game of tug-of-war with rope-toys.

After the weekend celebrations it's a thought to settle back into work mode. Reluctantly, I lay out my Dom-forms and start putting together a schedule.

By the time I've phoned them all, and made out NHS forms for them, it'll be lunchtime. Then I'll still have my Health Board statements to check, a pile of pricing to do, the cashbook to finish, new frame stock to process – since I've been re-building the business, the back-room work has been expanding at an exponential rate. I'm starting to feel like I spend more time pen-pushing than I do testing eyes.

When I finally finish the scheduling process, it occurs to me that I'd better pick up the post before starting anything else. Incoming post invariably generates more work, so I need to see it before I plan the afternoon.

Back in my workroom, I flick through the pile.

Glazing bill. Report from the hospital on one of my referrals. Rejected NHS claim form – date missed out, or maybe a comma - and another envelope also with Health Board franking, but not immediately identifiable by its shape and size. I open it, bring out the letter, and read it.

My heart sinks to the carpet. Freda's legacy has been making me feel invulnerable; what could possibly touch me now, I've been thinking?

How wrong I was.

Paperwork forgotten, I head out to the Club. Tom's usually there about now, and I need a drink.

'So what does it mean exactly?'

I rub my forehead before answering.

'They're very vague, all they say is that basically something's amiss, something serious, and they want to have an informal chat before pursuing it.'

'Have you been on the fiddle, then?'

'No Tom, I have not been 'on the fiddle.' Apart from anything else, I wouldn't dare. Claims-verification officers at the Health Board do their training in Al-Quaeda camps. Reading between the lines though, I don't think it's a financial problem, I think it's clinical.'

Tom looks blank.

'Like missing an eye disease in a patient, then they go blind and complain that I should have seen it,' I explain. 'Something like that.'

Now Tom's laughing.

'Naw, not you Mark. You wouldn't miss anything in an eye, you're completely obliterative.'

'Compulsive obsessive. Oh Tom, everybody in health care lives with this nowadays. We're only human, we make mistakes, errors of judgement, it can happen to anybody. Doesn't matter how good you are, it's down to luck - or bad luck.'

Tom scratches his head; I can almost see the static sparking.

'So, say you've missed something and somebody's gone blind - what happens then?'

'Well, they sue, but that doesn't matter because I've got professional indemnity insurance to pay for that. But if the Health Board decides that it's something I shouldn't have missed, then it gets nasty. First they pull my number, so I can't do NHS work, then the General Optical Council gets into the act and cancels my registration, so I can't practice at all.'

'Oh.'

Lost for further incisive comment, Tom orders me another pint. Then he asks:

'So what happens now?'

'Well, they've invited me to come in for this 'informal chat' tomorrow afternoon with some guy I've heard of but never met. Samuel Mayfield. Dr Samuel Mayfield. He's head of the Health Board's clinical monitoring team.'

'You'll probably get it all sorted out then. Bet it's some mistake or something.'

Yeah. I hope so.

The Health Board gave me a list of the patients they want to discuss, and by Tuesday I've been over the record cards about twenty times. I can't see anything that would warrant me being struck-off, but that probably depends more on what's happened since I saw them. There are one or two questionable little details, but everybody's records have a few of those. Real life and Health Board regulations aren't always compatible.

Before crossing swords with Doctor Mayfield however, I've got a patient to see: Derek Anderson in Gorseburn.

The drive down there is pleasant; quiet country roads bordered with sheep-filled fields are a welcome change from the chaos of the Edinburgh bypass. The fields are in the main unfenced from the road; either the sheep have great road sense, or a high mortality rate.

The journey takes me about half an hour. I've never been here before, and I love it on sight. Gorseburn is one of those little towns that oozes nostalgia.

Main Street is split down the middle by a grassy island sprouting a granite war memorial. The houses on either side are terraced, proudly exhibiting the terracotta-coloured bricks of their construction. The window-frames are wooden, not plastic, and they're all different sizes and painted in various warm colours, which lends a Disneyish feel to the scene.

The local shopping facilities comprise a Co-op general store and a Post Office, both on Main Street. The Co-op seems to have all the little Borders towns sewn up; they're becoming the Tesco of Tinytown.

Gorseburn feels very much like the middle of nowhere, and I can't imagine the bus service being up to much. Not an ideal place for housebound people to live.

Derek Anderson lives down one of the roads that criss-cross Main Street. He has a little bungalow, white-harled with rose-filled hanging-baskets dangling in a neat line along the frontage. A glance at the Dom-form confirms he's not on benefits.

No time to wonder if the doorbell is working; within seconds of pressing the button his door flies open and Derek welcomes me in. He's very excited, to the extent of jumping about. I hope he's not going to bring on an attack of asthma.

Because he's under sixty I don't have to dilate his pupils which are anyway wide with his relative youth, and possibly his excitement. We chat as I set up my equipment.

'Must be very frustrating for you, the asthma,' I comment.

He looks puzzled.

'Oh no, not really. It was more childhood asthma, it hardly ever bothers me now. Maybe a little wheeze once in a blue moon, and the inhaler soon gets rid of that.'

'But – I mean, the asthma is the reason you're housebound, isn't it?'

'Housebound? Me?'

'Well yes, that was what I understood…after all, you're having a sight test at home…'

'Oh, that's just because of living here. I don't drive you see, and the bus service is absolutely appalling – to get to Galashiels I would need to change twice, it would take me hours.'

I've stopped laying my equipment out. This is not looking good.

'Derek, I think we've got a bit of a misunderstanding here. NHS home visits are for people who can't get to a high street practice because of some medical disability, not because it's inconvenient.'

'But I really need my eyes done, and I've given your number to about six of my friends who're in the same position. It's not a problem, is it?'

Well yes, it is. As things stand, I can't claim any NHS examination fees for this. Under the rules for mobile providers, don't ask me why, it's examination fee plus visiting fee, or nothing.

Pragmatically however, I'm here now. Since Derek's not on benefits, I might as well do the test (for nothing) and take the profit from the private dispensing. But no way is it worth my while to repeat the exercise for his six friends. On the other hand, I hate turning business away. Maybe I'll just test the waters...

'Derek, under these circumstances it would be normal to charge a private examination fee...'

'I'm not very well off, Mark. I've put a bit aside for my specs, but ...I mean, how much would the fee be? I don't know if I could manage another, what, twenty pounds...?'

Seventy-five actually. Oh well...

'Alright Derek, it's nobody's fault, just a communication failure....'

I think?

'...so I tell you what, I'll waive the examination fee just this once.'

'That's really good of you. Of course, I'll tell my friends not to bother you ... I realise you couldn't keep on...'

I'm shaking my head slowly. I'm not quite sure where this next is coming from.

'No, don't say anything to your friends yet Derek. There might be a way round this, let me have some time to think about it...'

Well, it wasn't a total loss. Derek had put enough aside to finance a nice pair of designer specs with Transitions photochromic lenses. It's been profitable enough as a one-off, but I can't go on doing this for the whole population of Gorseburn.

My equipment's all loaded back in the car, and I've gone for a stroll around.

Doesn't take too long.

Down another street, again off the main drag, I find the town's third commercial venture. 'Ground-Down.' A coffee shop - though peeking through the window, the middle-aged female clientele all look to be drinking tea.

Until recently there were, it appears, five entrepreneurial ventures in Gorseburn. Number four across the street is the inevitable pub. Rather a nice example though, red stonework frontage with Dickensian windows, and a board advertising pub-lunches and a couple of rooms to let.

Number five however, sited adjacent to Ground-Down, has succumbed to the economic winter. The signage, which still looks new, proclaims the availability of hand-crafted pottery. The empty interior, and a large 'TO LET' sign, contradicts this claim. I recognise the name of the letting agent; they're based in Haddington.

The subconscious is a strange thing. Nose against the glass of the desolate pottery shop I find myself doing calculations, projecting a new interior on the abandoned space.

What a strange and unexpected idea this is, I reflect, watching the concept expand through the upper regions of my mind.

TWENTY-SIX

Moseying my trusty Impreza down to the barrier guarding the huge car park outside Health Board HQ, I feel like Clint Eastwood in the old Spaghetti Westerns.

One man against the forces of chaos, conscious of multiple gun-sights trained on his chest. A man facing unspeakable odds. Alone.

With the music dying in my mind I lower the window. A Parking Attendant is trotting over, his clipboard locked and loaded.

'Afternoon sir. Can I have your name, please?'

Health Board HQ being so close to Debenhams must necessitate the payment of bounty to clipboard-slingers, to protect their land...

Snap out of it, Mark.

'Mark Rogers, to see Sheriff – I mean Doctor Mayfield.'

'Sorry sir, you're not on my list.'

'Well, can't you phone in and get me put on your list?'

Woefully he shakes his head.

'Wouldn't make any difference now, sir. You have to be allocated a space at least twenty four hours in advance.'

'So what do I do?'

'Well, see the shopping centre over there?'

He points. I squint. WAY over there.

'...you'll be able to get into their car park, if you're lucky. Usually not too busy at this time.'

Great. Oh well, at least this didn't happen the last time I came, for my equipment inspection. With two cases and a visual field screener I'd have needed to take a taxi back. Today however, I only have a cardboard wallet of patient records to carry. It occurs to me only now how lucky I was not to come back to a clamped car last time; then again, that would have gotten me out of giving Tracy that ill-fated lift home.

By the time I've arranged finance to cover my stay at the shopping-centre car park and walked back, passing the half-empty Health Board car park on the way, my watch says I'm a quarter of an hour late. Tough. Not my fault if NHS administrators can't administrate.

Despite being late, I'm left to kick my heels for a further twenty minutes.

Retribution?

Finally an M&S-suited bellhop comes to fetch me. He shows me into an expectedly plush office; after dodging round the redwood rubber plants I come to an abrupt stop. Sitting behind the desk in front of me is – Tracy.

'I though this meeting was with Doctor Mayfield,' I say coldly.

Tracy looks happy. The purple ruffle on her diaphanous blouse trembles with polite laughter. Her eyes are narrow though; I've seen crows looking at worms with less appetite.

'I'm in charge of this investigation Mark. It's simply normal practice for communications to be signed by the boss, but be assured, it's me you're dealing with.'

Oh goody.

Tracy gets up and moves to a set of exquisitely upholstered damask armchairs flanking a huge knee-high walnut table with the sort of finish you might expect to see your reflection in.

'Let's sit over here Mark. It's a little less formal, easier to interact.'

Well, if that's what it takes to get me out of this, I'll just have to close my eyes and think of England…

To say we sink into the armchairs is like saying the Titanic ran aground. If only there were more money for medicines…

'Okay Tracy, what's this all about?'

'Mark.' Coy smile. 'I'm so sorry to have to be the one dealing with this. Unfortunately we've discovered a few little clinical discrepancies with some of your patients, and this necessitates further investigation.'

'Have I been targeted? On what grounds?'

'No, no, no. Routine clinical monitoring, nothing more.'

When patients sign the NHS sight test form, they agree to submit themselves for verification checks on demand. Few are aware of this. The usual procedure is to call a sample to a local examination centre; this is the first time I've heard of clinical checking being done on domiciliary patients. Someone must have gone out to their homes to re-examine them.

Now I wonder who that might have been?

'Who did the verification checks, Tracy? You?'

She nods smugly.

'Yes, it was an interesting experience. I don't know how you can bear to do this sort of work all the time. Nonetheless though, these patients are entitled to the same standards as anyone else.'

'I work to very high standards, Tracy. Perhaps we could get down to the nitty-gritty here – like, what's the problem?'

She opens the folder she brought from the desk; withdraws a sheaf of papers.

'Let's see now. First query I have is a young lady with learning difficulties. A Miss Emma Nugent. Do you remember her?'

'Yes, quite well actually.'

I reach into my own cardboard file, then slap Emma's record on the table.

'Fire away, Tracy.'

Whoops. I'm back to being Clint Eastwood.

'I examined Emma a couple of weeks ago, when I found a discrepancy between the spectacles she's wearing and the refractive result I obtained.'

'Really?'

I think I know what's coming here; I start scanning my own record, just to jog my memory.

'Yes, I'm afraid the spectacles you gave her were totally unsuitable. My refractive result was right eye minus one, left eye minus one. You gave her right eye minus one, left eye PLUS one. Being charitable, I'm assuming that first of all the spectacles were made up wrongly, and then the error was compounded by your not checking them properly before giving them out to the poor girl. With the lens you supplied, she can barely see the top letter on the chart with her left eye.'

Tracy sits back, awaiting my response like a dog waiting for a treat. I allow the silence to expand for a few seconds before speaking. Now, according to some ancient Chinese warmonger, attack is the best form of defence.

'You don't have the first idea what you're doing, do you?'

'I BEG your pardon?'

I spread my fingers in the direction of Tracy's notes.

'Your examination was flawed, to the point of incompetence... are you alright?'

Tracy's face has gone crimson, and she's spluttering.

How dare you…?'

'Yes, quite. Now, Emma has psychiatric problems. She also has an intermittent squint, brought on by stress – did you elicit that? No, obviously not. She started having huge problems with attacks of double vision, prism was not a viable treatment, her psychiatrist ruled out hypnosis, so the only answer was to block one eye out.'

I'm starting to enjoy myself.

'Double vision can be eliminated by wearing an eye patch, but that isn't a great solution for a nineteen year old girl. However, blurring the vision in the non-dominant eye – say by giving a plus one instead of a minus one – helps the brain to suppress the second image, thus treating the double vision. The technique was very successful in Emma's case, but obviously you didn't manage to figure any of this out. Did you?'

She's staring at me, moving her lips around words that wont form. She grabs my record card from the table, reads it several times. Finally she re-discovers her voice.

'Well, not exactly a conventional treatment...'

'Worked though. And you'll find plenty of reference to it in the literature...'

'...but I'm prepared to accept...'

'...it's called physiological occlusion in case you didn't know...'

'...the validity of your explanation. I'd like to move on to another case, if you don't mind.'

Sitting back, I fold my arms. Thirty-Love. I may, however, regret the way I handled that if the next case is different.

'Eighty year old man. Ronald Bishop. You charged the NHS for a tint, quite a deep one. Now, I held a very bright light to each of his eyes, and he didn't even flinch. What is your basis for believing he is light sensitive?'

I'm flicking through my records. Ah, here he is. I remember this one too. Tracy's still talking.

'Mr Bishop also has cataracts, they're pulling his vision down to six twenty-four, yet you didn't refer him for treatment. Would you also care to explain that?'

'The cataracts consist of very centrally-located opacities, right?'

She nods suspiciously.

'Can I ask, Tracy, did you question Mr Bishop about what medication he's on?'

Her eyes flicker, and she consults her notes.

'Yes I did, but Mr Bishop is not exactly lucid, so...'

Take aim. Fire. Oh Clint, get down...

'Tracy, you haven't got the foggiest notion of what Dom work is about, do you?'

I have to wait until she shuts up again.

'No, you really don't. Elderly confused patients aren't that simple to get a medical history from. You have to ferret it out, from relatives, carers - sometimes you have to go raking through their bathroom cupboards to find out what meds they're on. Mr Bishop is taking Warfarin to thin his blood - which as you know, well I presume you know, is a contraindication to cataract surgery. Mr Bishop's GP was not at all keen for me to refer him.'

'Oh. Yes well, you can't expect me to...anyway, that doesn't explain the prescribing of an unnecessary tint...'

'Think about it, Tracy. He's got central cataract, and he can't have it treated. So how do we get light round it? Make the pupil aperture bigger perhaps, so light can get around the cataract? Now, how do you dilate a pupil?'

She looks ready to spring; perhaps the other side of my face is about to get a matching pattern of nail-rake.

'Can use drops of course, but if it works, wouldn't a tint be preferable to medication? The tint makes his pupils dilate just enough to improve the vision by two lines on the chart. So can we agree the tint wasn't unnecessary?'

That last said with a sharp edge.

She nods mutely. I smile. She studies the wall behind me. Then she starts fumbling in her folder again...

'Tracy, what do you say we just leave it there? This is a personal vendetta, without basis in fact. If I was to take this further...'

Her bottom lip's started to tremble.

'Well, it looked like...'

'You mean you were looking, determined to find something to bring me down. Tracy I've got no grudge against you, but if you don't drop this now I'm going to have your job.'

Getting up, I start replacing records in my folder while turning for the door. Then I stop. Tears are spilling down Tracy's cheeks. Uncertainly, I reach out to place a hand on her shoulder; she covers it with her own, the nails digging in.

'It wasn't vindictive, Mark. It was just…your name came out of the hat, and I thought if I handled it, it would be…well…'

'What?'

'I wouldn't have let it go any further – and I thought you'd be grateful. I mean, these are unusual cases – you can't think…?'

'Tracy, I don't want to think anything about it any more. I've spent the last two days worrying about it, just…look, leave me alone, eh?'

Her face almost melts my annoyance, but I wont let it. Without another word, I leave Health Board HQ and set off on the odyssey to reclaim my car.

Walking back to the shopping mall a light rain starts spattering my face, but it doesn't dampen my spirits. I've got no doubt that Tracy was telling the truth; my name just came up for a random check and I've been very lucky.

The girl with the squint was an unusual case; it's easy to see how Tracy got the wrong idea there.

As for old Mr Bishop, well, I've no idea if he's on Warfarin. He's just one of those patients who don't want their cataracts treated because their vision is adequate for their needs. He's a bit of a boy though – really fancied himself in a tint, and I didn't have the heart to refuse him. That idea I came up with about a tint dilating the pupil around a central cataract is fascinating – I must try it sometime.

Taking a penlight from my pocket, I puff lightly to disperse imaginary smoke from the bulb-end. Quite a poker game that was; Clint would be proud of me. I know there were a few more minor infringements in Tracy's folder; nothing fatal, but all actionable in terms of reprimands and fines.

Yes, my luck was in today.

I think it's finally come back.

For the rest of the week Diane and I are too busy to meet, what with work and various other business. She's up to something though; I glean that impression from our phone calls, but she's not letting-on what. I just hope it's nothing to do with Matthew.

On Saturday morning I set off to pick her up from Gorebridge; I've got something else to tell her about now. She's surprised when I drive to Gorseburn; like me on Tuesday this is her first time here, and she immediately agrees the place has a lot of rustic charm.

I treat her to lunch in Ground-Down, where the home cooking is tasty if a bit basic. After she's laughed half-heartedly at my act of looking for my wallet we step back onto the street outside, where I stop by the closed-down pottery shop.

'What do you think of this?'

'What's to think? It's just a tatty little shop that's gone bust. What are we doing here anyway, Mark? Lunch was nice, but we didn't need to drive this far for soup and toasties.'

With a flourish I produce a key from my pocket, and unlock the pottery shop door.

'In you come, I'll show you round.'

I've seen that long-suffering look before, on other women.

'Oh what's this, Mark? You're going into the pottery business now?'

'No. You are standing in what will be the reception area of Mark Rogers, Optometric Practice. I signed a lease yesterday, and I plan to have it open by the end of next month.'

'What? You're giving up the Dom business?'

'Not a bit. See, since I've got things going again, the paperwork's got totally out of control. Now I can hardly take on clerical staff to work from my Caravan, can I? This is the perfect answer – I've got a small but captive catchment of patients, enough to give me a couple of half-days' testing a week. That'll pay all the running costs and still make a wee profit. Meanwhile I'll train somebody local as my assistant, and since the practice is part-time, they'll also be able to do all the Dom paperwork for me, leaving me free to…'

Diane was gaping, but now she's started to laugh.

'You're on a roll, aren't you? Yes, it's a great idea. Gives you a proper base, and expands your business at the same time. How can you afford it though? I thought all Freda's money was going on the flat in North Berwick.'

'Well, after giving the girls their share I wont have nearly enough, but I'll just go ahead and take that mortgage the bank offered me. This isn't going to cost as much as you might think 'cos I've already got most of the eye-testing equipment I need, even frame-stock for that matter.'

'You were really generous with the girls Mark, that was a lovely thing to do.'

'Not really, it was theirs by right. Freda would never have left me that sort of money and forgotten about them, it's obvious she expected me to pass a chunk on.'

'What about your Dom telephone number? Will you have it transferred here?'

'Best of both worlds – I can divert it to the new practice during opening hours, that in itself is a major advantage. I've never known how many new Dom-patients are being put off by the machine and not leaving a message – now they'll have a human voice answering the phone. And hey - I've already booked my first six Gorseburn practice-patients – though the dates I've given them are provisional on Tom finishing the shopfit in time…'

She grabs me in a hug.

'Nice one Branson,' she says softly. 'Right, come on – back to Greenacres. It's my turn – I've got something to show you too.'

When we arrive at Greenacres Diane directs me to A field. On her instructions I stop outside a boxy Pemberton where Diane jumps out of the car and trots up the verandah steps. Puzzled, I follow.

At the door she fumbles in her bag, then produces a…key? Opens the door. Disappears inside. Still feeling bemused, I step in behind her.

She's twirling in the kitchen space.

'What do you think?'

'What do you mean? You've…bought this?'

'No, but I've got first option on it. It belongs to the parents of one of my friends in the hospital; they're finding the running costs too much since the Site was taken over. Mark, it's the perfect answer – for now, anyway. You're scared of us jumping in too soon – no, come on, you know you are – so I'll come and live here, beside you but not with you. I'll sell my house and join the letting business, and…'

'Wait. The Site'll never wear it, if it's an outside sale…'

She's flicking her head dismissively…

'I've already spoken to Alf, argued that I've been down here as much as in my own place recently, and that you and I are…well, practically… and he agreed that the Site can't not approve me. He actually seemed to give in awfully easily, it was like he was scared of something…anyway if I want this, it's mine. Come on – you haven't told me what you're thinking.'

Now it's my turn to grab her.

'It's perfect Di.'

'Oh, one more thing...'

She's whispering now.

'…your problem with Horace is solved too – he can come and live with me, here. Somehow I've gotten quite attached to the big lug.'

'But what about Marcus…?'

'What about him? He accepted yours, and he's getting to move to a pussycat's paradise – no, Marcus can like it or lump it, I'm betting he'll like it.'

She feels good. I hug harder, feel her arms answering mine. Everything feels good.

Somehow I've gotten to a good place where everything's finally going my way.

I think.

EPILOGUE

Oasis Nursing Home,
East Kilbride.
15th June, 2011.

My dearest Mark,

It is so strange to be talking to you from beyond the grave.

Mark, you are the son I would have wanted. Knowing you has meant the world to me, sharing as we do a common thread - linked by opinion, outlook - it is unusual to feel such a strong philosophical connection.

I must be honest. On occasion I have actually been jealous of poor Sally; this before becoming angry at her shoddy treatment of you.

You must not think too badly of her - Sally's father spoiled her, and perhaps I too participated there, but her heart is in the right place. Sally's great fault is that she is too easily led. My hope was that this would be advantageous under your influence, but you're not forceful enough Mark, you're too quick to see the other point of view. Bluntly, not what Sally needed.

It gives me enormous pleasure to be able to help you in this small way, especially knowing that all you need is a little push in the right direction, a little assistance with the means to achieve your aspirations. Be careful Mark, but never be too cautious – set your goals and chase your dreams.

I cannot help but imagine the satisfaction were I able to watch as you tread the path, carving your way to fulfilment. Should you ever become aware of unseen eyes observing your endeavours…

Be happy Mark.

With fond love,

Freda

PS You may be tempted to think I have forgotten your adorable daughters - if so, shame on you – Kara and Zoe lit up many hours for me. I have made arrangements with my solicitors that the girls shall each receive a sizeable gift on their twenty-first birthdays.

AFTERWORD

I hope you enjoyed 'Eyes Up; if you did, it would be so good if you could leave a review on Amazon.
Please...

If you visit my website you can sign up to my mailing list and be the first to know about new releases etc, as well as bagging a free copy of 'Comical Short Stories'.

'Comical Short Stories' is a Mark Rogers Short Story entitled 'When Mark Met Molly', together with four funny flash fictions about a chef, a window cleaner, and a chap looking for a cheap pair of wellys. Oh, and a most annoying parrot. (The one about the window cleaner has previously been published in a It's available on Amazon, but you can get it free at: markrogersbooks.co.uk - come and have a look.

You can contact me direct on info@markrogersbooks.co.uk or via the contact form on the website - I'd love to hear from you, and will answer all messages personally.

'Eyes Up' was the sequel to your next read on Amazon -
'When Mark Met Tracy'
National Weekly Magazine.)

Mark and Tracy take their romance from the Scottish Holy Island to the canals of Venice; but underlying everything is the ever-present threat of Mark's psychopathic stalker...
In the final showdown, it's a Mark you haven't seen before...

Enjoy – and I'll be letting you know via the mailing list when my next book comes out, hopefully in the spring – tentative title, just to get the juices flowing, is

'WHEN MARK WED SALLY'

See you there!

Mark.

Printed in Great Britain
by Amazon